DANGEROUS DREAMS

Colin Stanmore and his sister, Diana, go to the wild and lawless Palestine of the 1930s to stay with their Aunt Harriet. Diana conceals her real reason for going—she is in love with David, a friend of her brother's, who is working on a Palestinian kibbutz. Colin loses his heart to Samira, only to find that she is promised to a local Arab chief. Diana must accept that although David finds her attractive, he will only take a Jewish bride. As war breaks out in Europe, Colin and David join the RAF and a heartbroken Diana returns home. But their time in Palestine is destined to haunt them all for years to come...

Dedicated to all men and women, on both sides, who are striving for peace in the Middle East.

DANGEROUS DREAMS

by
Eileen Stafford

Magna Large Print Books
Long Preston, North Yorkshire,
England.

British Library Cataloguing in Publication Data.

Stafford, Eileen
   Dangerous dreams.

   A catalogue record for this book is
   available from the British Library

   ISBN 0-7505-0974-0

First published in Great Britain by Judy Piatkus (Publishers) Ltd., 1994

The right of Eileen Stafford to be identified as the author of this work has been asserted in accordance with the Copyright, Designs and Patents Act, 1988

Published in Large Print January, 1997 by arrangement with Piatkus Books Ltd.

Magna Large Print is an imprint of
Library Magna Books Ltd.
Printed and bound in Great Britain by
T.J. International Ltd., Cornwall, PL28 8RW.

ACKNOWLEDGEMENTS

My thanks to Devon County Library for obtaining many books for me, and especially to the branches at Bovey Tracey and Newton Abbot.

I am grateful to The Parks Library at Southampton University for providing me with some wonderful old volumes concerning the time of the British Mandate in Palestine.

Thanks also to Dr Sebastian Poulter of the Faculty of Law at Southampton University, who gave me many details about the Muslim form of divorce and the consequences of this for a Palestinian girl in the thirties.

Also to Valentine Mitchel & Co for permission to quote from the poetry of Hannah Senesh.

Lastly gratitude to my husband who was willing to spend long hours alone so that I could complete this book.

TO CAESAREA

Hush, cease all sound.
Across the sea is the sand,
The shore known and near,
The shore golden, dear,
Home, the Homeland.

With step twisting and light
Among strangers we move,
Word and song hushed,
Towards the future-past
Caesarea...

But reaching the city of ruins
Soft a few words we intone.
We return. We are here.
Soft answers the silence of stone,
We awaited you two thousand years.

Hannah Senesh Sdot-Yam, Caesarea, 1941
(translated from the Hebrew by
Ruth Finer Mintz)
Hannah was executed by the Gestapo
in 1944 aged 23.

From the poem TO DIE...

...I love the warm sunny skies,
Light, songs, shining eyes.
I want no war, no battle cry—
No, no... Not I.

Hannah Senesh
Nahalal 1941
(translated from the Hebrew by
Dorothy H. Rochmis)

CHAPTER 1

Samira—Palestine—1938

Samira fetched towels and soap and set them down beside her father's chair. Then she took the bowl of warm water that had been heating slowly on the open fire and placed that too on the ground in front of him. She knelt and tested the water to see that it was the right temperature, and when she was satisfied that all was ready, she guided her father's large and calloused feet into the bowl. She washed them carefully, taking time, removing the grime of the day, and finally she placed the towel on her lap and wiped each foot in turn, making sure that they were completely dry and no moisture left between the toes.

Every evening before supper she performed this humiliating task, humiliating because Jebel el Hamid was perfectly capable of washing his own feet. Although she gave no outward sign, Samira was more rebellious than usual today for Colin Stanmore had talked to her about his home in England, given her a glimpse of a completely different way of life. He had shown her photographs of a large stone-built house in a place he called Devon. There was a print of his sister too. Samira had stared for a long time at the likeness of this girl. She was wearing trousers, jodhpurs Colin called them, and she was laughing. She held the bridle of a horse in one hand and the other was resting on the head of a large dog. Diana, for that was her name, was hoping to come to Palestine soon, he had said.

What was it like to be born English and free? Samira wondered as she fastened her father's soft leather sandals. She forced her reluctant fingers to be gentle and tried to suppress the anger and defiance in her heart, for those qualities were uncomfortable attributes in a daughter and they would be far from welcome when she was an unwilling wife to Eshref. They would only bring discontent and unhappiness. She knew she must do her best to banish all her impossible dreams. It was essential that her father should have no idea of the rebellion she felt, and she shuddered as she thought of the consequences should he ever be able to read her mind or to know of her friendship with Colin Stanmore.

Colin had come to Palestine because of his strange interest in the many ancient sites and ruins that were so plentiful here. Samira knew that Englishmen and sometimes women too were fascinated with these old stones. She'd met him first at Mrs Clayton's bungalow and had been amazed and delighted at the way he treated her. At first she hadn't dared address him directly, and had kept her eyes cast down, never looking at him openly, for men seldom held conversations with women here in Palestine, never acknowledged them as equals.

Thinking about Colin had, at first, filled her with happiness, given her a pleasurable, although vain sort of anticipation. She would recall the way he spoke to her, how his whole face came alive when he smiled, and she would be filled with delight, hopeless, but wonderful nevertheless. Recently however everything had changed and those things merely increased her despair, for the date of her marriage to Eshref had been fixed. Colin Stanmore was as unavailable to her as the stars she saw in the warm night sky and as the freedom that she so fiercely craved.

As she tied the final lace of her father's sandals he stood up, bringing her back abruptly to the present. His apparent lack of concern for her happiness reminded her forcefully of her lowly and subservient position in the family. He had not exchanged one word with her during her ministrations, but she was quite used to this, accepted it, knowing that he thought it totally unnecessary to smile his thanks. It was a woman's duty to serve a man in everything.

Jebel was a powerful character, both in his great physical strength and in his position in the village. He ruled with absolute authority and he allowed no one to remain in doubt of the fact that he had been appointed Mukhtar for the area by the British District Commissioner. This was in addition to being voted headman by popular vote of his own community. There was absolutely no chance that he would consider his daughter's wishes in anything. She would do his will, and soon that of her husband as well.

Allah had decreed it so for women, and so it must remain.

In spite of her gloomy thoughts Samira sprang to her feet in one lithe movement, picked up the bowl and carried it carefully, trying not to look in disgust at its sludgy contents. The water must be left in the yard to be used again.

Her mother was busy with the meal and later when it was ready Samira took the large plate of mutton and rice to the entrance of the room where her father and brothers were gathered. They sat in a circle on rugs and cushions and the youngest, seeing her, rose and took the plate. Assad was twelve and had recently been allowed the privilege of eating with the men.

When she had given the food to him she fetched a basket of pitta bread and, returning, stood again in the doorway holding it until it was taken from her as before. Women were not allowed into the room when the men and older boys were having their meal.

She waited for a moment watching her six brothers. They took food from the communal plate with their fingers, eating slowly in spite of their obvious hunger. As always they deferred to their father, seeing that he had the best pieces, the biggest share.

Fruit followed the first course, and when all was finished Assad carried the almost empty plates to his sister. He swaggered a little and grinned at her. 'Your turn,' he said. 'Not much left.'

Samira took the remains and turned away in anger. It wasn't like this at Mrs Clayton's

12

bungalow, nor, she had heard, in the dining hall of the kibbutz. Quietly she slid away and went through to the inner courtyard. She glared down at the few pieces of cold congealing mutton that were left for herself and her mother. She wanted to smash the plate angrily on the stones, scream out at the injustices of her life, of the lives of all the women she knew, but she did no such thing. She handed the plate to her mother, helped to clear the rest of the utensils and dishes away, and then sat down cross-legged on the mat and bunched her fists tightly until her fingers ached, but it was the only outward sign of her rebellion.

She thought of the Jewish girls who lived on the kibbutz. She had seen them again today. They reminded her of the photograph of Colin's sister, and their freedom amazed her. She was completely bewildered by it, but she was envious too. Her own life with its enslavement to the wishes of her father, and shortly to her husband, seemed quite unbearable since she had come to know of this other way. Those girls appeared to be almost equal to their men. They all ate and worked and laughed together. And in the evening they danced. She could often hear the music and then her heart would fill with a wild restlessness.

The small enclosed courtyard sometimes seemed like a prison and she felt that she resembled a caged bird or a small tethered goat ready for slaughter. But unlike the doomed animals, she had no way of showing her frustration and anger. She couldn't cry aloud

13

or flap agonised wings against the bars of her cage as she had seen trapped sparrows do. She had to appear calm and composed, had to accept her father's will without complaint. That was the lot of women. There was no escape.

Eventually her father and brothers left for a noisy evening in the village. She and her mother were alone at last. They usually preferred to delay their meal until the men had gone. It was more peaceful then. Samira looked up at her mother as she came into the courtyard and felt a stab of grief like a great knife wound. The parting that was soon to be forced upon them would be bitter.

Kaffa had taken the plate of stew and reheated it, added more vegetables and rice. She placed it now on a low table between them.

'They were hungry tonight,' she said. 'I should have prepared more. But there's plenty of bread and I made some fresh cheese.'

For a moment Samira was cheered for she too had a healthy appetite. She loved the little round goat's milk cheeses that her mother occasionally made. 'You didn't offer them to my brothers then?' she said, slightly amused.

Kaffa smiled at her conspiratorially. 'Not today,' she said, 'I made them just for us.'

After they had eaten the two women sat in the cool evening air each with a piece of embroidery, Samira's wedding clothes. They took great pride in the patterns and colours woven into every garment. Even their every-day clothes were bright and flamboyant with this traditional embroidery. Unlike her mother

14

whose figure had become shapeless with constant child-bearing, Samira wore a belt tied tightly around her slim waist, and her dark shining hair was covered with a thin scarf wound around her head and tied loosely at the back. For a Palestinian girl her skin was quite fair, but her eyes, bent now over her work, were large and dark, fringed by long upturned lashes. They could sometimes be full of fun and they sparkled with health and pleasure when she rode Jazi, Mrs Clayton's great stallion, but here at home they were often sad, nearly always downcast, deep pools of unhappiness.

For a time neither woman spoke, both guessing at the other's thoughts. Eventually Samira broke the silence. 'Do you think I'll ever get used to being the second wife?' she asked. She angrily pushed away the material she was stitching. She hadn't wanted to upset her mother but she couldn't hide her misery tonight. 'It's working for Mrs Clayton that has made me so unwilling to go on living as we do,' she continued. 'If I knew nothing of her way of life perhaps I shouldn't be so discontented.'

Kaffa sighed. She thought of the day seven years ago when the Englishwoman had saved her eldest son's life with some of her European medicine. Jebel has been so grateful that he had not been able to refuse her strange request, for Harriet Clayton had demanded that Samira, then aged ten, should go to her every day for lessons and should also learn to help in the animal refuge that she ran. Jebel had offered any one of his sons, for a boy should have the

15

advantages that this position would bring, but no, Mrs Clayton had insisted that it must be the little girl, and unwillingly he had agreed.

Ever since that day Samira had gone to work at Khanhaven, the long sprawling bungalow with its assortment of rescued animals, and between her and the eccentric Harriet a strong friendship had arisen. With Samira's marriage this was due to be broken.

'I sometimes wish that your father had never agreed to let you go,' Kaffa said sadly. 'I was always amazed that he did.'

'Mrs Clayton pays him well,' Samira replied bitterly, 'and I get nothing.'

'That's how it is, but you won't need money when you're married to Eshref. Your fiancé has great wealth.'

'I don't care about his money. It means nothing. After working so long for Mrs Clayton, how can I submit to a marriage like that? How can I, Mother? To have a glimpse of freedom and then to lose it is worse than living in ignorance. She's taught me to read and write English. I can read her newspapers, I know what's happening in Jerusalem, in London, in Cairo. I've more knowledge than all my stupid brothers put together. I can keep accounts, I can ride a horse as well as any of them, better probably, and I know how to cure sick animals because she has taught me. And now I must hide most of this!'

'Hush, child.' Kaffa was thoroughly alarmed by this outburst. She knew of her daughter's accomplishments, but she kept them carefully

16

secret from her husband and sons. 'You know quite well that you must never admit to being able to do all those things,' she said severely. 'You mustn't know more than your husband or any man. They think that we're only fit for work in the fields and house, and for child-bearing and pleasuring them. If you're wise you'll use your commonsense and knowledge to make life easier for yourself not harder.'

Samira sighed angrily. She knew that her mother was right and that if she didn't comply with the life that was to be forced upon her she would only bring grief and suffering to both of them. She hoped that her mother didn't know the depth of her love for Colin. It would greatly increase her disquiet and her sorrow, and if her father or brothers knew of it then it would mean a severe beating or even a secret and ugly death.

She took up her embroidery again and stabbed the needle repeatedly into the beautiful cloth. The gold thread and bright costly material had both been provided by Eshref, her wealthy bridegroom-to-be, but they gave her no pleasure.

Kaffa, watching her, was frightened for her most loved child. Like Samira she too had received some education, in her case, in an English missionary school, sent there because she was an orphan. But the years of marriage to Jebel had mellowed her early rebellion. He'd pleased her when he was young and she'd loved him in a way, still did perhaps, however incomprehensible this might seem to this young

17

daughter of hers, this girl with the impossible and highly dangerous dreams, the headstrong independent ways. She was well aware of the life she would be forced to live. Total submission would be demanded, not only to her husband but to the first wife and the mother-in-law, and there would be constant pregnancies. She fervently hoped that Samira's first child would be a healthy male baby, for this made a wife more valuable.

Her own sons coming quickly one after the other during the early years of her marriage had made her a successful and treasured wife, so for herself she was not altogether discontent. And there had been no second or third wife brought in to displace her. For that, in spite of the extra work it entailed, she was grateful.

There was little that she could say to comfort her daughter, nothing that would help her come to terms with her future life. She got to her feet and put her embroidery carefully aside, wrapping it in a white cloth. Then she kissed the girl gently on the cheek. 'You know there is no other way, Samira,' she said with a trace of firmness in her voice. 'Like all the women and girls of our family and our village, you'll be brave and strong and do what you must do. And it may not be as bad as you think. There are compensations. Eshref isn't old. He's handsome and rich.' She tried to show some optimism. 'When you've sons you'll find happiness, and I'm told that his mother is kind.'

Samira looked at Kaffa with incomprehension. So happiness only came with having sons did it?

18

Was this the supreme goal of a woman's life? She shook her head and tried to force back the tears. Into her mind came unbidden the strong smiling face of Colin Stanmore.

When she lay on her bed-mat that night she longed for sleep because it would bring the next day nearer. The happiest hours of her life were those she spent working for Mrs Clayton.

Harriet Clayton brushed back her curly hair, forcing it into its customary bun at the nape of her neck. She peered at herself in the full-length mirror behind the large door of her wardrobe. She had found this incongruous piece of furniture in a shabby second-hand store in Haifa when she first came to Palestine and had insisted upon having it in spite of the endless trouble caused in its transportation. She frequently laughed a little to herself when she remembered the girl she had been then and the vast amount of highly unsuitable clothes she had brought with her. The glowing well-polished oak of the wardrobe and its great size frequently reminded her of those early years. She had come as a young bride to this strange and fascinating country, had fallen in love with it and was resolved never to live anywhere else until she was a very old woman.

There was no door to her bedroom, merely a heavily beaded curtain, and it clattered comfortingly as she pushed some of the hanging strings aside and went into the outer room and then outside into the sun. 'Are you

19

ready, Samira?' she called. 'Where shall we ride this morning?'

Samira was standing between the two splendid horses, a bridle in each hand. She wore one of the dresses that Harriet had brought with her from England but it was hitched up around her waist with an embroidered girdle, and beneath it were the bright and baggy trousers fashionable now for the Arab women of this area. They were gathered just below her knees into tight cuffs round her legs and ended in an elaborate frill at her ankles. The outfit had caused Harriet much amusement when Samira first appeared in it, but it fulfilled all the requirements of modesty demanded by the girl's family, and she had to admit that it was splendidly convenient for riding. 'A Palestinian version of jodhpurs!' she had remarked with a laugh.

'Where would you like to go today?' she enquired again. 'And you must ride Jazi, please. I only feel up to Naama this morning.'

Samira blushed with pleasure. She loved the great white Arab stallion and rode him each evening before she went home, for Harriet was busy with her writing then and he needed prodigious amounts of exercise. Naama, the little mare, was nice, but the stallion gave her a sense of exhilaration and power that was denied to her in every other aspect of her life. And they were to be separated soon. She would never see him again after her marriage.

'Thank you, Mrs Clayton,' she said. 'I don't mind where we go as long as it's not back into the village.' She mounted easily and waited for her employer to climb more sedately onto the other animal.

Harriet knew that Samira was always apprehensive about being seen riding Jazi for he was the envy of every man for miles around. Her brothers particularly were passionately jealous and she had suffered many small cruelties from them after they had observed her on the stallion's back. They were well aware that she rode him most days, astride too. It offended them deeply, but if they should actually see her up there in the saddle the sight appeared to arouse a primitive male anger. Samira had, in earlier days, expected to be forbidden by her father to ride at all, but the command had never come.

It was almost unheard of for an Arab girl to be employed outside her home, to work for anyone apart from her family, but Jebel el Hamid was very proud of his position as Mukhtar. It was to his advantage to be well thought of by the British administration, particularly by the Assistant District Commissioner, and Harriet had not been above using her friendship with this important individual to get her own way.

It was this influence that had eventually caused Jebel to capitulate and allow his daughter rather than one of his sons to work for her. Harriet had been determined that she would take this bright intelligent child into her home every day and teach her to read and write in addition to all the other skills she would need if she was to be a useful assistant in the animal clinic. Even then, at ten years old, Samira had already spoken fairly fluent English, as did her brothers, all of them having been taught well by their mother who had learned the language in her own childhood in the mission orphanage.

At seventeen Samira was well beyond the age when most girls from her village were married, but now the wedding date had at last been fixed. Harriet guessed that Jebel would very much miss his daughter's substantial earnings and this was probably the reason for the frequent postponements, but Sheikh Eshref would wait no longer for his promised bride.

The two women walked their horses slowly out of the courtyard watched only by the four donkeys in the field behind the house. They were the latest that Harriet had rescued and nursed back to health, much to the amusement and secret admiration of the villagers. Soon they would be sold but their lives would be carefully monitored, their hooves regularly inspected and their well-being ensured. No animal that passed through Harriet's determined hands was ever abandoned to a doubtful future again.

The dusty track was bordered by olive trees, silvery grey in the summer heat, and here and there goats browsed trying to find pasture in the dry earth. Both women were silent at first, thinking of the coming separation, dreading it yet trying not to let the other know of the dread.

Samira spoke first. 'Tell me about your niece?' she asked. 'Colin's sister. I saw her photograph. Is she really coming here and will she be able to take over all my work?'

'Diana?' Harriet replied. 'If her father allows her to she'll come, and yes, I think she'll manage. From what I remember of her she's a very capable young lady. Her father says that she takes after me.' She laughed. 'That doesn't altogether please him. It'll be strange for her though, very different from Bagleigh. You'll have to help her at first, show her what to do.'

'Does she know about animals?'

'She should do. She's lived on a farm all her life, but her parents sent her away to school and I don't think she does much of the actual work. They have men to do it.'

'Then what does she do?'

Harriet wasn't sure how to reply. The worlds of the two girls were so different, so totally remote. 'She rides a lot, I think, goes to parties, goes shopping, that sort of thing.'

Samira did not in any way comprehend what 'that sort of thing' was. She couldn't imagine a world where women did no work. Certainly the men in her village thought it a great source of pride when they had enough grown sons to take over their own labours. They would then sit most of the day and all the evening in the shade of fig or vine gossiping with others just as well blessed. There was no such leisure for their wives and daughters.

The two women kept their mounts to a steady walk until the village was completely out of sight and then they turned along a narrow path that led through more olive groves and up into the open countryside. Once there Samira urged Jazi

23

to a canter and then to a gallop. The ends of her headdress streamed out in the wind as she rode and she bent low over the horse's neck as his flying hooves thundered over the ground. Galloping like this gave her no time to think, freed her for a precious few minutes from reality. Nothing mattered but the speed and the power of the horse gripped firmly between her knees.

She urged him into a great circle that brought her back eventually to Harriet, who, following on the quieter mare, felt her heart fill with sorrow for this girl whom she had come to love. She longed to take her away, somewhere, anywhere, far away, even to England perhaps, to any place where she could find freedom and fulfilment. But it was impossible for one woman, however influential her friends might be, to fight the customs of ages. It was a total way of life and religion which held Samira in its grip, a system and belief which regarded women merely as chattels of men, existing only for their pleasure and use. Harriet gritted her teeth in impotent rage as she frequently did lately, for now that the wedding day was finally drawing near there seemed no possible chance of any reprieve. She had explored many avenues, had many far-fetched ideas, but none had been fruitful.

And there was Colin to confuse matters further! She knew that Samira's heart was given to her nephew and the hopelessness of that situation dragged her spirits even further earthwards in spite of the beauty of the morning and her pleasure in the gentle little mare, whom if truth be told she preferred to the exuberant Jazi. In future she would have to ride the stallion herself unless, of course, Diana should be able to manage him.

They rode for many miles that morning, driven on by unspoken thoughts of the coming marriage when, for Samira, there would be no more long exhilarating hours in the saddle, no more freedom, and for Harriet a great loss.

Would James, that stubborn old fool of a brother of hers back in England, really allow Diana to come to Palestine? Harriet wondered. She smiled for a moment as she thought of her only brother. In some ways he was almost as bossy as Jebel el Hamid. At least he'd like to be! If he did let his daughter come it would only be for a few weeks probably, and then there would be another girl to find and train. An English girl this time though, she thought. There were quite a few horsey daughters of the various British officials here in Palestine, so the search to find one shouldn't prove too difficult. But she sighed nevertheless. Samira had become very dear. No one could ever take her place.

They crossed the great Plain of Megiddo and in the distance they could see the smoke of a train labouring along on the Damascus to Haifa line. They had never come so far before and at last the mare began to tire. Samira, who had once more galloped ahead unwilling to keep to a slower pace, now reigned Jazi to a halt and sat breathless and glowing with the joy of the ride, waiting for Harriet to catch up.

'That was wonderful,' she said.

Then Harriet, watching, saw the sparkle in her eyes fade suddenly, the youthful exuberance disappear.

'Thank you so much for lending Jazi to me to ride to my wedding,' she said quietly. 'It will make the day just a little more bearable.'

'I'll ride him over to your new home frequently so that you can see him again. Your Eshref can't object to that surely?' There was a forced cheerfulness in Harriet's words as if she was trying to give some sense of normality to the future, suggesting that she would call in for afternoon tea!

Samira's normally quiet and gentle voice was loud and angry when she replied. 'Don't call him that,' she ordered. 'Don't ever call him my Eshref. He'll never be mine, I tell you, and I don't want you to bring Jazi over either. It would kill me to see him, to touch him, and not to be allowed to get on his back and ride, ride, ride.' She almost screamed the last words and the horse, receptive to her mood, snorted anxiously and pawed the ground.

Harriet could think of nothing to say in reply and she turned Naama around, not wishing to see the girl's tears, the despair that must follow the anger.

Samira brought Jazi up so that the two horses were side by side and they walked slowly homewards, both women silent yet united in their shared grief. Then at last Samira leaned over and touched Harriet's arm gently. 'I'm sorry,' she whispered. 'I'm so sorry. Will you always be my friend?'

'Yes,' Harriet promised. 'I shall always be your friend.'

CHAPTER 2

Diana—Devonshire—1938

Diana leaned from her open window and saw the postman pedalling down the lane towards Bagleigh. He was early this morning, and she was anxious that her father should not intercept him before he reached the house for she expected a letter from David any day now.

Quietly she opened her bedroom door. There was no one else about. Her mother would already be downstairs, probably in the dining room. If she moved quickly she could reach the hall in time to examine the letters and extract the precious one that she longed for before any one else knew of its arrival.

She flew down the wide staircase and heard her parents talking in the dining room. Quietly she padded across the thick carpet and was just in time to pick up the letters as they fell onto the mat. She glanced at them, her heart beating rapidly, and saw that it was there. The usual blue envelope, the dear handwriting, and the stamp from Palestine. She put it in the pocket of her cardigan and looked at the others. Two more, and those from Palestine too, one from her brother and one from Aunt Harriet, her father's headstrong and fascinating sister.

She composed herself and took them into the dining room where her mother was pouring coffee and her father sitting in front of a well laden plate of bacon, eggs, sausages and fried liver.

'A letter from Colin and one from Aunt Harriet,' she said, placing them on the table.

James Stanmore wiped his hands and took up the envelope from his son first. He slit it open and read the three pages through to the end before continuing with his meal or making any comment. Then he passed it over to his wife. He frowned as he shovelled a forkful of bacon and liver into his mouth and Diana wondered what her brother could have written that displeased him. Colin was working on an archaeological project in Palestine, taking a year off after university. Their father had grudgingly given his consent in return for a promise that he would settle down when he came home and would learn to manage the farm.

Although Bagleigh could hardly be described as a large country estate it was more than just a working farm and James Stanmore seldom laboured with his men in the fields. He rode around his land on a splendid hunter and directed the work mainly from the saddle. He expected both his children to fit in with this way of life, and it had always been understood that neither would expect a career. Diana must help her mother and hope to marry well, while

28

his son, as heir to Bagleigh, would spend his life here under his father's direction. Colin's all-consuming interest in archaeology had caused much ill humour and disagreement. That he had eventually had his way, albeit for a year only, owed much to the persuasion of Aunt Harriet, the writer of the other letter, for she had ranged herself firmly on her nephew's side.

Harriet had lived in Palestine ever since her marriage, and even when she was widowed she had refused to come home and put herself under her brother's offered protection. James believed firmly that women should be dependent and subservient, always willing to be sheltered and protected. That this sister of his led such an outrageous life shocked him deeply.

'What does Colin say?' Diana asked a trifle nervously.

'Damned impertinent rascal,' James replied as he slit open the second envelope. 'Wants you to go out and join him for a few weeks!' He pushed his now empty plate to one side and prepared to read the letter from his sister.

Diana couldn't help a swift rush of hope, a flush of pleasure. This was what she wanted so desperately, had longed for ever since Colin went away. She put her hand on the thickness of David's letter in her pocket, for he was in Palestine too. She longed to rush to her bedroom and read what he said, but she knew that she must do nothing to arouse her father's suspicions.

Her mother had put Colin's letter down and was now clearing away the used plates on to the sideboard, carrying toast and marmalade to the table. Mary Stanmore's subservience irked Diana greatly. Even as a small child she had sometimes rebelled at the rules laid down by her father for all of them, and now that she was grown and expected by him to be little more than an ornament here in the house, she was becoming increasingly frustrated. They had a woman to cook and two maids to do most of the housework so there was little for her to do. Her father didn't like to see her working on the farm either. Not women's work at all, he insisted.

Colin, of course, being a boy had been given the freedom and education that Diana had constantly longed for, but now perhaps there was hope. She looked with disquiet however at the increasingly stormy frown on her father's face as he read Aunt Harriet's letter. Harriet was his only sister and Diana knew that he was very fond of her although she had been a constant thorn in his flesh. She was as stubborn and independent as he was himself and he couldn't rule her in any way.

Eventually he looked up. 'A conspiracy, that's what it is,' he announced. 'Harriet says she needs you to help in her ridiculous animal clinic for a few weeks.' He pushed the letter over to his wife, and then turned to his daughter. 'You know about this don't you, Diana?'

'I... Colin mentioned something about it in his last letter to me,' she said, hoping her voice sounded casual. 'I should very much like to go, Father. Would you give me your permission?'

'Absolutely not. No place for a girl. Dangerous, always has been, the Middle East. No. You stay here, and if it's this fascination with old stones you want, there are plenty up there on the moors.' He glanced dismissively towards the window where in the distance a great granite outcrop could be seen crowning the top of the steep heather-covered Dartmoor hillside that rose in splendour just beyond the front lawns of the house. 'Goodness knows why Colin should be interested in all this archaeology business. The sooner he gets it out of his head the better.'

'But, Father, Palestine is different, special,' she said quietly. 'There are so many things to see, so many ancient sites. It's the Holy Land. People go on pilgrimages there. Plenty of women go... It would be just the chance I need for my photography.' As soon as she had spoken those last words she knew that she had made a mistake.

'Photography be damned. Why can't you be content with snaps of the family and the moors? Wish I'd not given you that camera. I never thought it'd give you such fancy ideas.' He took another piece of toast and spread butter thickly and angrily upon it.

Diana was too exasperated to eat any more. She glanced at her aunt's firm unfussy writing on the envelope. It so perfectly portrayed all she knew of Aunt Harriet's character. She tried to take strength from it. Perhaps now was the time for the showdown that she knew had to come one day. She drew a deep breath. 'I'm

31

not content with taking family snapshots,' she said, 'because I wish to be a professional photographer, because I want a career of my own, because I think I have some talent. It's as important to me as Colin's wish to dig up ancient artefacts. And Palestine would be perfect, the lighting, the people, everything. It's the chance I need.' She didn't add, And David too is in Palestine! David of the flashing eyes and the Zionist passions. That would have been the knell of doom to all her hopes.

'Talent, pah! Just because a magazine published a few of your silly bits and pieces. Anyone could have taken them.'

She clenched her fists beneath the table and tried to keep her voice as calm as possible. 'I want to go very much, Father.' She had learned from her mother that with James Stanmore, diplomacy often achieved more than outright rage, and of course she could only go with his blessing for he saw to it that apart from a very small weekly allowance she had no money of her own. 'It's not like going alone,' she said, 'and plenty of women do that even. Aunt Harriet and Colin are there and will see that no harm comes to me.'

'No,' he said. 'I'm not spending all that money sending you to some outlandish part of the world. It's in the bank, young lady, ready to finance the wedding you'll no doubt want some day soon. That's a woman's place, getting wed. You find the right man and I'll be generous. But for this harebrained idea, most definitely no.'

'But you allowed Colin...'

'That's quite different as you well know. He's a man. He can look after himself.'

Diana pursed her lips in frustration and rage. She wanted to shout at her father that he was living right back in the last century and that it was 1938 now. Women were free and independent. But she looked at her mother and knew that it was not true, not for her family anyway. Her father would always dominate, always have his way.

Mary Stanmore was reading Harriet's letter now and Diana watched her carefully, wondering what she thought. She was a small fair woman, an echo of her husband, and she appeared on the surface at least to have no opinions of her own and few wants that were not amply supplied by the lovely spacious house and a generous clothes and housekeeping allowance. She frequently told Diana that she wondered how on earth she could have given birth to such a restless and discontented daughter.

She surprised both of them however by putting the letter firmly down on the table and glaring at her husband. 'Read it again, James,' she directed. 'Read between the lines. Your sister needs help. She's always been independent, and you haven't liked that, but now she's appealing to you for Diana's assistance for a short time. You should be flattered that she's asking you at last.'

James looked at his wife in amazement. 'Huh,' he grunted. 'I always knew that Harriet was crazy.' He took the letter again and looked at it in disgust. 'Enlarging her animal clinic indeed!

And what an outlandish place to choose. If she was so keen to help animals there are plenty here she could have concerned herself with. Damn silly name for a house too, let alone a donkey home. Khanhaven! What sort of a name is that?'

'She's bought more land,' Mary said, her voice returning to its more usual diffident tone. 'I've often felt worried about her all on her own over there. Couldn't you let Diana go just for a little while? She's always been good with animals, and Colin is there. Quite near anyway, I believe.' She smiled tremulously as if both surprised and pleased at her own courage.

Amazed, Diana waited for her father's outburst after such a daring suggestion from her normally passive mother. She longed to pick up both the letters and read them for herself. Whatever could Aunt Harriet have written to have inspired this unusual display of rebellion? 'May I read them?' she said quietly when no explosion came.

'If you wish,' her father replied, his mouth full of toast. 'I don't know where that foolish woman gets her crazy ideas from. Can't believe she's my own sister. I'd hoped she was coming home, not extending her stupid set-up.'

In spite of the words his tone was surprisingly indulgent and Diana knew that this exuberant younger sister had always possessed some power over him. It was a strange little chink in his armour. She remembered her aunt's visits long ago when she was small. She had come with her husband just before they went off to Palestine.

Uncle Edward was mostly a vague memory now, but she knew from the wedding photograph on the piano that he'd been a big handsome man, something in a British bank in a place called Haifa. He had been killed in some terrorist outrage and Aunt Harriet had come home alone. She had stayed with them for a month and then had firmly stated her resolve to return. 'I'm going to set up an animal sanctuary in an Arab village I know. I want to teach them how to love and care for their donkeys and goats and dogs, especially the dogs.'

Diana remembered her love for Cally, the old retriever they had then. Of course her father had been scandalised but Harriet had resolutely had her own way, and had only been home for one short visit since. But there were frequent letters.

As she read this last one a small measure of hope filled Diana's heart. The Arab girl, Samira, who had been her aunt's assistant for many years, was leaving to get married and she needed someone quickly she said. As Diana read she sensed a loneliness and an appeal for more than just practical help. She looked up at her father and saw that he too had felt the need behind the cheerful words.

Colin probably had something to do with the idea too, she thought. He visited their aunt frequently. In a previous letter he had said that he was working near her village. Then another thought flashed into her mind. David and Colin were close friends and often saw each other. Had he too suggested that she might go

35

out to Palestine? His letter was still unread in her pocket.

'Don't refuse outright, James,' Mary Stanmore persisted timidly. 'Harriet is your only sister after all.'

James Stanmore stood up and brushed crumbs from his jacket. 'I'll give the matter a little more thought,' he said. Then, turning to Diana, 'But don't get hopeful. I doubt if I can bring myself to allow you to go. It's a dangerous place to be, what with Arabs and Jews throwing bombs at one another, and there's going to be a war in Europe soon.' He picked up the morning's copy of *The Times* which was lying to hand and glanced at it. 'Good thing that Jewish friend of Colin's isn't living in Austria or Germany. It's bad for Jews in Europe just now. What was his name?'

'David,' Diana whispered, and hoped that her father was not aware of the beating of her heart or the flush on her face.

'Don't like Jews, never did,' he muttered. 'But that's no reason to kill 'em.' He looked at his daughter with sudden suspicion. 'Hope you don't intend to fall for that young man? Don't imagine that I was unaware of those silly eyes you fluttered at him when Colin brought him here last summer. You marry a Jew or a wog, my girl, and you're no daughter of mine.'

Diana had heard those words many times before and each time her sense of shock and outrage was as great as ever. Yet she said nothing. She dared not argue with him, must say nothing that might harden his resolve to keep her anchored here at Bagleigh. She cleared away some plates on to the side table.

'Don't worry about me, Father,' she said as sweetly as she could manage. 'There's more coffee. Shall I pour you some?'

Later, in the privacy of her room, she opened her own letter and read it. To her disappointment it was a very ordinary communication, no endearments, no encouragement to the romantic feelings she felt for him. He was settling into kibbutz life fairly well, David wrote, although after years at Oxford he wasn't used to heavy manual work. He had done a period of training in an agricultural school and that had helped.

He described the things he did each day, the Spartan accommodation, and mentioned that he and her brother met frequently at Mrs Clayton's house which was quite close. Diana read with amusement his descriptions of Aunt Harriet and the work she was doing, her endeavours to impart to the Arab villagers her very English middle-class values about animals. Then he mentioned Samira who worked at Khanhaven. Apparently she would never look directly at any man, but kept her eyes cast down as she spoke. Diana felt slightly apprehensive about the space he gave to this girl, but no Jew could be attracted to an Arab surely? Her brother too had mentioned Samira more than once.

Diana was far more worried about the girls who lived on the kibbutz. Colin visited there frequently and he had described them in one of his previous letters. They were mostly clever and full of ambition and energy, he had said, strong outdoor types, and all of them sharing David's Zionist dreams.

Later that day she rode up on to the hill above the house. There was a small nub of disquiet in her heart and she needed the companionship of her dog and the gentle chestnut mare. Both were comfortable to be with, giving a sense of love and security that she found nowhere else. She had owned Merryon for four years now and there was a deep bond between them. Her father frequently tried to persuade her to ride something larger and faster but she always refused. Rollo, the big labrador, was a true friend too, seldom allowing her out of his sight if he could help it.

Diana sat easily on the mare and let her have her head. Together the three of them took the winding path beyond the farm, where it curved steeply upwards out of the valley towards the wildness of the rocky hillside. There was no other person in sight in all that vast landscape and she shivered. Used though she was to these wild tors she always felt slightly intimidated when she was alone up here. It seemed that she became one with the sky and the heather-clad earth, but most of all with the ancient stones of the hut circles that lay just below the summit.

When the mare stopped and lowered her head to crop the short grass Diana slid down from the saddle and stood quite still, staring at the known and much loved landscape. She could just see the roof of her home surrounded by trees down in the valley below. She had grown up there in the security and beauty of Bagleigh Hall, and since leaving school ten months ago her life had been encompassed by the gentle rhythm of the countryside and its demands. Colin had been to Oxford, but her father had insisted that girls needed no education after eighteen. She had spent these last months reading, riding on the moors, helping her mother with various charitable events and, much against her father's will, working sometimes on the farm with the men. But now she was full of energy and ambition and longed for something more demanding.

She gave a lot of time to photography. Ever since she had been given a camera for her birthday three years ago she had been fascinated by its possibilities, and when *Picture Post* bought five of her Dartmoor photographs, the idea that she might one day make a career of her hobby had begun to take root in her mind.

It was an ancient Bronze Age hut circle that had featured in that first success and today she led her mare into the centre of the biggest one that crowned the summit of the tor. Leaning down, she ran her finger along the rough granite with its encrusting lichen and softer mosses. For a moment she felt a sense of oneness with the women who had lived here around three thousand years ago, whose home this had been.

Then she laughed at herself and tried to banish the eerie thoughts. These shadowy spirits must surely exist only in her imagination, but she had always had this instinctive empathy for times past. It was something that she shared with Colin and her thoughts travelled suddenly away from these wild Dartmoor hills to those others where her brother was working on another and quite different ancient site.

She dismounted, dropped the reins, and sat on one of the stones, warmed now by the spring sunshine. She took David's letter from her pocket again and her heart thumped as she held it in her hands. How clearly she remembered the day last summer when they had been here together. Colin had frequently invited his friend to Bagleigh during the university vacations, and last year, after they had both finished their finals, he had stayed longer than before. Colin spent some of his time helping on the farm and she and David had frequently ridden or walked together. She remembered one special afternoon.

The sky had been a brilliant brassy colour, she recalled, as it often was in high summer. David, staring at the great sweep of moorland, was obviously thinking of another landscape, the one that held his dreams. He had talked passionately about his hopes of a homeland in Palestine where Jews would be safe from hatred and persecution. He had shared his extravagant ambitions with her, and although she knew little about it she had felt honoured, flattered even. His eyes had burned with a ferocious zeal that she had never met before in anyone, and she had tried to enter into his enthusiasm while secretly wishing that some of the intensity she could feel in him was for her.

He had kissed her, just a quick kiss, almost brotherly, and she had longed to throw her arms around him and never let go. She wanted to say to him, look at me. I'm here and I'm flesh and blood and I love you. She knew that subconsciously she had resented his passion for a place, a faraway land. She had wanted to make him forget his precious Eretz Israel, as he called it, and think only of her.

But now she knew better, knew that this part of him was his very being itself and if she ever wanted him she would have to accept that too. Her brother had warned her later. 'Don't get any ideas,' he had said. 'David is a capital bloke, one of my greatest friends, but he's a crazy Zionist. He'd never marry a non-Jew.'

She read the letter twice over looking for some vestige of hope, but there was none. Its tone was friendly, answering the one she had sent to him. It was full of a vibrant living quality that seemed to spring from the pages, but she could tell that the ardour beneath the words was for the hills and plains of Palestine. There was nothing special for her alone.

She sighed and tucked it back into her jacket pocket. Then she remounted, and Merryon, responding to her touch, turned and walked carefully, placing her hooves in the grassy spaces between the stones. Rollo bounded in front, taking care to avoid the prickly gorse. It was still bare of blossom up here in this exposed place and Diana glanced down at it and felt that its barren state mirrored her feelings. The bracken too looked brown and dead, very little left of the tall waving fronds of last summer.

But as they went further down into the valley she saw that the gorse was coming into bloom, the yellow flaming against the duns and greens. She hadn't noticed it on the way up. The brilliant colour and the sudden call of a cuckoo, the first she had heard this year, sent her spirits soaring unexpectedly and she laughed at the dog as he wove his way backwards and forwards sniffing at every hole. Perhaps the cuckoo and the gorse were omens. She believed in omens, especially good ones.

For two weeks nothing more was said by her father about the longed for trip. Mary Stanmore indicated to her daughter that she thought he might be thinking about it favourably after all though. It was his sister's letter that had caused this unexpected change of mind.

'It looks as though there's going to be a war in the next year or two,' Mary explained as if some further excuse for his surprising switch of attitude was called for. 'He wants all the family back safe and sound in England. I think he believes that you might be able to persuade Harriet to come home.'

'Sounds crazy to me,' Diana said. 'But I won't argue if it gets me there.' She thought for a moment. The news coming out of Europe was certainly grim but so far she hadn't given it too much thought. 'But it won't affect the Middle East, will it?' she asked. 'I should think Aunt Harriet and certainly David Halprin would be safer in Palestine than here if Hitler isn't stopped in his tracks soon.'

'Whatever has David Halprin got to do with it?'

'Just...well, he's Jewish.' Diana realised, with a shock of dismay at her own carelessness, that she was not supposed to be at all interested in her brother's friend.

Mary however didn't pursue the matter further. 'I don't know, I'm sure,' she said. 'I'm not really interested in politics, but there always seems to be trouble of some sort in Palestine. I just wish Colin would come home, and Harriet too. Maybe you can all come back together in time for Christmas.'

Diana could hardly contain her impatience to know her father's will, but instructed by her mother she remained silent. Eventually she was rewarded. James Stanmore suddenly made his momentous announcement. 'I have decided, that as Colin and Harriet are both in Palestine, you may go and help your aunt for a month or perhaps two at the most,' he said. 'I have made all the arrangements. And I hope that you'll be able to persuade that difficult sister of mine to give up her ridiculous animal clinic and come home. That's mainly why I am allowing you to go, and I expect you to do your best!'

CHAPTER 3

Diana stood on deck in the early morning and stared at the mountains of Lebanon soaring in the splendour of sunrise behind the beautiful city of Beirut. All was bustle and apparent chaos as the boat made ready to dock. Full of excitement she pushed into the most advantageous places to take photographs. This was the kind of opportunity she had longed for.

Colin had promised to meet her, and as soon as she was near enough to distinguish individual faces in the crowds thronging the quayside below, she put her camera away and searched for him. It would be comforting to see his cheerful familiar face in this rather fearsome looking place.

He had written to say that Aunt Harriet had insisted that he borrow her old car for the journey. And he had suggested that they tour around a bit before going to Khanhaven so that she could see the countryside. She had been very thrilled about that.

But predictably her father had objected. 'It's not safe,' he had complained. 'Why can't you go straight to Harriet's?'

But Diana had been reading as much as she could about the Middle East. She had tried to reassure him. 'It's all right now, Father. With Syria in French hands and Palestine in

44

ours, it's safe to travel wherever you want. There are plenty of civilised police and troops around.' Then she had smiled at him with airy confidence, and knowing his patriotism and great pride in being British she had added, 'And with a British passport, whatever could possibly happen to me?'

He had made all the arrangements for her journey, choosing her route with care, insisting that Beirut was best, probably she guessed with a spark of amusement because it was the one place he knew. Better than Alexandria or Port Said, he had declared importantly. And now she was really here in this most exciting bit of the world.

At last she spotted Colin. He was waving enthusiastically and his tall figure was unmistakable. She pushed her fair hair back beneath the large hat that her mother had suggested she wear for the sun and gripped her small leather suitcase more tightly. Then she walked carefully down the gangplank from the boat, down towards her brother, towards the biggest adventure of her life, into the jostling crowd of Arabs and Jews, beggars and Bedouin.

Colin rushed towards her, pushing his way impatiently through. When he reached her he kissed her briefly on the cheek and grabbed her case. 'So he actually let you come!' he said. 'Jolly good show, Sis. I was afraid right up until the last minute that he'd make some excuse.'

Diana beamed at him. 'So was I. It was Aunt

Harriet's letter that did it though,' she said. 'Father would never have listened to you or me. He wants me to persuade her to go back to England for good, you know. Mother put in a word for me too, surprisingly.'

Brother and sister stood and looked at each other. He was tanned now and his dark hair was showing slightly gingerish tints here and there as it occasionally did in the summer holidays at home when he had been out in the sun.

'It's lovely to see you again, Colin,' Diana said. 'You look very healthy and fit. It obviously suits you here.'

'And we'll soon have you with a suntan and some of your famous freckles,' he laughed. 'It's a great country.'

'Come on then, show it to me. I can't wait. I could do without the freckles though!' She wanted to add, And when can I see David? but she forbore. Her father's awful words about Jews and wogs came suddenly and unwillingly into her mind, giving her an instant sense of guilt, almost as if she had spoken them herself. They made her feel foreign and out of place, pale and insipid among these colourful noisy crowds.

Colin found the rest of her luggage, and when all the formalities were dealt with he stacked the cases in the back of the car.

'You seem to have brought your whole wardrobe,' he remarked. 'We don't get much chance to dress up, you know.'

'It was Mother,' Diana explained. 'She insisted that I bring almost everything. She bought me a lot of new things too.'

46

Colin laughed. 'I daresay you'll find a use for them. You can always give some of them away like Aunt Harriet has done. Samira wears one or two of her dresses over Arab skirts and trousers!'

There it was again, the name of the Arab girl that she had read in his letters and in David's too. Diana turned her head to look at her brother but his expression gave nothing away. Well, she reflected, she would probably meet Samira soon. Then she would know if there was anything between the two of them. It was an uneasy thought.

Colin drove carefully out of the town and into the hills. They passed orange trees and olive groves and Diana breathed in the dry scent-laden air with delight. The little car chugged valiantly round hair-pin bends as they climbed higher and higher. They passed small villages of brown flat-roofed houses, and at a particularly beautiful spot they stopped to look at the view of Beirut and the sea far below.

Her first impression of the town had been of a large disorderly sort of place but charming and with a French look to it, reminding her of a visit she'd made to Provence a few years ago. And from up here it was exquisite, more beautiful than anything she had ever seen. The bay on which it stood was blue and sparkling and the houses rose up in tiers on the slopes of the hills like a great white amphitheatre.

'It's so lovely,' she whispered. 'I hope we can come back some time.'

'We will,' Colin promised. 'I should like to

explore Beirut properly, but we're staying at Baalbec for two nights now. It's a very special place with some spectacular ruins that I want to see while I'm in the area. A Greek friend of Aunt Harriet's runs a hotel there. Yes, there's a hotel,' he added, laughing at the look of disbelief on her face. 'In fact three or four, I believe. Aunt Harriet swears that her friend's is the best. She thought that you'd like a day in the mountains to relax before the drive south and I jumped at the idea. Once you get to Khanhaven you'll get no time to yourself, believe me, so make the most of it.'

Diana admitted to feeling tired after the long journey and she was glad of this respite. Later that day she looked with pleasure at the clean little room to which she was shown. There was a narrow bed and white-painted furniture. A window opened on to an interior courtyard, and the temperature was pleasant, the thick stone walls keeping out both the heat of the day and the cold of the night. She unpacked a few necessary things, washed and changed, and feeling refreshed, joined her brother for the evening meal. There was a bowl of rice and another of goulash. She helped herself liberally and found that the meat was tender and the sauce delicious.

'Kid, probably,' Colin remarked. 'We ought to get a herd of goats at home. Jolly nice animals.'

Diana stopped eating, her fork halfway to her mouth. 'Kid? Oh, how horrible. They're sweet little things.'

'For a farmer's daughter you're quite impossible! All the male kids are killed almost as soon as they're born. They wouldn't remain sweet little things for long.'

Slowly she put the food into her mouth. 'No, I suppose not.' She finished the first course reluctantly, her pleasure in it rather diminished. I mustn't be so sentimental, she told herself firmly. It's a luxury that won't do for abroad.

There was fruit and cheese afterwards.

'More to your fancy?' Colin asked.

'Definitely,' she replied. 'I could live on cheese like this.'

Colin laughed at her. 'That's also from the goats. But tell me about home. I'm dying for all the latest news. It seems a long time since I saw the folks.'

'Nothing very exciting to tell.' Diana's thoughts were jolted unwillingly away from her surroundings. She didn't want to think about her parents and all the restrictions of Bagleigh just now, but she glanced at his eager face and tried to comply. 'Mother and Father are just the same as ever, I suppose, and longing for you to go back and take over the farm. At least that's what Father says. He wants me to persuade you to return as soon as possible in fact.'

When Colin replied there was a slightly bitter edge to his voice. 'I'm only here for a year anyway. I shall have to go back when my money runs out, and that won't be all that long.'

'Couldn't you get a job?'

'I thought you said you intended persuading me to go home?'

Diana laughed. 'No, that wasn't what I said. That's what Father wants me to do.'

'Can you ever imagine him allowing me to run the farm?'

'Frankly, no. He likes the idea though. Says he wants to travel.'

'Travel? Father travel? That'll be the day.' Colin suddenly changed the subject. 'How's Major by the way? Have you managed to keep him exercised?'

'Yes, I hope so. Rob promised to take him out every day while I'm away. He's good with animals, the best worker we've ever had, Father says.'

Colin nodded. 'Hope he'll stay. The last time we talked he was thinking about joining the Army. Apparently they want men like him for the cavalry. They still use horses sometimes even now.'

Diana shivered in spite of the warmth of the evening. 'Do you really think there'll be a war? Father's sure of it. He says that the only way to stop Hitler is by brute strength.'

'I can just hear him saying it! He's probably right though. It's only twenty years since we smashed the Hun in the last lot.'

'Let's talk about something else, shall we?' she pleaded. 'It's my first night in the Holy Land and I want to think about...' She paused. 'Oh, thousands of things, your excavations, Jerusalem, my photography, Galilee, Aunt Harriet's endeavours.'

50

'And David perhaps?'

Diana sat bolt upright and stared at her brother. 'Yes David perhaps,' she repeated. 'When am I going to see him?'

'Soon, probably. He's just as intense as ever about his precious Jewish homeland here, of course. He lives on a farming settlement quite near Aunt Harriet's bungalow.' Colin took a sip of the strong black coffee that had been brought to them. 'It's a kibbutz actually, sort of communal living,' he explained. 'They call it Beth Haron.'

'Yes, I know. He writes to me.'

'Of course. I'd forgotten. So you don't need me to tell you all about his latest doings?'

'He doesn't say much. Tell me about the kibbutz.'

'I go over there when I'm in the area and need some company,' Colin said. 'They've made a small swimming pool—a bit of a misnomer really although they like to call it that. It's just a pond really for storing water but it's jolly welcome after a day's work in the heat.' Colin drummed his fingers on the table. 'You liked him a lot when he came to Bagleigh, didn't you? I've been worried about it. He's no good for you, Diana. He'll never give up his ideals, his passion for this place. I'm certain that he won't go back to England to live, unless there's a war of course. In that case he'd want to fight Hitler, but he's part of this land now, almost as though he was born here.'

'Then I shall live here too, if he asks me.' Diana blushed and looked down at the

51

tablecloth. Absent-mindedly she stirred more sugar into the thick brew in front of her. 'I love him, Colin. I knew it when you first brought him home to stay during that long vac, and then, when he came again last summer, I was quite sure.'

Colin shook his head. 'So it's my fault? I should have expected it. Girls were always falling for him in Oxford.' He was silent for a time and then he addressed her by the old affectionate name. 'Be careful, Dido. I don't want you hurt. You'd hate to live here permanently, whatever you think now. It's a tough land. It demands the very life blood of its people. Kibbutz life is no picnic either. You have to be dedicated, and you're not Jewish.'

'I could become Jewish, couldn't I? Would I have to adopt the faith?'

'I don't know. I'm not sure whether it's even possible, whether they would accept you.'

Suddenly the problems that she had pushed to the back of her mind became intrusive. She felt a strange heaviness as if a grey cloud had appeared from nowhere, covering her, replacing the happiness. She tried to turn the conversation to other things.

'And what about you then?' she said, forcing her voice to sound lighter, even slightly teasing. 'Any romantic attachments on the dig? There must be plenty of nice female archaeologists around as well as ancient bones.'

He failed to respond as she thought he would and her concern switched from herself to her brother. A shutter seemed to come down over his face and she winced for her own insensitivity. It was her turn to worry now. She found herself praying fervently, Please God, let it not be the Arab girl!

Eventually he forced a laugh, drank the remains of his coffee and got up from the table. 'Don't worry about me,' he said. 'One broken heart is enough in the family. Come on. You've had a long hard day and I want you to see the sunrise from the hotel roof in the morning. I'm told it's quite remarkable. You're tired. Go to bed soon. I hope you sleep well.'

'You sound just like Father,' she said, trying to reassert the previous easy banter between them. 'Patronising!'

'Sorry, old thing. I'll endeavour to remember your liberated status. Not easy in Palestine.'

'Not easy at Bagleigh either.'

'No, of course not.'

The guarded look was gone from his face but she knew that he was not going to talk any more about himself and she must be content to wait. He would confide in her eventually.

'See you in the morning then. Don't over-sleep,' he commanded.

The sky was aflame with the crimson light of the rising sun when Diana obediently climbed the outside stone stairway to the roof, early the following day. She gasped in delight at the distant snow-capped Lebanon hills tinged with pink and gold and at the nearer giant columns of the great temple ruins. Colin was already there and they stood together staring at the beauty on every side.

'I really could live in this place,' she whispered. 'In spite of what you said, I could live here for ever!'

'If you married David, you wouldn't be day-dreaming about old stones. You'd be digging the ground, learning to use a gun, tending animals from early morning to dark.'

'Here we are in one of the most romantic places on earth and you're spoiling it talking about work!' Her voice was teasing.

'I'm just being realistic.'

'I don't want realism today. This place is magical. I could do with some magic for a few hours.'

Colin laughed. 'Me too,' he said. 'We'll give ourselves up to Baalbec's treasures for the whole day.'

'I'm afraid that I shan't find our Dartmoor hut circles quite so enthralling now,' Diana said a few hours later as she ran her hand over the warm stones of the Temple of Bacchus. The entrance doorway was almost perfect. It soared above them and she stared at it with awe. 'However did they do it? Build places like this, I mean?' She focused her camera and took several shots.

Colin watched her activities with interest. 'I see that your enthusiasm for photography hasn't waned?'

'Photojournalism actually. I write about my photographs as well. I'm more keen than ever. I want a better camera than this and I'd like

54

to make a career of it.' She moved to another advantageous spot and he followed her.

'Career? That won't please Father.'

'I know. He wants me to marry and settle down as soon as possible. He thinks that's the only option for a girl.'

'To the right person, I presume?'

'Of course. I believe he favours Philip Briscoe.'

'Nice chap, rich too, and definitely highly eligible.' Colin laughed dryly. 'I suppose he's in for a shock then?'

Diana put her camera away in its case. 'The end of my film,' she said, not answering his query. 'I've lots more in my luggage.' She returned to her previous subject. 'These amazing buildings. How did they manage to build them without modern equipment?'

'Various methods,' Colin said. 'There are lots of theories. And they had plenty of cheap labour, slave and the like. They must have been more industrious than the inhabitants nowadays, judging by the state of the present villages anyway.'

His words made Diana think of El Admah, the village near her aunt's home which he had briefly described to her the previous day. 'Tell me a bit more about Aunt Harriet's set-up?' she said. 'What am I letting myself in for?'

'You'll like it. Aunt is a fantastic person. I'm constantly amazed that she and Father are brother and sister.'

'And Samira?'

'Samira is beautiful and good and clever!'

Diana was struck by the sudden intensity of her brother's words and she couldn't help being aware of the pain and anger in his voice. She saw him clench his fists and then he turned his back on her.

She was completely dismayed. It was more serious than she had thought. Not knowing what to say, she too turned away and walked through the ruins to the place where the busts of Venus and Diana, Minerva and Bacchus stood. She stared at them almost unseeing at first, and then a sense of peace began to take the place of the conflict. Just as the wild tors and the old granite stones of Dartmoor always seemed to help her to come to terms with whatever turmoil held her heart, so this magical place too brought a small measure of harmony. Perhaps it was only an illusion but Diana felt comforted as though the present reality was part of some greater plan, the smallness lost in the whole.

They reached the small Arab village of El Admah during the early evening of the following day and Colin drove slowly through the dusty street and straight out again on the other side towards Harriet's house which stood a mile away along the track.

There was a signpost, a rough wooden affair, that read 'Khanhaven'. Diana stared at it, fascinated. She had read it often on her Aunt's notepaper, and here was the reality.

'Why did she call her house Khanhaven?' she suddenly asked her brother. 'Father called it a damn silly name, but I've always liked the sound of it. Doesn't it seem a bit unusual here though? Isn't there a touch of Scotland about it?'

'Not to my knowledge.' Colin was watching the road carefully for it was more pitted and uneven than ever now and there were chickens pecking here and there. 'The Khan bit is Arab, I should think, and the haven is self-evident,' he said. 'Aunt Harriet fills the place with stray animals as you know. These chickens are hers by the way. We're nearly there.'

They rounded a bend in the track and Diana had her first glimpse of the sprawling bungalow that she had so often imagined. It was a comfortable welcoming place, well named and quite unlike any of the Arab houses she had seen. It stood alone, with a shaded balcony that ran the whole length of the front and there were tubs of flowers bright against the stone walls.

With a screech of brakes Colin brought the vehicle to a halt and they were enveloped in a cloud of red dust. He jumped out quickly and came round to open the passenger door. But before Diana could get out a dog rushed from the house barking furiously but then stopped, recognising him.

'Meet Ghazala,' Colin said. 'A saluki rescued by our aunt.'

The beautiful animal nuzzled his hand and he responded to her enthusiastic greeting, bending down and ruffling her long coat. Then Diana saw him suddenly look up. He straightened himself and seemed to forget both her and the dog. She followed his glance and saw a girl at the open door of the house. She had pulled the bead curtain aside and was standing there blinking in the sun.

Diana scrambled from the hot and sticky seat of the car and stared at the girl and then at Colin. She saw the look that passed between them, the longing as their eyes met for an instant, holding them both, excluding everyone and everything else.

She was shocked, horrified at what she saw, for now there was no room for any doubt. What she had suspected and tried not to believe was true after all. She saw at once that they loved each other. And she remembered that it was a totally forbidden love, for this could be none other than Samira, the Arab girl who was to be married soon.

Diana stood beside the car not wanting to move. She was gripping the door handle so tightly that her knuckles ached.

At last Colin came to himself. He turned to Diana and took her hand, pulling her gently through the small wooden gate. She noticed that the girl was not looking at them now, but standing quite still with bent head.

'This is Samira,' he said quietly. 'Samira, meet my sister.'

Diana wasn't sure how to greet her, what to say, but suddenly the girl raised her eyes shyly and they stared at each other for a moment. Then both smiled, and whether it was acceptable or not, Diana held out her hands and took Samira's. 'I know we're going to be friends,' she said. She had no idea how prophetic her words would prove to be.

CHAPTER 4

Kaffa pricked her finger and looked down in annoyance at the tiny swelling circle of blood. She was skilled with her needle and she surprised herself by her carelessness, especially now that she was putting the finishing touches to Samira's wedding garments. She thrust her finger into her mouth and sucked forcefully, then dabbed it on to her own multi-coloured skirt. She supposed that it was her grief over the imminent loss of her only daughter that was causing her to be so inattentive.

She had always been proud of her ability as a needlewoman. At the Bethlehem orphanage she had been taught many special embroidery stitches and patterns and the long and much resented hours of sewing in her childhood had borne fruit, giving her a valuable skill. The beautiful garments she made were a constant source of pride, and she was able to earn a little money which gave her added value in her husband's eyes. She often received orders for wedding clothes and these always had to be brightly coloured and patterned with gold and silver thread. The wives of some of the English Administrators too were beginning to discover how lovely her traditional embroidery was. Occasionally they would drive out to El Admah in their noisy motor cars and pay well for her work.

59

But for the past few weeks Kaffa had been concentrating on her own daughter's bridal garments. She paused for a moment until the tiny flow of blood from her finger should be staunched as she thought of Samira's birth. She had been the second child and Jebel had looked down at the tiny screwed up face of his new baby without much interest. He wanted sons. She remembered his words. 'Next time another boy,' he had said. 'One or two girls to do the work, but we want sons, Kaffa.' She had smiled at him weakly and prayed silently to Allah that it would be so. Zeid had been her next child, and then four more boys. Allah had answered. After Assad there had been no more children. Kaffa had no idea why but as long as her husband didn't bring home another wife to make up for her barren years she was secretly grateful.

She started to sew again, carefully now. She wanted Samira to have the very best for her wedding, almost as if her efforts could atone in some way for the girl's grief, and for her own sorrow too. Certainly the bridegroom had not stinted on any of the trousseau. He had provided money for material, and vast numbers of small shining coins to be stitched into the headdress. He had sent some beautiful jewellery too.

Kaffa knew that although Samira had seemed impressed by the presents they did nothing to lift her desolation. She had whispered to her mother, 'The present I most want is my freedom,' but Kaffa had not really understood. Freedom was a concept she couldn't begin to imagine. Even the men were not completely free. They owed allegiance to Allah. But a woman was in bondage from the moment of her birth. Samira must put her foolish ideas right out of her mind for ever. Kaffa had always known where her duty lay and her daughter must follow the same way. There was nothing anyone could do to rescue her from Eshref now. She surprised herself by this last thought. The word 'rescue' was out of place. She wondered why it had come into her mind.

The wedding preparations started early on the dreaded day and Samira was filled with a hopelessness that was in stark contrast to the excited chattering all about her. When it was time to put on the elaborate costume that she and her mother had prepared she stood passive and unsmiling as her cousins dressed her. She could not even have the comfort of her mother's presence, for married women were not allowed inside the house at this point. As she had no sisters it was her cousins who performed the ritual of placing each piece of clothing on her unwilling body. The only thing that cheered her, the only consolation, was that she would see Jazi once more.

The girls appeared to be oblivious of her misery. They remarked in pleasure and envy at the brightly decorated dresses and congratulated her on the richness of the coins and jewellery.

What's the matter with me? Samira thought. Why can't I be contented with my father's choice? Any one of my cousins would happily change places with me today. Eshref is handsome and rich as my mother keeps telling me.

'You're lucky, Samira,' the eldest cousin said, almost as if she could read her mind. 'I wish Sheikh Eshref had asked for me!' She giggled and brought the red veil which must now be placed on Samira's head.

'Your turn will come soon enough, Khadija. Make the most of your freedom while you have it.' Even as she spoke Samira wondered if any of her friends had any notion of what freedom meant, the kind of freedom she saw every day at Mrs Clayton's bungalow, the freedom she had glimpsed on the kibbutz.

'I think it will be much more fun and more enjoyable to wait on a husband than on my father and my brothers,' Khadija said. 'I hope to have more freedom when I'm married than I have now,'

'I hope you will,' Samira replied sincerely. 'I very much hope that your father chooses well for you.'

'As yours has,' Khadija said. She carefully fixed the red veil in place and then fetched the great white coat that must be draped over all the other garments. In this Samira was to ride to her bridegroom's village. It was traditional that the bride must ride, and must be heavily covered so that no evil eye could come upon her during the journey.

As Jazi was led to the door of the house she shivered in spite of the heat and the vast amount of clothes. His presence here seemed to symbolise everything that she was losing.

Jazi meant freedom and now he was carrying her into slavery.

Her father had announced some time ago that the stallion was the only horse worthy of the family and that he had hired him from Mrs Clayton for the wedding journey. The only other possibility was a camel, and he could not afford a camel. Samira guessed that Jazi came free!

She could see little through the heavy veil, but she heard the sounds of his hoofs, and she knew that he was nervous in the noisy throng. When she was brought out to stand beside him she struggled to release her hand from the constricting clothes and to touch his neck, gentling him, and she spoke to him quietly as she had done so many times before.

He hadn't recognised her at first, so covered was she in strange garments, but her voice calmed him immediately and he stood still and whinnied, nuzzling her softly.

Then, suppressing all her memories of their long rides together, the freedom and glory of them, she allowed herself to be lifted awkwardly on to his back and the procession moved off, the women and girls singing and dancing and Samira sitting tall and proud, determined that no one should know that her heart was breaking for her lost life, for everything that made living worthwhile, for Colin! She had determined that from now on her body would do, from day to day, and at night, what was required of it, for as her mother said there was no other way. But her mind and spirit would be entirely separate.

At least no one could enslave her thoughts.

For a second she allowed herself the luxury of thinking of Colin again. She had never before met a man who looked at her as he did, treating her as an equal with no condescension in either word or manner. He would be in her heart and in her dreams for the rest of her life, but she knew that those dreams were dangerous, more dangerous than anything she could imagine. No one but her mother must ever know of them.

As she rode she spoke to the horse from time to time, little endearments, but nothing that could be overheard. Her brothers were watching her critically, and she knew that they were jealous of her rapport with this beautiful animal. She imagined that she could see triumph in their faces, triumph that their clever and privileged sister had at last come to the end of her arrogant ways. They were obviously pleased that she was to be tamed at last.

A wave of fury swept through her, but she quickly tried to banish it and to control her wayward thoughts. Most importantly she must not allow any of her grief and anger to show.

When they reached the bridegroom's village she was helped down from her mount. She laid her head for a moment on Jazi's neck and then stepped back and stood silently as he was led away. She was glad of the thick red veil, for tears streamed down her cheeks, ruining the first layer of make-up that had been so carefully applied. For a second she wished, after all, that Jazi had not been chosen to carry her to her wedding. His going made everything even more terrible. Hope went with him down the village street. She thought of him back at Khanhaven with Harriet, with Colin.

But she knew that the veil hiding her grief must be lifted soon and she struggled to stop the flow of tears. Excited hands reached out to her and she allowed herself to be taken into the bridegroom's house. She sank on to the cushions that had been placed in readiness and strove with all her might to appear serene for the final ritual face painting, the transformation that denoted that her status was about to change. She tried not to flinch as red and white make-up was applied and gold leaf was pressed into her unwilling skin. She dared not cry now.

The older women were in high spirits as they worked, just as her young cousins had been, for everyone considered this an excellent match. The first wife had been sent away for the honeymoon period, they told Samira teasingly, so she would have Eshref all to herself.

Her mother had come over in the procession and when the work was complete she came into the house to make a final inspection. It was then that Samira knew that her grief was not hidden. Kaffa walked quickly to her daughter and took both of her hands in her own. They stood like that for a full minute and although no words were spoken there was a sympathy that passed between them, a bond which comforted each for that precious little time.

There had been much feasting during the celebrations both in her own village and here, but now everything was almost at an end. At last her new husband strode into the room and stood before her. Deftly he lifted her veil and she looked into his eyes. They seemed fierce and demanding and her heart beat for fear. Perhaps, had he been as young and inexperienced as she was, she could have made some effort, tried to salvage a little joy from her marriage, but she felt only a great weight of sorrow.

His mother had herself prepared a meal of delicacies which bride and groom must eat together as custom decreed. Samira looked at the dishes spread out on the low table and felt that she could not face any of it.

'Come,' Eshref commanded. 'You must eat. The food is given to us so that we should feel more comfortable together.'

She stared at him and wondered how she could ever feel comfortable with this man who would henceforth rule her life. 'I shall try,' she whispered.

At last when the sun was just rising in the morning sky the moment that she dreaded arrived. Eshref took her hand and led her into the special room that had been set aside for the consummation of their marriage. Slowly he took off his clothes and when she forced herself to look at him she was filled with both horror and amazement. She had never seen a naked man before. He was neither old nor fat and stood before her assured and powerful. He moved towards her and she backed involuntarily until the great bedstead was behind her and she could move no further away.

'Your clothes,' he said. 'Remove them.'

With cold fingers that seemed to refuse to do her will she obeyed and stood frightened and shivering in spite of the heat of the night. He looked at her for a moment and she blushed for shame as his eyes took in every line and curve of her body. Then he threw her back on the coverlet and forced himself upon her quickly and with no delicacy or thought for her pleasure, crushing her, cursing and wildly thrusting, enveloping her with himself until she thought that the world would end in the horror and the pain of it.

And when she thought she could bear no more and must at last cry out, cry for him to stop, he suddenly moved away and stood up unsteadily. He looked down at her and then roughly he pushed her aside and stared at the sheet on which she lay broken and bruised.

'There is no blood,' he said and his voice was icily cold and the anger in his eyes was the most terrifying thing she had ever seen. 'There is no blood. You have cheated me. You are no virgin. Your father has cheated me.' His arm swept towards her and she felt the stinging blow on her face and then he strode over to his clothes which were scattered on the floor. Roughly he pulled them over his body and went outside, leaving her shattered and trembling and even more terrified than she had been before. She heard shouting, angry voices and later her mother's wailing.

For a moment she sat unable to comprehend this terrible thing that had happened to her for she knew that she had never lain with anyone. She loved the Englishman but he had never touched her, not even her hand. No man had touched her before this awful night. With difficulty she pulled herself from the bed and looked down at it. It was soiled now but there was no blood, and blood was the sign of virginity. Her mother and mother-in-law would be waiting for the blood-stained sheet. It had to be proudly displayed to the entire village, a necessary sign that the bride was a virgin and that the marriage had been successfully consummated.

She took up some of the clothes that lay crumpled on the cushions and quickly pulled them over her head, covering her shivering body, and then she walked to the door of the tent.

Both of her mother's arms were held tightly by two of her brothers lest she should run to her daughter. 'She's innocent,' Kaffa screamed. 'I know my daughter, she is a true virgin. She has never lain with anyone.' She struggled to free herself.

Eshref was standing with her father whose face was contorted with anger. He looked at her and she cowered before his rage. 'You have cheated us,' he said. 'You, my only daughter have brought shame on your whole family.' His words were quiet, but fearful and deadly.

'I have never been with any man,' Samira shouted desperately. 'My father, my mother, I have never been with any man.'

'Then the sheets would prove it.' The last words were from Eshref. 'I want no tests done on the girl. No physician's documents will prove

68

to me what I know. She has deceived me. I want all my money and all my gifts back and you can take your daughter home. She is no wife of mine, nor ever has been.'

There was much heated argument between the two families and through it all Samira remained silent, knowing that any further protestations of innocence would be of no avail. No blood meant total disgrace, possibly death at the hands of her brothers. She had no idea why it should be, why she was not as other girls. And at last, after weary hours of wrangling, she heard the words called out loudly for all to hear, the words that every woman feared, the words of total disgrace: 'I divorce you. I divorce you, I divorce you.' Eshref stood staring at her as he spoke. His eyes were cold and he said the terrible chilling sentence three times as the law commanded. It was all that was necessary for any man to divorce his wife. Those words had the same effect, the same force, however long the marriage had lasted, thirty years or thirty minutes. A woman had no defence.

Samira felt numb with shock and horror and her legs shook as she turned away. They would hardly do her bidding. They seemed to belong to someone else. Then her mother, freed now, walked a few paces towards her, put out a hand and took hers and led her gently to the donkey cart for the return journey, the journey in disgrace back to her home. No word was spoken between them but she felt the understanding and the loving bond and because of it the tears began to flow once more. She climbed blindly into the cart and cared nothing about what would happen to her, but Kaffa sat close, stroked her hair now and then and wiped her face gently. There was fear in her mother's eyes, fear carefully guarded, but Samira sensed it and became fearful too.

It was after the middle of the day when they arrived back in the village. Her father had not spoken to her and she went into the small room that she had never thought to see again and threw herself on to the cushions and fell into an exhausted but fitful sleep. She was aware once or twice of waking and seeing her mother beside her, giving her a drink, stroking her hand, and then she slept again, longer this time, until darkness and silence fell upon the house.

She was awakened by a sudden noise in her room. She pulled herself from sleep and moved to ease her aching body, groaning as the memories of the day flooded back. Then she was fully awake for the noise came again and at first she thought it was her mother, for no man, brother or father, was ever allowed into her room. But then she saw, in the dim light of the lamp that always burned outside in the hallway, Gasim, her eldest brother. She sat up and pushed her hair from her eyes. 'What do you want?' she asked quickly.

'Bitch,' he whispered. 'Filthy disgusting bitch. You've shamed and defiled our whole family, and with a foreigner too! You've been with the Englishman.' He spat on the floor. 'My father was foolish to allow you to go out of our house every day. And I know about your reading and writing and fancy ways. Well, none of it will do you any good now.'

He moved quietly towards her and dragged her from the floor, putting his hand over her mouth and stifling her screams. Then she saw the glint of light on the curved knife in his belt and the fierce anger in his eyes. Zeid was behind him and he leapt at her throat, holding his knife so close that she could feel the coldness of the steel.

'No sound,' he commanded, and the flatness of the blade pressed closer on her neck. 'You come silently.'

Fear surged through Samira's body and although she struggled desperately it was without hope for she knew that she was helpless against their superior strength, just as she had been helpless before the violent lust and strength of Eshref. And the knife at her throat and the rough hand of Zeid pressing cruelly over her mouth ensured her silence.

She tried to call for her mother, but she could not, and she knew with a fearful certainty that it would be no use anyway. Kaffa would have been drugged so that she slept soundly. It had happened that way with Jamila's mother.

Together they dragged her out of the rear door of the house and down the village street. There was no one to hear their footsteps or to see their figures in the darkness for most of the windows of the small houses faced inwards towards a central courtyard, built like that for privacy and shade. She looked at each blank wall with rising hopelessness as with increasing terror she realised that they meant to kill her for the shame she had brought upon the family. It was always so. But they would not do it here. It would have to be done in some hidden and desolate place far away from the interfering eyes of the British Army and Police. Like Jamila...

She shuddered beneath their cruel hands as she remembered the mutilated body of her friend which had been found weeks later in the ravine on the other side of the valley, her neck broken and her body pierced through many times. Jamila's brothers had been suspected but there was no evidence. No one was ever accused of her murder. Harriet had told her that the British found it very difficult to interfere in these ancient family traditions. She had never thought those words would apply to herself.

Once beyond the village they stopped and tied her hands and put a rough gag round her mouth, and they walked swiftly, pulling her roughly as though she were an unwilling dog or an animal for slaughter. She could feel the sharp stones cutting into her bare feet. She wanted to cry out but the restraining band round her mouth was tight and she choked on it repeatedly. Suddenly she vomited and stumbled so that both brothers had to stop. Gasim angrily put his hand to her mouth to remove the gag and in that second she bit him like a terrified animal and as the cloth fell from her face she screamed repeatedly into the silent night. Zeid smashed his fist into her face and then the horror of the previous day and the terror of the present suddenly receded as she slid to the hard but welcome earth. She could feel it beneath her tightly bound hands before blackness overwhelmed her.

'What the hell...?' She heard the clear English words through mists of pain and terror and tried to raise her head, wondering where she was. She could see three figures now looming over her but they seemed to sway backwards and forwards and then faded into the all-encompassing blackness once more.

David Halprin let his bicycle fall to the ground and stared at the two men who were standing in the road. He could just see them in the moonlight and in the light from his lamp. He saw the girl lying on the ground too, but her face was turned away from him and he failed to recognise her. His first thoughts were that they were about to rape her.

'You bastards!' he said. 'I thought you Arabs were supposed to look after your women?'

'Just what we are doing,' Zeid growled. 'It's nothing to do with you, Jew.' He spat out the last word in contempt. 'Clear off. There's two of us.'

David laughed grimly. 'Two of you or not, I won't go until I see what filthy business you're up to.'

He quickly pulled the light from the front of his bicycle and shone it on to the face of the girl at his feet. He caught his breath in horror. 'Samira,' he said, and knelt beside her, feeling for her pulse. With relief he knew that she lived. He stood up and stared at the two men in disgust. In spite of their bravado they seemed temporarily nonplussed by his sudden appearance and he recognised them now as her brothers. 'I know this girl and I shall take charge of her. She needs a doctor.'

'It's you'll be needing a doctor,' Zeid said, quickly recovering himself. He pulled the jewelled dagger from his belt, but to David's surprise the other man put his hand on his brother's arm. 'We want no trouble at the moment with the kibbutz,' he said. 'Or with the British.' He turned to David. 'Our time will come. We'll avenge ourselves on your interference and your accursed presence in our land.' He spat angrily on the ground.

Zeid pulled free from his brother's restraining hand, and David, having no weapon, braced himself for an attack, but Gasim, much the bigger and stronger of the two, once again intervened. 'I have other plans,' he hissed to his brother. 'The girl's not worth the trouble. Let him have her for now. We'll bargain. He's a friend of the Englishman.'

David heard the words with relief. Although he was strong, had boxed at school and college, he knew that he could never hope to win in any combat with these two with their knives that glinted in the moonlight. They stood and looked at him menacingly.

'Take her,' Gasim said and kicked her savagely so that she moaned and, regaining consciousness, cried out and tried to struggle to her feet.

David helped her up and she leaned against

him for a moment for support. Then she stared around and shrank away from him and from her brothers. Even in the dim light he could see her swollen face and the terror in her eyes, and suddenly careless of his own safety, he turned in fury on the two men. 'Yes, I'll take her,' he said. 'To a place where she'll be cared for. Now go, both of you. Get out of my sight. You'll hear more of this.'

At once Gasim too pulled his knife. 'You only take the girl in return for your silence. Without that there's no deal.'

David looked at her, leaning now on a nearby olive tree, and concern for Samira's welfare overcame his desire for justice and revenge. 'All right,' he conceded. 'I take her and say nothing for the present.'

'Our father will come to see you. There will have to be a bargain.' Gasim spat the words at him and then both brothers turned and David watched them stride away down the road until they disappeared round the bend of the hill and he could hear only the gentle breeze in the branches of the tree above them, an owl hooting eerily, and Samira's frightened breathing as she stood terrified, swaying on her feet, watching him.

'Can you walk?' he asked her gently.

She nodded. 'I think so.'

David wanted to take her arm, to help her, but he knew that he must make no move towards her or he would terrify her afresh. If it was Diana or any girl from the kibbutz he would ask her to sit on the saddle of his bicycle

75

and would put his arm around her for support, but for an Arab girl that was impossible.

Samira could hardly take in anything that had happened to her during the last hour. She stared at David as though he were a figment of her imagination but gradually she began to realise that he had rescued her from her brothers, saved her from death in fact. Then suddenly she knew where she must go. There was only one place now where she would be safe, one person who could help her. 'Can I go to Mrs Clayton?' she whispered. 'Will you take me there?'

'Of course. It's not far, only a mile or so.' David had already decided on this course of action. But the girl looked so unsteady. He doubted if she would be able to manage the short journey. He decided to try the bike after all. 'Will you let me help you?' he said. 'You could go on the saddle.' He indicated the machine lying drunkenly on the ground.

Samira shook her head vigorously. 'I'm all right. I can walk.'

'OK then. Ready?' He picked up the bicycle and took a few doubtful paces. She followed, keeping a little way behind. He wished that at least she would walk beside him. But when he stopped she stopped too, so he walked steadily, looking back now and then. The night was very dark now, the moon suddenly hidden by clouds, and Samira kept fairly close to him. He could hear her crying, her sobs shaking her body and filling him with a monstrous anger. He had met her many times at Mrs Clayton's bungalow but they had seldom spoken. She had always been busy with the animals and usually kept her eyes cast down whenever he was there. He had once seen her at the kibbutz and had noticed her obvious amazement as she saw the girls in the new swimming pool. He had also been aware of the growing interest that Colin was showing in her and this had worried him. All these thoughts flashed through his mind as they slowly made their way back towards El Admah.

He was extremely apprehensive as they neared the village. He knew a way around it, but they had to go closer to the houses than he wished. There was no other possible route to Khanhaven. The brothers must have gone this way and he feared an ambush, a plot. Why had they released Samira so easily and without a fight? He didn't trust them. He wasn't particularly afraid for himself, but he was full of anxiety for the terrified girl trailing behind him.

CHAPTER 5

Harriet was awakened suddenly from sleep by the barking of her dogs. She sat up in bed and listened. She was seldom frightened, counting all the Arab families who lived in El Admah as friends, but she couldn't help a shiver of alarm at the sound of feet on the gravel path outside. But her fear subsided quickly and was replaced by concern when she heard David's voice calling

77

her name. She lit the candle that was always on her bedside table then slipped from bed, threw a shawl around her shoulders and went to the outer door. She placed the candle on a small shelf beside the door and pulled back the heavy bolts that were kept in place every night, commanded the still growling Ghazala, who was standing protectively beside her, to be quiet, and then opened the door. Suddenly, Samira was in her arms, sobbing and incoherent.

As she tried to calm the hysterical girl she was vaguely aware of David replacing the bolts with urgent haste. She glanced at him over Samira's head and as he turned to her she saw, in the flickering light of the candle, the grim set to his mouth. Numerous horrors flashed through her mind. 'What on earth...?' she said. 'What's happened?'

'I found her. Her brothers...' He almost spat out the last two words. 'Her brothers appeared to be about to murder her.'

Gently Harriet led Samira into the main room of the house and settled her on the long low sofa that ran the length of one wall. She sat beside her, cradled her in her arms like a child. 'You're safe now, dearheart,' she whispered. 'No one can hurt you here.'

Still holding her, calming her, she was aware of Diana, wakened by the commotion, standing in the doorway frightened and uncomprehending. Harriet forced herself to think, to be as calm as possible. 'There's been some sort of accident,' she said to her niece. 'Could you fetch warm water, please, Diana, and towels and something

78

to bathe Samira's face.' Then she turned to David. 'We need some more light. There are candles in the drawer beneath the table in the other room and you'll find matches for the lamp there too.'

She sat beside the terrified girl, holding her, calming her, brushing away the tears that streamed down her cheeks. Eventually the sobs began to lessen and Harriet felt Samira's tense frightened body relax a little in her arms. 'Don't try to talk yet,' she said, 'unless you wish to.'

'They might come for me. My father might come.' Samira glanced round as if she expected her brothers to materialise in the dark shadowy corners of the room.

'The door is bolted, David is here, and I'm quite capable of dealing with your father.' Harriet's words were however more confident than she felt. Jebel she could indeed deal with. He was a big blustering man but easily intimidated if she threatened the attentions of the British Authorities. Samira's brothers were a different matter.

There was a pause, quietness in the room. David had gone to look for the candles and Diana was heating water. Samira, seeing that she was alone with Harriet, bent her head low and whispered the awful shaming truth. 'They said that I was not a virgin. Eshref divorced me. There was no blood.' She gripped Harriet's hand tightly in hers. 'But I am...I was,' she corrected. 'No man had ever touched me before tonight. I had never been with any man. They wouldn't listen. My brothers were going to kill me. It is the custom when a girl dishonours her family.'

So that was it! Harriet could feel the slim body tense again in her arms and shuddered as she suddenly realized what must have happened. And she blamed herself for not having foreseen the danger. She should have known. This often happened to girls who rode a lot. Hadn't the same thing happened to her on her own wedding night? But with what different results! She remembered laughing with Edward over it, assuring him, in almost the same words that Samira had so desperately used, that she had never been with any other man. 'It's all the riding I do,' she had declared. 'You do believe me, don't you?' And he had pulled her into his arms again, loved her again. 'Of course I believe you, you ninny,' he had replied. 'It's a good thing you're not an Arab girl though. You'd be for the chop.'

She recalled the words clearly, was ashamed now by the remembered amusement it had caused them both. She had never thought that one day she would be involved in all the frightfulness of such a vicious law.

'Listen,' she said softly, 'I can explain what happened to you. Girls who ride as often and as energetically as you did frequently appear to lose their virginity. In England we understand this.'

Samira looked at her with wide-eyed amazement. 'So it was riding Jazi that caused it? Is that what you mean?'

'That's just what I mean. I should have foreseen it, told your father, even gone to see

Eshref.' Harriet turned her head away for she could feel tears in her eyes, tears of remorse and shame at her irresponsibility. Dear God, what had she been thinking about? Samira might have been killed, and the fault would clearly have been hers!

Diana returned from the kitchen carrying an enamel bowl of water which she set down carefully on the low table beside the sofa. There was soft muslin and a towel, and when all was ready and the lamp which David had lit placed nearer so that she could see, Harriet tilted Samira's face up to the light and gasped at the swelling and at the blood, some dried now, from the gash made by the large ring on Eshref's hand as he had swung out at her in anger.

Furiously she brushed her own tears away. She couldn't remember having cried since Edward's death. Crying was a luxury she couldn't indulge in, especially now. Her fingers were gentle as she bathed the wounds, but when at last all was done and iodine carefully applied, she discovered that she was shaking with emotion.

'What will become of me?' Samira's voice was scarcely audible.

Harriet tried to pull herself together, attempted to think of all the practical things that must be done. 'You must have something to eat, and then you must sleep,' she said firmly. 'And tomorrow we shall see. We'll talk about it when we're all rested, but you need not be afraid any more.' She stood up, outwardly determined and efficient now. 'No one will dare to cause you any harm while you're here with me, and no one is going to take you away again.' Her voice was firm, her resolve unflinching. She carried the bowl of water, the cloth and the towel into the other room, and then put some soup to heat on the primus stove.

Diana was standing there, a shawl thrown over her nightdress. She looked pale, horrified by what she had heard. Harriet tried to guess how she must feel. The Middle East was always a shock when you first came here, however well you might think you had prepared for it. 'Make us all a cup of tea, there's a love,' she said. 'We could do with it. Don't go outside. There's water in the pitcher.'

The soup was beginning to bubble and Harriet stirred it round and round slowly with a large wooden spoon while she pondered upon the various courses of action she might take. Gradually she began to feel a shred of optimism. The impossible appeared to have come about. Samira had returned to them! Harriet decided that she would go and see Jebel el Hamid as soon as she could and strike a bargain. No mention of the real reason for his daughter's presumed lack of virginity would pass her lips now, of course, in case he demanded her back. Let him believe what he liked. All that mattered was to give Samira her freedom.

Diana had to wait until the soup was heated before she could put the water to boil, for the primus only had one ring. During the day they cooked on an ancient wood-burning stove, but it was always put out at night and there was only this tiny flimsy thing, a remnant of her aunt's youthful camping expeditions. She waited impatiently, wanting something to occupy her hands, something to stop their trembling. She barely understood what had happened but she could imagine her brother's rage when he knew about it, when he saw Samira's injuries.

She fetched the old china teapot from the shelf, carefully set out cups and saucers on a tray and took the biscuit barrel from the cupboard and the jug of goat's milk from the cold box in the corner. When everything was ready she carried the tray carefully into the other room. David was sitting on the floor, a bowl of unwanted soup held awkwardly in his hands, and he turned when she came in. He put the bowl on the low table at his side and jumped up to take the tray from her. He smiled and Diana felt the colour rushing to her face as she looked at him, at the dark hair framing a tanned handsome face. And his hands! They were work-roughened now, sturdy and capable. His presence here in the middle of the night did nothing to calm her nerves. Embarrassed, she pulled one of Harriet's large shawls which she had borrowed more closely around her shoulders.

Harriet, with great satisfaction, watched Samira eat. She spooned the hot soup into her mouth slowly and nibbled at the flat home-made bread. As she looked at this girl whom she had come to love she thought again about what might have happened. She remembered the fate of Jamila and her heart lurched in horror.

The fact that David had been on the road so providentially seemed almost a miracle. She was suddenly curious. 'How is it you were in such an unlikely place in the middle of the night?' she asked him. 'It's a bit unusual, isn't it?'

Before he could reply Samira interrupted. 'Allah willed it so!' she said. She was staring at the bowl of comforting broth in her hands, stirring the remaining liquid round and round automatically. 'I'm innocent and I think that He sometimes protects the innocent,' she whispered.

Harriet was both surprised and a trifle nonplussed by the idea. In her experience of Palestine it was not often that God or Allah could be credited with protecting women. She had long ago decided that a male deity seemed more often on the side of the male sex, both in how he had ordained things and in the way everything seemed to conspire against most of the women with whom she came in contact. She looked sadly at Samira and then at David.

'Perhaps He does,' she said sceptically. 'But He had to use David, didn't he? Maybe I shouldn't doubt though. Perhaps Allah really did arrange it all!' If she could be sure that this was so, then she'd be grateful to Him for evermore, she decided.

David looked at the three women and wondered what each believed, and indeed what he believed himself. That his rather stern Jewish God could have had some concern for this Arab girl was a novel idea. 'Then He must have willed my puncture and my stupid incompetence!' he said. 'I'd been asked to make up a bridge four at Zikmina, the Brownstones' place. I hoped to get back to Beth Haron before dark actually, but we played longer than I expected and then the puncture happened before I'd gone more than a mile or two. I had nothing to mend it with so had to walk.'

He finished his soup with difficulty, placed the empty bowl on the tray, took a cup of tea and settled himself once more on the cushions on the floor. He crossed his legs easily as though he had been accustomed to sitting that way all his life. The silence that followed his words made him feel that further explanation was expected. 'My father was at college with Edward Brownstone,' he told them, 'And when he first heard that I was living at Beth Haron he asked me over. When he knew that I played bridge he was overjoyed. It's one of his main interests in life. I've been invited three or four times since.'

'Will you tell him about tonight?' Harriet questioned. She looked at him anxiously. She too was a friend of the Brownstones.

'Do you think I should?'

She pondered for a moment. 'Not yet. As he's Assistant District Commissioner for this area he would have to act immediately. I don't think that's the best way of dealing with the affair. I must talk to Jebel first.'

'But the British authorities should arrest the brothers,' David said angrily. 'Punish the swine as soon as possible. We can't let them get away with near murder.'

'And have the whole process of British justice swinging into action against El Admah? I don't

85

think so, David. It's Samira's family, our village, our people. It would affect Beth Haron too, make the animosity between kibbutz and village even worse. There are other ways. And of course they didn't actually carry out their evil intentions, thank God. You wouldn't have a very strong case in law. Don't forget that it's their ancient traditions that we'd be up against.'

'Damn their traditions! Are we to go along with murder just because it's always been done like that? It's an evil that should be rooted out.'

Harriet sighed. 'Of course you're right, but I still say that we must go carefully. Why did her brothers let Samira go so easily? Knowing them as I do, it seems a bit out of character.'

'They want money out of it, I think,' David said. 'They made me promise to keep silent, as a matter of fact. They would have killed both of us had I not given them my word.'

'So that's an end of the matter. You can't tell. An Englishman's word is always his bond, whatever the circumstances.'

'You really believe that?'

'Yes I do, very firmly, especially with Britain having the mandate to govern this ungovernable country.' Harriet took a gulp of her comforting tea. 'Leave it to me, for a few days anyway.'

Samira was quiet, but she had been listening with growing concern. They had been talking almost as if she was not there. Even here in this house she was being treated as someone without any opinion or influence in her own affairs. She had to speak, had to make sure that they wouldn't change their minds. 'You must never tell,' she declared passionately. 'You must keep it all secret for as long as Colin is in Palestine.' She looked at them anxiously, and in the flickering light from the candles and lamp all the terrible events of the past days and nights seemed to be dancing like black spots before her eyes. She shook her head, hardly seeing the faces staring at her, and then she brushed her hand across her own face and winced at the pain of the bruises there. 'Please don't tell.' She was full of terror again and this time it wasn't for herself. 'Colin will be in terrible danger if you do.'

'Why Colin?' Diana asked. 'What has my brother got to do with it?'

Three pairs of eyes swivelled in her direction.

'He's the one they blame,' Harriet said. 'They think that he was the cause of Samira's shame.'

Diana's face was suffused with embarrassing colour. 'I'm sorry,' she murmured. 'I hadn't thought.'

David smiled at her reassuringly. 'Of course you hadn't,' he said. 'None of us had.' Then he turned to Samira. 'I promise that I'll keep my word to your brothers,' he told her. 'So no more worries about Colin.'

'We won't talk about it any longer now,' Harriet said firmly. 'We've all had enough for one night. You can trust David, Samira, and I shall be silent as far as the authorities are concerned too.' She got up and put out the lamp and was once more the efficient organiser that they all knew. 'Now we must all try to get some sleep for what's left of the night,' she ordered. 'You can have the spare room, Samira. The bed is made and there's water for washing in the bowl. David, you must sleep here on the sofa. You can't possibly return to Beth Haron until morning, and Diana, try to calm yourself, child, and go back to bed.'

Harriet went into the kitchen and returned carrying two glasses. She handed one to Samira and the other to Diana. 'Drink it up,' she said. 'You need to sleep. It's a herbal mixture I keep for frightened animals.' She laughed at their startled faces. 'It's quite safe. I take it myself sometimes. It always works and won't do you any harm.'

Diana drank the contents of her tumbler a trifle unwillingly for she noticed the first glimmer of dawn around the edges of the wooden shutter that covered the window. The sun would soon be ablaze in the Eastern sky. She longed for this night to be over, longed for morning.

But eventually, in spite of herself and with the help of Harriet's potion, she slept, and when some hours later she staggered out of bed, David had already left, Samira was up and dressed and sitting in the kitchen, and Harriet was out with the animals. Life seemed to be resuming some degree of normality again although she guessed that it was only an illusion.

Samira held out her hands to her. 'Please don't be angry with me, Diana,' she pleaded.

'Your brother is innocent, I swear. He has never touched me!'

Diana blushed but took both her hands and kissed her gently on the cheek. 'Why should I be angry?' she said. 'Of course I believe you.'

CHAPTER 6

Colin pushed his few belongings into his rucksack and, with a sense of relief, dumped it in the back of his friend's tourer. The work he had been doing so enthusiastically for the past months had lost some of its glamour just lately, and for the first time he felt that he cared very little whether or not he found any more pottery shards, or artefacts of any kind. The weather seemed to drain every ounce of energy from him, and for once he longed for the mists and rain of his native land.

'Why so glum, old boy?' His companion looked at him with a perplexed grin. 'Homesick?'

'Perhaps I am. Stupid, of course. Anyway, let's get going.'

The two young men settled themselves in the vehicle and rattled and bumped their way along the track that led away from the ancient ramparts and treasures of Kefr Dor, the place that had held Colin's interest for many past weeks.

'I don't even know that I want to come back here!'

'That sounds a bit extreme. I thought you were enthusiastic.'

'I was. Until recently I felt that this was all I wanted to do for the rest of my life. To be an archaeologist seemed the most important thing in the world. There's so much to find out, so many things waiting to be discovered.'

'Then why the sudden change?'

Colin was silent, knowing perfectly well why his interest had gradually decreased, yet he was unwilling to share the ludicrous thing that had happened to him. How could he tell his friend, or anyone? How say, 'I'm hopelessly in love with an Arab girl, and she's wife now to some foul Sheikh!' It sounded too ridiculous to have any credence and he knew that he must forget her, force all remembrance of her right out of his life. There had been other girls, plenty in fact. He was silent, allowing his thoughts to stray back to Oxford. The choice of females there had been extremely limited, but he had never needed to look far. There was usually some young woman willing to smile upon him at the slightest invitation. It was the same at home. At functions in Exeter and even in the little market town near Bagleigh he was seldom without a partner. Yet none had ever taken his heart as had Samira. Thoughts of her filled his waking hours, and even his sleep was disturbed with her image. Just lately the dreams had been more like nightmares and he wondered how long he would remain in such bondage.

He stared at the road ahead, at the dusty earth and the barren scrubby hillside, and felt a deadness of spirit, a heaviness that he was unable to lift. The thought of her in another man's arms, a man she didn't love, was so abhorrent to him that he shuddered with suppressed rage and frustration, angry at his powerlessness. He knew that he must get home to England. Only in the wind and the rain, in long hikes over Dartmoor with Rollo, or riding Major furiously for miles, would he ever be able to find any kind of peace. But he would never forget her. He felt that she would always hold his heart until the day he died!

His friend was driving carefully over the stony track and at last they turned on to the main road, but here the surface was only marginally better. He repeated his question. 'I asked you why you've lost interest in the dig? Just as we're finding some really unusual things too.'

'Sorry. I know it must seem odd. It's...' Colin paused wondering what to say. If the complete truth sounded totally stupid and unbelievable perhaps he could tell half of it, make it sound more casual. 'Well,' he stalled, 'the usual thing—a woman.'

His friend laughed. 'Never worth it, old man. Give her up. How about a night in Haifa?'

He didn't elaborate further and Colin, taken aback by the suggestion, was glad to have a ready and quite truthful excuse. 'Not for me I'm afraid,' he said. 'I've an aunt and a sister expecting me for the weekend at El Admah.'

He had been deliberately out of touch for the past few days, ever since he'd left Diana in fact, for he had not wanted to hear about

91

Samira's wedding. He had worked every hour of daylight, trying to blot out the fearful images in his mind. But now, reluctantly, he could bear it no longer. He had to know how she was. Being at Khanhaven for the weekend would be painful beyond belief, but it was something he must do, a necessary torture. He had to see and touch the things Samira loved, ride Jazi perhaps, face the worst that those memories could do to him, and then try to purge the grief from his mind.

He had written a brief note to Harriet asking if she could meet him as she usually did, so he hoped that they were expecting him. There had been no time for a reply.

He was relieved to see, eventually, her motor car parked in the shade of a tree just where he had suggested, at the junction where the road swept on to Jenin. He felt an immediate surge of gratitude. He could always rely on Aunt Harriet, and she knew of his feelings for Samira so there was no need for any pretence. He was sure that she would be full of understanding and comfort as well as her usual bracing commonsense.

'There she is,' he said to his friend. 'Can you pull up somewhere?' The car shuddered to a halt in a cloud of dust and he grabbed his rucksack and climbed out. 'Thanks for the lift,' he called. 'I'll be in touch.'

'Cheers then. Enjoy yourself.' His friend roared away and Colin strode over to Harriet's car. 'Hello, Aunt,' he greeted her. 'How are things?'

She failed to reply at first, waiting until the noise and dust from the other car had lessened.

'Things, as you call them, could be a lot worse,' she said at last.

Colin stood unable to move for a moment, his mind filled with sudden dire catastrophes.

'Get in,' Harriet ordered with unusual impatience. 'The sooner we get to Khanhaven the better.' She started the engine with some difficulty and didn't speak again until they were satisfactorily back on the road.

'Something's wrong?' Colin felt tremors of alarm rip through his body.

'In a manner of speaking, yes.'

'Then for Heaven's sake, tell me. Diana? Is she all right?'

'Diana's fine.'

'Then what?'

There was a pause. Harriet was staring at the road with intense concentration, not once turning to look at him.

'Samira's marriage. Things went wrong.'

'What things?' Colin realised that he was shouting. 'What things for goodness' sake?'

Harriet's voice was quiet and controlled, comforting. 'She's all right, Colin. She's at home with Diana. You'll see her soon.'

'See her?' It was impossible. He was dreaming again. She was with that... He was suddenly aware of his aunt's hands gripping the steering wheel with unnecessary force.

'She's had some terrible experiences,' Harriet continued. 'Be careful what you say and...' She paused again, groping for words. 'Try not to remark on her appearance. She has some bruises.'

'Bruises! An accident? What happened?'

'No accident.' Harriet's voice was steady, carefully unemotional.

'You mean it was deliberate? My God, what kind of country is this? You'd better tell me everything before I go crazy!'

He listened with mounting fury as Harriet told the whole story. Then he was aware of the car jolting and bumping as they increased speed and he realised that they were in El Admah. The only practical road to Khanhaven from this direction led through the village. He wanted to jump out, find the brothers, the father, throttle them with his bare hands.

'Keep calm. Just sit there and keep calm,' Harriet ordered. She concentrated on driving. Getting Colin through this village needed all her attention.

He took no notice of her. Calm was the last thing in the world he wanted to be at that moment. 'Foul murdering bastards!' He spat out the words with all the venom and hatred of which he was capable.

But there was no one apart from his aunt to hear, or to see his fury. The walls of the houses glared blankly back at him. Everyone was inside resting during the noonday heat. The usual cloud of dust covered them as they rattled through, and Harriet didn't slacken speed until the last building was left behind and they were safely on the track that led to her own house.

There was a similar brooding quietness here too when they pulled up at the gate. Colin leapt out of the car and rushed inside, his

94

heart beating furiously with a mixture of both apprehension and hope.

'Samira!' he shouted. 'Samira, where are you?'

Harriet, carrying his abandoned rucksack, followed him inside. 'The horses are out so the girls must be too,' she said calmly. 'Samira wants to do nothing but ride lately. I won't let her go alone, but whenever she can persuade Diana to join her she's off on Jazi. It seems to purge her feelings of guilt and hopelessness and I prefer them to go at this time of day in spite of the heat. Most people are resting. They are less likely to meet anyone.'

Colin was horrified. 'Those damn' perverts might be out there!' he exclaimed. 'It can't be safe for two girls to be alone.'

'They have a small pistol and I've taught Diana to use it.'

He turned to his aunt in amazement. 'What did you say? Pistol! Diana! I don't believe it. She'd never dare kill anyone!' He immediately had a ridiculous picture in his mind of his sister carefully trapping a moth or a spider in an upturned tumbler and carrying the offending creature out to the garden rather than squashing it. He recalled the fuss she made when any of the farm animals went to market, and her steadfast refusal to hunt.

'I sincerely hope that she won't need to kill anyone.' Harriet stressed the last words. 'Just the sight of a gun would send them packing.' She laughed grimly. 'And that sister of yours has a lot of guts and commonsense. A girl

95

right after my own heart. Samira is quite safe with her. I really don't think there's any danger now anyway. The pistol is just an added precaution. It makes them feel better.' She dumped the heavy rucksack down on the floor. 'I've been to see Jebel el Hamid,' she said with a grimace. 'Wretched man. I've made an arrangement, and although he's still seething with rage he realises that he has to keep in with the British authorities if he wishes to retain his position as Mukhtar.' She paused and looked at her nephew thoughtfully. 'And he wants the money,' she added darkly. 'It's amazing what people will do for money.'

Colin digested this last piece of information. 'You mean you've bought Samira from him?' His voice was scathing.

'You could put it like that, I suppose.'

'My God!'

'Don't blaspheme, dear,' Harriet rebuked. There was a twinkle of amusement in her eyes now. 'You know I don't like the Lord's name taken in vain. In spite of my personal doubts about the deity, I like to keep my options open.'

Colin glanced at her as she kicked her shoes off and went barefoot into the kitchen to put water to boil. What an incredible woman she was, he thought, living here for years alone, capable of dealing with the most hardened Arab, and now she was actually telling him not to swear. Not to swear at a time like this when every foul word he had ever learned had rushed into his mind during the last half an hour. He had restrained himself, he thought, successfully. For a second he felt an affectionate amusement at her expense. 'Sorry, Aunt,' he said. 'I'll do my best!'

He still felt extremely sceptical about the arrangements she had made. He followed her into the kitchen. 'Her father might be satisfied, but what about the brothers?' He spat out the last word. 'Brothers! I can't believe it!' He thought briefly of his relationship with Diana and could in no way make any comparison.

'Things are different here,' Harriet said unnecessarily. 'Quite different. We have no conception of the way they think, of their values, of anything!'

'You're telling me!'

'The honour of the family is almost completely tied up with the purity of the women.'

Colin slumped down on the chair that stood beside the scrubbed wooden table and lit a cigarette. 'And who makes those rules?' he said half to himself. 'The men, of course, just for their own satisfaction and power. Good God, I almost feel ashamed to be male!'

It was Harriet's turn now to feel a trace of amusement. But she was worried too. She was extremely fond of her brother's two children and wanted their happiness above everything else. She busied herself with making coffee and eventually placed two brimming cups on the table. She stirred two large spoonfuls of sugar into hers.

'Don't be,' she said. 'Ashamed to be male, I mean. There's nothing wrong with you.' She

97

forced her tone to be more casual. 'The girls will be here soon and they won't want to see that angry expression on your face. And I don't think you need to fear Samira's brothers either. Jebel has a pretty firm grip on his sons. I'm sure he will have laid down the law very strongly and they won't dare go against his orders.'

Colin had smoked three cigarettes and downed two brimming cups of coffee before he heard the horses' hoofs on the stony path outside. He sprang up and was at the door before either girl could dismount. He pushed the bead curtain aside and cursed as he became caught up in one of its strands. Then Diana was rushing towards him, kissing him on the cheek. He returned her greeting, holding her for a moment, but his eyes were all for Samira who still sat on Jazi's back, still had not moved. He felt his sister release him and push him in the other girl's direction, but he needed no urging. He stood before the big horse. Looking up, he saw signs of suffering in Samira's eyes and ugly bruises on her face, but there was also a sudden flash of joy and a smile for him as quickly banished as it had come. After that quick betrayal of her feelings, she lowered her glance as usual.

Diana came over to them, taking Jazi's bridle. 'I'll see to both horses,' she said.

Colin had never touched Samira. She had always avoided any physical contact, but now he stood below her and held out his arms to her. She slid from the horse, hesitated for a moment and then he closed his arms around her and she sobbed as though she would never stop, her whole body shuddering in spite of his tight embrace. Each tremor went through him until he felt that he could hardly stand any more. He pulled off the embroidered cap she was wearing, letting it drop to the ground, and he stroked her hair, his fingers reverent and gentle on the shining black tresses that he had previously longed to touch.

Suddenly she drew away from him as though stung. She backed to the fence and stared like a small terrified animal. 'I am defiled,' she said. 'Defiled by Eshref and not fit for any man!'

Colin took a step towards her, but stopped as he saw her terror. 'What that swine did to you only makes you more precious to me,' he shouted. 'Don't you understand that, Samira? I love you. I love you. Do you hear me? Forget bloody Eshref, forget everything. I'll take you back to England. I want to marry you!'

His words were unconsidered, uttered in the emotion of the moment, yet he knew that he meant every one of them. His heart swelled with joy, and all the implications of what he was saying mattered not at all. He stood quite still, looking at her, longing to sweep her into his arms again, longing to carry her off to goodness knows where and make her his own for ever so that no one had any further right to her life.

'That can never be,' she whispered. 'Not after my disgrace. Not after what Eshref did to me.'

'I don't care if there were a thousand Eshrefs,' he shouted at her. 'I don't care, Samira. I love you. Eshref doesn't matter any more.'

She shuddered again and he realised what he had said. 'I don't mean that,' he corrected, quieter now. 'Of course I care about what happened to you. I want to kill him, and those brothers of yours too.' He paused and shook his head as he saw her fresh look of alarm. 'But I won't, I promise you. It's in the past, over, finished. Can't you understand that? You're free Samira, free!'

She stared at him, her eyes large with incomprehension as if she had no idea what he was talking about. Then his control snapped and he crossed the space between them and roughly pulled her reluctant body into his arms again. There was anger and frustration in him, replacing his previous gentleness, and he felt her struggle against him, felt her fear. Her hands were pushing him away, not accepting his embrace. 'Leave me,' she sobbed. 'Leave me Colin. You're the same as him, the same as all of them.'

Horrified by the terrible thing she had said, he released her and his hands dropped to his sides so that she almost fell. He was suddenly ashamed. Ashamed that he wanted to possess her in every way, to direct her life. He turned and walked into the house leaving her there leaning against the fence, still sobbing, her tears a terrible reproach.

Harriet pushed past him. 'Give her time,' she said. 'She's Arab, remember. She doesn't think as we do.'

He slumped at the kitchen table, hopelessness

in every line of him. This day with its amazing news should have been quite wonderful but it was going completely wrong.

Eventually Diana came in from the stable, washed her hands, tied a white apron round her waist and took a bowl from the shelf above the stove. 'I couldn't help overhearing,' she said. 'So you really want to marry her? Have you thought what it means? Are you sure?'

He looked up at her bitterly. 'Yes, I am sure. OK, tell me I'm totally stupid, that Father will turn me out penniless, that she doesn't want to marry me, that it might not even be possible. Tell me all those things, but I still intend to marry her.'

'Then marry her.' Diana's voice was firm. 'Her divorce was quite legal, you know. Apparently a man only has to say three times "I divorce you", and it becomes law.' She spat the words out in disgust. 'Divorced after only hours of marriage. They need a few suffragettes over here!'

She banged the bowl down on the table. 'For goodness' sake ask her gently though, Colin, properly, as you would someone at home. And wait a bit. She's not ready yet.' She paused and then suddenly smiled, her mood changing. 'She's one of the nicest girls I know. She'll agree, I'm sure, and you'll be happy eventually.'

'What do you mean, eventually?'

'Just what I say. It'll take time. She's not like us. As Harriet says, she's Arab. She's never even been allowed to sit at a table and eat with men. She won't look at them. Can you imagine dinner parties at Bagleigh? I'm not trying to put you off. It'll work in the end I'm sure, but don't be impatient.'

'She'll learn quickly. I love her. That's all that matters.'

'There you go, the bigoted male! Have you considered how she'll feel about giving up her way of life completely, going to live in a strange country?'

Colin snorted in disgust. 'Well, no, I don't suppose I have. I should think she'd be glad to be rescued from her "way of life", as you call it.'

Diana sighed. She was making bread, a seemingly endless chore since she came to Palestine. It had been set to rise while she was out riding and now must be kneaded again. She took the dough from the bowl and thumped and banged it on the table. Colin watched her with a glazed expression on his face.

'Just don't expect it to be easy. That's all I'm saying. And be careful about physical contact. She's still pretty wary of that side of things.'

Colin was shocked that his sister could speak easily of such matters. She had never been so relaxed in England. This country did amazing things to people, he reflected. But he knew in his heart that she was right.

He sat in a bemused and preoccupied way, watching his sister as she worked yet not really seeing her. He longed to be with Samira again, longed to do something to make up for his ill-considered and impulsive behaviour. He could hear Harriet talking to her in calm steadying tones, going on and on, and then sometimes Samira's lighter response. He couldn't make out any words.

Eventually they came into the room and he sprang nervously to his feet. Samira glanced quickly at him and then away again, but it was her appearance that surprised him. She had changed and was wearing a loose dress that fell to just below her knees. It was of some soft blue material, simply cut and plain. There was a string of bright beads around her neck and her hair was held in place by a band of matching ribbon. Her legs were bare and on her feet were a pair of leather sandals. Gone were the thick embroidered trousers, the heavy over-dress and scarf that she usually wore.

'Do you approve?' Harriet asked brightly. 'It was mine. A bit twenties, but Samira is the size I once was and I've a whole wardrobe full of the dresses I brought out here when I first came. She likes them!'

Diana laughed at the expression on her brother's face. She had just put a tray of small rolls into the oven and straightened up and wiped her hands on her apron. A sudden sense of happiness gripped her. Whether it was due to Samira's appearance in the new clothes, or the pleasure of making bread, she wasn't sure. But she felt illogically that the worst was over and everything was going to be all right. 'It's all this lovely bread that has spoilt your figure, Aunt,' she said. 'I hope it doesn't happen to me.'

Almost miraculously the mood of the day

changed, was reduced to simple ordinary things, like making bread and thinking about one's appearance. Colin caught a little of the atmosphere but he couldn't keep his eyes off Samira, the way she looked, and he noticed the colour rush to her face as she became aware of his admiration. Perhaps now he could repair a little of the damage he had done by that last rough embrace. 'You look lovely,' he said. 'Quite lovely.'

She smiled at him and there was no need for many words after all. Harriet had put things right, helped Samira to understand. He longed and yet feared to be alone with her again.

Then unexpectedly he felt hungry. There was a delicious smell of fresh bread. He looked at the tray of rolls cooling on the cupboard top. 'Any chance of some of that wonderful bread being ready soon?' he asked his sister. 'It's a long time since I smelt anything so good. I get fed up with endless flat pitta bread.'

'Pitta bread is good,' Samira said quietly.

Diana grinned at him. 'Don't disparage Arab food, will you?' she said. 'It's different, not worse or better.'

'You can have a meal in a few minutes,' Harriet interrupted. 'The soup isn't ready yet. Go and wash and put your things in the spare room, Colin. There's water ready for you, but if you want a shower you'll have to fill the bucket.'

'A shower would be wonderful. Thanks, Aunt.'

'I shall fetch the water.' Samira was galvanised

into action. She moved quickly to the door, but Colin sprang up and barred her way. 'I'll have no woman carrying a heavy bucket of water for me,' he said. 'Sit down, Samira.'

'But it's my job,' she whispered. 'I always fetch water for the men.'

'Not any more you don't.' Forgetting, Colin took her hand, forcibly pulling her away from the door. 'If you're going to wear European clothes, you'd better learn European ways. I shall carry water for you, understand, and never you for me.'

With a defeated slump to her body she sank on to the sofa and he was aware of her fresh misery as he resolutely pushed aside the bead curtain and walked out to the yard. He took one of the large buckets that stood there and carried it to the well, letting it down into the clear cool water below.

The second precious moment had gone, lost once more in a total lack of understanding between them, and he cursed himself again for his insensitivity. First the pitta bread and then the water. Yet how could he allow her to carry a heavy bucket for him? He pulled it up angrily so that water slopped all over his feet. He carried it back to the shower shed. It was a roughly constructed shelter with another bucket inside suspended on a thick rope. There were small holes pierced all over this second bucket and when it was filled the water spouted forth bringing welcome relief from the heat, and a great sense of luxury. It usually caused him great amusement for it was his aunt's own invention and also her pride and joy, but today he scowled at the inconvenience.

He divested himself of his clothes, hanging them on a hook behind a thick curtain that was meant to keep them dry. Then he carefully performed the difficult feat of pouring the water into the bucket that swung menacingly above his head. As soon as he had done so the cooling droplets fell over his skin and their cold shock restored him a little. He stood there, not bothering to soap himself but just allowing his tensions and his anger to dissipate, hoping they would vanish like the water sinking quickly into the earth beneath the wooden slats under his feet.

When he was dressed again he walked slowly back into the house. The women had prepared the simple meal, soup and bread, with fruit and cheese to follow. They were sitting at the table waiting for him. Samira jumped up as he entered.

'Sit down, girl,' Harriet said firmly. 'Men rise when a woman comes in. Not the other way round.'

Colin smiled. His tenseness had almost disappeared. He knew that he loved this shy Arab girl more than he would ever love anyone. He realised too that a long and difficult time lay ahead but he was prepared for it now. He went to the table. 'I can't sit down until you do, Samira,' he said gently. He moved to where she was standing and put his hands on the back of her chair, pulling it out a little further. 'Please!'

He held his breath as she struggled with this new situation. Then she turned to him and smiled and sat down again, allowing him to push the chair in for her.

'Thank you,' she murmured.

He felt his heart lift. It was a small thing, but a beginning, a very real beginning.

Harriet raised her glass, a shining beautiful thing, one of a set that she had brought with her from England. There was home-made wine for herself and for her niece and nephew, and fresh grape-juice for Samira. 'Here's to the future,' she said. 'And to peace and freedom!'

'Freedom,' Diana echoed, and Colin caught her glance and grinned.

'Freedom,' he said. 'For all of us.'

CHAPTER 7

'I expect you're going over to Beth Haron to see David?' Harriet said the following morning. She cleared the breakfast things from the table and poured more coffee for herself and Colin. 'Samira owes her life to him.'

'Of course. How do you thank him for something like that?'

'Just with a simple thank you, I should think. He'd be embarrassed by anything more.'

Colin had spent a night almost devoid of sleep but just before dawn had fallen into a deep slumber. He and Harriet were indulging in a late breakfast.

During the hours of darkness everything that had happened to Samira had assumed mountainous proportions. He had thumped the pillow angrily from time to time, wanted to get up and wreak revenge on the brothers there and then, and wanted Samira in his arms. Her very nearness had made any pretence of calm impossible. He thought, once or twice, that he heard her cry out in her sleep and had to force himself to stay where he was, gripping the narrow bed tightly so that he should not leap from it.

'It's Sabbath until sunset,' Harriet continued. 'So David won't be working. Borrow my car. I don't want you walking or even riding alone around here at the moment. And take the pistol. I'm sure that I've settled things satisfactorily with Samira's family, as I told you yesterday, but I don't know whether the amnesty extends to you. We only talked about Samira. There's no point in taking unnecessary risks. And get back before dusk.'

Colin felt impatient at these restrictions. 'You let the girls out alone. Why all the worry about me?'

'I've just told you, and they only go together, never alone. You're the cause of all the trouble, of course, according to Samira's family. Jebel firmly believes that you and Samira had a relationship.'

'You said nothing about the horse-riding?'

'Of course not.' Harriet smiled a little grimly. 'It occurred to me that Eshref might decide to take her back if he became convinced that it was

108

only riding Jazi that had made her as she is.'

'Doesn't she want her innocence proved?'

'Not at the risk of that!'

Colin hadn't thought of this frightful possibility. 'Best keep quiet about it then,' he said, embarrassed now. He was not used to talking about such personal matters to women, or much to men for that matter. He hoped that Samira and Diana couldn't overhear the conversation. They were both outside attending to the animals.

'You do believe me, don't you, Aunt?' he said. 'I mean Samira and I...'

Harriet finished her coffee and got up from the table. 'Of course I believe you, dear boy,' she said. 'But go and talk things over with David. He's very sensible, and knows about Arabs, a very nice young man in fact. We don't really want you around for the next few hours anyway. We're having an animal surgery this morning, and a lot of our customers will be from El Admah. Samira will have to stay in her room, but they know that she's here and it wouldn't be advisable to have you as well. We don't want unnecessary trouble.'

Colin remained where he was. He gripped his empty cup and stared down absent-mindedly at the sugar in the bottom. He was angry about the accusation that had been levelled at him by Samira's family even though it had secured her freedom. Yet perversely he wished that it was true.

Harriet looked at him a trifle impatiently. 'Off with you now,' she said briskly. 'I saw David a couple of days ago, after I got your letter, and told him you were coming. He'll be expecting you. They get up early there. No lying in bed at Beth Haron even on the Sabbath.'

There was an armed guard at the gate of the kibbutz but Colin was well known and was waved in. He parked the car and turned down the path to the communal hall where he was most likely to find David. The buildings were functional, possessing no aesthetic value, but there were flowers beside the path, and pervading everything the heavy aroma of oranges or orange blossom, combining strangely with rosemary and pines. Colin was not sure which scent was dominant and was only vaguely aware of them anyway. But they made a bouquet, a pleasing fragrance that he knew would always transport him to this place wherever he might be.

'Shalom!'

He repeated the greeting, not once but many times on his way to the hall. David was inside sorting through some books, as Colin had guessed he would be. He was in charge of the small library on the kibbutz and usually spent some time on Saturdays with his beloved volumes. 'It's not work,' he had said once with a laugh. 'To me books are pure pleasure, so I do it on the Sabbath.'

He looked up when Colin entered and strode over to him. 'Great to see you,' he said. 'I've been thinking about you a lot. I needn't do any more here. Come over to my billet. I've got

110

some coffee made. It only needs heating. How are they all at Khanhaven? How's Samira?'

'She's recovering slowly. The others are fine.' Colin watched while David returned briefly to his books and pushed them into reasonably tidy piles. 'I don't know what to say to you, David, except thanks. It sounds terribly inadequate.'

'Nothing more necessary, old chap. Anyone would have done the same. Come on, let's get out of here into the sunshine. It isn't too hot yet.'

Together they left the hall and walked along the path that led to the accommodation area. 'Tell me about it,' Colin said. 'Tell me what happened. Don't spare me. I want to hear it all.'

'We'd better sit here. We won't be overheard.' David indicated a rough wooden bench beside a rosemary hedge.

Colin flopped down upon it, and while David talked he found himself gripping the seat until his hands ached.

When the story was finished they sat for a time in silence and Colin was consumed with a terrible anger that forced a surge of adrenaline through his body, causing his heart to pound alarmingly. 'Those buggers,' he said at last between clenched teeth. 'Those bloody buggers. I want to get out there and throttle them one by one.'

'Steady on.' David's voice held a forced calm. 'So do I for that matter, but it's not the way. Harriet has a far better method.'

'I know that. That's what makes it so

frustrating. Having to leave it to a woman, and the family getting off without any punishment, with some advantages even!'

'Now you sound like one of them,' David said.

'So there's nothing we can do?'

'Not really. Just be around if we're needed. Your aunt is a very formidable lady.'

Colin sat quite still and saw vividly in his mind, Samira's bruised and haunted face, but there were questions to which he still needed an answer, doubts that worried him. 'How much do you know about...about the usual signs of a first time?' he asked sheepishly.

'Didn't Harriet explain?'

'Yes. She said it was all the riding, but to my shame I wondered about it. I've never heard of that before.'

'You mean you don't trust Samira?'

'Yes, of course I trust her.'

'Then what are you worried about?'

Colin shrugged his shoulders and felt more embarrassed and discomfited than ever.

'Well,' David continued, 'I must admit that it sounded strange to me, but I've made some of my own enquiries and apparently lots of the girls here are the same when they marry. They think nothing of it. An Arab girl wouldn't normally ride a horse or do any of the things that cause it to happen. It's something to do with the hymen, which gets broken by physical exercise.'

Colin digested this information slowly and was heartily ashamed of his early misgivings.

'I'm not much better than her brothers,' he said.

David laughed briefly. 'Don't be hard on yourself. It's just male ego. What are you going to do?'

'Marry her.' There was silence between them for a time before Colin could bring himself to continue. 'If she'll have me, of course. My sister reminded me in no uncertain terms that I have to ask, be humble. And there are problems. She was misused so badly by that monster Eshref that I shall probably have a mighty lot of trouble in more ways than one.'

David plucked a small shoot of rosemary that was pushing up between the planks of the seat and crushed it in his fingers, releasing its pungent odour. ' "Rosemary for remembrance",' he said. 'Hamlet. You're braver than I am. It's a big step. Have you thought about your parents?'

'Not really. There's been no time.'

'Then hadn't you better give it some consideration? Can you see her as mistress of Bagleigh one day?'

'To hell with Bagleigh. I love her, for God's sake. You sound like a headmaster. There's no one else. I'll never love anyone else. I know it's going to be a long haul. I'm aware of the difficulties, hundreds of them probably, but I've made up my mind. I'm going to marry her and sort everything out afterwards.'

'Muslims aren't usually allowed to marry Christians.' David's voice was flat, testing, probing.

'I know that,' Colin replied impatiently. 'But

113

she wouldn't want a Muslim ceremony, would she, not after the last time? I'll get the Assistant District Commissioner to do it, that friend of yours probably. Not in a Church, of course.'

Another long silence. Then David got up and looked away from Colin, away to the long low building that housed the kibbutz children. They could hear their voices, happy sounds mostly, and now and then a baby crying. There was a strange expression on his face. 'Have you read any newspapers lately, by the way?' he asked.

The abrupt change of subject took Colin by surprise. 'No, not really. My mind has been on other things.'

'Everything's worsening in Europe, especially for Jews. German Jews are forbidden to sell goods of any kind to non-Jews and their shops are daubed with the star of David. Austrian Jews aren't allowed to vote or marry non-Jews. Hitler is becoming steadily more powerful and his Jewish hate campaign is gaining ground.' He paused and lit a cigarette and inhaled deeply. 'And as if that wasn't enough, here in Palestine, as you must know, there are ever more terrorist attacks by Arabs on Jews. The Arabs will side with Hitler of course if there's an all out war.'

Colin was aware of the bitterness in his friend's voice. He could think of no response that would give any shred of comfort. 'And Samira is Arab,' he said. 'Are you telling me that I shouldn't marry an Arab?'

'I didn't say that.'

'But you still think it's foolish?'

'Not foolish. Just full of problems.'

114

They sat for a time, both thinking about the unknown and menacing future.

'It won't be so bad in England,' Colin said eventually, 'And I'm not Jewish so there's less conflict. I shall take Samira home as soon as we can get married and find a ship.' He stood up and together they walked in the direction of the wooden building that David called home. It always reminded Colin of the old summer house that stood in a corner of the garden at Bagleigh. It wasn't much bigger. Whenever he saw this place he couldn't help thinking of the big house belonging to David's parents. He had been invited to stay there one vac and remembered that he had been surprised at its opulence. Even by Bagleigh's standards it was luxurious.

'I'll get the coffee,' David said. 'Like to sit down?' He indicated the two rickety chairs that stood on the small balcony built along the front. He went inside to light the primus and eventually reappeared carrying two enamel mugs each filled with some hot brown liquid that smelt vaguely of coffee. 'Not as good as Mother makes,' he grinned as he placed both mugs on the floor. 'But the sunshine makes up for it.'

Colin felt slightly more relaxed now and managed to laugh. Then suddenly David took their thoughts back to college days, golden carefree times in Oxford when the whole world had seemed to consist of nothing more worrying than cricket, rowing and the University Air Squadron. 'The newspapers aren't all doom and gloom,' he said. 'I've been reading a piece about the Spitfire. It's a first-rate little fighter apparently. I remember seeing one a couple of years ago at Hendon Air Display. I was very impressed.'

'What made you suddenly think of that?' Colin asked.

'I don't know. Progression of thoughts, I suppose. Persecution of the Jews, defence, striking back. The article about the Spitfire fired my imagination. Super name for it. I wish we'd had a chance to get our hands on one at college.'

'Remember the old kites they taught us to fly in?' Colin said. 'The pilots could hardly get them airborne.'

David laughed. 'I certainly do. Frightful things! It was enough to put us off flying for good! Ruddy nearly pranged them a couple of times when I was up. I think the boffins have come up with something better at last though.'

As they talked their minds were far away from their surroundings, yet they could hear, in the background, the small comforting noises of the kibbutz, the occasional splash of water in the pond that they graced with the name of swimming pool, the sound of voices, a dog barking, the children still playing, and the cheerful tones of a mouth organ somewhere on the other side of the compound. All these sounds brought a sense of safety and peace, but both young men knew that it was illusory.

'Is there going to be a war in Europe?' Colin

muttered almost to himself.

'Pretty certain, I should say.' David finished his drink and replaced the mug on the floor. 'What will you do?'

'Join the Air Force, I suppose. I've never considered anything else. That's why I went for the Air Squadron at college, same as you. At least we're partially trained. They can't put us in any other service. You won't stay here, will you?'

David shook his head. 'Probably not. I've been giving it a lot of thought lately. Where do I belong? Palestine or England? Where is home, in fact? I feel part of both places. It'll have to be the old country though if it comes to war. If I'm needed I'll go.'

Colin considered his friend carefully as he asked the next question. 'What does it really feel like to be Jewish? Sorry if that's a bit impertinent, but I've often thought about it.'

Obviously surprised by the words, David took some time before he answered. 'I'm proud of it,' he said eventually. 'Yet my father was definitely not. He escaped from the pogroms in Russia when he was a boy and has lived with a kind of inferiority complex ever since, a sort of shame for having no place of his own, no country. Even though he's been successful and made a lot of money it always felt to me that he wanted to make an excuse for his very existence. In this land it's different though and if we ever get control of even a small part of it, then...' He stopped, groping for words, 'We were turned out nineteen hundred years ago, and for all

117

those years we've longed to come back. We've had nowhere of our own. Have you any idea what that feels like? Next year Jerusalem! It's our dream, and if I can do anything to make those longings come true I intend to do it with all my might.'

Colin looked at him, surprised at the vehemence in this long speech. He was deeply moved. 'Thanks for telling me, old chap,' he muttered. He drank the remains of the now cold coffee and leaned down to put his mug beside the other on the floor. 'It's the RAF then for us both?'

'I should think so.'

'Fighters?'

'I don't know that we'd have any choice, but if there was, then definitely yes, fighters.'

'Any reason?'

David ran his hand through his hair until it stood up straight on his head. 'It would be more...I can't think of a word to express what I mean...virtuous perhaps. In a fighter, alone up there, you'd be facing the other fellow in a kind of hand to hand combat, rather than dropping bombs on women and children.'

'I hadn't thought of it like that,' Colin admitted. 'But you're right of course.' He got up and stretched to his full six feet. 'It's going to be a bloody nuisance, this war.'

'That's a slight understatement, isn't it? What about Samira, by the way? Have you thought about how it'll affect your plans?'

Colin turned away and stared at the outline of the tall cypress trees just visible against

118

the unbroken blue of the sky, 'Well, no, I haven't really,' he replied. 'I keep on hoping it won't happen, the war I mean. I'm a great optimist. I suppose the true answer is that I have absolutely no idea how it will affect us. All I can think of is the first step ahead, that I have to marry her and get us both to England as soon as possible. Hitler's war will have to wait! And right now I'm going to have a swim.' He was suddenly galvanised into action. 'Come on. Life's exciting, a challenge, whatever happens!'

In quick response David jumped up, knocking both mugs over so that they clattered noisily across the balcony and fell on to the dry earth below. He laughed, retrieved them and fetched two shabby towels from a cupboard at the back of the room. He threw one to Colin. 'Let's go then,' he said. 'We can change over there.'

They both strode out over the grass towards the sounds of cheerful voices and laughter.

Colin put the towel round his neck and his spirits rose, his worries receding. 'If there's a war we're ready,' he said. 'Herr Hitler, here we come. When we're both in our Spits you just won't have a chance!'

While Colin was away at Beth Haron, Samira tried to concentrate on the animals. But during the morning clinic she went into her room and lay on her bed, leaving Diana to work as nurse and assistant to Harriet. It was better not to be around when the villagers from El Admah brought in their animals, Harriet had warned.

The thought gave her much pain for these were the people with whom she had grown up, her parents' friends, her friends. Had they all really turned against her so terribly?

She lay on her bed and thought about everything that had happened to her during the past amazing days. She longed above all for Kaffa's reassuring presence and for the familiar feel of her strong arms around her, a comfort she had known as long as she could remember. Being the only daughter, she and her mother were very close.

She shed a few tears on her pillow and then brushed them away guiltily and thought again of her friend Jamila, and the terrible thing that had happened to her at the hands of her brothers. No mother was strong enough to protect a daughter in the face of such male outrage. Family honour always had to be vindicated, and it was only to her English friends now that she could look for safety and protection. As she continued to think of her mother she knew that Kaffa would be comforted to know that things were as they were. And Harriet had promised that she would try to arrange a meeting as soon as it was possible.

Several days had passed since she had been rescued by David Halprin and with every passing hour she had begun to feel less threatened. She knew that a deal had been struck between Harriet and her father but little of the details had been told. She had no idea yet what was to become of her.

The overwhelming shame of her rejection

by Eshref had been fairly rapidly replaced by relief and gratitude that she was not to marry him after all. The ringing words of his divorce pronouncement brought only a feeling of deliverance now but the uncertainties of the future still worried her.

She recalled the details of that terrible night with absolute horror, the night of her defiling, the night that had made her an outcast, someone not worthy to be wife to any man or to have any honourable position. It wasn't possible that Colin fully understood what had happened to her, and when he did all his talk of marrying her would be forgotten. She was quite sure of that.

But there was something else too. It had been so awful, so completely terrifying, that she doubted if she could ever give herself willingly to a man again. And if she could not, then even if someone asked to marry her it would be impossible.

Her mind roved over all the possibilities and because she could imagine no worse fate she thought of the places she had heard of where men went to pleasure themselves, places in Haifa and Jerusalem where girls were used every night for money. She shivered and clutched the blanket closely over her body and felt her blood run cold as she recalled some of the things she had overheard her brothers talking about occasionally when they thought she and her mother were asleep.

Perhaps somewhere like that was the only place for a rejected wife, defiled as she now felt herself to be. It was the most hideous thing that she could imagine. She knew that she would rather Gasim and Zeid had killed her than that she should be forced into such a life, rather lie like Jamila, her body thrown into some distant ravine. At least her friend was at peace now. No man could hurt her any more. It was better to be eaten by wild beasts than to be treated so.

She tried to turn her thoughts to more cheerful things for she knew that she must not dwell on past horrors or be too frightened of the future. Surely she could trust Harriet to order her life? Resolutely she thought of her new clothes for these were a constant source of amazement and pleasure and if she concentrated her thoughts on them some of the frightening things lost a little of their terror. Harriet had given her a great number of dresses. She remembered the first time she had put on the straight blue dress and looked at herself in the long mirror that was one of the luxuries of Khanhaven. The sight of her own bare legs had shocked her immeasurably, but as she had stared at the newly emancipated girl looking back, a strange sense of freedom had filled her. There it was again, that word, freedom. She said it quietly to herself. 'Freedom, freedom,' and wondered what it truly meant.

Gradually her spirits began to rise again and she even smiled a little to herself as she remembered Colin's face when he saw her in the European dress. She had refused at first to wear these western clothes without any leg covering beneath. She used to put one or two of the sturdier dresses over some of her other things, mainly for riding Jazi, but this last week Diana had prevailed upon her to be more adventurous and she had weakened. She had few of her own garments with her at Khanhaven anyway so necessity had added to the persuasion.

The strange and meagre clothes gave her a new identity, helped forge the beginning of a new character, imparted confidence. But she would never wear them outside the house. When she rode Jazi she still added the thick trousers and the head covering that she felt was necessary. Harriet had procured them for her somehow from her home after she had refused the offer of a pair of jodhpurs.

Following these thoughts she began to consider her behaviour towards the various men she encountered at Khanhaven. It hadn't mattered before. She had kept her submissive ways intact. But now Harriet said she must change. Sometimes friends would call at the house, important-looking men with pretty wives, and she had always kept well out of their way and certainly had never spoken to them or lifted her eyes to theirs.

She sat up and plumped the cushions behind her head and thought for a long time about the way Diana and Harriet behaved, how they talked easily with anyone who called, and of course with Colin and David.

Colin! His arms around her had been frightening and disturbing, yet there had been a strange sweetness about that embrace, something she had never thought possible between man and woman. But she knew that between her mother and her father there was some attraction, something that made the awful thing that men needed to do not too terrible for Kaffa. After her own experience with Eshref could this frightful thing ever be anything but appalling? This was supposed to be what women were for, only that and the bearing of children, and of course the constant serving of their husbands' needs in every other way too. She shivered in spite of the heat, the unhappiness returning as her moods see-sawed violently from one thought to another.

Yet the feel of Colin's arms around her came back to haunt and disturb, and she heard his words again in her heart, those amazing inexplicable words. He wanted to marry her! But she knew that it could not be so. He would go away soon and she would never see him again. There could not possibly be any union between them now, not after Eshref! And did she even want it? Was there any other acceptable way for her now?

But then, a new thought occurred to her. It entered her mind suddenly like a ray of light in the dark. Perhaps there was a way. Eshref had defiled her, had given her a terror and a hatred of marriage. There was only one means to find out if she could ever pleasure a man again, ever give herself happily to anyone. If Colin lay with her she would know! If this act that was sometimes called love had anything pleasant about it at all then Colin would show her, for he said he loved her, and she was quite sure she loved him. Maybe the horror of her wedding night could be expunged, the memory washed from her mind.

She clutched her arms around her body with sudden resolve and new hope. But she knew that if Colin did to her what Eshref had done, in the way that Eshref had done it, then in spite of the love between them she could never marry him or anyone else. She knew instinctively that it was only in the embrace of this one man that she would discover whether it was possible to feel whole and clean and normal again. And after that? Well it was in the will of Allah.

She was filled alternately with panic and excitement at the turn in the direction of her thoughts and then, although it was still the morning, although there was the constant noise of animals and voices below, she fell into a light sleep, and she dreamed, a strange disturbing dream where she was sometimes a child again, sometimes unwilling wife to Eshref, and sometimes wife in a new and wonderful land, a land she had heard so much about where it was cool and green, where the hills were wild and wind-swept, a place where everyone was free and at peace!

CHAPTER 8

Colin stayed on at Khanhaven. He sent word that he wouldn't be returning to the dig for some time, and asked for most of his possessions to be sent to him. His life had changed so irrevocably that he occasionally doubted if he would ever go back to Kefr Dor. Perhaps there would be an opportunity after the wedding, though. He hated leaving anything unfinished, and although he'd told his friend that he'd lost interest, he knew it wasn't wholly true.

A week later he went to Haifa. He had liked the town when he first saw it, and now, although his mind was full of other things, he couldn't help feeling the sense of vibrancy and vitality in its busy streets. It suited his mood, for he was full of optimism and enthusiasm for the future. Perhaps he and Samira could stay here for a few weeks before they went home to Bagleigh.

The houses straggling around the shore and up the slopes of Mount Carmel were agreeable, inviting further investigation, and he wished that Samira was with him now and that they could enjoy a carefree day together like a couple of tourists. But that would have to wait. Today he had no time to spare. He had come to buy a ring for her and to make all the necessary arrangements for a speedy marriage and a passage to England. Not once during the past days, in spite of the difficulties ahead, had he felt any misgivings about what he was doing.

Samira's reluctance to accept him had not lasted for long. He strode through the narrow streets of the old town towards the municipal buildings, for there were many formalities to be dealt with. While he walked his mind returned, as it constantly did, to that amazing time a few days ago when she had finally and fully capitulated. They had been alone, Diana and Harriet attending some sick child in a neighbouring village.

'I want you to take me,' she told him. 'I want you to blot out Eshref and all trace of him. I want to know if I am acceptable to a man and also if I can...' She had not finished her sentence, but stood looking at him in a way that she seldom did, her eyes searching his face, pleading almost.

He had been repairing some fencing at the back of the house and he remembered the shock of her words and his initial lack of understanding. She was standing by the door and her face was fearful. She looked like some small terrified animal about to be sacrificed.

'Are you saying that you will marry me then, Samira? You've decided to marry me?' It was the only meaning that he could give to her strange request.

'Afterwards we shall both know,' she whispered. 'I shall know if you still wish to marry me.'

Then suddenly he understood. She was so frightened, so full of anxiety, that she wanted a trial run! He felt an immediate rush of protective love, but bubbling unwillingly to the surface was an affectionate amusement too. He could hardly believe it and he dared not smile for she was in deadly earnest.

He dropped the hammer on to the ground, wiped his hands on his trousers and with a few strides crossed the space between them.

'Of course I still wish it. I wish it more than anything else. But you must come to me of your own free will, because you want to. Do you...do you love me, Samira?'

She lowered her eyes. 'I love you,' she said. 'I think I've always loved you, ever since we first met, but I tried very hard not to because I thought then that it could never be.'

'I thought that too,' he said. 'And now the impossible has happened.' He longed to kiss her, to wrap his arms around her.

'Then you must take me,' she told him. 'Take me now, for I'm defiled and unworthy to be anyone's wife. It's the only way to be sure that you want me, to be sure that I can marry you.'

He still failed to understand her reasoning. Her words made him angry. 'Never defiled,' he said. 'Don't use that word. I forbid you to use it. And I want you more than anything else in the world. Nothing we do now will make any difference to that.'

'If you take me, then I shall be yours and not his. Take me now, Colin.'

At last he began to realise that she was quite seriously suggesting that they should lie together, as she put it. Lie together now, before they were married. She, an Arab girl, was asking this of him.

'But I can't,' he said. 'How to refuse I don't know, but...' He was about to take both of her hands, but he noticed the earth and dirt on his own and turned and immersed them in the water that always stood ready in a bucket beside the well. He scrubbed fiercely, aware all the time of her eyes boring into him. The small task gave him a moment's respite but he felt his whole body responding eagerly to hers. He took the old frayed towel that was fixed on a hook nearby and wiped his hands elaborately, each finger receiving special attention. Then he turned again to face her and for a moment their eyes held before she dropped her gaze once more to the ground, her customary posture. Slowly he replaced the towel and, still struggling with a welter of emotions, stood in front of her and gently put his hand beneath her chin tilting her head up so that she was forced to look at him.

'Thank you, Samira,' he whispered. 'It's a wonderful thing that you offer me. When we're married, yes. Then I shall teach you how much I love you...'

But he was unable to finish his sentence. She was suddenly in his arms, her body pressed to his, and he felt all his high ideals disappear. She led him inside, pulled him towards her bed, to the divan that was spread with a lightly scented cover. He knew that he would never smell fresh lavender again without thinking of this

129

moment. She stood before him in an attitude of submission and slowly she removed her dress. She was wearing nothing beneath it and he stared, riveted by her loveliness, her olive-tinted skin soft and taut, the breasts high and firm, and her eyes downcast still, allowing him to take in all of her beauty. In every line of her he could sense both fear and, strangely, her need of him. It was only for a brief moment that she stood so. Then she slipped beneath the bed cover, pulling the soft material up beneath her chin as some kind of armour between them.

His clothes were dirty, soiled from his work in the garden, and he let them drop quickly to the ground. She was looking at him with frightened eyes. He sat beside her on the bed and his heart seemed about to burst. 'Are you sure that you want it to be like this?' he murmured. 'Are you sure, Samira? I want you to come to me willingly.'

'I am willing,' she whispered. 'I do come to you willingly. Not like that other...that other time.' She shuddered and he could see tears on her cheeks. 'Don't you see, Colin? I'm defiled in my heart as well as in my body. In my heart I feel quite unworthy to come to you for the first time on our wedding night and I don't even know if I could marry you or anyone. If you take me now before that day then all can be made right and we shall both know, both be sure. I couldn't bear another rejection.'

He still wished it had not been like this but the feel of her body so close to his took away all his resistance. He tried to summon some gentleness but felt it evaporating in his desire. Yet he managed to prepare her for his love and she moaned a little, whether in fear or happiness he couldn't tell. He possessed her easily, and when they finally lay at peace together he began to understand a little of what was in her heart, what strange emotions lay behind her actions. It increased his love for her if that was possible. His arms tightened round her and he was filled once more with a fierce protectiveness that he knew would overcome every difficulty they might encounter. Finally he made love to her again, and hoped that he had at last made everything right for her. Perhaps now the horror of Eshref would be blotted from her mind as well as from her body.

The sweet memories of that hour filled his thoughts as he strode through the streets of Haifa. There had been no more time alone together, and he knew instinctively that even had they found moments of seclusion, her urgent need to banish the past before agreeing to marry him had been fulfilled. There would be no more illicit couplings and he was glad. He wanted to make sure that the night of their wedding would be precious, something to remember with joy for ever. He determined that it should be perfect.

While Colin was in Haifa, Diana and Samira found themselves alone, for Harriet had gone over to the kibbutz to give some of the children their weekly English lesson. Diana was grooming Naama in the yard outside the bungalow, while Samira was, for once, idle. She had put down the brush that she had been using on Jazi and there was a thoughtful expression on her face. 'When I marry your brother, I shall be a new person,' she announced firmly. 'I shall no longer be Samira el Hamid, no longer Arab. I shall accept his country, his name, his god, everything.'

'You mean you'll give up your religion?' Diana was taken aback.

'Outside of me, yes! Inside perhaps I won't be able to. But I've worked for your aunt for so long now that half of me feels non-Arab anyway. And don't forget that I've been reading all her books ever since she taught me to read. Jane Austen, the Brontës, Forster, even your long Dickens!'

'It's amazing,' Diana replied. 'Sometimes I feel that you're just the same as my school friends at home. Much cleverer than some of them, in fact. I can't believe that...'

'That my father is as he is, that my brothers were going to kill me, that I was about to be a second wife. No, I can't believe it myself when I'm here, when I'm talking to you and Harriet.' Suddenly the new confidence disappeared and she looked frightened. 'But I'm scared, Diana, truly scared of leaving in spite of what has happened to me. I often feel terrified of going to England. What is it like, really like? Colin has told me a little about Bagleigh, but mostly he talks of the farm, and of the place where he was at college—Oxford. Can you tell me anything else? Your parents? Will they accept me?'

For a moment Diana paused, resting her hand

on the horse's flank, and her thoughts travelled far from the stifling heat and Samira's problems, away to the moors and the grey rain-filled skies. The heather would be coming into flower soon, its purple combining in a magical pattern with the gold of the gorse. She closed her eyes and saw it, saw Merryon, her little mare, and Rollo dashing up towards the tor on the hill above Bagleigh. For a moment she was homesick. 'It's beautiful,' she said. 'Very beautiful. It's cold too. Even in summer sometimes it can be cold and wet, but beautiful still.' She looked at the girl who was watching her with anxious and troubled eyes and experienced a tremor of fear. She thought of her father, and of her gentle inadequate mother. How would these two cope with the sudden arrival of a strange new daughter-in-law, one who must be taught to fit in with the society of a small Devon market town, one who would need endless patience and skill and much kindness, a girl who perhaps based her ideas about England on Jane Austen or Charlotte Brontë, or even, horror of horrors, Charles Dickens? As far as her parents were concerned Samira might have come from a different planet, so at odds was her background to theirs.

'I wish you could come with me, Diana,' Samira said. 'I should have more confidence if you were there.'

'I'll come later on, but at first you need time with Colin alone. And Aunt Harriet wants me here until she's found someone else for company and to help with the work.'

Diana knew that she wasn't being quite honest on two counts. First she could in no way explain about her father's likely reaction to the marriage, so she purposely avoided giving any answer to the girl's anxious question. Colin would have to deal with that.

And then there were the dreams she had for herself. She couldn't bear to be whisked away from David so soon. Ever since he had rescued Samira a new understanding had developed between them. She'd been to the kibbutz a few times to swim in the pool and hoped that Harriet would ask her to help with the English lessons there too. Perhaps eventually she might be able to find a place at Beth Haron for herself, a niche that she could fill that would make her valuable. You're not Jewish and you never can be, she told herself gloomily now and then, but it made no difference. She knew that nothing could dislodge David from her heart. She had no idea what the outcome of this passion could possibly be, but Colin's love for Samira had seemed even more hopeless once. Perhaps there would be a miracle for herself too.

'When will you come?' Samira persisted. 'Don't leave me too long in England without you.'

'You'll have Colin.'

'That's different. He'll be my husband. I shall need a friend.'

Diana sighed. 'A husband is a friend. At least that's what we like to think in England.'

Samira picked up the brush and started to groom Jazi again, and the horse whinnied a little in pleasure. 'I've so much to learn,' she said half to herself.

'Colin will help you,' Diana said. 'He's kind and patient and he loves you very much.'

Samira looked at her with suddenly shining eyes. 'Yes.'

Hearing that one small word and seeing the flash of happiness in Samira's face, Diana knew a stab of envy. She thought of David and wondered if she would ever have such a wonderful certainty of his love for her.

CHAPTER 9

'Here's to the bride!' David lifted his glass to Samira. She stood beside Colin, radiant and very beautiful in a soft creamy satin dress. They were holding hands and for a moment he envied his friend his happiness. His own life seemed empty in contrast. Then he was aware of Diana. He turned to her and was surprised by the tears that he glimpsed before she speedily wiped them away. She smiled at him and raised her glass to his. 'To the bride and groom,' she said.

Harriet was busy with the refreshments. She had invited several guests to the wedding celebrations. The ceremony had been performed early that day in Haifa, at the office of the British District Commissioner. She had sighed a little at that. Everyone expected her to be sensible, lacking sentimentality, but today she

135

was constantly recalling her own wedding. The dress Samira was wearing had been hers. There had been bells pealing out over the Devonshire hills, flowers in abundance, her best friend Thelma for bridesmaid, and a vast reception to follow. For a second she was overcome with nostalgia and then, like Diana, she crossly wiped away two traitorous tears from her eyes.

She must concentrate on Samira's obvious happiness. Colin looked the perfect bridegroom, she thought, full of confidence, and inordinately proud of his lovely young bride. She was filled with love for both of them. 'They are my children,' she said to herself fondly. 'They're my family.'

She fetched another tray of delicacies and placed them on the table. Her guests were talking animatedly, standing around the room in small groups. There were a number of young people from the kibbutz, one or two of Colin's digging cronies and several English couples, friends of her own, and she had daringly invited some Arab neighbours too. Most had declined, but Doctor Raif Habib from Nazareth had accepted. He was a Christian Arab, educated abroad, and a great friend.

He came across the room and smiled at her, sharing her happiness. 'You've done a good job,' he said. 'They are meant for each other. I can see it in their faces.'

She was delighted at the comment. 'I hope you're right,' she replied. 'In fact, my dear Raif, I'm sure you are.'

Diana too was feeling sentimental, and angry with herself for being so. She had concentrated all her efforts on taking a vast number of spectacular photographs but now she had no more films left and had nothing to occupy her mind. She was very much aware of David watching her from across the room.

Their eyes met and he pushed his way through the crowd until he was standing next to her. 'Why do women always cry at weddings?' he asked with a grin. 'I take it that they're not averse to getting married?'

'No, nothing like that,' she replied, trying to match her tone to his. 'It's just sentiment, I suppose. Very silly. I don't think I'm crying am I?'

'I thought I saw a trace of tears just now.'

'You imagined it, my dear David. I never cry.' It wasn't true of course but she wanted to appear confident and perfectly in control.

'I won't believe that. But you're not eating either. Can I get you something?'

'No, thank you. It's I who should be offering food and drink to you. I'm supposed to be helping Aunt Harriet now that I've finished the photography.' She looked at the heavily laden table and felt slightly nauseous. 'I haven't been able to eat all day.'

He turned and picked up a plate of tiny sandwiches that stood untouched amongst the more traditional fare, barley bread, bowls of mutton and rice, yoghurts, spiced cakes and fruits of various kinds. He held them out to her. 'Come on,' he persuaded. 'Let's have one

137

each. They remind me of home and they look delicious.'

She felt for a moment as if everyone in the room could hear the beating of her heart. The lack of food, the heat, the emotion of the day, and most of all David's close proximity, all these things added to her lack of composure. But she took the proffered delicacy and nibbled it. He persuaded her to another and then another, and gradually she began to feel better.

'Now some wine,' he was saying, and when he filled her glass she obediently drank that too. And then she laughed, realising that she was enjoying herself.

'Will you be able to come over tonight?' he asked. 'We're having a swimming party. I'll borrow the old jalopy and deliver you safely home afterwards.'

The idea was splendid. Diana could think of no more fitting end to this wedding day than an evening with David and finally a ride home in the ancient open-top Ford. Bumping along the stony roads with the wind in your hair and the perfect companion at your side was a decidedly alluring prospect!

'If my aunt doesn't mind being left on her own, I'd love it,' she said. 'I'll have to clear up this lot though.' She looked around at the muddle of empty plates and glasses, mostly abandoned now on every available surface. 'Could you wait?'

'Of course. We'll see the happy couple off first, and then I'll help you,' David volunteered. 'Yes,' he said. 'Don't appear so surprised. I'm

138

getting used to doing household chores. No male privileges at Beth Haron!'

'Well spoken,' Harriet commented as she overheard his last remark. 'You'd better preach that message to our Arab neighbours.'

Diana looked up from the plates she was gathering together and noticed that her aunt's amused gaze was focused on the tall handsome figure of Doctor Habib. Then, seeing the look between them, she was suddenly surprised. Well, she thought in amazement. Perhaps Aunt Harriet might not need my company for much longer after all!

With that consideration firmly in her mind, and when all the work was done and Colin and Samira had been waved and cheered on their way, she asked if she might go to Beth Haron for the evening.

Harriet smiled at her. 'If David will bring you safely home in the motor car,' she said, 'then I don't mind. I certainly shall not be lonely. I'm too tired for that. Doctor Habib is staying for a while anyway and when he leaves I've got Ghazala.' She laughed and placed her hand fondly on the dog's head. 'I shall put my feet up and do nothing until you come home. Don't be too late!'

Diana and David walked to Beth Haron with the other wedding guests from the kibbutz.

'Speak English, please,' David ordered his friends. 'Diana doesn't understand Hebrew yet.'

Her heart gave a sudden lurch as she heard that one little word, 'yet'. So he expected her to learn this strange language, took it for granted that she would! Was it possible to read anything into that unexpected assumption? She glanced at him, but he seemed unaware of any deeper implication.

Apart from one of the girls who had recently come from Hungary they all spoke a little English, some more than others, and she felt at ease with them. Conversation was fairly easy, with David helping out where necessary. Then their talk turned to the coming day of Yom Kippur, and unwilling to show her ignorance, she walked along in silence until the subject was changed again. It was something she must ask David about when they were alone. She hated to be so uninformed about things which were obviously important to him and his friends. It made her feel different, alone, caused a barrier that she didn't like.

It wasn't until much later, after they had been in the swimming pool, that she had the opportunity. 'Do you all keep Yom Kippur then?' She had just climbed out of the water and they were standing together watching the others splashing merrily. There was no room in the pool for serious swimming. She draped her towel around her shoulders and pulled off her unbecoming rubber hat. The area was only dimly lit with a few candles, and the lovely velvet darkness of the night was all about them pierced by a million stars. There was a feeling of light-hearted festivity in the laughter and the shouting coming from the water. Everyone seemed to be carefree, not at all concerned with anything very serious.

From the discussion on the way here she had gleaned a few facts. Yom Kippur was a religious fast day and very solemn.

David looked at her in surprise when she brought the subject up again, wondering why she should suddenly ask about it.

'Yes, we keep it,' he said. 'I'm not too religious myself, but I keep some of the festivals. This isn't a very strict kibbutz though. Why do you ask?'

'You were talking about it. It sounded important to you.'

'Well, yes, it is. I suppose to some of us it's just an old custom to be kept for the sake of tradition, but for others it goes deeper than that.'

He spread his towel on the ground and they flopped down upon it.

'Explain it to me.'

'Well, we used to have sacrifices to atone for our sins, lambs usually.'

Diana shuddered. 'How on earth can the death of an innocent little animal atone, as you call it, for something a human being has done wrong?'

David laughed. 'Lots of folk wonder about that. And I really haven't any adequate reply. Probably not one that would satisfy you anyway. However you'll be pleased to know that we don't kill sheep any more, not since the destruction of the Temple by the Romans almost two thousand years ago. Except to eat, of course.'

'I'm glad to hear it. What do you do instead then?' She was genuinely interested, wanted to understand.

'Fast, repent, pray, and give to charity mainly.'

She glanced briefly at him. This was a side of his life that was a mystery to her. She felt suddenly excluded, a great barrier between them. 'How long do you go without food? I've never fasted in my life.' The idea didn't appeal to her at all although she was careful not to say so.

'We have a special meal the day before and then we eat or drink nothing from sundown until the same time the following day.'

'Nothing to drink? Not even water and in this heat?'

'Nothing unless you are ill or pregnant or have special dispensation for some reason.' David took her hand in his. 'But let's not be solemn tonight,' he said. 'We've had a long day. Life isn't all fasting and praying you know.'

They sat together in silence for a time and Diana felt depression descend upon her like a grey blanket in spite of the magic of the night, in spite of David's nearness, and the feel of his fingers intertwined with hers. How could she ever have any close relationship with this man, she wondered, how share the strange life that she was just beginning to realise meant so much to him? She had accepted his Jewishness, his Zionist ideals, but this religion was something different, something frightening and alien.

Perhaps sensing her fears, David bent over

142

her and kissed her gently. 'Don't worry about it, Diana,' he said. 'It's not so strange really. You have your customs too. Catholics have confession, don't they?'

'I'm not Catholic.' His kiss had been a brief fleeting thing, not giving any comfort, and she pulled away from him a little. 'I'm cold,' she said. 'Let's get dressed and go for a walk. Then I'll have to go home. It's getting late. I mustn't keep Aunt Harriet up.'

There was a fence behind which the women changed, and another for the men. Diana stood on the slatted wooden floor and pulled her bathing costume from her body, wiped herself vigorously and slipped into her clothes. The ugly bathing hat had kept her hair dry and the tightly plaited coil was still intact on the top of her head. She took out the pins and allowed it to fall in golden waves on to her shoulders.

David took her arm when she emerged and tucked it into his in a comfortable brotherly sort of way. Now that it was dark the walk could only be inside the high perimeter fence, but away from the pool and the living quarters it was almost quiet. She could hear the soft sound of the cicadas and the occasional barking of a dog somewhere out on the hills. She was still troubled, still full of a sense of difference, as though she didn't belong here, never could. It was always the same when she was with David. She was possessed of a deep yearning to be totally at one with him but at the same time she felt a separateness. There was always an invisible barrier between them, something that prevented complete accord.

'You all speak Hebrew,' she said, breaking the silence. There was almost a hint of complaint in her voice. 'It's a strange, difficult language. How on earth did you learn it so quickly?'

'Once you live here it becomes easier. I still find it hard to write though.'

'I don't think I could ever manage it. All I can say is Shalom.'

David laughed. 'It's a good word and sufficient for a lot of things,' he said. 'It means Peace.' He paused and a certain wistfulness crept into his voice. 'If only saying it could bring it about. The Arabs say something similar you know, Salaam Aleikum, and to you be peace.'

Then, without warning, he stopped and pulled her into his arms and kissed her full on the mouth. He held her tightly so that she was almost breathless.

She returned his fierce embrace just as enthusiastically and for a time nothing mattered to her but the sudden hope that perhaps he fully returned the love she had felt for him for so long. He had never kissed her like this before. But eventually she pushed away from him, held him at arm's length, saw his eyes searching hers.

What did it mean, this kiss? Was it, for him, just a diversion from the seriousness of his life here in this difficult place? She knew that she was ready to give all the support of which she was capable but it must be in return for love, and there was something in David that she couldn't fathom, something that forced her, against her will, to resist him. But in a strange way she was content for if the resistance came from her, that was how it should be. It gave her a certain power.

'Take me home,' she whispered. 'I think I'd like to go home now.'

He was surprised by her sudden rejection. For a long time he had felt a great affection for this girl, his best friend's sister, and he was sure that she was fond of him. She had shown it in many ways. Now there were the stirrings of something more. The depth of his feelings surprised him. He wanted to make love to her, but knew that he would not. What relationship could they ever have? How could he marry a non-jew? His children wouldn't be Jewish.

'I'll go and get Jezebel,' he said.

'Jezebel?'

'The motor. She's been christened!'

They both laughed in spite of their serious thoughts, or perhaps because of them. It was a releasing nervous laugh.

'With a name like that, she's sure to get me safely home,' Diana said.

'We shall need a couple more chaps to accompany us.' David's voice was slightly doleful. 'New orders. Safety precautions for after dark!'

Throughout the boisterous bumpy journey Diana's spirits rose gradually until the depression left her completely. One of the other men drove and David sat beside her in the back, his arm round her shoulders. She could smell the male scent of him, a clean washed smell blending with the evocative and pungent scent of the pines along the roadside. His thigh pressed strongly

145

against hers and she was filled with all sorts of strange and jubilant stirrings in her body that had nothing to do with commonsense and the reality of the everyday. Then their companions started to sing, quietly, some plaintive Hebrew song, and the magic of the night almost overcame her. Until she saw that the young man in front was holding a gun at the ready as he sang.

Harriet was waiting anxiously when she arrived. 'I don't like you out so late,' she complained. 'I know Samira's family have nothing against you and me, but they're not very partial to David or anyone from Beth Haron. Especially today!' She put down the newspaper she was reading. 'The pact I made with Samira's father was pretty firm, but I won't feel completely happy until she and Colin are out of the country. Not at night anyway. Zeid is the one I don't trust, nasty customer. But you're home safe and sound now. Nice time?'

'Lovely, Aunt. Sorry to worry you.' Diana busied herself hanging her damp bathing costume and towel over a wooden airer. 'We brought reinforcements with us in Jezebel, a couple of chaps with guns.'

'Sensible. I shouldn't have worried. Tell me about the pool. Although I go to the kibbutz a lot, I've never been to look at it.'

'It's a big pond really. They dug it out, lined it with concrete, and slightly diverted the stream that comes down from the hills. The water runs into it and out at the other end and irrigates some of their crops.'

146

'Cold I expect then?'

'A bit, but nice though. Refreshing.' She came back into the room where Harriet was sitting leafing through a pile of newspapers and magazines on the table. 'Where did these come from?'

'There's a new English family at Affula, English Jews,' Harriet explained. 'They came over for some herb plants just after you left and asked if we'd like the papers. There are some fairly recent copies of *The Times.*' She indicated the newspaper on the top of the pile. 'There's trouble over Czechoslovakia. Hitler is making threatening noises, and Mussolini is clamping down more strictly on Jews in Italy. It doesn't look good.'

Diana glanced at the headlines but her thoughts were still with David. She could feel the remembered strength of his arms around her.

'I often wonder if Mr Chamberlain is the right leader for us? Not strong enough, in my opinion,' Harriet mused half to herself. She got up and refilled her coffee cup and poured one for Diana. 'I'm sometimes quite fearful for the future.'

Diana fetched a loaf of bread, one of a batch that she had baked yesterday. She spread butter thickly upon a slice. In spite of the food that David had pressed upon her at the wedding she was hungry. She tried to concentrate on what Harriet was saying, but found it difficult. 'Don't be gloomy, Aunt,' she said. 'It's only twenty years since the last war with Germany. I'm

147

sure there won't be another.' She leaned over the table, dropping crumbs on the unpleasant words. 'I hope there isn't anyway, although Colin doesn't seem to mind the prospect. From something he said, I think he quite relishes the prospect of joining the Air Force.'

Diana finished her bread and then idly picked up another of the newspapers from the pile. 'Look at this,' she said. 'There's something here that suits my mood much better. It's about the biggest liner in the world, the *Queen Elizabeth*. She'll be ready for launching soon. I'd love to see her.' She gulped down her coffee. 'I've just had a wonderful idea. For my honeymoon, I'll go for a cruise on the *Queen Elizabeth!*'

'Silly girl,' said Harriet affectionately. 'Come on. I've never felt so tired in all my life. It's been a long day and we've to go to El Admah early tomorrow for the donkey surgery. No mention of Samira, mind. Just be careful.'

'Yes, Aunt.' Diana fetched another slice of bread and butter, and added some goat's cheese and yoghurt to her feast. When she was quite replete she got up from the table and carried her supper things to the sink. Her high spirits were still intact, fully replacing the earlier depression. 'Do you think we'll see those awful brothers of Samira's in the morning?' she said. 'If we do, I'd just like to...'

'You'll do nothing. We mustn't mention any of the things that have happened today.' Harriet's voice was grave and brooked no argument.

Thoughts of Gasim and Zeid were enough to

148

sober anyone, Diana thought. Visions of what they had been about to do when David came upon them on the road that night suddenly flashed into her mind. 'Why can't there be peace?' she asked half to herself. 'Why do men get so excited about war and killing?' she paused, 'And other things too,' she added darkly. 'It's men who cause almost all the suffering in the world, especially for women, isn't it, Aunt!'

Harriet laughed at her. 'Perhaps, but they bring a lot of joy as well. If we knew why some of them seem to delight in violence though, my dear Diana, then we could perhaps begin to re-model the whole of human life.'

'Not unless we were in power,' she said. 'Perhaps when we have a few women prime ministers around the world things will improve!'

CHAPTER 10

Samira had been nervous about her English wedding. Harriet and Diana had coached her well in the ways of western marriages, but she had still been anxious that she would do something wrong. However the day had passed successfully and she was almost sure now that she hadn't failed Colin in anything. But it had not been easy, and when she was safely in Harriet's old motor car with her new husband beside her, she felt a sense of dazed relief.

She had looked in amazement at the decorations daubed and tied on to the vehicle and especially at the old cans that must have been hidden underneath and which appeared on strings bumping over the stones as they drove away. The raucous remarks and noisy cheering of their friends had added to her bewilderment. Colin had laughed affectionately and eventually she had laughed too.

But now they were alone in the quiet of the hills and he pulled into the side of the road, kissed her, and told her that he loved her and that she had been wonderful, perfect, and that he was very proud of her. Then he got out of the car and removed all the trimmings that had clattered behind them for those first few miles.

Samira watched as he pushed them carefully out of sight in a hollow just below the road. He untied the pink ribbons that adorned the bumper and rubbed at the bright red lipstick which declared 'Just Married' on the rear window.

'There,' he said, surveying his handiwork from all sides. 'Now we shan't be quite so noticeable. And I'm going to carry you off to Tiberias for a few days on the shores of Galilee. My aunt has a friend who runs a hotel there. She has a host of very convenient friends all over the place.'

Samira smiled weakly but said nothing. This must be the surprise that he had told her about, a honeymoon he called it. She sat beside him as they drove away, her hands clasped tightly in her lap. In spite of her happiness there was still fear in her heart, two kinds of fear. One that wouldn't be diminished until she was far out of range of her family's wrath, and the other...? She kept telling herself that Colin was not like Eshref and he had proved it to her most certainly that day in Harriet's house. Yet he was her husband now and a husband had rights...both upbringing and experience had taught her to fear this night.

Colin sensed her nervousness but thought it was all because of her brothers. 'Tiberias is about sixty miles from here. You'll be quite safe there,' he said. 'But you're safe now anyway. You're my wife, Samira. My wife!' The words sounded sweet to him, sweet beyond words, and he took his hand from the steering wheel for a second and grasped hers.

Samira felt confidence returning a little. 'I can hardly believe it,' she whispered. 'Everything was so unreal today, so different from Arab weddings, and now, going away to a hotel as you call it...that's strange for me too.'

'Our honeymoon,' Colin said. 'Our honeymoon, sweetheart, and it'll be perfect. I'll make it perfect for you.'

'I like that word—sweetheart,' she said. She savoured it again slowly. The very sound of it comforted her. 'Sweetheart...it's lovely.'

The little hotel stood near the lakeside and she looked at it in amazement, marvelling that she was actually going to stay in such a place, be a guest there, have no work to do, be waited upon. Colin had explained all this to her but she had not really understood. Until this moment it had been just a beautiful dream. It was something so far removed from her experience that she could hardly visualise it at all.

The meal they shared together later in the cool white-painted dining room was another bewildering revelation. That a male cook should prepare the food was surprising enough but that men waiters should bring it to her was hardly to be believed. Was all this really happening? She twisted the shiny gold band on her finger and tried to assure herself that it was.

'Am I truly awake, Colin?' she whispered. 'Or am I about to find that all this is some wonderful dream?'

'No dream,' he said 'And you have a whole week to get used to being looked after and cosseted.'

'What is cosseted?'

'It means...' He was at a loss for a moment. 'It means being loved and protected and thoroughly spoilt.'

She laughed. 'You mustn't spoil me, Colin.'

'I shall spoil you as long as I live,' he said.

She thought about those words a little later when they stood alone together in the pretty bedroom. 'To spoil someone'. It was a strange English expression. What did it mean exactly? She really had no idea. But when she looked at the spotless white coverlet on the bed she started to tremble. It reminded her of Eshref, of that other night. She couldn't cast the memory away however hard she tried.

Colin sensed her distress, understood it. He took both of her hands in his and kissed her with

152

tenderness and reverence. He pulled her into his arms and was determined that he would do everything in his power to reassure her, to make this night a time that she would remember with happiness. Whenever he thought of that other wedding night of hers he was consumed with rage. She'd told him something of it and Harriet had filled him in on a few other nauseating details.

He knew that tonight he must be gentle with her, he must see that she enjoyed his love making. Tonight must change for ever her damaged view of marriage, eradicate all the hang-ups of her upbringing. So he kept his tremendous longing and need of her under control at first, fought with himself and was successful. She responded eventually and he knew then that he had truly won her body now as well as her mind. Their union was perfect beyond all his dreams.

When he awoke Samira was still in his arms. He saw that she was awake too. 'Happy?' he whispered.

She nodded. 'Completely happy. All my worries and fears have flown away and you have made them go.' She lay there in complete repose and then she murmured some words in Arabic.

He raised himself a little and looked at her. 'What did you say?'

She smiled at him and stroked his fingers which were lying over her breast. 'Peace be to your hands and your lips,' she translated. 'We say it when someone has been kind to us or has spoken kindly.'

153

'Teach me Arabic,' he said. 'I believe that it's a beautiful and gentle language.'

'No. I shall not speak it again.' Her voice was firm. 'From now on that part of me is dead!'

'Not dead, Samira. Just hibernating for a bit. Until the wounds are healed.'

'Hibernating?'

He laughed, realising that it was a word she probably wouldn't have met. 'Going to sleep for a while, but not for ever, waking up in the spring.' Then he kissed the tip of her nose and kept kissing it until she too laughed aloud and told him to stop. They made love once more and then reluctantly Colin got up from the bed, pulling her with him. 'Come on then, Mrs Colin Stanmore,' he said. 'We're going to do a bit of sight-seeing. All of Galilee is waiting for us.'

The name pleased her. 'Mrs Stanmore,' she said. 'That's what I truly am, isn't it? Mrs Stanmore. Samira Stanmore. It sounds...' She was lost for words to explain the freedom and emancipation she felt. 'It sounds English,' she finished. 'Completely English. I'm English!' She ran to the window and looked at the lake below, where the waters were ruffled by a welcome breeze. Little waves were chasing each other, one after the other breaking on the shore. 'I've never seen anything so perfect.'

'Neither have I,' said Colin, but his eyes were only for her.

The honeymoon was, for Samira, a joyful and wondrous experience, a constantly changing panorama of new sights and sounds, a gentle opening up of an unknown and fascinating world. Then followed a few weeks in a furnished room in a little place far away from Khanhaven while Colin worked on some assignments he had left unfinished and thought never to complete.

'You mustn't stop because of me,' Samira had told him. 'I shall be quite happy while you're digging up your old bits and pieces.'

His enthusiasm had returned a little, and he had laughed at her assessment of his work. He wouldn't leave her for long, just a few hours each morning. 'You're sure you'll be all right?' he said each day.

'Of course. No one except Harriet and Diana know where I am so I'm not frightened.'

But when their passage to England was at last confirmed he admitted to a sense of relief. 'We shall go to Khanhaven for a couple of days,' he said. 'Just to say goodbye, and then—home.'

'Home,' Samira said frequently to herself. 'England will be home!' It gave her a strange feeling, security mixed with quite a different kind of fear.

They were greeted with excitement and some celebration by Harriet and Diana when they arrived at Khanhaven. It was a strange time for Samira for she came as Mrs Stanmore, English now and expected to behave just as any expatriate wife. Diana laughed at her whenever she showed any glimpse of the old submissive ways and Harriet spent every minute that she could spare trying to coach her in all the things she would need to know when she arrived in England.

At last there was just one day to go, hours of trepidation and sadness as well as excitement. But on that day, just as the mid-day heat was passing, they heard Harriet's motor rattling along the track. It came screeching to a halt at the front of the house. There was nothing startling in that. She had been to the village to see a sick child and a lame donkey. They heard the slam of the door and then the clatter of the swinging beads. And suddenly Samira heard a voice she knew, a voice she had thought never to hear again. She ran quickly out to the verandah and then was in her mother's arms.

'My daughter,' Kaffa said. And there was no more either could say for the tears flowed and Harriet crept quietly away to the kitchen leaving them together.

'How did you do it?' Diana gasped. 'However did you get that fearsome old Jebel to let her come?'

'Don't ask questions,' Harriet said. 'Just make me some tea, nice and strong and lots of sugar!'

Diana rushed to put the kettle on the stove in the back courtyard, lifted the precious old china teapot down from the high shelf and measured tea leaves into it. By the time she had the cups set out on the table, milk in a jug, and the tea brewed, her aunt had recovered her equilibrium. She was seated on one of the hard kitchen chairs cooling herself with a large painted fan that was normally fastened decoratively to the wall.

Colin had come in from the back. 'Who's the visitor?' he asked.

'Just your mother-in-law,' Harriet announced.

'My...'

'Kaffa,' Diana said, her eyes dancing. 'I knew that Samira was very upset about not seeing her mother again before she left, and now our wonderful aunt has fixed it!'

It was a moment before Colin could collect his wits but then he swiftly crossed the room to where Harriet was sitting and kissed her exuberantly.

'Is there anything you can't do?' he said.

'Yes,' she replied. 'Plenty of things.'

Then the three of them were silent while the tall grandfather clock that Harriet had brought from England ticked away the precious minutes, minutes of parting for mother and daughter. They could hear quiet voices speaking in Arabic accompanied by the clucking of hens and the gentle sound of the breeze rustling the leaves of the old gnarled vine that twined itself over a trellis around the porch.

At last Samira pushed the bead curtain aside. She was holding Kaffa's hand tightly in hers. She led her to Colin. 'My mother,' she said simply. And then, and with infinite pride, 'Mother, this is my husband!'

They looked at each other, neither knowing how to react, how to greet the other. Kaffa appeared to be searching her son-in-law's face for some kind of reassurance, and then suddenly she smiled. 'I know you will be good to my daughter,' she said shyly. 'I can see it in your eyes and already you've made her happy.'

'I love her very much.' Colin knew that he mustn't stare at an Arab woman and certainly must not shake her hand or kiss her, but he felt sudden affection for this stranger standing uncertainly in front of him in her long heavily embroidered dress and elaborate head covering. 'I shall take good care of her,' he added, 'And one day we shall come back to see you. I promise.'

Samira looked at him with gratitude. 'And until then we'll send you photographs and I'll write to you, Mother, every week. I'll send everything to Mrs Clayton and she'll see that you get it.'

'I should like that,' Kaffa said. 'And especially photographs of your sons.'

'They shall come themselves,' Colin said. 'One day they'll come to you from England.'

'What about the daughters?' Diana objected. 'Don't they count, Samira?'

It was Kaffa who answered. 'Daughters too,' she said. 'I hope you have a daughter, both of you! To a mother daughters are just as precious!'

'To a father as well,' Colin added with a laugh.

They went through to the sitting room, the coolest place at this time of day and drank Diana's tea, ate the little biscuits that she had made. Samira knew that her mother would find it strange to eat in Colin's presence, but Kaffa said nothing. She remembered her years at the missionary orphanage as a child, and she rejoiced that her daughter was going to England, to the place where she'd heard that women were free and unfettered.

The precious hour passed too quickly. Eventually Harriet glanced at her watch. 'Sorry, but it's time to go back,' she interrupted. She got to her feet and went to the door. 'We daren't stay any longer!' Her tone was brisk.

Samira kissed her mother. 'Salaam,' she said, forgetting for a second time that afternoon her resolution not to speak her native language again. Her eyes were full of tears.

'And to you be peace,' Kaffa replied in English. Then quickly she turned and followed Harriet out of the room and they all stood in silence as if the power to speak had deserted them, until the sound of the motor car was just a faint murmur in the distance.

The following day Colin held his wife's hand tightly as though he feared that he would lose her for ever amongst the pushing noisy crowds that thronged the quayside at Haifa. With some trepidation he watched their luggage given over to the care of porters and then he helped her into the small boat that was to take them out to their steamer which lay at anchor in the bay. Diana, David and Harriet stood at the barrier watching and waving.

'Love to everyone,' Diana called. 'Kiss Merryon for me, Samira.'

This last remark broke the tension.

'Trust Diana to think of her horse before the parents,' Colin said as he waved to them.

'And the same for Jazi,' Samira called back to her. Parting from the white stallion had been a great sadness.

She turned to Colin as the boat pushed further from the shore. 'A horse is perhaps easier to kiss than a mother-in-law,' she commented wisely. 'I know that I shall love Diana's Merryon.'

Colin looked down at her and wondered privately whether she would ever get the chance to kiss either. He had written to tell his parents of his marriage and could only guess at the reaction to his letter. Every time he thought about Bagleigh lately he seemed to see his father's face and the words that he always used to describe anyone who wasn't European, white and fully acceptable. Those words had always sounded shocking to him. Now they seemed to be much worse than that, sickening and loathsome.

But England was the only place now where he felt Samira could begin to live a new life. He must go there and face his father's wrath. If he couldn't take her to Bagleigh, then he would find somewhere else. 'I shall join the Air Force,' he had reaffirmed to David before he left. 'Then I'll have a reasonable income and we'll be able to afford a house of our own.'

1 'And meanwhile,' Harriet had said, 'there's my little cottage down in Cornwall, everything all shrouded in dust covers and probably nothing at all working, but you're welcome to it for as long as you need it. I'd thought of selling the place, but couldn't bring myself. I'm keeping it for my old age, and it has some precious memories!'

160

She had given him a large key wrapped in a piece of musty white muslin. 'Use it with my love.'

Once on the steamer they stood on deck and watched the mountains of the Carmel range fade gradually into the distance.

'We'll come back, Samira,' Colin told her. 'We'll definitely come back one day, I promise you. We shall bring our children as we told your mother and we shall show them your beautiful country.'

His arm lay around her shoulders and she felt the warmth of him and his strong protective love, and as the ship took her further and further away from all that she had ever known, her apprehension gradually gave way to a fierce exultation.

'Our sons,' she whispered, and gently touched the soft folds of her skirt. Beneath Harriet's bright twenties-style dress she was sure already of the promise of new life.

CHAPTER 11

Samira thought she had prepared herself for England, for the new sights and sounds and for the cold. Under Harriet's guidance she had selected warm clothes, read slightly more up-to-date books than Dickens and looked at photographs of London, of Devon, and a few of Bagleigh. But she had not anticipated the noise and the crowds, the rushing and shouting at Paddington, and the wind that whistled chillingly round the draughty platforms even though this was supposed to be summer.

'The end of summer,' Colin said, excusing his country's difficult climate.

She kept as close to him as she could, not wishing to let him out of her sight. 'There are so many people,' she said. 'I have never seen so many people in my life.'

He was preoccupied with the luggage, with organising porters, finding the right train and the first-class carriage in which they were to travel, but when at last they were settled and the train steamed its ponderous way out of the station he linked his arm through hers and smiled at her. They had the carriage to themselves. 'There won't be any crowds where we're going,' he said. 'You'll like it. I promise.'

'If you're there, then I shall like it!' Samira was quite confident that she would be happy anywhere if Colin wished it and as long as he was beside her.

When they reached Devonshire she looked with fresh interest as he pointed out various landmarks. She kept her eyes fixed on the changing pattern of fields and hills as the train lurched its way noisily towards their destination. Then suddenly she saw the green give way to a grey expanse of water and they seemed to be almost in the waves. She gasped in fright and Colin laughed.

'The railway line goes right along the edge of the shore here,' he explained. 'This is Dawlish.

It's not far from Bagleigh. I'll bring you here to walk on the beach one day.'

She turned to him, away from the desolation outside, for that was how it appeared to her. The sky was grey and the waves looked angry and cold. She remembered the warm blue waters of Galilee. But this was her husband's land, she told herself sternly, and it must be hers too. It would definitely be hers for she had no other now, and she was determined, in time, to love every inch of it. But in compensation for the strangeness of the countryside there was the novelty of a husband who wanted to walk with you, walk at your side beside the sea, on those unknown moors he talked about, even in the town, anywhere. The joy of it sparkled suddenly in her eyes replacing the apprehension.

She knew that they were to stay in this place called Newton Abbot for the night, in a hotel. Colin had explained that he had to talk to his parents before he could take her to his home. It was the only sadness, the only thing that had any power to spoil her happiness.

She looked out of the window again at the sea. It gave way to a wide river, and then Colin got up and started taking their things down from the rack. She sensed tension in him. It had been present from time to time ever since they had arrived in England. He was doing his best to conceal it, but because she loved him and was sensitive to his moods, she was aware of his anxiety. She guessed that his parents' probable reaction to their marriage was the cause but she couldn't talk to him about it. It was the first thing that had come between them, and her happiness was marred because of it.

He was holding out her coat for her as the train came to a shuddering halt, and she slipped into the garment, marvelling again at this thing he called 'just normal courtesy' which made a man perform services such as this for a woman. It was one of the aspects of life that she least understood, and one which gave her both embarrassment and pleasure.

The coat was a beautiful thing, a soft wool with a big fur collar that had made her laugh in delight when Harriet had retrieved it from the depths of the wardrobe at Khanhaven. There was fur at the hem and cuffs too and she had remarked, in the afternoon heat of Palestine, that surely it wouldn't be cold enough for that anywhere!

But in London even the summer wind had been cold to her and now, when Colin lowered the window of the carriage door, letting in the evening air, she was glad of it again. He stepped on to the platform and then held out his hand to help her down and she took it and gingerly followed him. He called to the porters who were waiting for custom, and directed one of them to assemble their bags and take them to the hotel across the road.

Samira stood still and looked at the swirl of people all around. As in London there were girls and women travelling alone, and those who were with their men were either walking in front of them or beside, usually arm in arm. She marvelled at the way the men carried the heaviest loads. There were no women carrying anything more than a handbag or a hatbox and she was saddened, thinking suddenly of her mother with her endless burdens.

'The end of our journey for today,' Colin said breaking into her reverie. He led her out of the station and pointed to the hotel where they were to stay. It looked solid and grand and she felt intimidated as they walked over to it and went inside. She watched as he signed the visitor's book, and then they were taken upstairs to their room.

'Do you want to bathe?' he asked her. 'I intend to.'

He flung open a door and she gasped in amazement at the splendid bathroom beyond.

'I asked for a room with a bath adjoining,' he said.

'You mean that this is just for us?'

'Just for us. You can have as many baths as you like. I'm sorry that the London hotel had no rooms vacant with private bathrooms.'

Samira had little experience of such luxuries. The hotel in Tiberias had not possessed any bathrooms and Harriet only had her home-made shower.

She stood beside Colin and looked down at the shining bath, saying nothing. He fiddled with the gas geyser above it and a stream of hot water gushed forth. She jumped back in panic. There had only been a slow trickle of water in the few bathrooms on the boat and their use was strictly limited. Colin put in the plug and turned on the cold tap as well and she watched, fascinated as the water ran in abundance.

'So much water,' she said. 'And all for one person to get clean!'

'I'll come and scrub your back,' Colin teased.

Swiftly her nervousness disappeared and she laughed. Life was fun again. She clutched her arms across her body. 'No you most certainly will not,' she told him. 'I shall lock the door.'

'You might drown!'

She considered for a moment and looked at him with a sparkle of merriment in her eyes. 'Then perhaps you had better come and wait here while I bathe. But you will not look! You must sit on the little stool and turn your head away!'

For reply he pulled her into his arms and kissed her while the water ran steadily on and they were enveloped in a vast cloud of steam.

Samira enjoyed her first English bath. 'I want to bathe every day,' she said, the soapy water coming right up beneath her chin. 'It's the nicest thing in the world.'

'Nicer than me?'

'No, not nicer than you,' she whispered to him later when they lay together in the cosy warmth of the big feather bed. 'Nothing at all could be nicer than you!'

Exhausted she soon slept and Colin held her in his arms marvelling at how much he loved her. But he lay sleepless for a long time and his thoughts were of tomorrow, when he must go to Bagleigh without her.

His parents were expecting him. They had

recently had the telephone installed and he had been able to talk to them briefly from London. The conversation had not been easy. They were still shocked and angry about his marriage. The fact that his wife was a Muslim Arab was so unthinkable, so horrifying to them, that Colin had very little hope of ever being accepted into the family again.

And she was pregnant! He hadn't told them that. They were bound to think that she had forced him into marriage. He slid his hand gently down over her stomach. And then the chill entered his heart again as it so frequently did lately. Was the child growing there his, or was it Eshref's? Whoever was the father, the child was Samira's and therefore precious. He wouldn't entertain for a moment the thought that it wasn't his! Yet he knew that however strong his resolutions, however determined his mind, the kernel of doubt would always be there.

He recalled yet again the time that she had beseeched him to lie with her. It was only a week or two after the terrible rape by her so-called husband, that monster as Diana called him. She had said that she wanted him to purge away all memories of Eshref, to make herself clean in her heart and in her body. She had been so persuasive, so determined, quite unlike the normally shy and modest girl that he knew her to be. Had there been another stronger motive for her uncharacteristic behaviour? He hated himself for his thoughts. His lovely pure Samira surely couldn't have had such scheming plans? And if Eshref had implanted his foul seed within her then all his own love making couldn't displace it. He knew enough about biology to be sure of that, whatever Samira might persuade herself to believe.

Gently, so that he wouldn't disturb her, he turned over, turned away from her, and wondered, not for the first time, how he was going to come to terms with the future, with his parents' wrath, with having little money, with an Arab child to bring up who might inherit Bagleigh. To inherit Bagleigh! He said it again to himself under his breath. His father had threatened to cut him out of the will, but Colin was not sure how things would stand legally. The house might go straight to his son... His son? Eshref's son? Bagleigh, the house and farm that had been in the Stanmore family for generations. He would have to stand back and see this alien child take his inheritance from him.

He laughed bitterly with the irony of it and slept at last, a disturbed sleep from which he awoke in the morning feeling as though a thousand drums were beating a tattoo in his head.

And this was the day he must go home. He must leave Samira here, must not let her know anything of his apprehensions and worries. He loved her. He reminded himself fiercely that he loved her more than he loved anyone, more than he loved Bagleigh. He stretched out an arm to feel for her, but she was not there. He heard the water running in the nearby bathroom. He grinned a little in spite of his unease and tried to think of comfortable ordinary things, of Rollo and Major, his horse and his dog, both of whom he would see today. Perhaps there would be time to ride up to Greatcombe Rocks. The thought cheered him, even imparted a little enthusiasm for the day ahead, and he got out of bed and did a few exercises in front of the open window, breathing deeply of the fresh morning air. After Palestine it felt invigorating and made him glad to be back in England.

Samira came into the bedroom already dressed. She was wearing a navy blue and white patterned dress, another of Harriet's for there had been little time to buy any new clothes. Her head was bare and her dark hair cut to shoulder length was loose, clipped back with two kirby grips just above each ear. She kissed him and he could smell the strange spicy perfume that she had bought before they left. It reminded him of the Middle East and of those first heady days when he knew that she would be his. He pulled her into his arms and held her close for a moment. The feel of her young body healed, for a time at least, all the wounds of the night, all the tensions that had overcome him in the hours of darkness. In the freshness of the new day and in her nearness the problems seemed lighter, bearable. Only their love mattered.

It was past midday before he was able to get to Bagleigh. The bus that went infrequently to Widecombe dropped him at the end of the road and there were still over two miles to walk down into the valley where the house lay surrounded by its own lush green fields, and by trees which were now in all their late summer glory. He stood quite still on the hillside when the house first came into view. He stood and gazed down at the old weathered stone walls and lichen-covered roof, and in his heart was a great swell of pride, but of apprehension too. He wished that Samira was with him to share this momentous home-coming. He wanted to take her by the hand and lead her along the drive, between the six great yew trees that stood guard on either side, and then see his mother gather her into her arms, kiss her and welcome her as she was worthy of being welcomed.

He adjusted the rucksack, heavy with presents chosen carefully in Palestine. He had photographs too, all taken by Diana. She had sent home with him a number of clever ones that she hoped he would be able to sell to various magazines, but the ones he carried now were snapshots of Khanhaven, of Harriet, and some of the wedding. He thought of them with a small measure of hope and then purposefully strode out down the hill.

A rather frightened little maid let him in, a girl he didn't recognise. He smiled briefly at her and then stopped as a large dog hurled himself out of the dining room. Rollo barked and growled at the supposed intruder and then paused, unsure of himself. Colin called him gently and suddenly the dog rushed towards him in a frenzy of delight. He bent and allowed the animal's exuberance full rein, the boisterous welcome cheering him. But he was suddenly aware of his father standing watching the exhibition with disapproval. Colin straightened and looked his parent full in the face. He brushed the dog hairs from his trousers and then held out his hand.

'Father,' he said. 'You look well.'

'I'll not even shake your hand,' James Stanmore boomed. 'You can arrange to get your things, any possessions you left here, and then you can clear out, you and your, your...' he snorted in disgust. 'Your native woman.' The last two words were filled with such venom that Colin blanched, but he stood his ground.

He slowly lowered his hand and laid it on the dog's head, for Rollo, sensing that his master was being attacked in some way, had seated himself firmly at his side. He could feel the animal's distress. It matched his own anger. 'Then you refuse to meet my wife?' It was more a statement than a question.

'Of course we refuse. I don't know how you can ask, how even suggest that you bring some primitive creature here to offend your mother and shock the whole neighbourhood.'

For a moment Colin wanted to laugh out loud. Did they imagine someone swathed in black or even perhaps wearing feathers and a grass skirt?

'She's educated and not much darker than you are,' he said. 'She speaks English as fluently as Diana and reads *The Times*.'

His mother had come quietly, almost un-noticed, to stand beside her husband. James turned to her.

171

'Here he is then,' he said. 'Here's your precious son who has disgraced us all.'

Mary Stanmore walked uncertainly past him and over to Colin. Then suddenly she held out her hands to her son and kissed him gently. 'It's lovely to see you, my dear,' she whispered. 'Your father is quite adamant that you shall not stay, but I've prepared a few things for you. And I've persuaded him to allow you to have tea with us—with me that is.'

Again Colin, because he was tense and nervous and terribly distressed, perversely wanted to laugh. He was to be allowed tea! But he returned his mother's embrace and wondered at her courage. 'Thank you, Mother,' he said. 'I shall be grateful for a drink. And I have some presents for you, and some photographs. Letters from Aunt Harriet and Diana too.'

'I don't suppose Diana has persuaded that stubborn sister of mine to come home at last and live a decent respectable life as I directed her? That's the only reason I let her go to Palestine.' James Stanmore's voice had lost none of its exasperation.

'I'm afraid not, Father. Aunt Harriet is very happy there.'

Mary Stanmore ignored her husband's outrage and smiled nervously at Colin. 'Come into the sitting room, dear,' she said. 'I shall ring for tea. I think Lily has made cucumber sandwiches. We have our own cucumbers, you know. I grow them myself in the conservatory.'

If she was aware of the eccentricity of her

speech she did nothing to show it, but led the way from the hall into the comfortable room that he had always loved. It was not a place kept sacred for visitors. He and Diana had played childhood games here, ludo, lexicon and snakes and ladders, and as they grew older, draughts and chess. There had always been a story read to them beside the old granite fireplace each night too and he remembered the smell of woodsmoke from the logs brought in each day by one of the men. The haunting aroma was still here and all the memories came flooding back. There was a beautiful arrangement of flowers and branches in the fireplace today, and he remembered his mother's care over such things.

Rollo, obviously comforted somewhat by the mellowing atmosphere, followed them in, made for the sheepskin rug in front of the fireplace, and turning round two or three times to obtain the position of optimum comfort, settled himself with a grunt of satisfaction.

'I'm sorry, Mother.' Colin said when they too were seated. 'Sorry for so many things, but mainly that you won't be able to see Samira. She's gentle and kind and beautiful and I know that you'd love her. She and Diana are great friends and Aunt Harriet considers her almost a daughter.'

Mary Stanmore was more at ease now that the door was firmly closed between herself and her husband. She looked at her son with compassion. 'I'm sorry too,' she said. 'But nothing will budge your father. However, I shall manage somehow to meet your wife, I'm quite determined on that. I'm not quite sure yet how I shall achieve it. I still find it very difficult to defy your father openly.'

'But why?' Colin was indignant.

'I know that you and Diana both think that I am quite incredibly submissive. Well, perhaps I am, but I've found that it's the easiest way to manage your father, and it makes for harmony, which I like. I've always needed to scheme a little to get my own way over certain things.' She smiled at him and then leaned over and patted his hand comfortingly, and he felt an overwhelming affection for her. They had never been close, in fact he had always believed that she had no deep attachments to anyone. Now he was not so sure. Perhaps there was more to his mild little mother than he and Diana had discovered.

He was suddenly sad, realising with amazement that it was possible to live for years in the same house with someone and not to know them at all. He determined that it would never happen to him again. He and Samira would share everything about each other, and their children...the child she carried? He was unprepared for the depth of his disturbance about this child, the feelings of alienation that yet again swept through him catching him completely unawares. He saw his mother looking at him with surprised concern and he swiftly composed his features as best he could.

'I hope you'll manage to meet Samira soon then,' he said. 'We're going down to Aunt

Harriet's house for a while until I've sorted out a job and somewhere of our own. You remember that I told you in my letter that she had offered me the loan of Chy Morvah?'

'Yes, I'm glad for you. It's a very pretty place.'

As she spoke the maid knocked and then entered the room with an elaborately laid trolley. There were delicate sandwiches, scones and cream, fruit cake and a plate of creamy fancies.

'Now you must eat,' Mary Stanmore said. She poured him a cup of tea. 'Cook and Lily have made a special effort in your honour.'

Colin looked at the spread laid before him and at the intricate patterns on the shining silver teapot in his mother's hand and realised that all this effort had been made just because he was home. She must be trying to tell him that he was still important to her, and that as far as she was concerned he still had a place here in this house. He was very moved. In spite of what she said about deferring to his father, she had defied him this afternoon.

'You have money?' The unexpected question surprised him.

'A small amount,' he said. 'The legacy from Grandma. It brings me a little income each month, but I shall try to do some teaching, and I hope to join the Air Force eventually.'

'Flying?' There was immediate concern on her face.

'Don't worry,' he told her. 'If there's another war, I'd rather be in the air than in the trenches.'

'Your father says there won't be trenches this time.'

'No.'

There was a long silence between them and Colin realised that he was hungry after all. He ate one tiny sandwich after another, and when he had finally had enough he looked across at his mother. He had to know about Major. Realising now the depth of his father's displeasure he wondered if the horse was still considered his. 'Major?' he questioned. 'I hardly dare ask.'

Mary hesitated for a moment before she replied. Eventually she said, 'Your father rides him now. Since he heard about your marriage he has ridden him every day.'

'So I have to lose Major too!'

'He won't be sold. I was relieved when James decided to keep him. At first I was afraid he'd want to sell him.'

'I suppose I must be glad for small mercies!' Colin's voice was bitter.

'It's better that he should be ridden regularly. Your father is a good horseman. No harm will come to Major.'

'I'd hoped to ride him this afternoon.'

She smiled a little sadly. 'Have patience, my son. Perhaps the next time you come.'

'Next time? I thought I was banished for ever.'

'For ever is a long time.'

'I wish I could share your optimism.'

'Without optimism I couldn't live,' Mary said. 'And now, if you've quite finished your tea, I shall ring for these things to be cleared away and you can give me the rest of the news from Palestine.'

Colin waited until the new maid had carried the remains of the meal away and then he retrieved his rucksack from behind the chair where he had left it. 'I've brought you some presents,' he said. 'But first I expect you want the letters.' He took a small package from the side pocket and handed them to his mother. She held them for a moment and then got up and put them into her bureau. 'I shall read them later,' she said. 'I miss Diana. You've not told me anything about her yet.'

He had been instructed to say nothing at all about his sister's relationship with David and indeed he knew little about it himself. She hadn't confided in him as she usually did. 'She's very well,' he said briefly. 'And Harriet relies on her a lot now.' But his words were absent-minded, for his attention was on the next package that he was about to open, the photographs.

His mother was looking at him expectantly and he was dismayed to discover that he was trembling as he placed, first of all, the wallet of wedding prints in her eager hands. He stood watching her as she looked at each one and then sat awkwardly on the edge of the chair, his tension mounting with each second that passed. She examined them all carefully and then returned to the first one again.

'This is your wife?' There was surprise in her voice.

'Yes, Mother. That is Samira.'

There was silence in the room broken only by the grunts of Rollo who was dreaming happily, totally unaware of the jangled emotions of the two people sitting either side of him.

'But she isn't at all what I imagined,' Mary Stanmore murmured at last. 'Your father would accept her, Colin. I am sure he would if only he had seen her before he knew that she...'

'Is foreign!' The words were angry and full of contempt.

His mother appeared to ignore his remark. She continued to stare at the photograph and then went through them all again. At last she looked up and he saw that she had put the one of Samira standing alone beside Jazi on top of the others.

He remembered so clearly the taking of that odd snap. There had been no careful posing. It was one from a film Diana had taken on their return from honeymoon because Samira realised that she had no photographs of the horse. She was wearing Harriet's jodhpurs and an old shirt. Her head was bare, the long dark hair in a neat bun at the nape of her neck. After her marriage she had deliberately cast off every possible evidence of her Arab inheritance. But Colin remembered her reluctance to wear the jodhpurs instead of her elaborately embroidered trousers, and to go bareheaded too was another milestone. She had laughed a little grimly when she saw this particular photograph, calling the clothes uncomely and ugly. Yet this was the one his mother had chosen from all the rest.

'She looks like one of Diana's friends,' she said. 'I shall put it in a frame and place it on the piano. Your father will see it and ask who she is!'

Colin was full of admiration for his mother's scheming and discernment. 'Do you want any of the others?' he managed.

'I should like the one of the two of you. I'll put it in my drawer beneath my clothes. Have you any of Harriet and Diana? Your father might grudgingly look at those.'

'Yes, of course.' He handed her the second envelope containing photographs of his sister and aunt, of Khanhaven, and some of the rescued animals. 'You can keep as many of these as you want,' he said.

She selected some. 'I don't suppose your father will change his opinions about Harriet's work when he sees them, but we can at least try.' She handed the rest back to him and smiled. 'How is Diana getting on with her photography?'

'Splendidly. I have a lot more of the towns and countryside that she wants me to try to sell for her. She's very determined.'

Then he pulled another parcel out of the rucksack. 'I have a little thing that I found on one of the digs,' he said. 'It's slightly chipped but very old, thousands of years perhaps. I thought you'd like it.'

He handed the box to his mother and she held it for a moment before opening it. Then she unwrapped the outer paper and carefully pulled the layers of tissue aside. The object that lay within was a clay lamp, beautiful only in its simplicity and precious because of its antiquity and associations.

'They put olive oil here.' Colin leaned over and indicated the main body of the vessel. 'And a wick. It was all the light they had.' He felt that he had to make excuses for his choice but was totally unprepared for his mother's reaction.

'It shall be a symbol of light to me,' she said softly. 'Perhaps some light might come from it into your father's heart.'

He gasped. What had happened to his mother that she should say such things? He looked at her in amazement again. Then carefully he unwrapped the remaining presents. There was a silver chain and a cross of olive wood. 'From Bethlehem,' he said. 'And an Arab dagger for Father! A bit incongruous, I know, but I thought he might like to hang it in the dining room along with his other bits and pieces.'

The bits and pieces he referred to were swords and duelling pistols. Collecting these had been one of his father's consuming interests for many years.

'I shall give it to him when he's in a good mood,' his mother said. 'I know that he'll like it, but of course he may not admit to doing so! And the cross is lovely, my dear. Thank you. But most precious of all is this photograph of Samira.' She looked at it again and he could see that she was almost crying. 'I have a perfect little silver frame for it.'

Then she became suddenly more practical, more the mother he knew and could cope with.

'Now you had better go,' she said. 'We mustn't strain your father's patience too far. And try not to worry. Leave things to me. I'll come to you somehow as soon as I can. I shall write to you at Chy Morvah.'

While Colin was away Samira was too frightened to go out. The streets of Newton Abbot looked quite fearsome now that she was alone. Until this morning Colin hadn't left her at all. She felt a deep sense of alienation with everything around her as she sat in the hotel room and watched the busy scene below her window, and wondered if she would ever become like the women she could see. She marvelled at the free untrammelled look of them. Yet she noticed that some had worried frowning faces, and their clothes were drab and dull compared to the bright embroidered dresses she wore at home. She thought of her mother and longed to share all of these new experiences and to hear the remarks Kaffa would make if she could see these women.

There were a few girls in uniform. Samira looked at their short straight skirts and square box-like jackets and thought the clothes most unbecoming.

The morning wore on and the sun at last crept round to the small room, warming her and helping to defeat her homesickness. Lunch was brought at one o'clock as Colin had ordered and she picked at the potatoes swimming in an unappetising sea of brown gravy. She looked with suspicion at the cake-like object that was also anointed with the liquid, and the meat, which she guessed was beef, filled her with nausea. She knew that it wouldn't have been prepared according to Muslim laws. She told herself fiercely that she had vowed to take her husband's God as well as his country, but in spite of her determination, the meat defeated her. She pushed it to the edge of the plate and thought of the tender mutton at home, and remembered how she and her mother always ate what the men had left. She smiled to herself a little bitterly.

When she had eaten as much as she could manage she lay down on the bed and had at last drifted into sleep when Colin returned. Then she started up and rubbed her eyes, trying to remember where she was, what day it was.

He came over to her and took her hands in his pulling her into his arms. 'Sorry I've been so long, sweetheart,' he said. 'Are you all right?'

'Yes, I'm fine.' She searched his face for signs of gladness and found none. 'It wasn't good then, your visit to your home?'

'No, not really. But my mother was kind and longs to see you.'

'I should like to meet her.'

'She promised to come to us at the cottage.'

'Then we can't go to Bagleigh?'

'Sorry, sweetheart. Not yet.'

She was filled with disappointment, and fear too. 'Will your father allow your mother to come to see us then?'

'She'll manage it without his permission, I think. She's changed. I found her more assertive than I've ever known her.'

Samira hardly understood. The relationship between husbands and wives in this new country of hers was still a mystery, and this terrible news of Colin's made her very frightened of her unknown father-in-law.

'Then we have to go to this place with the funny name?' Samira tried not to show how miserable she felt. 'Harriet told me a lot about her little cottage near the sea. It sounds lovely.'

'Chy Morvah is very beautiful. We had some holidays there when I was little. I loved the beach. There are long stretches of sand and huge towering cliffs.'

'Like Mount Carmel?'

Colin smiled. He knew what she meant. She had gone one day, with Harriet, to a small village on the coast to look at some donkeys there. They had taken the long route back, going beside the sea to Haifa. There, where the road ran around the foot of the famous mountain, were miles of firm golden sands and great waves crashing onto the beach.

He had arrived at his aunt's house just as they had returned from the expedition and he remembered the colour in Samira's cheeks and the sparkle in her eyes as she described the day's events.

'Not as hot,' he said. He too had often driven that particular route. He recalled the sultry heat, the burning sun, and he wondered for an uncomfortable moment how she would survive the tearing winds and rain of North

Cornwall, and especially the sea mists that frequently rolled in from the Atlantic. 'No,' he said shaking his head. 'I don't think it bears any resemblance to Mount Carmel!'

'But I shall like Chy Morvah.'

He heard the determination in her voice. 'Of course you will. And we shall be happy there, Samira.'

She reached up and kissed him and he knew that the gesture took much courage for she seldom initiated any endearment. He wrapped his arms around her more tightly in a fierce protective hug. His father's unreasoning hostility only made her more precious. Without her there would be nothing.

CHAPTER 12

'Can you do without me for a couple of days, Aunt?'

Diana and Harriet had just returned from their daily ride. Harriet dismounted and led Naama through the outer gate. 'Where do you propose going? Sorry to be inquisitive but...'

Diana laughed. 'I won't say that you sound like my father. You've every right to ask. David has suggested a trip to Jerusalem. He has to go on some business for the kibbutz and wondered if I'd like to go along.'

Harriet didn't look at her niece but concentrated all her attention on the mare, unbuckling the bridle and carefully removing the saddle. 'Of course I can spare you, but do you really think you should?'

Diana ignored the guarded criticism. She slipped from Jazi's back and patted him absent-mindedly. 'I want to see Jerusalem,' she said. 'It's a place no one should miss.'

'Yes,' Harriet replied thoughtfully. 'It's certainly a place no one should miss. How are you going to get there?'

'Motor, of course. David has the use of Jezebel.'

'Jezebel? Is that what they call that terrible old Ford?'

'Yes, they've painted her red now and christened her. Someone had the brilliant idea of calling her by the name of the wicked Queen in the Bible! I thought you knew.'

'You spend more time over in that kibbutz than I do nowadays.'

Diana could detect a trace of disapproval in her aunt's voice. 'You think I shouldn't go?'

'I didn't say that.'

'I can feel it though. You don't seem keen on the idea. Is it because of David?'

'My dear child,' Harriet said, 'I consider David to be one of the nicest men I know. I should fall for him myself if I were a few years younger, but I also know how strong his feelings are for this place. He wants a Jewish homeland here. He's a Zionist. Very little else matters to him. He'd make a terrible husband. At least he would for anyone who didn't care just as much about the same things.

I don't want you hurt! When you first came I thought that his friendship might be a little diversion for you. I knew that you'd met him before in England. I was very foolish and short-sighted.' She straightened up and stared at Diana, shook her head slightly. 'Whoever marries David Halprin will have to make a lot of sacrifices.'

'I don't mind the sacrifices. Please, Aunt, agree to my going with him to Jerusalem this once? It'll help me to make up my mind! Perhaps when I see him there, spend two whole days with him, I'll know what to do. Maybe I'll find out that he's not right for me after all!'

Diana knew of course that she wasn't being completely truthful. She hoped desperately that two days in David's company would have the opposite effect, would seal their relationship. And then there was the perfect bliss of being alone with him for such a long time. Usually there were multitudes of other people around.

Harriet returned to her careful grooming of Naama, her hand sweeping in long strokes of the brush down the horse's side. 'You don't need me to agree,' she said. 'As you implied, I'm not like my dear brother, all rules and regulations. You do just what you want to do, but be careful. I feel responsible for you while you're here. Don't do anything foolish that you'll regret. And take your pistol.'

'Pistol?' Diana wanted to laugh. She thought that her aunt's concern was merely with David and what might happen between them.

'Yes, of course. It's a long way. There are some funny people about.

'David will look after me,' Diana said, her voice full of airy confidence.

'We join the main road at Jenin,' David told her. He had brought the old motor car, newly washed and gleaming in its bright red paint, round to Khanhaven before the sun had quite risen. Diana was in a fever of excitement. He tucked a blanket around her legs when she was settled in the seat beside him. 'You won't need that for long,' he said. 'But it's cold just now.'

She looked up at him, at his dark hair, longer than he had worn it at home, at his brown eyes smiling down at her, and at the ruggedness that had not been there when they first met in England. His skin was tanned, and she thought it suited him. She was well used by now to this quite different version of the young English gentleman that he had been when her parents met him at Bagleigh. She wondered how they would like the rugged idealist that he had become. The smart suit had given way to a casual shirt worn with shorts or shabby unpressed trousers. Although his hands on the steering wheel were still scholar's hands, they were tougher now. She stared at the long sensitive fingers that she had heard playing the violin so brilliantly in the sitting room at home. They were rough and calloused and seemed larger, stronger, and the nails, although obviously well scrubbed, had small traces of earth beneath them. He had laughed about it to her recently when he held her hands in his. 'Precious earth,' he had said. 'The earth of Eretz Israel, my homeland!' She remembered wishing that he had applied the word 'precious' to herself, but no, it was to the land. That was typical. Perhaps that was what worried Harriet.

The motor car bounced and rattled its way along the track and conversation was difficult because of the noise. They passed several villages, picturesque tumbledown places, and eventually they crossed the railway line.

'Soon be on the main road,' David shouted as he drove carefully over the crossing. 'You can go all the way from Damascus down to Gaza and eventually across the Suez Canal to Cairo on that line. I want to go some day. It's safer than going by road.'

'I remember Colin telling me about it when I first came here,' Diana said. 'But what do you mean, safer? Is going by road very dangerous then?'

'Well, it could be, the route we're taking anyway. We're meeting up with a couple of chaps from Affula at Jenin. They'll have rifles. And an Army truck is coming along too. Nablus isn't the nicest of places to drive through. A bit hostile from time to time. We usually go in convoy if we can.'

Diana was more disappointed than scared. So they weren't to be alone, and perhaps Harriet had been right about the pistol after all.

'My aunt told me to be careful, but she didn't say exactly why it was dangerous,' she said. 'At least I didn't take her seriously.'

'Harriet? Oh, she's not frightened of anything. She'll go alone anywhere. I believe she always has a pistol in her pocket though.'

Diana put her hand on the bag in her lap and felt the bulge of the little weapon. 'She gave me one some time ago and taught me to use it. I have it here.' She produced the gun nervously and held it out for his inspection.

David glanced at it and then at her and the car swerved a little. She thought she detected a look of approval in his eyes.

'How good are you?'

'I've never needed to fire it for real, thank goodness, but I know how. I've had lots of target practice. Aunt Harriet wouldn't let me have a thing like this without being sure that I was competent.'

They drove for some time in silence after that and at Jenin picked up David's two friends. The Army truck was waiting too and led the way out of the little town and onto the road that wound its way beside the railway for a few miles and then south through the hills of Samaria down to Jerusalem.

'We usually say up to Jerusalem, not down.' David corrected her later. 'It may lie to the south, but it's built on hills and it's special anyway, so it's "up" like London or Oxford.'

The comparison was odd, funny even, and Diana laughed to herself. Never had she known anything more unlike London or Oxford and the English countryside, than this wild and beautiful land, a place where you had to carry a gun,

189

where ideals appeared to matter more than people, a place that could capture a man's heart, where a girl might be murdered by her brothers because... She shivered and thought of Samira in England. She would be there by now. What was she doing? What did she think of Bagleigh? Had her father allowed them to stay? Without warning she felt alone, in the wrong place, felt as though she didn't belong here at all. And amazingly she could feel tears sliding down her cheeks. Angrily she brushed them away with the back of her hand.

'Jerusalem!' She said the word over to herself with reverence. If Jenin and Nablus had instilled fear into her heart, Jerusalem gave an overwhelming sensation of timelessness and survival. Those other towns were Arab but Jerusalem belonged to everyone. The long hot and uncomfortable journey had been worthwhile.

She climbed out of the motor car, brushed the dust from her skirt and looked around at the great golden walls of the old city. So this was the place of a million dreams, of endless prayers and conflicts.

David smiled at her. 'Happy?' he queried. It was an odd question, not the right word at all for how she felt. She nodded in silent assent and they went through the Jaffa gate into a different world.

They walked in the narrow streets, bargained for treasures at little Arab stalls, and at her insistence went into the dark mysterious Church of the Holy Sepulchre. The heady scent of incense, the chanting monks, the candles, all increased her feeling of unreality.

'The centre of the world,' David said, and she turned to him, wondering if he was laughing at the tradition, but there was no hint of amusement on his face. 'Here.' He pointed to the place. 'They say this is the centre of the world.'

'I think I can believe it,' she whispered. There were police everywhere, armed guards round each corner. It seemed symbolic somehow.

Outside again in the stifling heat she found the military presence disturbing, an intrusion into her ideas of what such a special place should be.

'I know it sounds naive, but why, David?' she asked. 'Why is there so much strife and unrest? This is the Holy Land after all.' They had been joined by the other two members of their group now and together they plunged down through the maze of narrow alleys that led to the ancient Temple Area.

It was a little while before he could answer her question. 'Because it is just that, I suppose,' he said at last. 'Holy to lots of different groups of people. And religion produces high emotions and consequently conflict. Sad but a fact of life.'

Eventually they descended a narrow passage way, and giving immediate weight to his words, they came suddenly upon the Wailing Wall. Diana stared fascinated at the worshippers there. They were facing the great stones which she knew were the only remains of Herod's temple and although she couldn't see their faces their devotion was quite obvious.

This was their most holy place. Some were silent and still but many were praying with a strange bowing movement of their heads that went on and on. Diana could feel the passionate intensity herself as she looked on. They were all men, some of them with their hair in long ringlets hanging on each side of their face, and they were inappropriately dressed for the climate in long black coats and wide-brimmed hats. She saw them touching and kissing the wall as though taking inspiration and hope from its enduring strength.

Although she had read about this special place, the reality was more impressive than anything she had been told. She looked at David and their two companions. They were all three standing quite still, their eyes fixed on the scene before them. She felt that she dare not speak.

It was David who eventually broke the silence. 'These are mostly orthodox Jews,' he explained, indicating the heavily clothed worshippers. 'They're very religious and not really interested in a secular state here. They think that God will bring that about when the Messiah comes. They're praying for his coming and for salvation of course.'

The spell was broken. Diana came to her senses but forbore to say that as far as she was concerned the Messiah had come almost two thousand years ago and been rejected. It

192

was another source of friction, another cause of disunity with David, with everyone she met lately. She had never thought deeply about her faith, had even considered giving it up if David should ask her to marry him, but now she saw just what it would mean and was suddenly afraid.

'But you and your friends are not like that?' she stated desperately, hoping for a strong denial.

'No. These men are more concerned with their religion than with anything else. They're very strict and live in a settlement called Mea Shearim. The boys spend hours studying the Bible and the Sabbath is kept very strictly.'

'What about the girls?' Diana had learned that most highly religious sects kept their women in a state of subjection. It irked her greatly.

'Important in the home,' David said. 'But there it ends. They are expected to stay very much behind the scenes, bear lots of children, and have no say in anything outside. The marriages are arranged, of course, and when the girls marry they must shave their hair off and wear wigs for the rest of their lives. Incredible to me, and I've no idea why they persist in such ideas.'

Diana looked at him with utter horror. 'Are you joking?' she said. 'About the wigs? You must be.'

He shook his head. 'Afraid not, but don't worry. We don't expect such sacrifices from our modern pioneers.'

She detected amusement in his tone and was

slightly relieved. She looked down again at the wall, and then noticed that a small section had been set apart for women and a few were praying there. She wondered about their lives. But at least they weren't so heavily clothed in this heat as their male counterparts.

'Why do the men wear those awful clothes?' she asked.

'I think it's a sort of hangover from the European countries they originally came from, Poland and Russia and the like.'

Diana sighed and was silent again. As she watched the strange panorama before her she tried to make some connection with the men there, some of them quite young, and with the freedom and the gaiety of all the friends she had made on the kibbutz. They were all Jews! But there was no obvious likeness, none at all that she could see.

David had become quiet again too and she guessed that his thoughts might be something like her own.

'Prayers are all right,' he said at last, 'but we need action as well. The most important thing to me is a homeland here in Palestine.' He looked beyond the worshippers to the Temple Mount and the great Mosque that was built upon it, and Diana heard the bitterness in his voice. 'Almost the whole world thinks it has a religious claim on Jerusalem but for us it's more than that. It's the ancient capital of Israel. There isn't any other place that would do.'

Their companions had gone down to join the worshippers at the Wall and for a few minutes they were alone but David hardly seemed aware of her presence.

'All those who claim it have other holy places, other lands,' he said. 'Except the Jews. Muslims have Mecca, Christians have Rome. We've nowhere except here, no country to call our own, no place where we can be sure that we'll not be persecuted or discriminated against.'

'You can't say that about England surely? Being discriminated against, I mean.' Diana didn't want a political discussion but she sensed how strongly he felt and tried to respond. 'Or America,' she added.

'Oh, yes, you can.' He turned angry eyes upon her so that she almost flinched, feeling that his hurt was somehow directed at her, as though just by being gentile, being non-Jew she was committing some offence.

'Do you know that Jews are excluded from lots of organisations in England, tennis clubs, business clubs, things like that? You haven't been to Oxford as a Jew, heard the jibes, felt the antagonism.'

A bit like being a woman, she thought privately, a second-class non-person! But she didn't say the words aloud. Instead she felt for his hand and pressed it in hers quickly in a gesture of accord, of oneness with him. 'I believe I can understand a little,' she said, thinking of her father, of his rules for her life that differed so much from those laid down for her brother, and remembering his frightful racial comments too.

He didn't answer her or return the pressure of

her fingers on his. 'And what about Germany?' His voice was tense. 'What about the persecution that's getting worse every day? We've nowhere to run but Palestine, and even here we're blocked by rules and regulations.'

'What do you mean?'

'By endless White Papers and the like. The British don't want too many of us settling here for fear of offending the Arabs.'

A great weight of hopelessness descended upon Diana as she listened to him. This day to which she had looked forward so much appeared to be widening the gulf between them instead of forwarding their relationship as she'd hoped.

'Oh, David,' she whispered, her voice near to despair. 'Isn't Britain your country too? You're British, or had you forgotten?'

He didn't reply or look at her and she felt cold and alone again as she'd done in the car. It was a feeling she'd experienced at other times too when she was in David's company and she shivered with apprehension.

When their companions returned from their prayers, he left her with them and went to perform his own devotions. She watched him and her heart plummeted. She saw all her dreams fading rapidly away down there beside the great golden wall and longed to run down and throw her arms around him, pull him back to her, back to normality. Back to England.

That night they stood together in the garden of the house where they were staying. It was outside the city on the slopes of the Mount of

Olives. The darkness of the Judean hills was all about them and the lights of Jerusalem shone dimly across the Kidron valley.

' "A city set on a hill cannot be hid",' Diana quoted.

'Why do you say that?'

'It's in the Bible.'

'I've never read that bit.'

She looked up at him. 'Wrong testament,' she said bleakly.

Their hands were joined but there was no harmony between them, no feeling of unison.

'It's my homeland,' David said. 'My true homeland. The place where I really belong, Diana, not England any more. Can you understand that?'

And suddenly she knew that she could not understand, could never be part of his burning ideals. The conflicts, the passionate loyalties, the anger and the strife could never be hers too.

'No, David,' she whispered. 'I love you, but I can't marry you.'

As the impact of what she had said came home to her she suddenly realised that he had not asked her to marry him, or even declared his love. For a moment she was embarrassed but then she realised that it didn't matter now anyway.

'I'm going home,' she said. Home to where I belong, to *my* homeland, to England.' Her heart cried out that it was his home too, the place where he had been born and raised, but she said nothing of that.

He put out a hand to detain her as though he

was expecting her to run from him at that very minute. And he was right. She did run, ran as swiftly as possible along the dark path lined with its sweet-smelling rosemary hedge, back to the house, back to desolation of spirit and misery of heart. Yet there was an odd peace within her too that was totally at variance with the grief, for the facts that she had known and not acknowledged for a long time had been made clear to her at last.

She went straight to her room not wanting to speak to anyone. 'Shalom,' she said to herself over and over again through her tears. She said it almost like a mantra until she slept. 'Shalom, shalom, shalom.'

CHAPTER 13

Diana knew that she would never forget these last few days in Palestine. She felt herself to be a mass of conflicting emotions. I'm doing the right thing, she affirmed constantly to herself, but my heart is breaking nevertheless.

She talked to Harriet about it on her first evening back from Jerusalem. They were sitting in the courtyard in the cool of the evening, the work of the day done, the sound of cicadas all about them and the occasional braying of a contented donkey coming from the field behind the bungalow.

'As soon as you can find someone else to help,

I shall go home,' she said. 'You were right of course about David, and as long as I remain here I shall never manage to put him out of my mind.' Not that I ever shall, she added silently. Aloud she said, 'I'm sorry, Aunt. I've loved getting to know you and working with the animals.'

'You've made the right decision,' Harriet said dully. 'I shall miss you, of course, but ever since you arrived I've been telling myself that you were only here for a short time.'

Diana laughed. 'Sounds as though you wanted to get rid of me!'

'Not at all, child. The exact opposite. I shall feel quite bereft when you've gone.'

'Now that I've decided to leave Palestine, everything here is suddenly more precious,' Diana said, realising that the country itself was beginning to have meaning for her.

'It's always the way,' Harriet said. 'We always seem to want what we haven't got. It's the human condition.' She patted Ghazala who had put her silky head on her lap. 'And of course Samira will be pleased to have you in England.'

'I shall go down to Chy Morvah as soon as I can.'

Diana's words caused Harriet to think of her little house in Cornwall. For a moment she thought that she heard in her imagination the sound of the waves crashing against the breakwater there, but it was only the wind in the olive trees. It was difficult to visualise the wild and bleak cliffs of Cornwall while she was sitting here beneath this warm starlit sky. You could seldom sit outside at night in Porthmead. For a fleeting second she was almost homesick for England.

Then she pulled herself together. She had work to do. Life must continue as before. A vast number of animals needed her care and devotion, and tomorrow there was a visit to be made to an animal sanctuary she had set up some miles away. The village was very lovely, beside the sea and straggling the road to Haifa. It was one of her favourite places.

They set off early the next morning visiting other tiny villages on the way, and by the middle of the afternoon Harriet was weary. They had just finished the last donkey's hoof which, having been neglected for years, had been a difficult one to put right.

'Well, that's a good job done,' Harriet said rubbing her aching back. She stared fiercely at her Arab helpers. 'See that you carry on with all the treatments I've ordered, and if you see any other donkeys with hooves like that, take them in if you can.' She opened her bag and paid the arranged wages and inspected the stores of animal food. 'I shall come back in four weeks time.' She spoke in fluent Arabic and her voice was authoritative, expecting to be obeyed. 'Don't allow any animal to suffer if you can do anything about it,' she directed. 'On my next visit I shall reimburse whatever you've spent.'

Diana, listening, smiled to herself. She could

see a likeness to her father now in Aunt Harriet. She wondered if she too had inherited this bossy streak.

'Let's go then,' Harriet said briskly. 'Eight more donkeys rescued.' There was a glow of pride in her voice as she settled herself into the little car. 'Work's over for today. Now we can enjoy ourselves. Shall we go straight back, or into Haifa for an hour or so? I think we just have time to do some shopping in the market.'

'Oh, into Haifa definitely,' Diana replied. 'It'll probably be my last visit and I remember Samira saying how lovely this road is.'

'Not much of a surface though. A bit of a struggle for the old banger.' Harriet gripped the steering wheel firmly and gritted her teeth as the sturdy old car bumped its way out of the lane and onto the main road which was only a little better.

'Never mind, Aunt. Could we have a look at Colin's castle? It's on the way, isn't it, not far from here?'

Harriet smiled. 'You mean Athlit? I should think so. Your brother loved that place, didn't he? He was always going on about the excavations he wanted to do there when he'd finished at Kefr Dor. He'll never get to either place again, I suppose.'

'We have to turn off the road shortly, don't we?' Diana said, her finger on the map. 'I hope we don't miss it. The light's just right for some good photographs. I must make the most of my last few days here.'

'Don't worry, we won't get lost. I know the

201

place. It's right on the shore. You don't need the map.' As in everything else, Harriet was completely confident.

When they reached the ruins of the old crusader castle Diana saw, with surprise, that it was surrounded and infiltrated by ramshackle little Arab houses.

'If you really want to get out and wander round,' Harriet said, 'we'll have to get someone to guard the car and pay him well too. We daren't leave it.' She pulled the vehicle to a stop but left the engine running. 'I'm not so sure about getting out after all,' she said. 'They don't look very friendly, do they? They're not usually like that. I wonder what's wrong.'

A crowd of men and boys were staring at them and the usual smiles of welcome were missing. Suddenly a small stone bounced against the side of the car, just missing the window. 'I think we'd better get out of here,' Harriet said unnecessarily. She had parked in a spot where the road widened and quickly she swung into a great circle and revved the engine hard, driving back the way they had come. More stones spun after them, some hitting the car again. One crashed through the rear window and as Harriet automatically ducked, the vehicle swerved alarmingly, but she soon had it on a straight course again.

'That was a near thing. Can't understand it.' Harriet's voice was steady. 'They're normally glad to welcome visitors even if only to get money out of us.'

Diana was silent. It was the first time she had

seen any violence although she was always being told that she must be prepared for it. They drove without speaking for a long time. Harriet coaxed as much speed as she could out of the Austin but it shuddered and groaned over the rough uneven surface of the road. Then they rounded a bend and Diana saw a scene of such beauty and such contrast that she gasped with sudden delight. It was just a camel caravan walking on the sand at the sea's edge. Little waves frothed and gambolled at the animals' feet, the sun was shining as it almost always did, and for a fleeting moment everything looked quite perfect.

'Oh stop, Aunt, please! I must photograph that.'

Harriet laughed and watched as Diana leapt out of the car and focused her camera. 'It's just the people who spoil things,' she remarked philosophically. You'll give me a print of that one won't you?'

'Of course, if it's any good.' Diana stood for a moment, breathing in the scent of the sea, the beauty of sky and land, and the peace imparted by the rhythmic movement of the camels' bodies. At moments like this she wanted to stay in Palestine for ever.

As she climbed back into the car her thoughts forced her to think about the future again. 'Are you glad that I've decided to go back to England?' she asked suddenly.

Harriet looked at her in surprise. 'That's a silly question,' she said. 'Of course I'm not glad. I've already told you that I'll miss you dreadfully.'

'I mean,' Diana paused, 'are you glad that I've decided to finish with David? Staying here would probably have meant our getting married eventually.'

Harriet was aware that if she had been totally selfish she would have liked her niece to stay in Palestine, to marry and settle here, but she had done everything she could to discourage just this outcome. Her voice was very firm when she replied. 'You know my thoughts about it,' she said. 'You're just a goy, my girl, horrible word but that's what the Jews call us. Gentile it means, but goy sounds more...' she shrugged her shoulders 'hard, more modern, I suppose.'

'I don't like it,' Diana said. 'It's disparaging.'

'Perhaps it is, but a Jew is a Jew and a goy is a goy. You saw the hatred on those Arab faces, didn't you? It's a lesson perhaps. Races don't mix—a fact of life.'

'Aunt!' Diana was shocked. What about Samira and Colin she wanted to add? And you and Doctor Habib? but she refrained.

'There are exceptions,' Harriet said, probably guessing at her thoughts. 'But only some. Go back to Bagleigh, my dear, take your photographs and make a career of them if you can, or marry some nice Englishman and have children.'

'Are the two things mutually exclusive?'

Harriet laughed. 'Some people think so. It's up to you.'

'I don't want to marry some nice Englishman.'

'That's in the lap of the gods.'

'Then I haven't any say in the matter?'

'Of course you have, but I'm sure that there would be little happiness for you with David. He cares too much for this place to make a comfortable husband.'

Harriet had said all this before but Diana wanted to hear it again, wanted her aunt to affirm once more what she already knew quite well. They were hard truths and needed saying more than once if they were to settle resolutely in her mind, erasing all the doubts that still assailed her.

They heard the explosion as they reached the outskirts of Haifa. Then there was the sound of gunfire, and in the distance, screaming. Harriet pulled the little car to a violent stop. 'Dear God what was that? Sounded like a bomb. I'll go and see. You stay here.'

'No.' Diana stumbled out of the vehicle. 'I'm coming too.'

All was confusion, smoke and terror when they reached the Market Place. The explosion had torn through the little stalls, wrecked houses nearby, sent wounded donkeys and mules galloping panic-stricken through the narrow alleys, and scattered the streets with dead and dying.

Suddenly Harriet's free hand went to her pocket. 'Don't look,' she ordered, but Diana looked, watched in horror and then in shocked admiration as her aunt strode over to a wounded donkey that lay bleeding and panting nearby. She went down on her knees, felt the animal's legs, looked at the gaping wounds, and then gently stroked its muzzle, talking quietly all the time. She took a firm grip on the pistol, held it expertly between the creature's terrified eyes and fired. A great convulsion seized the agonised body, and then, peace. Harriet knelt there for a few seconds and finally stood up. When she turned Diana could see the tears that streaked her face. 'No hope for that one,' she muttered.

Hours later they picked their way wearily back to the outskirts of the town. 'If the car's still there it'll be a miracle,' Harriet said.

'It is, Aunt, it is!' The little vehicle was just as they had left it and Diana looked at it with a surge of relief. Her head swam and she was faint with weakness. She had been sick several times as she helped to bandage gaping wounds, put more animals out of their misery, and comfort screaming and bleeding children.

She looked down at her blood-stained clothes and shuddered.

'You did a good job,' Harriet said, and in spite of her weariness and continuing sense of shock, the words gave Diana a glimmer of comfort. Praise from Harriet was worth having, something to be proud of.

Eventually they were on the road away from the town. Harriet kept her attention firmly on the way ahead for the drive back to Khanhaven would take a long time. They had come out of their way to visit Haifa. They took the inland road home for neither wanted to go near Athlit again. 'Perhaps the bomb plot was hatched there,' Harriet observed grimly. 'That could account for our unpleasant reception earlier today.'

Diana shivered. 'Your cottage,' she said suddenly. 'Chy Morvah. Don't you ever long to go back there and live in peace?' A cottage by the sea in Cornwall seemed a very oasis of tranquillity just at this moment, a highly desirable place to be.

Harriet gripped the steering wheel more tightly. 'Most certainly not,' she replied. 'Not until I'm in my dotage. I've work to do here, and as long as I can do it, I shall stay.'

Diana glanced sideways at her and was filled again with admiration. They said little more to each other and she was lost in her own thoughts until they reached El Admah. The village had seemed to hold a threat ever since Samira's marriage to Colin. Harriet didn't slow down more than was necessary to avoid various hens that clucked and scratched between the houses. Then at last they were at Khanhaven.

'Good to be home,' Harriet said with great understatement as she climbed out of the car. 'Now where on earth are we going to get the old jalopy repaired?' She went round to the back of the vehicle and examined the damage. 'Best just to take out all the remaining glass and leave a space. I always said we needed more air!' She laughed almost as though the past few hours had never happened. 'Wouldn't do for England, but out here...well, anything goes.'

Diana looked at the shattered window, at the dents made by the stones, and then down at her blood-stained clothes once again and wondered for one crazy moment what on earth her father would think if he could see the two of them now? 'Persuade that sister of mine to come home,' he had directed. A trace of a smile crossed her face.

'I'll get some water and make us a cup of tea,' she said.

Harriet looked at her. 'No dear, not just now. Whisky, I think. Yes, definitely whisky. I have a little secret store.'

They smiled at each other and went inside.

CHAPTER 14

Samira could hear the sea as soon as the taxi deposited them at the cottage gate.

'Chy Morvah,' Colin said. 'Our first home.'

'House with a view of the sea,' Samira quoted. 'Harriet told me the meaning.'

She looked at the white walls and tiny windows with delight, but then she felt a small and unexpected shiver of apprehension. Colin had talked more of Bagleigh than of this little cottage, and it was because of her that they were here. Although he said little about his disappointment, she knew that he felt the loss of his home acutely. Could she ever hope to make him happy now, make up to him for the loss of Bagleigh? It was an awesome responsibility.

Yet she knew that she must be grateful for

Chy Morvah, and it was after all a place where she and Colin could be alone. She could make the great leap from her old life to the new without Colin's family to complicate matters. So there were compensations.

Harriet had shown her some old photographs of the cottage and she had talked about it with great affection, but now that the reality was here before her eyes Samira could only marvel at a place so different from anything she had ever known. It was smaller than she had pictured and it stood in a row of others. In fact it was joined to its neighbour on one side and there were lacy curtains at the windows and a tiny garden beyond the front gate. And it was tall. She had little experience of what Harriet had called 'upstairs'. There were only flat roofs on the houses in El Admah. Some had stone steps outside leading to little built-on sheds on the roof, but there was none that looked like this. And the weather! She shivered and pulled her coat more tightly around herself for there was a cold prickly mist enveloping everything. She had been warned about this. 'It blows in from the sea, sometimes even in summer,' Harriet had said. But Samira had not understood that either.

She could feel sudden tears in her eyes and was at once afraid that Colin should notice. She brushed her hand angrily over her face and then, composing herself, turned to him and smiled. 'It's beautiful,' she whispered.

He pushed open the gate with his foot, his hands occupied with as much of their luggage as he could manage. Then he dropped the biggest suitcase and groped for the key that Harriet had given him. He looked down at it and for a moment it reminded him of Khanhaven, of Palestine, of the heat and the dust. 'Different from El Admah,' he replied unnecessarily. 'We shall need to do some shopping, I expect. No one has lived here for a while.' He looked with impatience at the gloomy sky. 'It might be damp too. I hope there's some coal. Even though it's meant to be summer I'll have to light a fire.'

He didn't understand why he was saying these depressing things. He fitted the key into the lock and it turned easily. He pushed impatiently at the door and a musty unused smell assailed him as it opened. For one betraying moment he thought of Bagleigh, of the shining wooden floor in the big hall and the smell of polish and flowers, the scents mingling to greet him whenever he arrived. His mother always saw that everything was bright and clean and she was proud of the huge arrangements of boughs and blossoms that she placed in each room.

But once inside he felt his spirits lift a little. Obviously a neighbour had been in and prepared for them. Someone must have been thoughtful and sent a telegram announcing their arrival. His mother? He could think of no one else. He was filled with gratitude. There was a loaf of bread in the larder, milk in a jug carefully covered with a beaded cloth, a caddy of tea and a fruit cake sitting in splendour on a china plate complete with lace doily. He stared at the cake and laughed. 'Afternoon tea, Samira.

210

You're really English now. Look, we can have afternoon tea!'

She was standing behind him with a trusting yet slightly frightened look on her face. Then he remembered! He took her hand and led her back into the hall and out into the front garden again. He heard a sea-gull calling and waves crashing onto the breakwater. The sounds filled him with a sense of peace, dispelling his previous foreboding. He put his arms around her and picked her up. 'A bride must always be carried over the threshold,' he told her.

Once again he saw that startled look as she clung to him and was filled with the urge to protect her and to make her happy in this place which must seem so very alien to her. Just inside the door he set her down and hugged her slim body to his and kissed her on the lips. 'Just another quaint custom of ours,' he said.

And then, suddenly as bright as the sunshine of her native land, she smiled at him and returned his embrace and his kiss. 'I like your quaint customs,' she whispered. 'And as long as you are with me, I shall be happy.'

Diana's last day in Palestine had arrived.

'I shall miss you very much,' Harriet said to her. 'I wish things had worked out differently. You've been a wonderful help.'

Diana looked at the throng of noisy porters jostling and shouting for the chance to carry luggage out to the waiting boat. She searched for her handkerchief and wiped her eyes. 'Your new girl, Elizabeth what's-her-name, isn't likely

211

to be as stupid as I've been, and get a broken heart,' she said. 'She's firmly in love with her nice suitable English lieutenant.'

'Broken hearts mend, my dear,' Harriet replied. 'Elizabeth will do for a while. She's good with the animals.'

They were interrupted by the arrival of Raif Habib. He pushed his way through the crowd towards them. 'Everything is in order,' he said. 'Your bags are safely stowed in your cabin. You only have to board.'

'Thank you Doctor Habib,' Diana said. 'I'm grateful.'

Harriet smiled a little sadly at their companion. 'I'm so glad you could come,' she said. 'I must admit to feeling very sad. You'll be a comfort and it's good to have a man around in a situation like this!'

The steamer on which Diana was to travel all the way to Marseilles was anchored outside the little rock-girt harbour of Jaffa. A smaller boat was necessary to get out to it. She looked at the line of breakers that were visible just beyond the harbour wall. 'Was it very rough?' she asked. 'I'm a bit scared of the little boat that has to take me out to the ship. It seems rather fragile.'

Doctor Habib gave a great booming laugh that immediately cheered her. 'Not rough at all, my dear. And the boatmen are very skilled. You have no need to worry on that account. And your cabin is very pleasant, an outside one, so you will be able to see where you're going from its porthole!'

Diana was dreading this journey, each long mile of it taking her further from David, back to a life which she expected would prove to be tedious in the extreme. Yet there were compensations. She tried to think of Merryon and Rollo, the moors, and the continuation of her friendship with Samira. She at least would be a link with Palestine, for now that Diana was to leave she felt a great yearning to stay. My contrary nature, she told herself. I always want to be in some place other than where I am.

Her father had not been pleased about the choice of her route home, but Harriet had decided upon it and arranged everything. 'The boat will take you right to Marseilles,' she had said. 'I have friends there who will meet you and see you safely on the train to Paris.'

Once in Paris Diana would be met by her brother and escorted to Exeter. Philip Briscoe, a neighbour who owned a motor car, would meet them there for the last stage of the journey. She had argued against all these elaborate plans. 'I can get from Paris on my own,' she had declared. 'There's no need at all for Colin to come all that way.' But it was not to be. Her father had declared that Europe was no safer than Palestine now with Hitler rampaging everywhere. She and Harriet had laughed at that letter. 'Austria certainly, and threats to Czechoslovakia,' Harriet had said. 'But that's hardly everywhere, and you're not Jewish.'

'No, I'm not Jewish,' Diana had agreed thoughtfully. 'Perhaps if I were...' She had not finished her sentence and Harriet had ignored it.

She brought her thoughts back to the present, to the little town which was to be her last memory of Palestine. Jaffa was built on the sides of a hill and most of its houses had a view of the sea. It was a bit like a great amphitheatre, she thought, and still encircled by its ancient ruined walls. 'I could live here,' she said quietly almost to herself, but Harriet heard her and smiled.

'I like it too. I've always wanted a house with a view of the sea.'

'Chy Morvah,' Diana said. 'You already have one. A house with a view of the sea. That's what the name means, doesn't it?'

'Just so. Porthmead, the place where I shall take my weary bones when I'm really old. Not until then, of course, but it's nice to think about sometimes. Quite a contrast to Jaffa, but just as lovely.'

'I wonder how Samira likes Cornwall?'

'As long as the mists don't blow in too often during her first few weeks, she'll be all right.'

'I shall write to you and give you all the news just as soon as I've been down to see them both.'

These last moments were difficult. It seemed necessary to make polite inconsequential conversation. Then suddenly the two women threw their arms around each other. 'Thank you for everything, Aunt,' Diana murmured. 'I shall come back. I just know that I shall come back one day.'

'I think I know it too,' Harriet said.

David Halprin had been working all day in the fields. Since Diana had left he had tried to stop thinking about her by working even harder than usual. He hadn't realised how much he would miss her, how much he had come to care. Work helped to dull his senses, helped him to forget a little.

But even after all this time in Palestine he was still unused to backbreaking physical toil. He looked ruefully at his hands as he walked back to his billet, hands that were no use now for playing his violin. He wondered again what exactly he should do with his life. Since Diana's return he had been possessed by a feeling of dissatisfaction and loss. Yet he knew that he couldn't marry her, not if he wanted to stay here anyway. He kicked angrily at the stony ground and thought of his parents, the home in England with its luxuries, its servants, and the privileged life he had led before he came to Beth Haron. His father had made vast amounts of money as a banker and he was willing to pour much of it into the creation of a home for Jews, a land of their own, a new Israel. But this place needed more than money. It demanded your very life blood.

When he reached the building which served as both dining and community hall for the kibbutz, he glanced at the newspapers that were spread on the table. These were in various languages and from many countries, some of them quite stale, but the Jerusalem ones were more up-to-date. He glanced at the headlines and then sat down and read them again to make sure he was getting the right message. Considering the news coming from Europe during the past months this didn't make sense.

'Mr Chamberlain declares "Peace in our Time",' he read. Then he read it over again, this time aloud.

'What do you think of that then?' The questioner was a tall fair girl who often reminded him of Diana. Her name was Rachel and she came from England too. 'I heard it on the wireless, but seeing it in print makes it seem even more unbelievable.'

David stood up and threw the paper back on to the table. He shook his head in disbelief. 'Chamberlain making peace with that monster! What do you suppose is going to happen to Europe's Jews now?'

'I daren't think. If we don't stop Hitler, who on earth will? I've relations in Holland. My mother was Dutch.'

'I didn't know you were half-Dutch?' David said with interest.

'Yes. We lived in Amsterdam for most of my childhood. There are a lot of Jewish families there. It's a good place to be. At least it is at the moment. Perhaps I should say it *was* a good place, past tense!'

David looked at her, understanding the fear in her voice. Then he glanced down at the newspaper again. 'The Czechs want to fight Hitler apparently,' he said, reading on down the page. 'So our dear Mr Chamberlain's treaty isn't good news for them.'

'Not good news for Jews anywhere probably, but in England everyone seems pleased. He's been greeted like a hero.' Her voice was full of scorn. She leaned over David's shoulder and pointed to the bottom of the page. 'Look, even the King and Queen joined in the jubilation. Can you imagine it? Crowds going mad, Buckingham Palace floodlit, everyone cheering, while our people are...'

'What do you want then?' David interrupted. 'War? A great bloody war like the last one, because that's what it'll be.'

'I don't know. But Hitler has got to be stopped, defeated, assassinated or something, hasn't he, or what hope is there for any of us?'

David turned away from the table with its disturbing news. He looked at Rachel yet hardly saw her. 'This is why we must have a homeland,' he said. 'News like this makes it more important than ever that we should have somewhere of our own where every Jew can come and be safe.'

Rachel sniffed. 'Of course, but easier said than done. Those are dangerous dreams. Can they ever come true?'

'The pessimistic part of me says that no, they can't, not in our lifetime anyway, but miracles happen sometimes.'

'We need a miracle,' Rachel said.

The grim far away expression faded from David's face. Suddenly he really saw the girl who was staring back at him. She was attractive in a fierce sort of way. This was the kind of girl he ought to fall in love with! She would perfectly share his ideals and his dreams. But immediately he saw Diana in his mind, saw her fair curling hair, her smile, and the freckles that she hated.

Rachel seemed to read his thoughts. 'Your friend?' she questioned. 'Colin's sister, the girl who was working with the animals? I haven't seen her for a bit.'

'Gone home to England.'

Rachel's face held an expression he couldn't fathom. 'A bit sudden, wasn't it? I thought she liked it here.'

'She only came for a short time. Her father wouldn't allow her to stay indefinitely.' David knew he was making excuses for Diana. He couldn't tell the painful, hurtful truth, couldn't say, she was in love with me, and she rushed off home because I couldn't wholly return her love.

'And how is your Arab girl liking England?'

David had had enough of her questions. He was beginning to feel irritated. 'Samira isn't *my* Arab girl,' he said. 'And I haven't any idea how she likes England, Cornwall actually. Colin will write eventually, I suppose.'

'OK. Sorry I asked. It was a lovely wedding though.'

David remembered that she had been one of the guests at Khanhaven and felt slightly contrite. 'Samira won't like the weather,' he said.

'I don't suppose she will.' Rachel flounced

to the doorway. 'I'm going to have a swim now to cool off. Bet they'd all like a bit of this sunshine at home. My mother was always moaning about the climate in Holland, and England is no better, probably worse.' She grinned at him. 'Cheer up. Work's done for today. Forget about Hitler and relax.'

David followed her out. Could he do as she said? Forget Hitler? And had Chamberlain really abandoned Czechoslovakia and all of Europe's Jews to their fate?

Suddenly he wanted to fight, wanted to put into practice much of what he had learned in the University Air Squadron, wanted to get up there in the skies and fight the Germans with everything he had. His sense of depression left him. Perhaps this was what he must do, go home to England and join the RAF as soon as he could without waiting for the war that he and Colin had talked about a few weeks before. Peace, Chamberlain had said. He just didn't believe it. And even if there was no European war after all, then a training in air combat would stand him in good stead for whatever lay ahead in the future, in Palestine.

He ran all the way to his billet, threw off his clothes and pulled on his swimming costume. Then he charged over to the pool and dived in, almost landing on top of the indignant Rachel.

'Steady on,' she spluttered, 'you nearly drowned me.'

'I'm going to join the RAF,' he said.

CHAPTER 15

'You'll wear yourself right out,' Mary Stanmore said looking critically at Diana one morning at breakfast. 'I wish you wouldn't work so hard.'

Diana sighed and helped herself to a large portion of scrambled eggs. 'I need to work, Mother,' she replied. 'And at least it makes me eat a lot and that pleases you.'

Her father looked up from his newspaper. 'Can't think what's got into you, girl,' he grunted. 'That trip to Palestine did you no good at all. If you want to do something to fill your time, you could teach yourself to type. That would be more suitable, a useful accomplishment for a girl.'

'I'll do that as well,' Diana said. 'It's almost too dark to be outside for long in the evenings now. I'll do it then.' She laughed to herself. It was seldom that her father's wishes and her own coincided. For a career in photojournalism, which was what she wanted, the ability to type was essential.

She was only just getting used to being back in England. Almost as soon as she had arrived, she had started working on the farm. I can never forget David, but I can work until I'm too tired to think any more. Until I drop, she had told herself savagely. Even when work was finished for the day she refused to sit still. As long as there was a little light remaining in the sky she was out again, usually riding Merryon up to Greatcombe Rocks, Rollo always bounding ahead, cheering her with his exuberance and high spirits.

Her father had reluctantly come to terms with seeing her labouring in the fields. Harriet's influence and the period of independence in Palestine had worked wonders for Diana's ability to assert herself. But both parents were concerned at the number of hours she spent in, what they called, back-breaking toil.

Mary Stanmore had never needed to do any hard work. Although one of the maids had left there was still a cook at Bagleigh as well as Lily and a woman from the village who came in twice a week to do the rough work. Consequently Mary was frequently very bored and often lonely and she had been looking forward to her daughter's homecoming, hoping for some companionship. Diana's preoccupation with the farm disappointed her and she was continually saddened when she saw her dressed in the slacks and old shirt that denoted another day to be spent outside.

'We'll have a day in Exeter soon, I promise you Mother,' Diana said on this particular morning. 'I need some things for my camera.'

James snorted in disgust. 'Waste of money,' he grumbled. 'Get yourself some decent clothes, girl. Look more like a woman for a change.'

Diana was not afraid of her father now, but to her continuing fury, he still resolutely pitted himself against any suggestion that she might

221

want a career. He told her frequently that in his opinion marriage was the only choice open to women.

Diana's lack of money combined with her love of Bagleigh, still held her captive in Devon, but she knew that one day she would get away. The details were not yet clear to her and for the moment anyway she considered that she was as content as she would ever be without David. Her grief over his loss made any decision about the future too big a burden to tackle just now.

Mary Stanmore blamed herself for her daughter's obvious grieving. David Halprin was a personable young man. During his visits to Bagleigh she had noticed the attention he paid to Diana and she had not been happy about it even then. Unlike her husband she had no aversion to Jews, but Colin had told her that David was a Zionist, and that was a different matter. She had read something about them, about their nationalistic tendencies, and had decided, too late, that this made David altogether undesirable. If only she'd thought about it before Diana went away, if only she had not encouraged the visit to Palestine, her daughter might not now be suffering from a broken heart.

Perhaps a break away from home might be a good idea for Diana? she thought on this bright October morning. It would suit her own plans too. She had been wondering, for some time, how she was to get to Porthmead to visit Colin and Samira. Suddenly she made up her mind.

She and Diana would go together as soon as it could be arranged and whatever James said!

She took a spoonful of marmalade and put it on the side of her plate and then spread it with exaggerated care on her toast, and all the time her thoughts were focused on the right words to say to her husband. She took a bite of the toast and finished it slowly, then she wiped her hands on her serviette and summoned every ounce of courage she possessed.

'I have decided to go to Porthmead,' she announced to both of them. 'I have to see how things are for Colin. I can't rest any longer without knowing if he's happy, and I should very much like your support, Diana. I should be glad if you would come with me.'

Diana, looking from one parent to the other, nearly choked on her coffee. She had been alone to Porthmead to see Samira and her brother, but her mother had not dared to suggest that she might go too, not until this moment. Diana said nothing, waiting fearfully for her father's outburst.

He put his newspaper down and the seconds that passed seemed endless to the two women watching him. 'You'll do no such thing,' he growled decisively, glaring at his wife. 'He's made his bed. He must lie on it. His concerns are of no interest to any of us.'

'But they are to me.' Mary insisted. 'I'm sorry, James, but my mind is quite made up.'

Diana couldn't believe that she was hearing correctly. She stared at her mother in sudden admiration. She wanted to stand up and cheer!

Instead she said quickly, before her father could recover his wits, 'I think you should go and I'll certainly accompany you, Mother. We could go next weekend. Philip will drive us to Exeter if I ask him. We can get a train from there.'

The mention of Philip Briscoe surprised Mary, but she knew that it was a brilliant piece of diplomacy. It would deflect her husband's anger a little. He looked upon this particular young man with great favour, almost as a surrogate son since Colin's defection. The Briscoes were a very respected family, owners of land on the other side of the moor, and Philip was an only son. James kept talking about him, about his prospects, his excellent education, and even, in Diana's presence, his good looks. Mary often secretly thought how convenient it would have been if Diana could have fallen in love with the amiable and eligible Philip instead of David, for this was definitely what James wished. But life was seldom convenient.

Diana's strategy had the desired effect. 'Philip?' her father enquired suspiciously. 'What has he got to do with it?'

'Nothing, Father,' she replied innocently. 'But he has a motor car and is always telling me that he would like to drive me somewhere.'

James sniffed a trifle derisively. His own inability to drive was the one thing that dented his self-esteem. He had never learned, preferring his horses. 'I doubt he means both of you.'

'He'll do anything I ask.'

'Then telephone him at once,' Mary directed, quickly taking advantage. 'Perhaps Philip would like to come all the way with us. He used to be a friend of Colin's, you remember. They went to school together.'

Diana had no intention of asking him to drive them right to Porthmead. Just to Exeter would be quite sufficient. He was persistent enough without any added encouragement. That she might be making use of him to persuade her father to be a little more lenient occurred to her, but she rapidly banished the thought.

'All right,' James said somewhat mollified. 'If Philip will take you, I'll let you go. Just this once, mind.'

Diana was surprised at her father's quick change of mind as well as being incensed by his phrase 'let you go'. He's almost as bad as Samira's father, she thought and he must be quite determined that I should marry Philip. I'm glad I'm not Arab. He'd command it!

'Go and make your telephone call,' he ordered, repeating his wife's words and confirming Diana's suspicions. 'But I'm not having Colin back.' His voice assumed its old belligerence. 'So don't give him and that native wife of his any ideas that might raise their hopes.'

Diana seethed with anger at the word 'native'. She couldn't imagine how her father pictured Samira. She knew that one day, when he did meet her, he was in for the shock of his life!

Philip of course was delighted that Diana should ask him to take her to Exeter, as she had known he would be, but to her dismay he insisted on driving the whole way.

'Porthmead isn't far,' he said. 'Only about fifty or sixty miles. It's silly to take you to Exeter and put you on a train. How about making a little holiday of it before it's too late? We could go on Friday night and come back on Sunday. I'll find myself a hotel.'

'What do you mean, too late?' Diana asked.

'Well, Hitler and all that. There won't be many more holidays if we go on letting him have his way.'

She gripped the telephone receiver more tightly. 'I don't know,' she said. 'Thanks anyway. I'll talk to Mother about the final plans and ring you again. We'll have to get in touch with Colin.'

Slowly she put the receiver down on its cradle and thought about his last chilling words. He was probably right about Hitler. The advance of the Nazis into Czechoslovakia was frightening, and Mr Chamberlain's famous promise of peace seemed rather fragile. Whenever she saw the headlines in her father's newspaper her own small concerns appeared less important. She wondered what Colin would do should there be a war, and what would happen to Samira? Her thoughts turned to David. He had talked of joining the RAF and that meant coming home! She gripped her hands together and tried to banish the hope.

Yet in spite of all the momentous happenings in Europe, just now it was still Palestine that interested her most. She had recently discovered that the plan to divide the country into two, one part for Arabs and another area for Jews, had been abandoned so David wasn't going to get his dream state yet. Britain would be in control for a lot longer. She was inclined to consider this a good thing, yet when she thought of Beth Haron and the bright hopes of all the friends she had made there, she had doubts. She was longing to talk to Colin and Samira about it, for no one else here appeared to be very interested in the Middle East. There was enough to worry about in Europe.

Samira was terrified when she heard about Mary's imminent visit. Mothers-in-law were to be feared. However much Colin tried to reassure her, he couldn't stop her frenzied preparations. She cleaned the house from top to bottom, arranged the guest bedroom with great care and spent hours poring over an ancient cookery book that she had found in the bureau, and then more hours preparing several elaborate dishes.

'If your Mrs Beeton is the expert for English food, then I shall do what she says,' she told Colin.

'Why don't you make some Arab food?' he suggested. 'My mother would like that.'

She looked at him incredulously. 'But she's English. I couldn't give her those things. It wouldn't be polite or hospitable.'

She refused to discuss the subject further and Colin left her to her preparations. The day was pleasant and he would have liked her company on his walk along the coast-guard's path. It was wild and beautiful, one of his favourite places, but Samira wouldn't leave her tiny kitchen. Their guests were due to arrive in time for the evening meal, and to his disgust he began to feel nervous too. It was not that he feared his mother's reaction. He was more apprehensive about Samira. She had such strange notions of family relationships.

And then there was Philip Briscoe. Why was he coming? There was a perfectly good bus and train service from Exeter. Was there more to this arrangement than mere convenience? he wondered. He strode over the short springy turf and had to admit that it would be a good thing if Diana could be persuaded to look favourably on someone else and forget about David, but he was amazed that this had come about so soon. Philip was all right, a decent chap but not a close friend although they'd been at school together, and his presence just now was bound to be an intrusion. Colin expected this weekend to be extremely difficult. He wished they were coming alone and swore to himself over his father's obstinate refusal to buy a motor car. Diana had learned to drive in Palestine and wouldn't have needed Philip's company if she had her own vehicle. He walked for an hour and then abruptly turned round and walked back to the house.

He waited almost as anxiously as Samira for their guests to arrive, and as soon as he heard the car pull up outside he leapt nervously to his feet and flung the front door wide open.

Diana was the first out. She bounced over to her brother and threw her arms around him.

'Colin, you look well, even better than last time I came. Marriage suits you. We've had a lovely journey. It's a super car, an Austin Ten, the same model as Aunt Harriet's but new and open and quite glamorous. We drove for the first half an hour with the hood down.'

He returned her embrace and then experienced a quick pang of envy as he looked at the vehicle. But Philip was helping his mother out of it and, ashamed of his thoughts, Colin went to greet her. He took her hands in his and kissed her. 'It's wonderful to see you, Mother. I'm so glad you've managed it,' he said.

She was obviously nervous and he thought he saw tears in her eyes. 'I've been longing to come,' she whispered. She released herself from him and turned back to the car and retrieved her handbag, gripping it tightly as though it were some sort of talisman giving security and confidence. Then she glanced beyond him to the open door through which Diana had already disappeared.

Samira was standing in the kitchen, frightened and undecided, not knowing what she should do, how she should greet this unknown English mother-in-law, when Diana burst into the room.

The two girls embraced and then stood back and looked at each other. 'Marriage continues to agree with you, I see,' Diana said. 'Come on, meet my mother.'

Before Samira had a moment to calm herself, she was propelled through the door and into the hall.

Philip was still tactfully outside, busy removing suitcases from the back of the motor car, and Diana led Samira past Colin and pushed her towards her mother. 'Samira,' she announced, 'this is my mother. Mother, your new daughter.'

Mary Stanmore looked at the girl who was standing before her with downcast eyes and figure slightly rounded with Colin's child and her heart immediately warmed towards her. She held out both her hands and grasped Samira's. 'Welcome to our family, my dear.'

The weekend passed swiftly with cliff walks, endless talk, and sharing of recipes, for Samira, warming to Mary's friendliness, soon lost her fears and had eventually been persuaded to prepare some Arab food. Contrary to Colin's and Diana's fears Philip had been no problem. 'I want to do some walking,' he had announced on Saturday morning. 'Mind if I take myself off? I'll drop in now and then.'

Diana was pleased with his tact. 'Nice bloke,' she commented in an aside to her brother when they were alone. 'I just wish I'd fallen in love with him.'

Colin grinned at her. 'So you haven't? I wondered. A pity, but it might happen. Give it time.'

Diana shook her head. 'Nothing so convenient could ever happen to me,' she said ruefully.

Mary was enchanted with her daughter-in-law. 'Just wait until I get home,' she said to Diana in the privacy of the little bedroom they were sharing. 'I shall pluck up courage to tell your father just how ridiculous he's being. Samira is delightful.'

'Yes, she is,' Diana agreed. 'He'll come round eventually.'

'Perhaps when the baby arrives.' Mary's voice was wistful. 'We could do with some new life at Bagleigh.'

On Sunday afternoon Samira and Mary were busy discussing baby rearing over the washing up. Their conversation was happy and animated as if they had known each other for years. Diana, listening a trifle bleakly, suddenly felt left out. She had hoped for long gossiping sessions with Samira. It was only Samira who might understand how she felt about David. But there had been no time. 'Like to go for a walk?' she suggested to her brother. 'Let's leave these two for an hour.'

He needed no persuading. 'Right,' he said quickly. He turned to his wife. 'Mind if I go out for a while?'

She smiled at him. 'Why do you ask? I shall never understand your English ways. It is I who have to ask permission of you, never you of me.'

Colin didn't respond with the laugh that Diana expected. He shrugged his shoulders and went to get his jacket. When they were outside on the cliff path that led up to the lighthouse, she turned to him.

'Do I detect a slight irritation in you, brother dear?' she said. The autumn afternoon was bright and sunny and the sea at its best with lazy waves rolling languidly towards the shore. There was hardly any wind and the sun was warm. 'Gosh, it's so peaceful here,' she continued, thinking suddenly of that terrible day at Haifa and her conversation with Harriet about Chy Morvah. 'You must be quite perfectly happy.'

In spite of her words she knew him well enough to sense that he was not, that there was something troubling him, and her comments were meant to goad him into talking about it, for she knew from her own experience that when a problem was shared the pain was halved and sometimes even disposed of completely.

They walked in silence for a while and she had to take little running steps now and then to keep up with him.

'The trouble is,' he said eventually, 'that everything is just too perfect and I feel a complete swine for *not* being happy.'

'Any reason?'

He shrugged his shoulders again. 'Just that there's no challenge, nothing to do in fact.'

'I thought you liked your teaching job?'

'Hell, Diana. Teaching! I never wanted to teach. It's just that we have to eat!' His voice was scornful.

'It won't be for long. There's probably going to be a war. That'll be challenge enough.'

'And what do you suppose Samira is going to do all on her own down here if I join up?'

'Things change. A war might make a lot of difference to many things.'

'Like Father having her to live at Bagleigh?'

'Perhaps. She'll have her baby by next

232

spring. Mother thinks that he'll want to see his grandchild.'

'If it is his grandchild.'

Diana stopped in her tracks and it was a moment or two before Colin too slowed down and looked back.

'What on earth do you mean?' Diana's voice was cold and shocked. She glared at her brother without understanding.

'I shouldn't have said that. Forget it.'

They stood on the cliff top and faced each other. There had never been any secrets between them. They had always been close.

'How can I forget such a dreadful thing?' Diana said. 'Tell me, for goodness' sake, what you're talking about.'

There was a bench set into the rock just below the headland at a point where the cliff sloped gently down to the sea. Colin turned away from her and strode towards it. He slumped down and put his head in his hands.

Diana was quite shattered. Even the events she had witnessed in Palestine hadn't made her feel so horrified as those awful words she had just heard. Could she indeed have heard correctly? She followed him slowly and sat down too but at the other end of the seat.

Colin raised his head and stared out to sea and then westwards where headland after headland stretched away into the distance. They could be seen clearly today in the bright afternoon air. 'I hate myself,' he murmured, 'but I have these awful doubts. The child could easily be Eshref's.'

233

Diana's heart thudded and she felt herself go cold with shock. But, yes, it could be so, she acknowledged silently and in sudden astonishment. Of course it could be Eshref's. Why did I not think of it before? Did Harriet never wonder either?

She hadn't spoken a word aloud and when she managed to regain some shreds of composure she tried to reassure him. 'You mustn't think that way, Colin,' she said decisively. 'This child is yours. You must believe that.'

'Even if it isn't?'

She was silent for a further moment, considering. 'Yes,' she said eventually. 'Even if it isn't. There's no other choice for you or for Samira.'

Then quietly he told her of the time, just a week after her disastrous marriage night with Eshref, when Samira had come to him and asked him to make love to her. 'She said it was because she felt unworthy to marry anyone,' he said. 'I believed her, but the ugly thought persists sometimes that it was a calculated plan, so that the fatherhood of her child, if she had conceived one on that terrible night, would always be in doubt. It could be mine as easily as Eshref's.'

Diana was horrified. For some reason she had never doubted that the child Samira carried was her brother's. It had not occurred to her to count up the weeks, and she realised that no definite date for the birth had yet been given anyway. Now there was no point in any calculations. The revelation she had just heard

234

would make it impossible to know for sure.

'What about the baby's colouring?' she queried. 'Do you know what Eshref looked like?'

'Yes. Samira told me. He wasn't dark-skinned like some. Not any more than Samira anyway, and she's quite fair for a Palestinian.'

'And you're dark-haired,' Diana said. 'Mother always said that you must have taken your colouring from our Cornish ancestors. The Celts are dark.'

'What are you trying to say?' He glared at her. 'How does all that help?'

'It does help,' she said. 'The child won't be too dark. He'll probably be just like you, and even if you have doubts you must keep them strictly to yourself and accept him as yours. If you don't, then too many people's lives will be completely shattered. Can you imagine what it would do to Mother? She and Samira are getting along splendidly. It seems to have given her a new lease of life. And Samira, and the child? What would they do? And Father? I think he'd have a heart attack immediately. And it would be the end of any hopes you have of coming back to Bagleigh. There must be no glimmer of doubt in anyone's mind, ever.' Her voice was decisive. She stood up. 'You love Samira. You chose her and brought her here. Whatever happens it was not her fault. She's quite blameless. You'll love the child because he's hers, and as he grows, your doubts, if you had any, will vanish.'

Colin sat there refusing to move. He looked up at her with a stony expression on his face.

'You seem very sure about my life, about what I should do.'

Diana too was surprised by her own words, but she knew that if Colin refused to take any notice of what she was saying, then his marriage would be wrecked, and there would be anguish for all the family. 'I'm sure about it because I can see that there's no other way,' she said. 'And I know you pretty well too. You're good and fair and sensible. You can't possibly bring misery to so many people just because of something that might not even be true anyway.'

'What do you mean?'

'This baby might not be Eshref's, is probably yours in fact.'

'I wish I could believe that.'

She almost shouted at him as she replied, 'You've got to believe it! Got to, do you hear me?' She wanted to shake him, but she glared at him instead. 'For goodness sake, Colin, can't you see that?'

He got up slowly. 'Yes, I can see that you're right of course.' He grinned at her a little sheepishly. 'I'm being stupid and selfish, and I do love Samira. I'll do my best to take your advice, Dido.'

'Come on then,' she said. 'Let's finish our walk. After all the food Samira's been giving us, I need some more exercise.'

They walked in silence for a long time after that. In spite of her firm assurances to her brother Diana was nevertheless full of anxiety. Although she would never admit it to anyone, she knew that she wouldn't be able to banish the doubts that Colin had voiced either. Her first glimpse of her baby niece or nephew would be marred. She would try to identify the Stanmore eyes, the gingerish tints of Colin's dark hair, even perhaps her own hated freckles. Or would she see an imagined look of the frightful Eshref?

I must fight these silly fears with all my might, she told herself firmly as she tried to match her strides to Colin's. The child will be my brother's. I must never doubt it. Then one horrifying thought entered her mind. If he really is Eshref's son will he inherit Bagleigh one day? Dear God, that would be the final irony. But she said nothing at all. For the moment there was nothing to be done about it.

CHAPTER 16

Colin looked at the child in Samira's arms and knew at once that this was not his son. Afterwards he could never say just why he was suddenly so sure, for he could only see the baby's little screwed up face. I can never love it, he told himself, yet I shall see that it has everything money can buy. I owe that to Samira. He stared down fiercely into the big brown eyes that appeared to be challenging him and he could give the child neither gender nor name. It was just 'it'.

Samira felt tears in her eyes as she held her son towards him, for this was her moment of triumph. The birth of a firstborn male child was always a cause for great jubilation and pride in her homeland. 'I should like to call him James,' she whispered. 'James Stanmore.'

Colin was shocked. His father had still not seen Samira, adamantly refusing to allow her to visit Bagleigh in spite of Mary's pleading. Even if this baby had been his true grandchild Colin was sure that he wouldn't be pleased to have it called after him. 'You can't do that,' he said. 'You can't possibly call him that.'

Samira recoiled. 'What then should I call him? Jebel, Gasim, Zeid?' She could hold the tears in check no longer and buried her face in the baby's shawl. When the nurse had first put the tiny scrap into her anxious welcoming arms she had looked at him for a long moment and she too had known that he was Eshref's son. The knowledge had come with initial shock and horror, but she had quickly put it aside, banished it from her mind, refused to believe the terrible damaging truth. This child must be Colin's. To everyone he must be her husband's true-born son. And indeed her coupling with Eshref had been so terrible that she couldn't imagine anything as perfect as the baby she held resulting from that night of terror. In complete contrast the memory of Colin's lovemaking a few days later was so beautiful to her that in spirit this baby must surely be Colin's child even if the hair, the eyes, and look of him was of Eshref. She had decided to hold to that belief whatever happened, for only by doing so could she and her son survive.

Colin saw the tears and guessed at her despair. He was immediately filled with shame for his behaviour, with pity for her, and with love too. Nothing has changed, he told himself fiercely. I love her passionately and I always shall. He had lived with the fear of what this moment might reveal for a long time and he had tried to come to terms with it. In fact he thought that he'd succeeded. He remembered his sister's words, her firm advice. He must act upon that now, quickly, before he wrecked his marriage and brought more misery on his family.

With this resolve firmly in place, he bent down and put his hand beneath Samira's chin, lifting her face to his. 'My precious girl,' he said, 'don't cry. You've given me a wonderful gift and we'll choose a name together.' He gently brushed the tears from her eyes and kissed her. Then, forcing himself, he pushed the shawl gingerly further away from the baby's face and saw the tiny hand, suddenly free, move before his fascinated gaze. He had never imagined anything so small. The fingers bunched into a little fist and Colin actually smiled. Perhaps love might come after all, he thought, for this helpless scrap was entirely dependent on him now. 'He's waving a fist at me. I'll teach him to box one day.'

Samira felt relief wash over her. So her son was accepted. Colin would love her again. She had sensed a slight withdrawal of his affection during the past weeks and had been consumed with a dreadful uncertainty about her life and her future. But now all that was past. She had given her husband a son and everything would be well. She vowed that she would never mention Eshref, would not remember him, would banish him from her thoughts for ever. If she could successfully do this then no harm would come to her child. And Eshref had not been too dark-skinned. For one of his race he had been fair-complexioned as a few Palestinian Arabs were. She remembered having been surprised by his colouring.

'If James won't do, then perhaps another name from your Holy Book?'

Colin looked at her, surprised. 'Holy Book? What do you mean?'

'Your Bible. Our son will be baptised as a Christian, and I want him to have a real Christian name.'

Colin noticed the hospital Bible on the table beside her bed. 'You've been reading it?' He indicated the sombre-looking volume.

'Yes, of course. I am your wife and I shall take your God, as I told you.'

Colin's religion was not very personal. It contained nothing he felt to be of great importance to the way he lived his life, and for the second time during this visit he felt ashamed. 'You don't have to, Samira,' he said. 'I don't mind if you remain Muslim.'

She shook her head. She had made her decision on this point a long time ago. 'If I still lived in Palestine, then it would be difficult, impossible perhaps. But here in England I am

240

Mrs Stanmore and I shall be C of E.'

He was amused at these last words, but his face showed no trace of it. He wondered just what C of E meant to her. And in a more serious vein, what in fact it meant to him? 'All right then,' he conceded. 'You do what you wish. But what name from the Bible were you thinking of?'

'James was your first martyr. I've been reading your New Testament. Then there was Stephen, but that doesn't go very well with Stanmore. Could we have Matthew? He wrote about your Jesus Christ. Then your name next?' She looked up at him tremulously. 'Matthew Colin Stanmore sounds very nice.'

Yes, very nice, very English, he thought. He looked down once more at the child sleeping peacefully now, the little hands tucked warmly into the shawl. So Matthew Stanmore, Eshref's son, would go to an English public school one day, and...and might inherit Bagleigh! The thought chilled him so much that he clenched his hands automatically and then unclenched them, forcing himself again to accept the unthinkable. 'Matthew Colin Stanmore it shall be,' he said as calmly as he could.

The news of Matthew's birth reached Palestine at the beginning of April. Harriet looked at the letter written by Samira and wondered. March 17th, she said to herself. That tells me nothing. Samira had written that he was to be called Matthew Colin, and stressed that Colin was delighted with his son. So perhaps all was well,

Harriet thought, perhaps her worst fears had not come to pass.

She told the news to David when she next saw him. He had come to visit her for no reason that she could at first define.

'I'm pleased for them,' he said. 'Samira will be happy that she has a son. Arab women always want sons.'

'They're their own worst enemies,' Harriet said dryly. 'Even the women count boys more valuable than girls. No wonder they win no rights.' She shrugged her shoulders. 'They need a few Emily Pankhursts. I can never understand why such a vast number of women all over the world are so passive.'

David laughed. 'You'd have been out campaigning for Votes for Women if you'd been old enough, wouldn't you?' he said. 'I can just see you throwing stones through shop windows.'

'I certainly would,' Harriet said. She handed David a cup of tea and some flat pitta bread that she had made herself. 'I was born just a fraction too late though.' She looked at him critically. 'But you didn't come here to discuss women's rights, did you? There's something more on your mind.'

He stared down at the bread in his hand without really seeing it. 'Lots of things,' he said. 'Weeks ago I decided that I should join the RAF, war or no war. I let things slide and did nothing and now, well, I don't know who I am, where I belong.'

'That's a pretty devastating statement. Explain.' Harriet sat down opposite him and took a sip of her coffee. She was used to young people coming to her for advice. Listening seemed to be one of her functions in life.

'Am I British or am I a Palestinian Jew?'

'Both, I suppose. Are they exclusive?'

'In a way, yes. If I had been born here, I'd be in the Haganah. We need weapons and men to defend ourselves from Arab terrorists.'

'And the British have declared the Haganah illegal!'

David put his bread back on the plate and clenched his fists in anger. 'Yes. With the death penalty for carrying illegal arms. I can't believe it.'

Harriet sighed. She had so many friends of all persuasions. She could see the point of view of both Arabs and Jews, but the attitude of the British just now completely dismayed her.

'You've heard about the latest White Paper, of course?' David continued without waiting for her to reply.

'Yes, a limit to the immigration of Jews. Britain is frightened of the Arabs.'

David slammed his fists down upon the table. 'Then where are we to go, for God's sake? Anti-Semitism is rife all over Europe, more now than ever before probably.'

Harriet shook her head. 'I expect you heard that the British Government wants to settle Jewish refugees in remote parts of the Empire?'

'Africa!' His voice was full of scorn. 'Can you imagine it?'

'Frankly, no.' Sometimes Harriet felt quite

ashamed to be British and now was one of those times.

'You could join the Palestine Police Force,' she said at last in an effort to be practical. 'At least you'd be official and you'd get military training.'

This suggestion was greeted with further disgust. 'That's all right for those who can't get into a proper fighting force, but I want something better. I want to fight Hitler first and then come back and fight for a Jewish State here.'

'Then what's stopping you?'

'The British aren't too keen to accept Palestinian Jews in the forces. That makes me mad. I have friends who are as loyal to the Mandate as I am and desperate to have a go at Hitler. Because they were born here they seem suspect, untrustworthy somehow. So of course they feel frustrated. It's OK for me, but I'd have to go back to England and more or less forget that I was Jewish.'

'It won't last.'

He looked at her in surprise. 'What won't last?'

'Britain will need all the men she can get when the war really gets going. Not many questions will be asked eventually. You mark my words, your friends will be wooed, not rejected.'

He was thoughtful. 'I suppose you're right. I can't wait that long though.'

'You've kept your British passport?' Harriet looked at him in some alarm. 'That's the most

244

valuable thing you have at present.'

'A slight overstatement, but yes, of course I have. I'm as British as you if I want to be.'

'Then forget about the others and go and join the RAF. That's what you've always wanted. You'd be fighting for all your friends as well as yourself.'

David relaxed and started to eat his pitta bread, crunching the olives and savouring appreciatively the goat's cheese with which it was filled. He looked up at Harriet and grinned. 'I'd decided to do that anyway,' he said. 'I just wanted to hear you telling me to do it!'

'Fiddlesticks,' she said. 'You'd never listen to a woman.'

'Your bread is superb anyway and the cheese just perfect.'

'That's why you came then.'

'Not entirely.'

She watched him eat and experienced a wave of pleasure. My frustrated maternal instinct, she thought to herself. 'Tell me more about your plans then,' she said.

'I intend to learn as much as I can from the British, help to smash Herr Hitler—and then smash the British if they continue to stop us coming to Palestine!'

'But you're British yourself.'

'Jewish first.'

Harriet finished her coffee. 'Of course,' she said thoughtfully, and wondered how it felt to be a member of a race that had no home of its own, hadn't had one for almost two thousand years of persecution.

She got up and fetched the coffee pot and refilled David's cup, trying to fend off her gloomy thoughts. Then suddenly she wondered, in a lighter vein, if there was any other reason behind his visit. Perhaps he wanted news of Diana?

'Well, we've decided that you didn't really need my advice about the RAF haven't we?' she said. 'I've a feeling that something else is on your mind.'

He finished eating, took a drink of coffee, and then put the cup and plate on the low table between them. 'Yes. There is something else,' he said quietly. 'More your department, a girl whom I like very much.'

Harriet felt a sudden sense of loss. This was strange for she was aware that she had not truly wanted this personable young man for Diana. She'd decided long ago that if her niece were to marry him there would be endless trouble and heartbreak for both of them. She knew that Diana had no pioneering zeal for the cause of the Jews, and there was no reason why she should have. Yet, hearing his last words, Harriet felt foolishly rejected. Just as if it was myself, she thought grimly.

She betrayed none of this to David. 'A girl?' she said. 'Who?'

'Rachel Meyerson. She's suitable, pretty, very Jewish, shares all my hopes and aspirations, and from England too, half-Dutch, English father.'

'And you want to marry her?'

'I've thought about it.'

'Are you in love with her?'

246

There was silence in the room broken only by the sombre ticking of the old clock that Harriet had brought from England so long ago and which never ceased to remind her of home.

'Perhaps,' David said at last.

'And Diana?' Harriet hardly dared say it. 'She was very much in love with you.'

'I know. It makes me feel unworthy. She's...' He didn't finish the sentence and Harriet was never to know what he meant to say.

'Rachel is Jewish.'

'And that's important to you.'

He looked at her with a trace of impatience. 'Of course it's important. My children would be Jewish, sabres in fact if they were born here. Yes, that's mighty important. If I marry a non-Jew they won't be. The mother determines the race in Jewish law.'

'Would Rachel go back to England with you if you join up?'

'I don't know. We haven't discussed it. She's a nurse and doing valuable work here. I'd want her to come with me, of course. Her mother is dead and her father has married again, so she has no ties anywhere really.'

Harriet was suddenly weary. This land and its problems, its people all struggling for the same tiny bit of earth, overwhelmed her as it never had done before. She thought for a moment nostalgically, of Chy Morvah. Perhaps she should go back too and help with the war effort if there was going to be a war. And it looked increasingly certain that there would be one soon. But no, she said firmly to herself.

247

My animals need me here. I've pledged myself to them and I won't desert them.

'She sounds very suitable,' she said. 'I met her at the wedding, didn't I, and I've seen her from time to time at Beth Haron. A nice girl.'

Harriet thought for a moment of her own marriage. It had been a perfect love match. She twisted the ring on her finger and tears almost started to her eyes. Stupid woman, she said indignantly to herself. Aloud she said, 'Make sure that you love her, David. Don't marry anyone just to get Jewish children. Love is more important than anything.'

After he had gone she sat for a long time thinking about his visit, thinking about Diana, wondering if David had any love left over at all for any woman while he was so passionate a Zionist. She felt very sad. She got up slowly and cleared away the coffee cups, gave Ghazala the remains of the food along with some goat meat, and then went out to attend to the other animals.

Raif Habib's motor car bumping down the track to the bungalow disturbed her gloomy thoughts. She was more pleased to see him than she'd thought possible. She ushered him inside and made yet more coffee. They sat facing each other with the small table between them and their talk at first was all of small inconsequential things. Then inevitably the conversation drifted towards the happenings in Europe.

'No good news, I'm afraid,' he said. 'I've been reading the papers this morning. There's definitely going to be a war soon.'

'And the Arabs will be on the side of Hitler. You will be on his side!' Harriet shocked herself with the thought.

He shook his head. 'Never,' he said. 'Remember, my dear Harriet, that I am Christian, not Muslim. We Christian Arabs are different.'

Harriet smiled at him. 'That's the best thing I've heard today,' she said. 'I knew already, of course, but hearing it again makes me feel better. Do you think it will be a long war?'

He shrugged his shoulders. 'Who knows?' he said. 'But yes I fear it will be very long.' He finished his coffee and then got up and went over to the low divan that ran the length of the room. 'May I sit here?' he asked. 'I find it very comfortable.'

'Of course. What about something to eat?'

'I should very much like some of your admirable pitta bread. Your beautiful Ghazala would like some too.' The dog had followed them in and was staring into his face with rapture.

'She's already eaten. She's very greedy.'

'Perhaps because she never had enough before she came to you.'

'Probably.' Harriet prepared some olives and cut more cheese. 'She likes you very much and she's a very good judge of character.'

She handed the food to him and gave the dog some too and then sat down beside him on the divan, but with a respectable distance between them.

She felt comforted by Raif's visit, but not a

little surprised at the sudden turn her wayward thoughts were taking. What a mix-up my life is, she mused. I'm British and I fear that I'm falling in love with an Arab.

'What is it that you say? "A shilling for your thoughts"?' Raif said.

'A penny,' she corrected, and blushed. 'No, I couldn't reveal my thoughts for all the wealth in the world.'

'Then I shall have to earn more than all the wealth in the world,' he said.

I think he's in love with me too, she commented to herself in amazement. At my age, almost forty! What on earth am I going to do about that and whatever will my dear brother say? The thought of James' fury made her suddenly laugh aloud.

'Why do you laugh?'

She shook her head. 'One day I might tell you.'

He finished most of the pitta sandwich, gave the dog the last little bit, and then took her hand in his and kissed it gently. 'I'm glad that I've cheered you,' he said, misunderstanding.

'Yes, you have cheered me,' she replied. 'You always do, and that is perhaps the greatest gift anyone can give another.'

She marvelled at what she had just said, but it was true. In Raif's company she invariably felt happy and secure.

'I should like always to make you happy,' he said quietly. 'I should like to marry you, my Harriet.'

CHAPTER 17

August–October 1939

When Harriet received an invitation to David's wedding at Beth Haron she felt again a strong sense of rejection on Diana's behalf. In spite of the commonsense which told her that the match would never have worked, she still admitted to a secret foolishness, a longing to see Diana and David together in a sort of happy-ever-after idyll. But more seriously, she was worried now for Diana, for she knew that her niece had loved David very much.

She stood quite still after opening the envelope. She held the invitation in her hand for a long time before she could bring herself, eventually, to sit down and pen her congratulations to David and Rachel. Yes, she would certainly attend.

It was a very Jewish celebration and both bride and groom seemed happy and in love. Harriet looked, at first, for some sign of doubt or hesitation in David's eyes when he greeted her, but there was none that she could see. Rachel Meyerson, now Halprin, was very pretty—handsome might be a more suitable adjective, she thought. She was tall and capable-looking and sparkling with good humour and fun, altogether an excellent wife for David.

As Harriet drove home at the end of the long day she admitted to herself that her commonsense had won the battle over those secret romantic delusions she had harboured. This marriage was probably the best thing that could have happened. She felt slightly traitorous for thinking so, and she knew that her niece would be devastated for a time. But grief seldom lasted for long when you were young. When Diana got over it she would be free from the forlorn hope that David would marry her, for forlorn it had probably always been.

That evening she sat down to write to Diana. It was a difficult letter to compose, one which she knew was bound to cause great distress. But I have to be like a surgeon, Harriet told herself. I must be cruel to be kind. She'll find someone much more suitable in due course.

Diana greeted the news of David's marriage to Rachel with shock and outrage. She held Harriet's letter in her hand and trembled so violently that the paper shook. How dared he? She wanted to scream aloud, but instead gritted her teeth and said to herself over and over again as she read to the bottom of the page, I loved him, still love him, and I thought he loved me! She knew that she was being illogical for she had left Palestine of her own free will, but the knowledge brought no comfort.

Her mother was reading her own mail but Diana's distress was so obvious that she paused and stared at her daughter. 'What does Harriet say?' she asked anxiously.

Diana threw the letter down on to the table. 'That David's married some girl on the kibbutz, a nurse—Rachel something or other. Very Jewish, very Zionist. Just what he wants, all the things that I am not.' Her tone was scathing and she forced back her tears.

Mary looked down at Harriet's letter and longed to pick it up and read for herself just what her sister-in-law had said, but she resisted. The suddenness of the news shocked her and she was filled with concern, and with irrational anger—anger with David and pity for her daughter who had allowed herself to fall in love with such an unsuitable man. She was sure in her own heart that he could never be the right one for Diana, yet she knew that the hurt would be as deep and as real as if he had been totally suitable. She reminded herself that commonsense had nothing to do with love. Gently she said, 'You told him that you couldn't face his kind of life, didn't you?'

It was not a question, more a statement of fact, but it made Diana feel worse, made her sure that she was foolishly responsible for losing the only man she had ever wanted.

'But he needn't have done it so soon,' she said. 'It's only a few months since I came home. I still hoped...'

'That he would follow you, put you before his precious ideals?' Mary finished the sentence for her. 'Men aren't, on the whole, like that. Women usually have to take second place in their lives. If we can't accommodate ourselves to them and their wishes, then we're likely to be pushed aside. Men seldom want to fit in with a woman's way of life. We have to make the sacrifices. It's always been so, and I suppose always will be. Unless we fight!'

For Mary it was a long speech, but she had been doing a lot of thinking lately, and knew that in her own experience every word was true. Only during the past few months had she begun to fight a little. And she was still fighting. She had been to see her new grandson, was entranced with him and completely determined that he and Samira should come to Bagleigh before too long. She had plans, but she was waiting for the right time. Fighting and scheming had to go together when you had a husband like James! But Diana was of a different generation. Surely she would want to keep her own identity rather than let it be swallowed up by a man, however much she might love him? With David she would have needed to conform.

Diana was aware, while she struggled to keep back her tears, that her mother had summed up the situation perfectly, but she was in no mood to listen. She wanted David. Not freedom, not independence, just David. And he was probably coming back to England soon to join up. He would be here, with a wife! She felt that she couldn't bear it, that her heart would break. She wanted to tear out of the room and give in to a frenzy of weeping.

With supreme effort she forced herself to pick

up the letter again and read to the end once more as if she needed further confirmation that something so awful could really have happened, was not just a dream.

She looked at her mother with pain-ravaged eyes. 'Read it for yourself,' she managed. She let the pages flutter down on to the table this time, dropping them as though they had a loathsome, almost untouchable quality of their own, and then, feeling that she could hold her tears in check no longer, she fled upstairs to the sanctuary of her bedroom and gave herself up to her grief.

A few days later came the news that made everything else fade into near-insignificance. Britain was at war with Germany. Diana, still grieving, still feeling that life would never hold anything of interest again, was nevertheless jolted a little out of her glum resignation.

She and her mother were in the big kitchen at Bagleigh preparing Sunday lunch when they heard the announcement on the wireless. This room had become the centre of their lives lately for Cook had retired and Lily had left to join up. Mary had joyfully taken over much of the running of the house, for apart from the woman who came in to clean now and then, there was no more help to be had.

They had known for some time that war was inevitable. The Evacuation Warden had been round the village and the farms warning that children were to be brought from the towns and would be billeted wherever there was room for them. And preparations for a black-out had been going gloomily ahead. All curtains that were not thick enough to hide every vestige of light from the expected enemy bombers were taken down and stored away, their bright colours almost a reproach. 'Just as if we were in mourning already,' Mary had commented as she and Diana had cut and stitched the twenty-six yards of sturdy black fabric that they had bought during a recent shopping expedition in Exeter.

But when the official announcement of war came it was still shocking. Diana was at the sink peeling potatoes and her mother was gathering ingredients together for the pie she was about to make when the Home Service programme was interrupted for the Prime Minister. Both women stopped and stood quite still while Mr Chamberlain's voice dominated everything in the quiet room. '...I have to tell you now that this country is at war with Germany.'

Rollo, lying on his special rug in the corner of the room, lifted his head from his paws and looked from one to the other, aware as dogs often are of the sudden tension, the sense of moment and drama.

The disembodied voice went on ' "It is the evil things that we shall be fighting against—brute force, bad faith, injustice, oppression and persecution... The right will prevail. The right must prevail." '

Neither woman spoke. The dog slowly got up and pushed his wet nose into Diana's apron. His tail wagged slowly from side to side and Diana wiped her hands and stroked him absent-mindedly.

Mary went to the wireless set and switched it off and a great well of silence fell upon the room. She sat down heavily on the rocking chair that stood beside the Aga. 'Well,' she said eventually, 'that's it then. A second war in my lifetime and with Germany again too. I suppose Colin will have to go.' There was a deadness in her voice that didn't at all match the sudden lift to the spirits that Diana felt.

For she was not depressed. Instead she was filled with sudden excitement. Here was something that would certainly change the boring domesticity of her life. She would get away from her father, away from Bagleigh. A war might even help her to forget a little... New horizons beckoned alluringly.

'Colin wants to fly fighters,' Diana said, and her eyes glowed for a moment as they hadn't done for days. 'I'm going to do something too, no stopping here rusting away for me. I shall join up as well.'

Mary looked at her as if she were quite mad. 'Join up? Your father won't hear of it.'

'He'll have to get used to the idea. I shall be called up probably and then there'll be no choice. I think they're going to conscript single women of my age pretty soon.'

Mary shook her head in disbelief. 'It doesn't seem right to me,' she said. 'Women in the forces. What do you think you'll be able to do, for goodness sake?'

'Something exciting, I hope. I've had a good

education, and I can drive. I'd like to be a war correspondent perhaps. I could use my photography then.' She glanced out of the window at the small portion of sky that showed blue above the mass of the hill. 'I think that some women are being trained to fly so that they can deliver planes from the factories to the airfields. Just think of that! I might get to fly a Spitfire.'

Mary was horrified. 'I sincerely hope not. Flying isn't natural! Too dangerous.'

Diana laughed. 'Oh, Mother, how can you be so old-fashioned? Air-power is the thing of the future.'

'Old-fashioned or not, I don't like the idea. You'd never get me up there. No time anyway. I'll be busy here, I suppose, managing a house full of rowdy evacuees while you and Colin are gadding about enjoying yourselves.'

Diana felt a moment of guilt. Her mother would need help. There were plenty of empty rooms at Bagleigh, and the Evacuation Warden had told them that they had ample accommodation for five or six children.

'Half a dozen for sure,' Mary continued. 'Think of it, six small children running all over the place. Your father will go mad.' Then she too laughed. 'But I think I'm quite looking forward to it actually.'

'How will you manage?'

'What do you mean, manage?'

'Well, all the extra work?'

'I have an idea!' Mary's voice was mysterious. She got up and went back to the table and took

258

a bowl and tipped flour into it. 'Samira will be alone, won't she? Fetch me the butter dish, Diana.'

'You mean?' Diana went to the larder where a bowl of their own home-made butter had been placed earlier on the slate shelf. She carried it back to the table and set it down in front of her mother.

'You mean that you hope to have Samira here at last?'

Mary carefully cut several pieces of butter from the block and added them to the flour. Before she replied she chopped each piece into smaller nubs and then plunged her hands into the bowl to rub the butter into the flour. She did it delicately with her finger tips so that the pastry would be light and fluffy.

'Yes. Everything is different in wartime. People have to make sacrifices. Not that having Samira and our grandson is a sacrifice, but your father might think so at first. But he'll give in eventually. Especially if I take to my bed with a mysterious malady for a few days and leave him to look after six noisy children. Even Samira might be welcome reluctantly then!'

Diana was amazed and delighted. 'You're wonderful, Mother,' she said. 'I've always underestimated you. I wait with bated breath to see how it all works out.'

Mary continued to work as she talked and Diana watched, slightly mesmerised, as the butter and flour became transformed into a fine breadcrumb-like consistency under her mother's deft fingers. Then suddenly everything seemed slightly unreal. Events were moving at such speed that she could only think of the pie that they were having for lunch. 'Where did you learn to make pastry like that?' she asked.

'I used to come in here and watch Cook. I was determined that I would learn how to prepare meals. My life was so useless, Diana. I think that at last I'm actually beginning to live. I was only a child in the Great War, and it was the same then. I saw my mother and lots of other women suddenly come into their own, suddenly realize that they were as good as men and could do all sorts of things they had never imagined. Then afterwards they were all thrown back into their kitchens or parlours. I hope it won't be the same after this one.'

Diana laughed. 'But it's only led you into the kitchen so far,' she said. 'Not out of it.'

'I want to do all sorts of other things too. I might join the ARP.'

Diana gulped at the idea. 'Air Raid Precautions? But isn't that only for men, and only in towns? Wouldn't the WVS be more suitable?'

Mary was now rolling out the pastry. 'Perhaps, but hurry up, dear,' she directed. 'Not so many questions. Get the plums out, will you, or your father will be in and nothing will be ready. Cut them in halves and take the stones out.'

Diana washed the big luscious fruits that she had picked the day before, eating a number of them as she prepared them for the pie. The sticky juice ran down her chin and through her fingers. Then she watched thoughtfully as her mother placed the pieces on the pastry and sprinkled sugar liberally over them before placing another circle of pastry on top.

'I wonder what differences the war will really make,' she said. 'We might be short of food of course.' She helped herself to yet another plum. 'But the worst thing is Hitler's hatred of the Jews. I wish David would stay in Palestine. He'd be safer there. Supposing he was shot down over Germany!'

'He'll be all right,' Mary said firmly. 'Stop thinking about him. He belongs to someone else now. And I don't know that Palestine would be safer anyway. By the way, your father has asked Philip Briscoe over to supper tonight.'

David and Colin were to report to the Air-Crew Receiving Centre at Helton, a small town in Sussex, in the middle of October. Both had been called up, both were Acting Pilot Officers, and both were full of excitement. They met in London and travelled down together.

'Any qualms about leaving Palestine?' Colin asked when they were settled in corner seats in a first-class compartment.

'Lots, especially with Rachel staying on.'

'When's she coming over here?'

David lit a cigarette and inhaled deeply before he replied. 'Can't say. She's nursing, as you know, and thinks that her work is badly needed where she is.'

'Needed everywhere.' Colin's voice was grim. 'There'll be plenty for her to do here before long.'

'I suppose it was a shock, the news of our marriage.'

'You're telling me. Diana...' He stopped himself. He had been about to say, Diana threw a fit, hasn't been the same since, but he knew that this would be disloyal to his sister, and wasn't quite true anyway. On the surface she seemed to have come to terms with the inevitable. He had deliberately not talked about her to David before and he immediately regretted mentioning her now especially in the context of his friend's marriage.

But David looked at him and spoke sharply. 'What about Diana?'

Colin shrugged his shoulders and tried to sound casual, tried to repair the damage. 'I suppose it was more of a shock to her than to anyone else,' he said, 'but she's over it now, I think. She goes out from time to time with a chap from home, Philip Briscoe, a decent sort. I was at school with him. His family farm on the other side of the moor, a big place, lots of money.'

David appeared to digest this information carefully for a moment before he replied. 'Are they serious?'

'I couldn't tell you. Can anyone be serious about anything in wartime?'

'Is she still at Bagleigh?'

'For the time being. She's working on the farm. She'd rather be in one of the services doing something she sees as glamorous, but the country needs food. Farming is a reserved occupation. She wants to be a war correspondent, she told me, but she's rather young and inexperienced for a job like that apparently.'

'I was very fond of Diana, a little in love with her in fact.'

The words took Colin by surprise. 'I thought it was more than a little.' He allowed a trace of condemnation to creep into his voice.

'Perhaps it was, but I fought against it towards the end.'

'Was that quite fair?'

'It was for her sake mainly. At least that's what I tell myself. She belongs here, not in a place like Palestine with a fanatic like me for a husband. Rachel is as dedicated as I am to our cause, and the sacrifices I might ask of her she'd want to make anyway.'

Colin was silent for a while. He knew that Diana had been much more than a little in love with David, and he partly blamed himself for her grief. He wondered too if his friend's marriage to Rachel would work. Had the marriage been on the rebound? And would Diana fall into the arms of Philip Briscoe for the same reason? He stared out of the window and thought about the tangled strands of all their lives. David jolted him out of his reverie.

'You haven't told me much about yourself?' he questioned. 'How did you manage to get your parents to relent and have Samira at Bagleigh?'

Colin too took out a cigarette. 'My father was very unwilling at first, but the house is full of evacuees, my mother was exhausted, went down with a mystery germ in fact, and he was persuaded eventually that another pair of hands was vital.'

'How are things working out then?'

Colin smiled. 'He's taken to Matthew.'

The baby, now seven months old, had been the catalyst, the means of a partial reconciliation. It was ironic, the biggest surprise of Colin's life, that his parents, especially his father, should so adore this supposed grandchild, the little boy who was in fact no grandchild of theirs at all.

He had brought Samira to Bagleigh because of his mother's illness, an indisposition from which she very quickly recovered once they were installed in the spare wing of the house. Then he had joined up and there had been no question of sending them back to Chy Morvah.

'What about Samira?' David asked. 'I'll bet she was a surprise to your father.'

'He kept his feelings very much to himself, but I could tell that he was quite nonplussed when he first saw her. When she rode Major out on the moors I don't think he could believe the evidence of his eyes. She's a very competent rider, as you know.'

'Yes. The beautiful Jazi!'

'Anyway, things seem to be settling down. My father is very proud though. He finds it impossible to say that he was wrong, or that he's sorry. Consequently I don't know if he's forgiven me, or if he'll reinstate me after the war.'

For a time Colin was silent, thinking about the amazing events of the past weeks. But he was not entirely at peace even now. Samira's happiness, and his own, was built on such a fragile base. Sometimes, in the night, he would wake up drenched with sweat and shivering with fear, and the nightmare was always the same: the discovery by his parents that Matthew was Eshref's son.

Apart from himself and Samira only Diana knew. He had given no sign to David, and his friend appeared to have no suspicions. Harriet was the only other person who might speculate now and then but she was a long way away, and he could count on her silence anyway. Yet the secret was a constant source of anxiety to him. It plagued his waking hours as well as his nights and he constantly feared the eventual outcome. And now Samira had told him that she was pregnant again. If this second child should be a son, a son of his own flesh, what would he do? How could he reconcile his inevitable love for the one and his sense of loyalty to the other? He prayed every night for a daughter. A girl would cause less conflict.

The train rumbled on through the quiet countryside and David also was absorbed in his own thoughts and dreams. He looked at the panorama of sleepy villages and peaceful wooded hillsides. This was his country too, he mused. He had been born here in Sussex, loved the richness of it, the sounds and scents of the autumn fields and hedgerows. He could just discern some evocative fragrance now and then as it was carried through the open carriage window on the breeze, mixed with the smuts and smoke of the labouring engine. If only he could have settled, accepted his English heritage, then he might have married Diana, followed his father into the bank, become rich instead of... He quickly pulled himself together and banished the traitorous thoughts. Eretz Israel, that was where he belonged, and Rachel was waiting for him. When Hitler was smashed he would go back, have a string of little sabres, prickly pears, the affectionate nickname for children born in the ancient land of Israel. And he would fight in another war, a war for Israel!

He dozed and dreamed for a few moments and then awoke with a start. What had they been talking about? Matthew, Colin's son. 'What made you choose that name Matthew?' he asked suddenly.

Colin grinned at him. 'First book in the New Testament,' he replied. 'Samira has become religious, wants to join the Church of England!'

David suddenly saw the funny side and let out a great bellow of laughter. 'Well, that's a turn up for the books,' he said. 'I'd like to see old Jebel when he gets that news!'

'He's not likely to get it is he!'

'Unless Harriet tells him.'

'She has more sense that that.'

Further conversation was cut short by their arrival at the seaside resort that was to be their home for the next few weeks. They pulled their bags from the racks above their heads and stepped on to the platform. 'This is it then,' Colin said. 'We're in for the duration.'

'It'll be a piece of cake,' David remarked casually. 'A jolly old piece of cake.'

CHAPTER 18

Diana stood up to stretch her aching back and looked at the sombre November sky. She wondered how much longer she would be here at Bagleigh. She was working in the kitchen garden, a place that had grown in importance lately. Posters everywhere told of the necessity to dig for victory and Bagleigh was doing its bit but she knew that next year the garden must do better, produce larger quantities of crops, support more hens. She spent long hours on the farm too, working with the land-girl who lived in the village and came over every day. Even her father had abandoned his position of gentleman-farmer, and now worked as hard as anyone else, of necessity since most of the available young men were in the forces.

Diana had given up hope of joining the select group of women trained to transport aeroplanes from factory to airfield. She had made enquiries, but there was too much competition. She had been told that she was too young, and that as a farmer's daughter, she must work on the land. It was a job ready-made for her. Yet she still yearned for a career and real fulfilment. In spite of everyone's discouragement she was determined that this should be through her photography. But it was not the right time yet! She had complete confidence that with patience she would succeed in getting what she wanted eventually. Meanwhile there were many compensations at Bagleigh.

Since Samira and the enchanting little Matthew had come to live here life had been far from humdrum. Samira had needed help to settle for she had been terrified of her father-in-law. Diana had smoothed the way for her and the two girls had become very attached to each other. Neither had ever had a sister or even a close female friend and both found the new relationship rewarding and precious.

The evacuees certainly livened things up as well and three of them had taken to Samira very quickly. Perhaps they sensed that, like themselves, she was there on sufferance. There were four now, Ben, Dougie, Will and George, four snotty-nosed and appallingly behaved little boys from some unimaginable London slum.

Diana was thinking about all this while she shovelled manure into the trench she had been digging for next year's potatoes. She grinned to herself as she recalled the day the children had arrived. The shock and outrage had been so clear on her father's face. And two days later her mother had taken purposefully to her bed! The ensuing chaos had ensured that James Stanmore had agreed to the suggestion that Samira be temporarily installed, for Diana, falling in with her mother's schemes, had declared that she couldn't take any responsibility for the children. There was far too much to do in the garden and on the farm.

James had been determined not to speak to

Samira, thinking of his daughter-in-law as a kind of nanny-cum-servant. But the cunning strategy had worked exactly as Mary had carefully planned, and there was no question now of Samira going back to Chy Morvah.

She had proved invaluable, dealing efficiently with the children and helping wherever help was most needed. 'I've always worked hard,' she was sometimes heard to say. 'And I understand boys. I've had brothers!' Diana thinking of those brothers had looked her straight in the eyes and she had stared back and then turned away.

When the pile of manure was finished Diana wheeled the barrow back to its place against the wall, wiped her hands on a dirty piece of cloth and gathered up her spade and fork. Then she looked up into the darkening sky and her attention was suddenly drawn to a buzzard circling overhead. His majestic flight was causing great disquiet to a number of crows who were flying around him filling the otherwise peaceful late-afternoon with their raucous cries. Eventually, giving up his search for a meal, the buzzard suddenly swooped out of sight behind the hill and Diana turned to watch the crows as they too flew away, calmer now, into the distance, until they were mere specks of black, becoming finally invisible against the night clouds that hid the setting sun.

The buzzard made her think of Philip Briscoe for just yesterday she had been riding on the moor with him and they had slowed their mounts to a walk in order to watch a similar display. But then the buzzard had been successful, falling to earth and soaring up again with some small terrified creature in its claws. She had closed her eyes for a moment, not wanting to see, and Philip had laughed affectionately at her. 'It's nature,' he had said. 'Red in tooth and claw. For a farmer's daughter you're remarkably sentimental.'

'I always have been. Do you know, I can't even kill a spider or moth. I trap them in a tumbler and carry them outside!'

'Where they promptly die of cold!'

'I suppose so.'

Then they had talked about the war, and Philip had told her that he was to go into the Navy soon. 'Unlike your brother, I have no great inclination to fly.' He had looked up at the scudding clouds and the gulls which were inland because of storms at sea. 'No. Flying doesn't attract me. The sea now, that's different.'

She wondered agonisingly and frequently about her feelings for Philip. There was still an ache in her heart, anger too, whenever she thought of David. He and her brother were together training to fly. Colin had written recently with the news that David's wife was pregnant and was to stay in Palestine until the baby was born. It was important that this child should be born in the sacred land. Diana had clenched her fists and been filled with a frightening jealousy when she read those lines. And now, whenever she thought of this unborn Jewish baby for whom David had longed, she was consumed with a destroying and ugly repugnance. Surely I cannot feel hatred for a baby still in the womb? Is it Rachel then? Is it David's wife whom I hate? The questions had been going round and round in her head agonisingly ever since she had read that letter. Hatred destroys everything it touches, she told herself. I must never hate.

She was horrified that she could feel such terrible things, and distressed by her continuing inability to erase David from her most secret thoughts. Philip was so pleasant, such good company, fun to be with. 'I like him a lot, so why can't I be content with him?' She hardly realised that she had spoken aloud.

As the night clouds began to sweep over the woods Diana, still pondering in her mind, saw three small aeroplanes come out of the western sky. She stared at them entranced. Perhaps it was Colin? Maybe it was David? Not very likely, of course, but just possible. The 'planes were heading back to an airfield somewhere in England after a training flight possibly, or even after a sortie over France. She knew that they were fighters but that was all. She shivered and tightened the belt of her old working coat, and then, as they, like the birds before them, disappeared into the distance, she pulled her spade from the earth and strode back to the house.

Three of the evacuees settled in well, but George had been a problem from the start. He was an undernourished and pathetic little scrap, only five years old and quite uncomprehending about what had happened to him. Where was Mum?

he asked repeatedly. Why had Gran deserted him too? He'd slept with her, he told them, ever since Mum brought home his new Uncle. Diana, looking at him, had visions of the small boy cocooned in some slatternly woman's vast yielding shape. She was sorry for him, but unable to do much about it. She'd never been easy with children, much preferring animals. It was to Samira he turned for comfort.

To Mary he seemed to cry or grizzle for almost twenty hours out of each twenty-four. He wet the bed once or twice most nights and frequently wet himself too during the day, and in spite of all their best efforts he would not be comforted.

Eventually Mary and Samira, beside themselves with sleepless nights and stress-filled days, decided that enough was enough, he must be returned to his mother. If he was not, then they were both convinced that he would die, for surely no child could sustain such grief and live?

His mother was contacted by one of the welfare workers and her reaction was reported to Mary over the telephone almost word for word.

Yes, of course the little perisher must come home, she'd said. She'd always known he wouldn't be no good in one of them posh country places, and them Jerries hadn't been over with their bleedin' bombs yet. She reckoned they wouldn't be neither. They was too frightened of our brave boys in them fighters, that's what. But how was Georgie to get to London then?

She couldn't come, what with another on the way any day now. Could the lady bring the little tyke?

When this tale was relayed to Diana her eyes sparkled and she volunteered at once. London! Yes, she would certainly take George back to his loving family, and hopefully stay for a night or two in the capital herself. Perhaps she could see her brother. She had heard that London was full of excitement, servicemen everywhere, and maybe she could make some enquiries that might further her future career.

'Come straight back,' Mary said, worried. 'The bombing may start any time.'

'Don't be so pessimistic, Mother,' she replied. 'They've only managed one bomb so far, and that was up in Scotland. I often wonder why the authorities were in such a hurry to get the children evacuated.'

'Never underestimate the Germans,' said Mary severely. 'I remember the last time. They've got something up their sleeve, you mark my words.'

Diana had never been to London's East End, never seen the worst of its poverty. At Paddington she managed to hail a taxi and then suffered the driver's odd looks when she gave the address. Eventually she found herself in Georgie's road.

' 'Ere you are then, Miss,' the cabbie said. 'That'll be 'alf a crown.'

Diana ushered the now silent child out of the vehicle and found three shillings in her purse.

Was sixpence enough for a tip? She handed it over and was thankful when the man pocketed it, said nothing and drove off. She hadn't the courage to ask him to wait for her.

'We're home, George,' she said. She took the child's sticky hand. 'Show me which is your house.'

To her surprise he didn't respond, just stood there hanging on to her as though he was in a dream world. She looked at the row of tiny houses all joined together. The front doors, right on the street, stood mostly ajar.

But suddenly there was an eruption of noise and a heavily pregnant woman in a large dirty apron burst from number forty-three.

'Well, if it ain't our Georgie,' she said. 'Come 'ome to yer old Mum, 'ave you, luv.'

In spite of the squalor and the smell issuing from the grubby passageway, George was immediately galvanised into action. He seemed to spring into life like a greyhound released from its trap at the start of a race. He dropped Diana's hand, rushed into his mother's arms and was folded into her ample curves. Diana was deeply moved.

When the embraces were over the woman looked at her. 'Comin' in, love? Like a cuppa tea, would you? Kettle's on the boil. I reckon you've 'ad a long journey.'

'Thank you, but I won't take your precious rations.' Diana felt inadequate, totally out of place. All she wanted to do was get away as quickly as she decently could. She handed over the suitcase that her mother had provided. It was

274

full of clean and neatly pressed little garments that had been unearthed from trunks in the Bagleigh attics, Colin's clothes from years ago. Diana hoped that they wouldn't end up in the pawn shop.

'Cheerio then, love. If them Jerries gets nasty after all, perhaps we'll 'ave another go at sending 'im away, but me and Gran and the new one'ull try to go as well. See you again, p'raps?'

Diana shuddered inwardly. 'Perhaps,' she said.

She was to meet Colin at Christie's Hotel. He had managed to get a thirty-six-hour leave and had promised to take her to a show. He'd fixed accommodation with a friend whose parents had a house in the West End, he'd told her, so she need not rush straight back to Devon. She was looking forward to it greatly, her first proper visit to London.

She had walked through the dirty noisy streets for some time almost getting lost twice before she managed to get a taxi. When at last it left her outside the hotel she hoped that she didn't show too many signs of the traumatic day she'd had so far. Her feet were uncomfortable in the smart shoes that she had chosen, her coat and gloves had suffered from George's sticky closeness, and she felt her fashionable little hat to be at quite the wrong angle. She had wanted to grab it from her head and stuff it into a bag when she was in George's street, but at least here it wouldn't attract any undue notice. She walked slowly up the front steps, glad that it was only her brother who was to meet her. Colin was a comfortable sort of person, just what she needed at the moment.

But it was not Colin who strode towards her, took her overnight bag, and kissed her in a brotherly way on the cheek.

'Well, hello. Sorry it's me. Colin couldn't make it. Soaring temperature and shaking legs. The MO confined him to bed this morning. There's a particularly virulent 'flu bug doing the rounds.' David smiled down at her. 'Hope I'll do instead!'

For a moment she couldn't trust herself to answer. Would he do? How could she possibly manage with this married version of the man she loved to distraction? Oh Colin, Colin, how could you do this to me? She had not seen David in uniform, was more used to the regulation kibbutz gear of shabby trousers and crumpled open-necked shirt. This new David was something quite different and her treacherous heart thumped like a piston. He was immaculately groomed, tall and so handsome and powerful that she could hardly breathe.

'I'll order tea and cakes,' he was saying. 'They do the most wonderful fancies here, almost pre-war style. I expect you'd like a wash and brush up first? Colin told me about the little horror you were escorting to London.'

Did she then look worn out and scruffy? 'Yes. A wash and brush up would be fine,' she heard herself mumble.

In the rather opulent ladies' cloakroom she

took stock of the situation. She removed her hat, combed her hair and re-applied her bright new lipstick. Then she surveyed herself critically in the mirror and her reflection stared back, telling her to take advantage, to enjoy every minute of this amazing and unexpected reunion. 'I can't. He's married,' she told the brazen face that was looking at her. 'Why worry about that!' The image shrugged its shoulders. 'You have no special loyalty to the woman he married.' She realised that she was talking aloud and laughed and shook her head. Whatever is happening to me? she thought. I'm going mad. Seeing David again has touched my brain!

The door opened and an older woman came in. She glanced at Diana and smiled. 'Chilly for December, isn't it,' she remarked. 'Still, what can you expect with a war on!'

She disappeared into the lavatory and Diana grinned again. Everything could be blamed on the war, even the weather apparently, and what did one expect in December anyway? She replaced her hat on her head, speared it with a long hat-pin, a bit of left-over Victoriana of which she was rather fond and which she had found in a junk box at Bagleigh. She looked at her reflection again. 'All right,' she said to it, aloud. 'I'll enjoy myself and try not to feel guilty. After all, there's a war on.' She hoped the woman in the lavatory wouldn't think she was completely batty.

David stood up and held out both hands to her when she returned to him. 'What a lovely little hat,' he said. 'You look quite ravishing.'

Her shoulder bag slid down her arm annoyingly as she took his hands. My God, he's changed, she thought. What has happened to him? Where's the rugged pioneer now? Aloud she said, 'Thank you, David. You look quite personable yourself. That uniform makes a great difference.'

'So I wasn't personable before?' He laughed, his great noisy laugh which she had forgotten. It was one of the many things she liked about him.

'Yes, but different.'

'I often wonder if Rachel would like the new image.'

Diana was suddenly angry. Rachel! Why did he have to mention her now? Oh, please God, let him not think about Rachel. 'I don't expect she would,' Diana said with hidden venom. 'Too glamorous for Palestine.'

'Glamorous? Not the adjective I would use for a fighter pilot.'

'Oh, but yes. Didn't you know that fighter pilots are the most glamorous men on earth?'

He dropped her hands gently and she readjusted the troublesome shoulder bag.

'Tea,' he said. 'Over there. Come on, I'm starving.'

They sat in the darkness together in Drury Lane Theatre. Diana heard little of the ENSA concert that they had come to enjoy. The presence of David so close to her was too disturbing, altogether too sad. She groped for a more suitable word but could find none. Sad was exactly what she was just now in spite of her brave words to her reflection. All around her couples were laughing, holding hands, enjoying the jokes, the songs, the skits about Hitler. Most were in uniform and she felt out of place, alone, more miserable than she had been for weeks. David was careful not to touch her, not to take her hand again. In the hotel it had been a friendly greeting, meaning nothing to him. A closeness, a caress in this place, in the dark, was obviously something quite different, something he wouldn't allow.

She couldn't think afterwards how she managed to eat her way through the supper which he bought for her or how they got to the house in which she was to stay for the night.

'Colin gave me the key,' he said, groping in his pocket. 'This place belongs to parents of a friend of his. Someone he met in Palestine, I believe, another archaeologist.'

'You mean they're not here?'

He looked down at her. 'No. They're away in the country most of the time.'

'And I shall have to...' She couldn't finish her sentence, couldn't say, Stay here alone, as though she was frightened, or worse, as though she wanted him to stay with her. Which of course she did, desperately.

'I'll come in with you,' he said. 'Make sure everything is all right, no bogey men under the beds.' He laughed and unlocked the door and she followed him nervously into the dark hall. He felt along the wall for the first doorway and fell over a chair on his way to the window to

279

pull the blackout curtains. Then suddenly the room was flooded with light as he found the switch.

Diana looked around. The room was small but attractive, and smelt of fresh polish. 'Nice,' she murmured.

'I'll just check the other rooms,' he said. He took a torch and held it with its narrow beam shining on to the floor.

She stood quite still listening to his footsteps on the stairs. She heard the swish of curtains again, and then again, and saw more lights.

'Two bedrooms and a bathroom,' he called down to her. 'All blacked out now. Have you found a kitchen?'

Coming out of her dream, she pushed at a door which led from the hall. Quickly she pulled down the blind, and then she shivered, realising how cold she was.

Back in the tiny sitting room David was stooping to light the gas fire. She followed him in and then stood watching the flames. She heard them popping as they spread from the middle of the fire outwards until the whole thing was red and comforting. 'You could sleep in here,' he said. 'The sofa looks comfortable enough, and you'd be warm. It's freezing everywhere else.'

Then, quite suddenly and without warning, he crossed the room towards her, gathered her into his arms and she was completely lost in the strength of his embrace. She felt a moment of complete confusion in which all the carefully repressed emotions of her life disappeared in the face of shattering conviction that she couldn't do without this man.

They sank on to the welcoming sofa and she knew that the girl in the mirror was smiling, was completely happy, was about to be fulfilled after all. But abruptly she felt his hands, those long delicate fingers that she loved, lose their magic. They became bunched fists instead. His body froze in her arms. She opened her eyes and looked at him and was terrified by what she saw. There was suffering in his face, and fierce resolve.

He pulled himself away from her. 'I'm sorry. Oh, my God, Diana, I'm sorry!' He rushed from the room and stormed up the stairs. She heard a door slam, and then water running in the bathroom. She sat quite still, stunned and frightened, outraged too. When he returned he didn't look at her. He went over to the window and stood with his back to her as though he could see through the heavy brown curtains. 'I've always loved you,' he said in a strangled voice. 'Ever since that first visit to Bagleigh.'

They were words she had dreamed about, words she had longed to hear. He loved her, had always loved her. But her first heady reaction was quickly followed by a violent rush of disappointment and a fury that surprised her.

She wanted to scream and shout, ask him why in hell's name he had married Rachel? She wanted to throw something big and hard at his foolish back, but when he turned and she saw his ravaged expression, his haunted eyes, she

281

wanted instead to gather him in her arms as she would a little boy.

'I'll go,' he said. 'I must go. Now.' He walked unsteadily to the door, picked up his things from the hall stand. 'Will you be all right?'

She clenched her fists and looked him straight in the eye. 'All right? What is all right? How do you think, in God's name, that I can be all right when I've just lost what I want most in the whole world?' She tried to make her voice sound quiet and controlled, but beneath she felt a boiling cauldron of agony. 'Go then, David. Go back to your aeroplanes and your wife, and leave me alone for ever.'

He hesitated, his hand on the front door. 'I can't leave you like this,' he said. 'Diana...'

Then her delicately preserved control cracked. 'Get out, get out, you lying bastard!' she screamed. She picked up her handbag and threw it at him. 'I never want to see you again. Get out, for God's sake.'

After he had gone she gave herself up to a frenzy of weeping, making no attempt to staunch the flow of her tears for a long time. The gas fire was making the room hotter and hotter and she flung off her coat and lay on the sofa, hoping for sleep to blot out the misery. But after only a few minutes of blessed oblivion she awoke with a start and was suddenly in quite another place, a Jerusalem garden, where she heard her own voice, clear as a bell. 'No, David,' she had whispered to him on that hot still night. 'I love you, but I can't marry you. I'm going home, where I belong, to *my* homeland, to England.'

She sat up, wondering for a moment where she was. Then the details of the evening flooded back to her, and she wanted to weep all over again. She had said terrible things to him, called him a bastard, when of course he was no such thing. She was to blame for what had happened. It was her own pride and foolishness that had wrecked their lives.

She swung her feet to the ground, padded out to the kitchen and looked for something to make a cup of tea. Her head was throbbing and she swayed as she opened one cupboard door after another. At last, with an unappetising brew before her, she sat down at the kitchen table. She jabbed angrily at the blobs of dried milk floating on the top. 'I shall marry Philip,' she said aloud. 'Even if I'm adding one foolish action to another, that's what I must do. We'll become engaged before he goes to sea. With his ring on my finger, perhaps I'll be free of David Halprin for ever.'

She knew, of course, that she could hope for no such release.

CHAPTER 19

'Four ounces of butter for each of us a week,' Mary Stanmore grumbled. 'A fine way to begin 1940. That won't go very far. You know how much your father likes on his toast, and what about cooking? We'll have to try and find the old churn. We haven't made butter at Bagleigh for years.' She was rolling out pastry, one of her favourite tasks. 'Thank goodness we've a house cow.'

'I've heard that the authorities are going to investigate farms. We shan't be able to keep as much milk or as many eggs as we'd like.' Diana's voice was gloomy.

'Your father won't take kindly to being told what to do.'

'He'll have to put up with it. He'll need to get used to a lot of things he doesn't like during this war.' Just like all of us, thought Diana ruefully. She was still unsuccessful in her attempts to get work on a newspaper or with a London photographer. She had written many letters and the replies were always the same. 'You have no training, no experience. We cannot take on untrained staff during wartime.' The official position was similar. 'Stay and work on your farm. You know about farming. You're of more value there.'

For once Diana was idle. The weather prevented her from doing any but the most necessary tasks outside. Now she watched her mother making pasties. There was very little meat, but this way the lack was hardly noticed. Mary put little heaps of potato and onion on each circle of pastry and added a teaspoon of minced beef, pepper and salt and a little milk. Then she moistened the edges and folded them together, crimping them skilfully so that they were sealed. 'At least your father's pleased about you and Philip getting on so well,' she said as she worked.

Yes, Diana thought, and for a contrary moment she wished this wasn't so. Her father usually opposed everything she wanted to do, but finally she appeared to be falling in with his wishes. The feeling was unusual, giving no challenge.

She gathered up some of the utensils that her mother had finished with and carried them to the sink where she looked out of the window at the steadily falling snow. Philip had promised to come over later tonight. Perhaps he wouldn't manage it. The road across the moor might be blocked. Did she feel relief or disappointment? She poured water into the bowl for washing up and then refilled the kettle and put it to heat again. Her heart was full of confusion, a familiar state lately.

At seven o'clock she heard his knock.

'A bit of cold wouldn't keep me away,' he said shedding snowflakes everywhere as he stood on the mat and took off his overcoat. 'The road's just passable and the blizzard's eased off for the moment.'

She ushered him into the sitting room and he looked appreciatively at the huge log fire in its great granite fireplace. He stood in front of it and warmed himself and then turned to her. 'I'm in,' he said, 'the Navy. I heard today. Some training first and then straight in as a Sub Lieutenant if I'm successful in the exams. Destroyers, I hope.' His eyes gleamed with excitement.

Diana was surprised by the sudden chill she felt at hearing this news. Soon he would be gone, lost to her for months, years perhaps. She sat down on the large comfortable settee, pushing Samira's embroidery out of the way.

He glanced at it. 'That's beautiful. Where is she, by the way?'

'Putting the children to bed. She adores them all. She's a natural mother.'

'A good thing, if you ask me.' He grinned and sat down beside her. Then his tone changed. 'And you, Diana? Are you fulfilled and happy like Samira?'

She was surprised for a second time and didn't quite know how to answer. 'It depends what you mean by happy,' she managed after a few moments. 'I'm digging for victory. Everyone tells me that it's an honourable occupation.'

'Of course. We all need to eat. You're keeping the nation fed. Reserved occupation even for men, in fact.'

'Yes.' She gazed into the flames. 'You could have stayed, and so could Colin.'

'It's different for men.'

'I suppose so.' She sighed audibly. There it was again, this certainty that everything in life was determined by whether you were male or female. Pre-determined pathways, she thought, that we all have to follow. Aloud she said, 'But I'm not going to stay here very much longer either, Philip. I can't desert Samira until her baby is born, but I shall be twenty-one in March and then I'll no longer have to consult my father over what I do with my life. I shall try to start my career at long last. I get a small income from my grandmother when I come of age, as Colin does. At least I'll be slightly more independent.'

He seemed taken aback by the words and Diana was aware that she had spoken with an air of determination, even perhaps a trace of aggression. She tried to make amends and smiled at him. When she spoke again her tone was light and frivolous. 'When your ship comes in I'll be there to take photographs and report on how brave and handsome you were.'

'Were?'

'Are,' she corrected. They both laughed.

'So you're still set on becoming a photographer?'

'If possible, yes.' The logs were glowing red now and she remembered how she had imagined magical pictures in the grate when she was a little girl. The future then had seemed a golden glow, full of wonderful promises just like the enchantment of the fire.

She forced herself back to the present, to the resolution she had made to herself to marry Philip if he should ask her. Would that private declaration still hold?

She added another log and the flames curled and flickered, giving comfort, a sense of security. Those were the things that marriage would give, weren't they, and a bulwark between herself and David? That's the truth of it, she thought. I need a defence against my feelings for David Halprin. Can I possibly marry Philip on those grounds? And what about this career I want? Would he be willing to put up with that?

287

Philip too was quiet. He was looking steadily at her. 'You'll make it eventually if you're determined enough. I wish you'd stay here though. I prefer to think of you safe and contented like Samira. Selfish, I suppose.'

She shook her head. 'Not really. I can understand how you feel perhaps, but I'm not like Samira, not one bit. I want to be a war correspondent.'

She was aware that this sounded more ambitious than just a photographer, but if Philip was taken aback he showed no sign. He settled himself more comfortably before replying and didn't automatically trample on her dreams like most other people did.

'That's a pretty enterprising idea,' he said, 'and not impossible. I read a couple of reports today in the newspaper, both by women.'

She looked up at him, surprised and full of gratitude. Here at last was a man who didn't underestimate her; neither did he expect her to subjugate all her own wishes to others. She felt a surge of affection for him, and at the same time a sense of unworthiness. 'Thank you, Philip,' she said quietly. 'Not many people believe I could do it.'

'I'll be proud of you when you're famous.' He lit a cigarette and drew the smoke slowly into his lungs before he continued, changing the subject abruptly. 'Any more news of Colin?'

'He's been selected for pilot training. They send them to America for it now. Did you know that?'

'Yes. I heard something about it.'

288

'Colin wants to fly fighters. His friend too.'

'That Jewish fellow, d'you mean?'

'Yes. David Halprin. For some reason they hope it won't be bombers.'

'We're going to need all the fliers we can get soon, both kinds.'

They were silent again for a time, faces glowing with the heat from the fire, but in spite of Philip's presence so close to her and her great liking for him, Diana's heart was suddenly full of David again. Whenever she thought of flying she thought of David. She'd had one short letter from him since that disastrous London meeting and had been both amazed and hurt by its tone. He'd apologised! It was I who was the guilty one, I who said such terrible things, she affirmed angrily to herself. The words had gone round and round in her head and remorse for her clumsy handling of their relationship was an ever present source of bitterness.

And while it was only David's face she could see, David's voice she wanted to hear, Philip suddenly took both her hands in his and pulled her towards him.

'Diana, will you marry me?'

She hesitated, gently released her hands and brushed some imaginary strands of hair out of her eyes. Although she had expected this she hadn't planned her answer, and now was full of guilt. Was it really fair to marry this good man on the rebound from David? The perpetual question!

'I don't think I should, Philip,' she whispered.

'You're such a good person and I'd be a terrible disappointment to you.'

He looked at her with a tenderness she hadn't seen in him before. 'Never! You could never be a disappointment.'

She knew that she must be honest with him. 'But I'm not really in love with you.'

'I know that. But my love is enough for both of us. I'm content to wait. You like me, don't you?'

She was near to tears. 'Oh Philip. Of course I like you. You're about the best person I've ever met.'

'Then don't worry. Marry me. Love will grow.'

Diana had heard those words before. Her mother had said them, and so had Samira and Samira's mother. Perhaps they were right. Perhaps her earlier decision to marry Philip if he should ask her had been wise. She gave herself into his arms, and was surprised by her own enthusiastic response to his embrace. 'Yes, I'll marry you,' she whispered.

They went to Exeter and bought a ring, a splendid three diamond affair, and there was a big party to celebrate. Throughout it all and during the following weeks Diana felt a sense of otherness, as if she was floating on some unreal cloud, as if all this was happening to someone else and she was a slightly bemused spectator. Then he was gone, and a trifle restlessly she settled down again at Bagleigh to wait for the time of her freedom. When she was twenty-one, when Samira's second child was born, when they could get another land-girl, then she would go to London.

Meanwhile Samira needed as much help as possible. This pregnancy was not as easy as the first one and Diana found herself frequently wondering why her brother had shown so little restraint, for Matthew was only thirteen months old. There were ways of preventing pregnancy now. She was quite determined that after she married Philip there would be no babies until she was ready, until her career was firmly in place. She resolved to make her sister-in-law wise about such matters as soon as the opportunity offered.

But Samira was completely appalled at the suggestion. 'It's just the way of men,' she said when Diana implied that Colin could have been more considerate. 'And I could never ask him to...' She blushed and turned away. 'It's women's work to bear children, the more the better. What is the value of a wife who refuses to do her duty?'

They were alone in the kitchen, a favourite place lately. Diana sighed and looked up from the bowl of potatoes she was peeling. 'Oh, Samira! I'd hoped you had learned to be more independent and free since you came to England.'

'But I want to please Colin more than anything, and this is the only way I can do that.' She was sitting in the rocking chair where she had been sternly directed by her mother-in-law, and the creaking of the runners as she rocked backwards and forwards was slightly irritating to Diana.

'Is that really what you believe?'

'Yes. We've so little in common, Colin and me, that to bear children is the only way I know of pleasing him.'

Diana shook her head and wondered how this marriage would work after the war when Colin was home for good. In spite of everything that had happened to her Samira was still a product of her upbringing and tradition. Could she and Colin ever be truly happy? Diana loved her brother and Samira. She longed for their contentment as much as she wished it for Philip and herself.

With the passing of the long bitter winter a new optimism seemed to grip everyone at Bagleigh. The news of May 10th particularly pleased James Stanmore and he boomed his pleasure the following morning when they were all gathered for breakfast. 'We've got a splendid chap at the helm now,' he said. 'With Churchill to direct things, the war is as good as won. A real fighter.'

The frightening fate of the allied armies in France seemed totally to have escaped him for the moment.

The following week Samira's daughter was born, a little girl whom she promptly named Kaffa Mary. 'After our two mothers,' she told Diana proudly. 'Mine and yours. But I should like her to be called Kaffa. It's not too foreign-sounding is it?'

'It's lovely,' Diana said. 'And Colin will be home soon to see his baby daughter.'

A shadow passed over Samira's face. 'I wanted a son for him though. Do you think he'll be angry?'

Diana wanted to shake her. 'Angry? What are you talking about? Kaffa is beautiful. He'll be thrilled to bits.' But then suddenly a chilling thought swept over her. Perhaps Colin would have preferred a son, for Matthew was not...she banished the traitorous thought as quickly as it had come. 'Just you wait,' she finished. 'If you think he won't be pleased, you're in for the surprise of your life.'

Diana normally loved the month of May. In other years she had used the sunshine and the evenings with their long shadows for some of her more spectacular photography. But this year there was too much to do, and only a week after the birth of little Kaffa came news that brought a chill to everyone and banished all the previous optimism. They were listening to the wireless, a frequent occupation lately, when the mellow tones of the announcer confirmed that the Germans had advanced through Belgium and France surrounding the French First Army, the Belgian Army and the British Expeditionary Force. Thousands of men were trapped on the beach at a small seaside town called Dunkirk.

Sudden horror gripped them all. The reality of war arrived in their midst at that very moment like an explosion. Everything that had gone before was almost a game compared to this.

Mary was the first to speak. 'The Jerries are getting too near,' she said. 'I'm frightened.'

'They'll never cross the Channel,' said James. He stretched himself to his full height and looked as though he was prepared to defend all his family personally.

Diana thought he resembled the cockerel in the yard, but felt a sudden surge of affection for him.

'Like I said a few weeks ago,' he went on, 'with Churchill leading us we'll win in the end. And we'll get our lads home from France, God willing. You mark my words.'

Mary shook her head slowly. 'I hope you're right, my dear. I just hope you're right or Heaven help all of us.'

Diana was working in the field that bordered the lane later that afternoon. The hedge was misted with bluebells and a multitude of butterflies flitted around her as she worked. It was hard to believe that there was so much suffering and cruelty in such a beautiful world.

The cheerful sound of the postman's bicycle bell broke into her rather gloomy thoughts and she looked up, glad to stand straight for a few moments. He was bringing a second delivery. He propped his bicycle against the hedge. 'One for you, miss,' he called. 'Do you want it now or shall I take it on up to the house?'

She wiped her hands on her old trousers and went to the gate. 'I'll take it. Save you going any further if it's the only one.'

'From the Holy Land,' he said as he handed

it to her. His voice was full of respect. ' 'Tis a place I've always wanted to see.'

She smiled at him and looked down at the envelope. It was addressed to her in Harriet's writing and she pushed it into her jacket pocket. 'Nearly time for my tea-break,' she said. 'Thanks for bringing it.'

She decided to take the flask and biscuits that she had brought from the house and go down to her favourite place by the old clapper bridge and read it there. She always tried to make the receiving and reading of letters something special. It was a small ritual that she enjoyed. There were sometimes pages from Philip, neatly written and often censored. Colin wrote too from time to time, but for some reason that she couldn't understand Harriet's letters were special. They breathed a sense of freedom and space, a glimpse of more carefree times and what might have been.

She called to Rollo who was sleeping in a sunny spot at the foot of the hedge. 'Lazybones. We're going for a walk.'

He leapt up and bounded ahead. It was a perfect day. The hillsides were flaming with yellow gorse, the cuckoo was calling his wicked delight to the world, and in every remote hollow beneath the trees there were great white swathes of wild parsley contrasting with the bluebells that she had already noticed in the hedge. When she reached the ancient bridge over the stream she sat down on a large flat piece of granite and took the letter from her pocket. Rollo frisked into the water, came out and shook himself all over her, and then plunged in again.

Usually she laughed at him and threw a stone or stick into the deepest part so that he needed to swim to retrieve it. But today she ignored him as she read Harriet's words. Her aunt wrote that Rachel had given birth to a daughter at the beginning of May.

So David had his Jewish child at last! Diana held the pages in her hand and read them over and over, and instead of the bluebells and the gentle river at her feet she saw in her mind the scrubby hills of Palestine, the kibbutz and its little houses, and imagined Rachel's face full of pride looking down at her baby. Diana knew that David would have wanted a son, a little sabre to fight for Israel. But a girl would be better than nothing, a girl to breed future citizens of the Promised Land.

This child was the reason she hadn't been able to marry the man she loved. She would never be able to produce Jewish children because she was a goy, and the race of the mother determined the race of the child in Jewish law. She had thought about this thousands of times. Because she so much wished it to be otherwise she considered it a stupid tradition, an unfair and preposterous law. She thought of it again now, and then laughed bitterly. It was one of the few ways in which a woman was important, and it had worked against her. She clenched her fists angrily and almost threw the letter into the swirling water.

Rollo barked, sensing that he was soon to

have something to catch. He was watching her, his whole body poised and expectant. Drops of water were glistening on his coat and falling from his long tail which swept majestically from side to side.

She looked at him and jumped to her feet. 'No, you can't have this.' She smoothed the pages out, refolded them and put them back into her pocket for she always gave Harriet's letters to her parents to read. 'That's that then.'

Rollo barked and wagged his tail harder.

'It's all finished,' she told him. She looked round for a stick and threw it into the water, and after he had retrieved it, called him to follow her as she took the path up on to the top of the tor. Her work could wait, she decided. She needed to think. It was a steep climb but she walked swiftly and once there she stood and looked down at Bagleigh, almost hidden now beneath its canopy of trees in fresh new leaf. Then she looked in the other direction, over the desolate wastes of the moor. There was no other human soul to be seen and in a contrary way she was suddenly exultant. 'This is my place, mine and Philip's, she said aloud. 'I shall grow to love him deeply, and one day we shall have babies, English babies. I made the right decision. I could never have made David happy, nor he me. Palestine is no part of my life nor ever will be.'

With this thought firmly in place she strode purposefully down the well-known track, pulled off her shoes at the door of the house and padded into the sitting room where her mother was doing some mending. She handed the letter to her.

'I suppose she'll be coming to England then,' Mary said when she had read it. 'David will want to see his baby. He and Colin have finished their training. They're fully fledged pilots.'

Diana was nonplussed, not sure how to react. Her feelings and resolutions, carefully marshalled just a few minutes before, fell in tatters.

'You've heard from them?' she managed.

'Yes. A telephone call from London just since lunch. Colin is coming here at the end of the week. They've both got their wings.'

Samira carried baby Kaffa into the room. 'And they've both got new babies as well,' she said happily. 'So it'll be a double celebration.'

'How will David's wife get here, I wonder?' Mary sounded worried. 'Now that France has fallen, she can't come that way.' She had picked up her mending again and appeared to be concentrating on it. 'I suppose she might get a place on a military flight,' she said thoughtfully. 'There must be some, and with her husband being in the RAF I should think they'd manage it somehow. Why didn't she come over with him?'

'The child had to be born in Palestine.' Diana couldn't prevent an edge of bitterness from slipping into her voice. 'That's very important to both of them.'

'By the way,' Mary said, 'what do you think

298

of Harriet's suggestion?'

'What suggestion?' Diana was washing her hands at the sink. She turned to her mother.

'About this friend of hers, Thelma something.'

'What are you talking about?'

'The PS on the letter,' Mary explained patiently. 'Don't tell me you missed it. She has a friend in London who might help you.'

Diana finished drying her hands and eagerly took up the letter again. The postscript was scrawled on the back of the last page and in her distress over the rest of the letter she had indeed missed it.

I have a friend in London who might be a useful contact for you. Thelma Barrington-Smith is an old school friend of mine, came to Bagleigh once as a matter of fact when we were young. Your father might remember her. She's a photographer. I've written telling her about you.

Diana stared at the lines as if in a trance, then she came to life and did a pirouette round the kitchen, hugging her mother on the way. 'Thanks, Ma,' she said. 'You're a wonder. Just think, I might have missed the most important news of my life!'

James Stanmore read the letter later that day and snorted with disgust when he reached the postscript. 'Yes, I remember Thelma whats-it,' he said. Then grinned suddenly. 'Good-looking woman once.'

The remark was so unlike her father that

299

Diana blinked in surprise. But she was filled with hope. The day which had seemed so black in spite of the sunshine was transformed.

When Colin arrived at Bagleigh at the beginning of June Samira felt a mixture of excitement and apprehension. She had made herself a new dress from some material bought in the market at Newton Abbot, and had been persuaded by Diana to experiment with lipstick and powder.

'I look like...what's the right word? A tart,' she said as she surveyed herself in the mirror.

Diana laughed at her. 'You look modern and just right—and here he is, I think. He's early. Mother and Father aren't back from Exeter yet.'

They both heard the car on the gravel drive outside and rushed to the window. A small Austin Seven pulled up and Colin sprang from it.

'Yes, it is him,' Diana said. 'Go on then. Go straight down and greet him, you silly girl. I'll fetch Matthew. It's you he wants to see before the rest of us.' She pushed her sister-in-law from the room, and once Samira was at the top of the stairs her reluctance disappeared and she ran down to the hall and into his arms.

He crushed her to him and then held her back and looked at her, devouring her with his eyes. 'You're beautiful, Samira,' he said. 'I'd almost forgotten how beautiful. And where's Matthew and my new daughter?'

'Here.' Diana had roused the little boy from

his lunch-time nap, and held his hand tightly in hers, reassuring him. 'Go and give your daddy a kiss,' she said. But he hid behind her skirt and refused to go.

'Hi, Sis,' Colin said to her, and then directed his whole attention to his son. He groped in his pocket. Bringing out a bright red wooden aeroplane, he held it out. 'For Matthew,' he said.

Diana held her breath, but the child released her hand, looked at the toy and slowly toddled forward. Then, as he took it, Colin knelt down and gathered him up in his arms. 'That's my swell guy,' he said. 'And where's your new sister?'

'Asleep in her pram.' Samira's face was full of happiness.

'Then she'd better wake up and see if she approves of her daddy. Lead the way, Mummy.' He put Matthew on his feet and took Samira's hand and the three of them went out into the garden.

For a moment Diana felt a pang of jealousy, but it was quickly banished. They would be all right, she was sure of it. And herself? She wasn't needed here any more. They had just had word that another land-girl was available and Samira was well again. Diana had waited until past her birthday, allowing the needs of her family to come first, but now was the time to think of herself.

'London here I come,' she said aloud as she went into the kitchen to prepare their next meal.

CHAPTER 20

Diana packed her suitcase carefully, discarding everything she considered irrelevant to her life in London. Her determination to travel with as little luggage as possible increased her sense of adventure. Her camera and a portfolio of all her best photographs were the most important items. They were her passports to the new life she hoped to lead.

Her clothes had caused her some trouble. She wanted to appear efficient and capable, but not dowdy. In the end she decided to travel in her best suit. She had bought it to celebrate her engagement to Philip and he had helped in the choosing. It was made in a soft wool material patterned in deep blue checks and with fashionable padded shoulders and a neat straight skirt. She put away the frilly blouse that had complemented it on that weekend and wore a white shirt instead with a tie borrowed from Colin. A small hat shorn of all ornament completed the outfit.

Her brother was to drive her to the station on his way back to his Squadron.

'You look very smart,' he said as he dumped her luggage on the back seat.

'Thank you.' Diana climbed quickly into the vehicle, not wanting to intrude on his goodbyes to Samira. She was standing at the door, baby

Kaffa in her arms and Matthew clinging to her skirt. Their one remaining evacuee was there too and Diana felt a little sorry for him. She'd become fond of Dougie, the little cockney boy who apparently had no home to return to now. Ben and Will had speedily followed George back to the comfortable squalor of their London homes. She waved to Dougie and he blew her a kiss.

Colin slammed the car door and went back to them and Diana looked away towards the rise of the hill at the end of the drive and the rocks that crowned its summit. For a moment her regrets of leaving were mainly for Rollo. She'd shared so many walks up there with him. She knew that he was sitting obediently beside Samira, but she was aware too of his reproachful eyes watching her. She'd kissed him on his wet nose and told him that he couldn't come, that he was to behave and that she'd be back one day and take him out again.

'Just as if he could understand every word you say,' her mother had remarked.

'He can,' she had replied indignantly.

When Colin eventually came back to the car she turned towards the house again. 'Look after Rollo for me, won't you?' she called to Samira.

Colin laughed at her. 'Trust my sister to think of her dog before anything else. You take after Aunt Harriet.'

He started the car with some effort and they were eventually on the narrow track that led away from Bagleigh, away from the moor. He was concentrating all his attention on the road, for sheep and ponies frequently wandered across it. 'A bit like Khanhaven,' he said.

'Do you really think that I take after Aunt Harriet?'

'Of course.'

'I think I'm flattered.'

'You should be. She's one of my favourite people.'

Thoughts of Harriet sent Diana's mind winging back to Palestine.

'Will you ever be able to go back there now that you're married to Samira?' she asked.

'Back where?'

'Palestine, of course. You're not concentrating on our conversation.'

'Sorry, Sis, but your butterfly mind does skip about a bit. Why do you ask that now?'

'You mentioned Aunt Harriet and that made me think of Khanhaven and El Admah and Jazi. And I definitely have not got a butterfly mind!'

'Sorry again. No, perhaps you haven't. You're very superior to most females.' He turned briefly to grin at her. 'But whether or not I'll ever go back to Palestine is in the lap of the gods. The war is bound to change things a lot. Samira will want to see her mother one day, though, and we did promise to take our children.'

'Will it ever be safe?'

Colin shrugged his shoulders. 'From what point of view?'

'I'm not sure. Samira's brothers, the unrest. Aunt Harriet and I saw the horrors of that bomb blast in Haifa, remember.'

'Yes, you had a narrow escape. No one knows what will happen after the war. Let's get Hitler dealt with first.'

'What does David think about it?' She couldn't help the question, for whenever she thought of Palestine she thought of David.

'Dying to get back, of course.'

'Of course,' Diana repeated bleakly. 'It's his only reason for living.'

'Do I detect a trace of bitterness?'

'I suppose so. I try to reject it.'

'You're not still in love with him, are you?'

'No.' Her reply was too fierce, too quick.

The road down from the moor was steep and Diana felt her ears popping slightly with the rapid descent. She wasn't at all ready for Colin's next question.

'Why did you promise to marry Philip?'

She lit a cigarette and drew on it slowly. Ever since he'd gone back to his ship she had been asking herself this, not with regret, but with curiosity. There had to be some rational answer and she tried now to give it, both for her own satisfaction and for Colin's. 'I'm very fond of him,' she said a trifle over-enthusiastically. 'I respect him and like him a lot. I enjoy his letters and write vast amounts to him. We get on well, have plenty of things in common. I once told Samira that a husband should also be a friend. Philip and I are very good friends. We enjoy each other's company enormously.'

'Not bad,' Colin commented. 'Very important

in fact. I wish Samira and I could say the same.'

Diana was alarmed. 'You love her though?'

'Yes. A lot.'

She was silent for a long time after that, pondering what indeed was the best basis for marriage, any marriage—a great flaming romantic passion that wouldn't let you rest, or a comfortable friendship.

'Marriage is supposed to give women status,' she said, 'but I hope I'll achieve that for myself.'

Colin obviously found this amusing. He laughed aloud. 'And if you don't manage it, then as a naval officer's wife you'll get a position in life and a generous marriage allowance! So it's a kind of safety net.'

'Not at all.' She was indignant. 'And I may not marry him until after the war anyway. I'm independent now even if I don't earn very much. I get my small yearly legacy from Grandmother's estate, as you do. I have no need of a husband at the moment.'

'Sorry, Dido. I'm only taking the mickey. I read somewhere though that to have a husband is to occupy an island of permanence in an uncertain world.' He was suddenly serious. 'I remember the words exactly because they impressed me and I think they're true for men as well as women. Having a wife, I mean.'

Diana was surprised by the sentiment. 'Perhaps,' she admitted, but silently considered that an island of permanence was the last thing she wanted just now when life was full of unknown promise and potential. 'I don't want to tie myself down just yet,' she said. 'Life's too uncertain.'

'Isn't it better to be Mrs than Miss though? Doesn't it give you more status?'

She considered carefully before answering. 'Unfortunately, yes,' she said at last. 'I wish we had some title that women could use that wouldn't identify us. A man isn't immediately labelled married or not, is he?'

'A wife is a possession though.'

Colin's tone had changed again and she knew that he was teasing once more.

'I'll only refrain from thumping you because you're driving,' she said, glad that the bantering was back. She didn't want to be serious today.

They passed through little straggling Bovey Tracey. 'The gateway to the moor,' she said, glancing at its white-painted cottages and small shops. 'I wouldn't mind living here when I'm old and can't manage to walk far.' She remembered saying the same thing about Haifa, or was it Jaffa? She couldn't remember which. 'There are so many lovely places in the world,' she added reflectively.

'Don't think about being old,' Colin ordered. 'It's stupid with a war on. Tell me about your immediate plans instead. You haven't talked about them too much.'

'You've been too busy to listen.' There was slight reproach in her tone for during her brother's brief visits to Bagleigh lately they had found little opportunity to talk together.

Their close friendship had been slightly dented by his marriage.

'Well, it'll take quite a while to get to Exeter in this old jalopy, so get cracking. I'm all ears.'

Diana relaxed and sat back in the uncomfortable little bucket seat. 'You know that I'm going to stay with a friend of Aunt Harriet's, a Mrs Barrington-Smith, a widow?' she began.

'Actually she came to Bagleigh years ago when she and Aunt were girls. Father remembered her. She's a photojournalist, I believe, knows some of the editorial staff of *Picture Post* apparently. I'm hoping to show my pictures to her and...who knows where that might lead?'

'And if it doesn't?'

'Don't be so pessimistic. I shall stay in London for a bit. She has a spare room that she's prepared to rent to me. I shall have to do some war work eventually, but I want to keep all my options open.'

'You could be a driver and take your camera along with you. That's probably the best way of getting to where the action is.'

'As a last resort perhaps.'

'What does Philip think of all your flighty plans?'

'He'd rather I stayed at home, of course. He admires Samira, wants me to be like her, but I told him that I'm not at all that kind of person.'

'And he's happy about it?'

'Not really, but he accepts that I'm free to do what I like at the moment.' Diana wanted to change the subject. She'd had enough of Colin's probing. She turned her thoughts to him instead. 'How about you?' she asked. 'I don't know much about your life lately either. Except that you were jolly lucky to get posted to a squadron in Exeter. How do you like Hurricanes by the way? You always yearned for Spits?'

'They're OK. Different, but pretty good on the whole.'

'And David didn't get fighters at all, did he?' She couldn't help mentioning that name again.

'No. Bomber Command. Wellingtons, great bumbling things, but knowing David he'll get the best out of them.'

'And his squadron's in Scotland.'

'That's right. A long way away!'

Diana turned to look at her brother. Was there a trace of satisfaction in his voice, a warning perhaps, or was she just imagining it? 'I suppose Rachel will go up there too,' she said glumly.

'Stop torturing yourself, Dido. Don't think of him any more, or her. You've got yourself nearly hitched. You're going to be happy. Philip is a capital chap, a comfortable sort of guy, the exact opposite of David.'

'I know and I'm not torturing myself, honestly. I'm only curious. I *have* forgotten about him.'

Colin grinned. 'Liar.'

The train from Exeter was crowded and hot. Posters everywhere demanded 'Is Your Journey

Really Necessary' and by the time Diana reached Paddington she was beginning to wonder if hers was. The wild tors of Dartmoor suddenly seemed very desirable. But she thought of the precious photographs in her suitcase, especially those of Palestine, straightened her back and strode out towards the underground.

The house was one of a terrace of five or six. Diana stood and looked up at its three stories in something of a daze. Number ten alone had plants in tubs decorating the tiny front garden and there were steps leading to the door. The three identical windows, one above the other, stared down on the road completely unsheltered by the net curtains that protected all the others in the row. Eventually, summoning all her courage, she rang the bell and then stepped back and waited.

A dog barked, purposeful footsteps sounded from inside, the door was flung open and Diana felt herself being examined critically by a tall middle-aged woman wearing slacks and a man's shirt tightly belted round a slim waist. She immediately felt over-dressed in her smart suit.

'You must be Harriet's niece.'

The words were flung at her and she nodded, put her suitcase down and held out her hand. 'Yes, Diana Stanmore.'

Thelma Barrington-Smith's grip was firm and hearty. 'Been expecting you this last hour,' she said in a brisk cheerful voice, 'but trains aren't what they were, always late nowadays. Come in, child. No point in standing out there.'

She turned and led the way inside and then

paused to look at Diana again. 'Yes, I can see the likeness. You're supposed to take after Harriet, I'm told. Well, I hope so. Admirable woman. My best friend for umpteen years, y'know. She says in her last letter that you'd like to live here for a bit, keen on photography?'

The statements and questions were fired one after the other like bullets giving Diana scarcely a moment to reply. She followed her hostess through a small entrance hall and then up two flights of stairs.

'Here's your room.'

Diana looked through the open door at a pleasant attic room with sloping roof and white-painted furniture. The bed was covered with a colourfully woven bedspread that reminded her immediately of Palestine.

'It's lovely,' she murmured. 'I'm very grateful.'

'No need for gratitude. I'm glad to have company. Sure we'll get on as you come with Harriet's recommendation. If Jerry starts to bomb us, of course, it won't be safe up here, but then nowhere will. We'll cross that bridge when we come to it. There's a Morrison shelter downstairs just in case. We'll cram into that if the sirens ever do go, Bounder included of course, so we'll have to share his fleas!' She laughed loudly and bent to pat the shaggy little dog who had followed them up. 'Like dogs, do you? Harriet said you were good with animals so I presume you do?'

'Oh, yes,' Diana managed. 'I've a dog at home, and lots of animal photographs.'

'I've been to Bagleigh, y'know, years ago

311

when your aunt and I were girls. Met your father, of course. A young blood he was then.' She gave a deep throaty laugh and changed the subject. 'Get unpacked and washed and come down when you're ready and we'll talk. Bathroom down a flight. Temperamental geyser if you want hot water. I've a report to finish. See you later.'

When she was alone Diana collapsed on to the bed and chuckled to herself. Her father, a young blood! The idea was incongruous. And this was Thelma Barrington-Smith, her aunt's schoolgirl friend, the woman whom her father said had been a good looker.

It was all quite amazing, but exciting too. Diana felt that she was at last at the beginning of a new life, a completely fresh beginning that had nothing whatsoever to do with Devon, with being engaged to be married, with farming and the countryside, even with David. She stood up again and struggled with the leather straps around her suitcase. Then she quickly unpacked her few clothes, found her way to the bathroom, washed in cold water and eventually presented herself at the open door on the ground floor where she could see Bounder standing guard. He growled.

Thelma Barrington-Smith looked, on closer scrutiny, to be not so formidable as Diana had at first supposed, and yes, she might once have been a good looker, was still quite handsome in fact.

She jumped up from her desk, scolded the grumbling dog, and led the way into a small

312

sitting room at the back of the house. It had french doors leading to a pleasant enclosed garden and she flung these open and indicated two deck chairs set at the edge of the lawn.

'Time for a break,' she said. 'Sit down and make friends with my hound and I'll get some tea.'

The tranquillity took Diana by surprise. Birds were singing, and the flower border beyond the lawn was a rainbow of lupins. A dragon-fly hovered above a small pond. Sweet peas had been trained on a trellis close by and she closed her eyes for a moment and leaned back, breathing in the scent of them, so evocative of summers at Bagleigh. The sun shone full on her face and she was filled with a sense of peace and wondered for a magical second if she could be imagining all of this. Or perhaps it was the war that was just a bad dream and she would wake up to find...

'Don't fall asleep, dear child. No time for that in wartime.'

Diana came back to reality with a jolt and struggled to sit upright in the relaxing canvas chair. 'Sorry, Mrs Barrington-Smith,' she said. 'It's so lovely here though.'

'Yes. I'm keen on the garden when I get the time.' She placed two mugs of steaming tea on the top of a low wall beside the chairs and sat down. 'Enough of the Barrington-Smith, by the way. Thelma please. And now tell me all about yourself and what you want to do and how you think I can help you.'

Diana gulped down a mouthful of the scalding

313

liquid before she could bring herself to reply. 'I've always been interested in photography and I write a bit too. I should like to be a war correspondent eventually, or get into photojournalism. Aunt Harriet said you were in that sort of thing.'

Thelma laughed. 'Did she indeed? It's a long time since Harriet and I saw each other. I make my living from portraits mostly. Very mundane, but they pay. I need an assistant. You can work for me if you like and I'll teach you all I know. You'll learn more that way than you would at one of those Polytechnic places, and if you want to do something more ambitious later on I'll be right behind you. Hard work mind. Hope you don't mind hard work?'

'No, of course I don't. I should love to work for you.'

Although taking portraits wasn't exactly the exciting beginning she had envisaged, Diana knew that this would be a start, and hoped that she sounded suitably appreciative.

'There's plenty of opportunity now for portraits, y'know. Rushed off my feet in fact. Mostly servicemen, poor devils, wanting a last photograph. All that sort of thing.'

'I thought you worked for *Picture Post?*' Diana hoped that Harriet's assessment of her friend hadn't been over-enthusiastic.

'Freelance, dear child, newspapers too. I do anything and everything. Portraits are the bread and butter.'

This sounded better. 'I have a lot of photographs of Palestine,' Diana said.

'I'll look at them. We might find something saleable. Jews trying to get out of Europe and all that, rather topical just now.'

Her staccato style of speaking was amusing and seemed to demand some suitable response. 'My sister-in-law is a Palestinian Arab,' Diana said hopefully, 'and my brother's friend is a Zionist Jew.'

'Well now, that sounds like an interesting scenario.'

She felt she had managed to impress her hostess at last. But how can I look at the pictures of the people I love most in the world and think about selling them? she asked herself. How can I make money and a career out of David's dreams and Samira's heartbreak?

'Might help a few refugees,' Thelma said providentially, answering Diana's unspoken question. 'Lots of 'em are on the move just now. We need to do a bit of propaganda, get people kindly disposed towards Hitler's cast-offs. Nasty little man! That's what wartime photography mostly is, propaganda of some sort or another. Very important. Wars are won and lives saved through the right kind of propaganda.' She jumped up purposefully. 'No time like the present. Fetch your albums down and we'll see what we can do.'

As Diana ran up the stairs, her remaining doubts completely vanished and she felt supremely optimistic. Even if everything wasn't quite what she had imagined, she was on the path to her chosen career at last. Untold possibilities lay ahead, all of them better than growing vegetables and looking after a few sheep. Inspired and taught by Thelma Barrington-Smith, she would wield her camera and her pen in a great array of noble causes.

'You can begin by helping me with a commission for a women's page item,' Thelma said late that same evening. 'They want pictures of a market stall, would you believe, vegetables ready for sale and so on, and captions about women's work in wartime. Ludicrous, but it pays the bills. We have to get there very early. Go to bed now. I'll give you a call at five tomorrow. All I shall want you to do is hold things so don't worry.'

Diana laughed at herself a little ruefully as she climbed into bed. So much for her high ideals and great expectations! She was just to hold things, help to photograph vegetables on a stall and write about women doing menial jobs. But it was a beginning. She would watch and learn.

In the darkness of the London black-out she eventually fell asleep only to dream of David and the kibbutz pool, the sound of cicadas, the splashing of water and children laughing.

CHAPTER 21

'Leave the children with Mother, Samira. I want to talk to you.' There was an unusual trace of impatience in Colin's voice and Samira looked at him in sudden alarm.

'Talk? What about?'

'I'll tell you later, and please don't start making excuses. Just get some sensible shoes on and we'll go for a walk.'

Unlike Diana, Samira didn't enjoy walking on the moor. It always seemed to threaten. Those great empty wastes stretching away into the distance gave her a sense of loneliness and awe, feelings she had never experienced in the hot and arid hills of Palestine. When she rode Major or Merryon it was slightly different, but on foot even the presence of Rollo was only of limited comfort.

'It's nearly time for Kaffa's feed,' she said.

'For God's sake, Samira, put me first for once. I've only a couple of hours before I have to leave. I want to talk to you. Seriously.' He stressed the last words.

Hearing the urgent tone of his voice, her years of submission to father and brothers overcame her reluctance. She hurried from the room, put on the tough and ugly shoes that Colin had insisted upon buying for her when they first came to Devon, and told Mary that she was going out.

Ten minutes later they were on the track that led away from the house and up towards the tor. Samira could see these frightening rocks from her bedroom and when the moon was behind them and the wind tearing round the house they looked like the outline of a great beast, a menacing hound that sent shivers of superstitious fear through her body.

Colin was striding out in front of her making

317

straight for the top. Then suddenly he stopped and turned to her, held out his hand and took hers and she was comforted a little, but there was still a tension about him that she failed to understand. The weather was strangely still, unusual for Dartmoor, for however warm and sunny it might be in the valley there was usually a cold wind higher up. But today was lovely. The sun was warm and the heather and gorse blooming together now made a brilliant kaleidoscope of colour that belied her fears. But when they reached the top Colin paused and looked down at Bagleigh. There was a good view of it from here. The house stood foursquare and solid amongst its trees, and the fields around it were lush and green.

It was some time before he spoke and then his voice was full of emotion. 'I want to talk to you about Bagleigh,' he said. 'I'm flying on lots of ops as you know. Pilots sometimes don't come back, Samira.'

She pulled her hand from his and flung her arms round him. 'Don't say it,' she cried. 'Please don't even think it or you'll make it happen.'

He kissed her and then gently disentangled himself. He sat down on the grass and pulled her down beside him. He didn't know how to bring himself to say what was on his mind, to speak about the problem that had been gnawing away insidiously ever since Matthew's birth. At last he forced out the words. 'I want Bagleigh to go to a Stanmore,' he said slowly. 'You understand what I'm trying to say, don't you?'

A wave of dismay swept through her. So the shocking nightmare was happening in reality. The terrible truth against which she had shut her mind was about to assume its destroying power in all their lives. She couldn't speak.

Colin groped for words. He loved Matthew and longed to forget that he wasn't his own flesh and blood. He had even contemplated saying nothing, allowing events to take their course, but that was passing the responsibility to someone else, to Diana most likely. He could imagine the complications and heartbreak that would occur if he should be killed and had not revealed this appalling secret, or at least made arrangements of some sort.

'I love Matthew,' he said at last. 'You know that I love him, Samira, just as if he were my own son.'

'Then why must you denounce him?'

'My dear girl I'm not denouncing him. Nothing that has happened in the past is either your fault or his, and if it wasn't for Bagleigh no one should ever know.'

Samira realised she had used the wrong word but it seemed, in her distress, almost as apt. 'Disowning him then. That's what you're doing. You are going to disown Matthew publicly and bring disaster to all of us. Is that what you want? Is a house more important to you than our son?'

Colin sighed. How could he possibly expect her to understand? 'The house and land have been in our family for generations,' he tried to explain. 'They're entailed to go only to a male heir. It wouldn't be fair to Diana. If she had a son and we hadn't then it should by rights go to him.'

'But she has no son, and isn't likely to have for a long time, and we'll have other sons, lots and lots, like my mother did.'

Colin shook his head and continued to stare ahead down into the valley where he could just see Major cropping the turf in the field beside the house. 'The problem would still be there though, don't you see? If we had another boy then everything should be his. It should never go to Eshref's son.' He paused for a moment on that repugnant name and closed his eyes in disgust at what he was saying, but forced himself to go on relentlessly. 'Matthew has no title to Bagleigh at all.'

He knew that he was being heartlessly cruel, but his own mortality had been brought home forcibly to him lately. The war in the air was increasing in ferocity. Just a couple of days ago his squadron had been defending a convoy at sea from a fierce Luftwaffe attack and two of his closest friends had not come back. The RAF had lost nineteen aircraft in that one operation. It had shocked him and he knew that he had to set things right at home while he could. It was the honourable thing to do, however distasteful.

But he couldn't say all this to Samira. Instead he said, 'I may be moved to Dorset soon. Once I'm there I shall not be able to come here so often. I want to get things settled.'

In spite of the warm day Samira felt cold. She

shivered and looked down at Bagleigh, hating it. There seemed to be nothing that she could say or do that would stave off the impending doom, the end of all her hopes. Her mother-in-law would despise her and James Stanmore would be completely outraged. Their relationship was just beginning to warm a little. If he found out about Eshref all that would change. He would hate her, might even kill her. Certainly in her own country something as dreadful as this would merit total dishonour and probably even death.

'If you must tell, then I shall have to go away,' she whispered. 'They won't want me here. I shall be too frightened to stay.'

'Frightened?'

'Of course. Do you remember what my brothers wanted to do to me when they thought that I had been defiled?'

'But this is England.'

She shook her head. 'It may be, but that makes no difference to me. I shall go away. I don't know how or where, but I shall go Colin. I should like to go to Harriet.'

'Impossible,' he said irritably and without thinking. 'Don't you know there's a war on?'

Samira seldom felt angry but now she was filled with despair and anger in equal measure. 'Of course I know there's a war on, but I shall still go, somehow.'

In his distress Colin felt his anger rising to match hers. 'For God's sake, stop being so stupid! And I won't have you taking our children away anywhere dangerous, do you hear

321

me? They stay here at Bagleigh.' He wanted to shake her, but bunched his fists instead and thrust them into his pockets.

Samira looked at him in disbelief. Her good English husband who had told her that he was friend as well as lover was behaving just as she had been taught to believe all husbands behaved. 'Oh, yes, I hear you,' she said coldly, 'but I thought you had just rejected Matthew. If so you have no rights in him at all. And it must be possible to get to Palestine. David's wife came here somehow, didn't she, so I should think I could go in the other direction. If you betray Matthew and me we shall go, all three of us!'

She paused and thought about what she had just said. Was it possible that those words had come from her lips? Was she really standing up to Colin, laying down the law? Yes, I am, she told herself in amazement, and I'm glad. Harriet's teaching is bearing fruit at last. Then with some relief she thought of the Cornish cottage beside the sea where she had spent those first idyllic weeks of her marriage. To go there was a far more practical proposition.

'If I cannot go home,' she added, 'I shall go back to Chy Morvah. Harriet wouldn't mind my having her cottage again.' But as she spoke she remembered the mists that came in from the sea and it seemed that a great grey blanket of despair descended on her soul and the brave stance she had taken a moment ago began to slide away, leaving her vulnerable and alone.

Colin had been staring at Bagleigh as he listened to her tirade but now he turned to her and with a shock realised they had just had their first quarrel. He saw the pallor of her face, saw that in spite of her brave words tears were edging down her cheeks. He realised that everything she had said was probably a façade to hide her distress and cursed himself for the clumsy way he had handled things. His anger evaporated as quickly as it had come and he suddenly felt unequal to the task of balancing the problems and complications of his marriage with the stresses of life as a fighter pilot. That alone demanded all his energies, all his concentration. In the air every nerve and sinew was stretched to full measure.

For a moment he was at a loss. He thought of his aircraft and the Stuka he had shot down in that last operation. He had been triumphant for a while, but recently during the nights when he should be sleeping and recharging his batteries, he found himself agonising over the problem of Matthew. It had become an obsession, and in order to achieve a measure of peace he had come here today with his bombshell.

Now, too late, he realised that peace was the last thing he or anyone in his family would have if he made any impetuous declaration. Quickly contrite and not a little ashamed he said slowly, 'Perhaps there is another way, a kinder way, than making the facts known just now. I really had no definite plans when I asked you to come up here. I wanted to talk about it with you, find a way out of the problem together, but we both became angry.' His anger now was only at himself.

She glanced at him in sudden hope. She too was horrified by the bitterness of their first quarrel, but tried to understand. She guessed that it was fear of dying that had made him broach the subject of Matthew and Bagleigh at this moment. Her heart was filled with sorrow because she had brought him this added worry.

'You won't die, Colin,' she said bravely. 'I pray to Allah every night for your safety. Now I shall pray about this thing too, about Matthew, and I shall pray for more sons. It will all come right.'

He didn't share her faith and smiled a little at her reference to Allah. He remembered, with another pang of conscience, and with further remorse, her enthusiasm about joining the Church of England and her firm wish to have Matthew christened.

She continued desperately, 'It will be a long long time before you die, fifty or sixty years perhaps. Many things can happen in that time. Your parents won't be alive then, and this truth couldn't hurt them. Please, Colin. Would you leave it a little while?'

He stood up, his mind in a turmoil, his firm resolutions of only an hour ago in tatters. Perhaps a letter to Matthew to be read many years hence, possibly on James Stanmore's death, left with a solicitor, might be a better solution? He wondered why he had not thought of that before.

Samira got to her feet and they stood looking at each other, both uncertain.

'I shall think of something,' he murmured.

'I've been too hasty. Please, sweetheart, forgive me. We'll talk about it next time and find the best way.' He took both of her hands in his and leaned forward and kissed her.

'There's nothing to forgive,' she said.

But he was sure that there was. Guilt consumed him, yet as he looked at her he wanted to make love to her right there on the hillside and in her eyes he thought he saw an answering fire. He glanced around at the wastes of the moor stretching out desolate and empty on every side.

'We could make another son for you, Colin,' she whispered, and he knew that he had been right. Her desire for him was as great as his for her, but her words made him hesitate, brought him back to reality, to his responsibilities.

He shook his head. 'It's too soon,' he said. 'I love you, Samira. We mustn't risk another baby. You're not strong enough yet.'

She smiled, happy over his care for her, yet determined to dismiss his worries. Since Kaffa-Mary's birth she had unwillingly given in to his insistence over the delicate matter of...of preventing babies...she couldn't even bring herself to name the things he used every time they made love, and she rejoiced that now perhaps they could do without. He wouldn't have brought them up here.

'Please, Colin,' she said. 'I'm fit and strong and I hate those...those disgusting things.'

But still he hesitated and Samira suddenly remembered what her mother had told her. 'Feeding a baby can sometimes make it more difficult to start another one.' It hadn't always proved true but it might do to convince Colin. 'I'm still feeding Kaffa,' she said.

He too knew something of this half-truth and grasped at it thankfully. He was beside himself with wanting her. His life lately was lived on a knife edge and the present moment seemed suddenly to be more important than any other consideration. Every blade of grass, every branch of every tree and bush, appeared to be animated with a strange new vitality.

'There's a special place,' he said, and led her over to the rocks, to a secret spot where the sun shone between two great boulders. He took off his jacket, put it on the ground and pulled her gently down beside him.

They made love with urgency and passion and it was more wondrous than either had ever experienced before. Then they lay quietly looking up at the deep blue of the sky and the few gentle fluffy clouds.

Samira didn't like what she saw. The sky was a threat, a rival for her husband's affection but Colin, at peace now, rejoiced in its challenge. His mind and his body were satisfied and he was eager to get back to his squadron, back to the action. He wanted to be up there amongst the clouds rather than lying here looking at them.

He rolled over, sprang up and pulled Samira gently to her feet. He shook out his jacket and put it on and brushed the grass and moss from his trousers. Hand in hand they walked down from the summit and neither spoke until they reached the brook with its ancient stone clapper bridge.

Then Samira stopped and stood quite still staring into the clear swirling water. 'I shall make a promise to you, Colin. I know that Matthew has no right to have Bagleigh. It wouldn't be fair to Diana or to Kaffa-Mary, as you said. I don't understand your law, but Eshref's son shall never inherit your Bagleigh. If you don't do anything about it now but keep it a secret still between us, then I promise you that if you...shouldn't come back...' She paused and her eyes filled with tears.

He wiped her face carefully with the back of his hand and then put one finger on her lips. 'I trust you completely and I give you my promise too,' he said. 'It shall remain a secret between us until the right time.'

He wasn't quite sure when the right time would be, but he determined to visit his solicitor during his next leave, probably at the end of the month. He would take Samira with him for she must know exactly what he proposed to do and agree to it.

He returned to his Squadron happier about his marriage than he had been for some time. He and Samira had survived their first quarrel and he felt more in love with her than ever. They had made love wonderfully together up there on the moors, but he was glad that they had talked, really talked. In marriage, he reflected as he drove back to Exeter, talking to each other was important too. He grinned to himself and in confident mood parked his motor-car in its allotted place at the edge of the airfield and swung over to the mess.

The following morning he was up and outside in the early dawn and he watched as the 'planes were being refuelled and everything brought into readiness. He felt a rush of new life and excitement. He too was ready, straining at the leash in fact, for whatever the day might bring.

An hour or two later, conveniently after a hearty breakfast, and when he and the other members of his flight were lounging outside in the sunshine, there was a loud yell from the telephone orderly. 'Scramble "A" Flight, Angels 10.'

With more enthusiasm than he had felt for a long time he tore across the runway to his aircraft and strapped himself in. His ground crew helped him and he felt sorry for them. Terrible to be left earthbound, he thought momentarily, instead of heading up into the sky, meeting Jerry head on, beating the hell out of him.

He saw his leader soar upwards, followed by number two, and then he was away in a great roar of power racing towards the action. He could hear the ground controller's voice, 'Bandits approaching at Angels ten, Yellow Leader, more Bandits at Angels one five, over.'

He saw the convoy they were to protect. The ships were like placid sitting ducks and he was filled with fury as he spotted the Heinkel bombers ahead with their deadly Messerschmitt escort, at least two formations of them. All he wanted to do was kill those murdering bastards sitting behind their black crosses...

Samira held a telegram in her hand. Three words would be seared into her memory for ever. 'Missing, believed killed.'

The letter from his commanding officer came later.

...during an engagement with the enemy, Pilot Officer Colin Stanmore's Hurricane was hit by cannon shells. Instead of abandoning his burning aircraft he was seen to attack and shoot down an enemy fighter before crashing into the sea. He will be recommended for a posthumous award for bravery.

'I'm very proud of him,' Samira said through her tears to Diana who had come home from London as soon as she heard the news. 'And now he may never have sons of his own to inherit that brave spirit.'

Diana looked at her, startled. Then she saw, with relief, that the sitting-room door was closed. Her parents couldn't possibly have heard those damning and dangerous words.

CHAPTER 22

September was a golden month of blue skies, a blaze of yellow gorse on the moors and rowan berries bright on the trees, but at Bagleigh there was a blanket of grief as thick and damp as a winter fog.

'We can't have a funeral,' Mary mourned. 'He won't be buried alongside his ancestors in the churchyard.'

'We'll have a plaque on the wall of the church though, Mother,' Diana comforted. 'Colin would have approved of that, and he'd have been proud of the memorial service tomorrow.'

Mary sniffed and dabbed her eyes. 'I can't believe it. With no coffin and flowers, I can't believe he's dead. I expect him to come roaring up in that old motor of his any moment.'

'So do we all,' Diana said. 'So do we all.'

The memorial service was to be held in the ancient parish church, and the following morning the family drove the few miles from the house. In true English fashion they all tried to hide their emotions.

Samira, leaning heavily on David's arm, for he had managed to get leave, stood for a moment as they entered the churchyard and gazed at the cross with the inscription to those from the parish killed in the Great War. She knew little about that war but read the top few names over to herself and felt their ghosts beside her. She wanted to wail and cry her loss aloud, but knew that this was not the correct behaviour here in this strangely inhibited country, so she forced back her heartbreak and walked bravely on.

David, supporting Samira, thought of the night he had rescued her from her murdering brothers. He felt protective of her just as he had on that other occasion and wondered what she would do now that Colin was dead, how she

330

would cope with the coming empty months. Colin, dead! Like the others he couldn't quite believe it. To be so young, so full of vigour and life one moment, and then within minutes... He shivered in spite of the warmth of the day and thought of some of the members of his own squadron who had not returned. It was always happening, the empty places at table in the mess, the car or motor-bike left just as it had been parked, the new young men brought in to replace those missing. He should have become used to it, but each time there was shock, a fresh grief.

James Stanmore, walking a few steps behind, felt vastly older than his fifty-one years and his glance fell upon the village cricket pitch which lay just beyond the wall of the churchyard. He and Colin had played there often before the war. For one moment his mind blocked out the fact of his son's death and he thought of the pleasures to come when baby Matthew would be old enough to have his first bat.

Mary Stanmore could think of nothing but her loss and wept quietly the whole way along the gravel path between the old gravestones. She was wearing a hat with a black veil and was glad of its protection. She held tightly to her husband's arm with one hand and crushed her handkerchief to her face beneath the veil with the other.

Diana, walking behind her parents, stared at the long panorama of the moor beyond the sports field and the road. The craggy rocks that she knew so well were etched against the clear blue of the summer sky and she thought of the many times she and her brother had ridden there in happier days. Then she brushed a tear from her eyes and looked instead at the tall handsome figure of David just about to turn into the church porch with Samira. She had been devastated when he had telephoned to say that he had managed to get a lift in a 'plane that was coming south and had asked for some long overdue leave so that he could be at the memorial service.

She longed suddenly for Philip. In spite of her independence and the new confidence that her job in London was giving, a fiancé to walk beside just now would have been a very great comfort indeed.

After the simple service they returned to Bagleigh and sat around in an awkward group trying to make inconsequential conversation, to drink the cups of tea and to eat the sandwiches that Diana had made before the service and which none of them wanted. There were a few friends and neighbours present all of whom said how proud of Colin the whole community felt.

The three children, Matthew, Kaffa-Mary and Dougie, the one remaining evacuee, were in the kitchen with the girl who had been brought in from the village to help on this difficult day.

'I must go and see to the baby,' Samira said. She longed to escape from the room, longed most of all for the night when she would be able to be alone and so give full vent to her grief in the manner of her own people. But for now she must seem to be composed.

'May I come?' David asked. He too was anxious to leave the charged atmosphere of the sitting room.

Matthew at eighteen months was beginning to say a few words. He was sitting at the big table with a fat wax crayon held in his hand, the baby fingers clenched tightly round it so that it appeared to be a weapon more than a colouring tool. He was scribbling forcefully from side to side on a piece of paper and he looked up as his mother entered. 'Da-dad kiy,' he said jabbing at the blue lines of his picture.

Samira wanted to snatch him up and press his sturdy little body to hers but instead she planted a kiss on his dark curly head and nodded. 'Yes, Daddy in the sky,' she said, with double meaning, and then added half beneath her breath, 'Salaam Aleikum.'

'What d'you mean?' six-year-old Dougie asked. 'Them's funny words.'

David had followed Samira into the kitchen. 'She means, peace be to you,' he said.

'Sounds daft,' said Dougie as he added a few more violent bursts of gunfire to the picture he was drawing.

David looked at it. 'That's good.'

'Them's Messerschmitts,' the child said pointing to the two planes about to crash in flames. 'And that one up there's the Spitfire what got them.'

Samira turned away and David put his arm around her. She crumpled against him and cried, really cried, for the first time that day.

Diana knew that she would have to offer to drive David to Exeter. He had been asked to bring Colin's car back to Bagleigh and this he had done. She guessed that it had been a difficult thing to do, and she was glad that he had been thoughtful enough to come quietly round the back way and not bring it up to the front door as Colin always did. Her mother's remark about expecting Colin to drive up in his motor car any minute had made her grateful for this thoughtfulness. She wasn't sure whether she would have the courage to drive her brother's disreputable but much loved old vehicle so soon but there was no other. Petrol for private motoring was not allowed any more.

David looked at her with surprise when she made her offer. 'Are you sure?' he said. 'Yes, there is enough petrol in the tank, but I could get a taxi, couldn't I?'

'Not very easily. Everyone's busy with the harvest. You'd have to wait a long time.'

'Then I accept if you don't mind too much?' He had noticed the deep circles beneath her eyes and remembered that she and her brother had been very close.

'We all have to face things sooner or later,' she said. She lit a cigarette and drew on it deeply. 'Say your goodbyes to the parents when you're ready and come round the back. We'll go that way. Did you lock it?'

He shook his head. 'No, the keys are in the ignition.'

'Right.' She dreaded using those keys. Colin

had always rattled them about, tossed them from one hand to the other before putting them in his pocket. There was a big leather fob attached with his name embossed upon it.

During the journey they talked mostly of unimportant things or of nothing at all. It was the only time during the day that they had been alone together.

Eventually she pulled up at the railway station. 'It'll be a long journey,' she said unnecessarily. 'Couldn't you get a 'plane back?'

'No chance. I was jolly lucky to get that lift down.' He made no effort to get out of the car, and she felt the colour begin to creep into her face. She wished he would go.

Then suddenly he put his hand over hers and turned to look at her. 'Are you happy, Diana?' he asked quietly.

She remembered that he had said something similar to her before. Why was he so concerned for her welfare, her happiness?

'A strange question to ask when my only brother has just been killed.' Her reply was bitter.

He shook his head. 'Not strange really. I mean in your own life. Are you content?'

She wanted to shout rudely that it had nothing at all to do with him, but instead she answered as calmly as she could, 'Moderately so. Yes, David, on the whole I believe that I am happy.' She slid her hand from beneath his. 'Are you?' she asked.

He repeated her own answer. 'Moderately so.' Then he quickly opened the car door and got out. He strode over to the station entrance and she watched him, watched every step, wanted to run after him and throw herself into his arms. Instead she sat there, her hands still clenched on the steering wheel, her heart pounding with annoyance that he should still disturb her so. Before he disappeared into the throng of people he turned, looked directly at her and then raised his hand, waved once and then was gone.

I'll never see him again, she told herself fiercely. Bomber pilots aren't very high up in the survival league. But I'll remember him for ever. She started the engine and drove bleakly back to Bagleigh.

'You'll stay here now, won't you?' Mary Stanmore said hopefully to Diana the following day. 'I mean, we need you. We all need you.'

Diana sighed. She'd escaped to a new life only a few short weeks ago and now her freedom was threatened again. Yet she didn't want to be selfish. 'Nothing has actually changed, Mother,' she replied. 'I mean, we all miss Colin dreadfully but there's no more work or anything, nothing that I can do...' She tailed off miserably, realising how trite the words must sound.

'Just having you here is a comfort. I know Samira would like you to stay.' Mary dabbed at her eyes. She looked pathetic and Diana put her arms around her.

'I'll stay for a week or so,' she conceded, 'but I must go back. There's work to be done.'

'Taking photographs?' Mary said scathingly. 'How's that to win the war?'

'Propaganda. We have to try and cheer people up, encourage them by printing cheerful pictures.'

Diana had talked about this to Thelma. It was against the older woman's principles to record only the brave and the good. She wanted to show the full horror of the bombing and the cruelties of war. 'But,' she had said firmly, 'we have to win the war first. Only the noble must get into the papers. The people must be buoyed up, given confidence. We'll save the rest and publish it later, in a book, so take it all, Diana, every horrible obscene bit of it. Perhaps one day we might convince the world that war isn't glorious at all but just a bloody abomination.'

Diana remembered the words now and longed to get back to London. Here in Devon life was too easy, too quiet. In London she could lose herself in her job, and forget, or at least submerge, her grief for Colin and her longing for David.

She stayed for another two weeks and then returned to the horrors of the blitz.

'Glad to have you back, dear girl,' a grey-faced Thelma boomed at her when she arrived after a long and tedious journey on a train jammed with servicemen. She ushered Diana into the sitting room. 'You look tired out,' she said. 'I'll make us some tea.'

'Had to stand all the way.' Diana flung off her coat and draped it across a chair and sank thankfully on to the sofa. Bounder sniffed at her suspiciously. 'He can smell Rollo,' she laughed, and felt a moment's home sickness, quickly banished.

'How are things here then?'

There was no reply for a time as Thelma clattered about in the next room, but she reappeared eventually carrying a tray set with two large mugs and cake. 'Carrot cake,' she explained. 'Next-door gave it to me. It's very good actually.'

Diana ate appreciatively and realised that she was hungry. 'My mother makes it,' she said. 'Tell me about the bombing. It looks pretty terrifying.'

'Number twenty had it a few days ago. Did you see?'

Diana nodded, her mouth full of cake. 'Passed it on the way. Anyone hurt?'

'No. Saved by the Morrison shelter. Nice people.'

'Are you frightened?'

'Me, frightened?' Thelma laughed and cut herself another wedge of cake. 'Yes, of course I'm frightened. Bloody terrified, dear girl. But that doesn't stop me. Once the adrenaline gets going I'm out there with the old camera. Got to keep the press happy and beat Hitler with nice cheerful shots of people smiling while they're being pulled out of the wreckage.'

'You sound like Churchill.'

'It's important. "Fight on the beaches" and all that. I've come to realise it lately. The other side must wait, like I told you before. But now go and get a lie down. I shall too. Always try to get an hour's kip in the afternoon.'

'Lie down?' Diana couldn't believe it.

'Yes, dear child. A lie down. You'll be up most of the night!'

She realised how wise this instruction was the following day, and the day after that, and during the amazing horrifying nights of October. November brought hardly any relief and in December the death toll was in many thousands. The raids appeared to send great surges of energy coursing through Thelma's wiry body and as soon as the sirens sounded she was out with her camera in the thick of the action.

Diana followed her example, although with some trepidation. They were constantly being shouted at by Air Raid Wardens, policemen and various other characters in authority, but Thelma shouted back at them. 'Press,' she would state, waving her camera importantly, and in the noise and destruction she usually got what she wanted: photographs of courage and of terror, of blazing buildings, of the kindness of individuals, and endless reels showing the terrible carnage of war. These she mostly put away in a great steel box in the cellar.

When they stumbled home in the mornings through the shattered streets, picking their way over broken glass, fire hoses, piles of rubble, and avoiding great craters or perilous-looking remains of just-bombed houses, Diana at first marvelled that they were both unhurt. But later she began to take their survival for granted.

'A charmed life, dear girl,' Thelma would frequently say. 'Lucky old me. Hope I'm passing it on to you as well.' Her concern was often for her dog. 'Hope poor old Bounder is all right,' she often said amidst the raging fires and the endless bombardment, and then Diana would laugh a little, the tension broken. The dog was always shut into the Morrison shelter when they left. 'Perhaps he should be evacuated to your Bagleigh,' Thelma once said. 'But I couldn't get along without old Bounder.'

Samira tried to settle into life again at Bagleigh. With Colin dead her hold on the family seemed, in her own mind, to falter. The only true link was baby Kaffa-Mary.

Whenever she looked at her son she felt that she was living a falsehood, a lie that one day would be revealed and cause her life to come crashing about her in tatters. But as each day passed Matthew became more and more enchanting and James Stanmore was increasingly besotted with his supposed grandson. The child responded and Grandpa was beginning to be one of the most important persons in his young life. Samira shuddered inwardly whenever she thought of the horror that the revelation of his fatherhood would bring to everyone concerned.

She would go over all the consequences in her mind and the promise she had made to Colin on that last precious day would come back to her with deadening reality. When was she to fulfil those things she had said? When reveal the ruinous truth? She was sure that her father-in-law, in his distress and disappointment would change completely in his attitude to Matthew and even more to herself. His love for the child would be displaced by searing anger.

Remembering her own father and brothers, she imagined that he would even harbour murderous thoughts that could easily be translated into action. And Mary? Her mother-in-law who had become her friend? Mary was bound to reject her too. She imagined, if she and Matthew lived, fleeing back with him to Chy Morvah, staying there in Harriet's little cottage until she could arrange to go back to Palestine, back to Eshref perhaps, for that would be the only thing she could do for Matthew. She would present him to his real father. But what of her daughter, Colin's true child? She could never condemn her to life in a Palestinian village. Perhaps Harriet...

In her more rational moments Samira completely rejected this sequence of events. Matthew was English, she told herself, born in England, baptised into the Church of England, his name down for what Colin called public school. He would play cricket, ride to hounds with his grandfather, learn to take his rightful place here at Bagleigh.

It was at night when she was alone that the fears returned. 'If only I had someone to talk to,' she occasionally sobbed into her pillow, 'but there's no one. Harriet is the only person in the world who would understand, the only person who could tell me what to do.'

Usually, as she thought of Harriet, her mind would begin to grow calm again, and eventually she would sleep until Kaffa-Mary woke for a feed and a nappy change. Then she would clutch the baby to herself in gratitude. In spite of her name, Kaffa-Mary was as English as any Stanmore. Samira always joined the two Christian names together now so that they sounded less foreign, and occasionally she considered dropping the first one, but then thought of her mother and felt disloyal.

Occasionally there was news from Palestine for Harriet wrote from time to time. Abdulla, the only one of Samira's six brothers to keep in touch with Harriet, sometimes took messages, so there was a flow of secret news from El Admah. Samira had always liked this younger brother. He was the only one with whom she had managed a semblance of friendship and she hoped that he wouldn't become like the others, like his father. He was sensitive and clever, worthy of better things.

Samira knew now that Gasim and Zeid were married, and her mother had sent a message through Abdulla to say that their wives were good girls and were learning to take Samira's place so the work load was not so great. She had sent her love to Samira and congratulations over the births of the children, and had said that she was happy and hoped one day that Allah would reunite them all again.

Samira had cried a little over that last letter and wished that she could write directly back to her mother instead of always through Harriet. She was angry at a way of life that restricted women so much and laid down rigid laws, all of them dictated by men. When her thinking went along these lines she was quite sure that whatever happened to her she would stay in England. Matthew and Kaffa-Mary should never be brought up like that.

'You're quite free now,' her mother-in-law had said to her recently. 'We used to think that widows were poor things and to be pitied, but in these modern days it's different. You have a small pension from the War Office, and freedom, Samira.'

She said those words over and over to herself when she felt most alone and most miserable. Freedom! It was what she had always wanted. She remembered sitting in the courtyard at home long ago and telling her own mother that was what she desired above all else. It had seemed an impossible and dangerous dream then. But now she had it, and sometimes she wondered if it was so wonderful after all. She would rather have Colin back than all the freedom in the world.

CHAPTER 23

1942

David's promotion to Flight Lieutenant meant a new posting.

'The South of England,' he told his wife triumphantly. 'You said you'd had enough of Scotland after this last winter.'

Rachel smiled at him. She was immensely

proud. 'Yes,' she said, 'I shall like to settle in England for a while. After Palestine, Scotland is cold!'

There were some drawbacks to the arrangements however. In Scotland, officers' families had been housed near the airfield, but in England it would be different and David wondered how she was going to like the change to the small isolated cottage he had found for her in Devon. It had been offered to him by a friend to rent for as long as he needed it but it was more than two hours' drive from his new base.

'Why so far away?' Rachel asked dubiously when he first told her of his plans.

'Anywhere near an airfield is a bit risky for families,' he explained. 'There's also been a directive from headquarters that wives shouldn't live within forty miles of any Bomber Command Base.'

'That's a bit tough, especially for the newly-weds, isn't it?'

'I suppose it is. It doesn't apply to those with houses of their own, of course.'

'Then we'd better buy a house.'

David grinned at her. 'You know you don't mean that. Neither England nor Scotland could be our home now, surely!'

'No, my dear, of course they couldn't. Eretz Israel. I don't mind where I am for the present as long as we get back there one day.'

There was a flush on Rachel's face and a gleam of enthusiasm in her eyes that matched his own. He put his hand beneath her chin and raised her face to his. As he kissed her he knew that this marriage had been the right one. They shared the same longings, the same ideals. It could never have been like this with Diana. Diana... He thought about her often even now. It was a secret shame and he guessed that he would never be able to shut her totally out of his heart.

By March all the arrangements had been made and they began the long journey south. With baby Deborah to consider, with no signposts to help find the way, and with the old car grumbling much of the time, it took them nearly three days. As they crossed the county border into Devon Rachel looked about her with interest. 'It's very pretty, but do you really think we'll be safer here?' she said. 'From invasion and bombs, I mean? We're closer to the Germans than we were in Scotland.'

'Children were evacuated here because it's supposed to be safe,' David told her. 'And you needn't fear an invasion any longer. The Germans haven't got the air power, thanks to Colin Stanmore and a lot more like him.' He hoped his voice sounded more confident than he felt.

'Churchill's few,' Rachel said. 'But you were in the Battle of Britain too. Don't be modest.'

He laughed. 'Yes, but it was the fighter squadrons that bore the brunt.'

Rachel was silent for a time and her thoughts were unusually gloomy. She was seldom dispirited, but sometimes, when she considered the odds against her husband living through the war, she would find herself filled with fear.

To dispel it she quickly changed the subject. 'How far is this cottage of ours from Colin Stanmore's home?'

'Bagleigh? About twenty miles or so.' David felt sudden apprehension. He hoped that his wife had never suspected the strength of his feelings for Diana. If they went to Bagleigh and if Diana should be there he couldn't imagine a very comfortable meeting between the two women. He kept his eyes carefully on the road ahead. 'Why do you ask?'

'I thought you might take me to see Samira. I feel sorry for her, being so far from her family. She must feel lonely since Colin was killed.'

David was slightly relieved, but at the mention of Samira's family he snorted with disgust. 'Family? Have you forgotten about her brothers?'

'Perhaps I had for a moment. But I should like to meet her again. I remember she was slim and pretty with dark hair and constantly downcast eyes. I don't think I ever talked to her when we were at Beth Haron.'

'Well, you wouldn't, of course. She was Arab, we were Jews.'

'Why the past tense?'

David laughed briefly. 'It doesn't seem to matter so much here.'

'I wish it didn't matter in Palestine. Perhaps it won't in the future.'

'You are joking, of course?'

After a few minutes' silence Rachel said,

346

'What about Colin's sister?'

David felt alarmed again. 'Diana? The last I heard she was working in London, taking various semi-official photographs of the blitz. She wants to become a war correspondent. She's working with a photographer, a friend of Harriet Clayton's. You remember her, of course?'

'How could anyone ever forget Harriet and her wonderful animal clinics? Are there any women war correspondents?'

'Some, I believe, here and there. Americans mostly.'

'And will your Diana achieve her ambition, do you think?'

David was tired. He had been driving for a long time and didn't want to think about Diana just now. He glanced quickly at his wife. 'I've no idea. Why are you so interested? She isn't my Diana. She's engaged to be married to some farmer, in the Navy at the moment.' He couldn't keep the sharpness from his voice.

Rachel grinned at him and shrugged her shoulders. 'I know you had a certain feeling for her,' she said. 'Shall we call it a pash, that funny old schoolgirl word?'

'All right,' he said in some relief. 'A pash. Yes, perhaps I did, but that was all over a long time ago.' He hoped that she believed him. He hoped that he believed himself.

They reached the village of Starton in the late-afternoon and David pulled up outside a tiny thatched cottage. 'Here we are,' he said proudly. 'All ours for the duration.'

347

'It's beautiful,' Rachel said. She gently woke Deborah who had been sleeping on her lap for the past hour and climbed stiffly out of the vehicle. She put the child on her feet beside the wooden gate which stood open, welcoming them. The little girl rubbed chubby fingers into her eyes and was about to cry but Rachel quickly diverted her. 'Look, Debbie,' she said. 'Daffodils. See their golden heads smiling at you?'

Deborah had never seen daffodils before. She cupped her hands over the first bloom and then paused and slid her fingers down the stem and broke it off. 'Daff-daff,' she said, but she didn't squash its fragile beauty. She held it daintily so that the petals nodded at her and she laughed, delighted.

'We'll come out and pick some more later on,' Rachel said. 'And put them in a vase. They'll cheer us all up.'

There were a great many of them lining the path, their bright golden heads making a splash of vivid colour, and Rachel noticed rose bushes too that promised glories to come. With a pang she remembered the few precious roses at Beth Haron. The plants had been taken out by an English couple, both keen gardeners, and in Palestine they would be in bloom now. For a moment she stood quite still, remembering, and then quickly pulled herself together, but not without a fleeting twinge of dismay. Could she really be happy here in this beautiful isolated place? Would her energetic restless spirit be able to settle here until this awful war was over? She

348

took Deborah's hand and walked up the path to the front door. Then she turned and waited for David.

He was staggering behind her with two huge suitcases. He set them down and searched in his pocket, eventually producing a large key which he fitted carefully into the lock, but before opening the door he turned to her and smiled. 'Thank you for coming here, for leaving Palestine and then Scotland. I'm sorry to uproot you so much.'

She reached up and kissed him. 'I love you,' she said, 'and I shall be the good little wife waiting here for you to return from war. Who could ever want more than this?' But in spite of the brave words, she knew that it was not enough. In Scotland it had been different. On the base there had been plenty to do. She had not felt superfluous. She suddenly thought of Diana and her photography with a certain envy.

As David opened the door and stood back for her to pass, he too experienced a twinge of foreboding. Her words about being the good little wife just waiting for him were so unlike her. Did they hide something that he failed to understand?

Rachel had not been in Devon for more than a few weeks and she was only just beginning to feel a little settled when the first bombs fell on Exeter. The morning after the air-raid she took Deborah for their usual walk, and called in at the village shop as she did most days.

349

'You'll be all right here, me dear,' the shopkeeper told her. 'Starton be safe as houses. 'Tis well outside the city.'

'I hope you're right,' Rachel said. Privately she was inclined to laugh a trifle ruefully at the statement. 'Houses' were certainly not safe. The announcer on the wireless had said that a number on the outskirts had received direct hits.

During the second raid she felt, at first, very alone and vulnerable. She heard the bombers overhead, listened to their relentless throbbing flight and shivered, not for herself but for her daughter sleeping soundly in her cot beside the fire. She had decided that they would sleep downstairs now nearer the Morrison shelter and tonight she hoped fervently that the village shopkeeper was right and Starton would be spared.

She heard the whining of falling bombs followed by ominous explosions, and put out the light and went to her window. She saw the flashes of anti-aircraft fire and searchlights criss-crossing the night sky. Then suddenly her apprehension changed to excitement. Here was action at last. She was part of the war, part of David's war. Horrible though it all was, she felt a sinister thrill and in that moment knew that she must do something for the war effort. She could no longer sit around uselessly here while Hitler rampaged over Europe, murdering Jews, her people, and now bombing indiscriminately.

As she continued to stand at the window, almost mesmerised, like a rabbit before a stoat, she was filled with anger on behalf of her child and millions of others like her. She wanted to be up there in the skies or manning an ack-ack gun shooting down those bastards in their throbbing menacing 'planes. She had no idea what she could do, but was quite sure that she wouldn't remain in a state of passive inaction much longer.

Then Deborah awoke and cried and Rachel was ashamed. She doused the last embers of fire in the grate, grabbed the child and crawled into the Morrison shelter.

A stray bomb hit the shed at the side of the cottage and the old cob walls crumbled with the impact. Beams fell from the ceiling, showering the room with ancient plaster, covering the sturdy shelter, making a tomb of it.

But Rachel cradled her screaming child, sang to her, saw that the beams had fallen across leaving spaces where air could penetrate, and the hearth-fire was out. She sighed with relief as she thought of the water she had unwillingly put on to the comforting embers.

Some hours later Rachel and Deborah were pulled out, shocked but alive.

David, rushing home on compassionate leave, found them in the small cottage hospital. He was filled with contrition. 'I brought you here,' was all he could say at first. 'It's my fault. In Scotland you would have been safe.'

Rachel, with her commonsense and good humour revived now, put her finger on his lips. 'Of course it wasn't your fault,' she whispered. 'And we've survived. It was the Morrison shelter

351

that saved us. I thought it a total irrelevance when I first saw how ugly it was, how much space it took up in that tiny room, but, David, it saved our lives.'

He had insisted on getting it installed during the first week in Devon in spite of her objections. It had been difficult finding one at this stage in the war, but his perseverance had been rewarded and now as he looked at his wife and daughter his heart overflowed with thankfulness.

'I've made arrangements for you to go to Bagleigh, temporarily,' he said. 'Colin's mother contacted me and offered you a home until we can fix something.' He had been amazed at the offer coming so quickly but Mary Stanmore was working for the Women's Voluntary Service and as soon as she had seen the name 'Halprin' on a list of survivors she had made enquiries. Any friend of Colin's was important to her.

'So we are to go to Bagleigh after all,' Rachel said. She had sensed David's unwillingness to agree to her earlier suggestion that she should visit Samira.

'Yes. It's a big house. You'll like it. But I'll do my best to find you some place of your own as soon as I can.'

Rachel smiled at him. 'Don't worry too much,' she said. 'I can look after Deborah and myself. You just concentrate on winning this bloody war.'

She wasn't a swearing person and he looked at her in surprise.

'Yes, I mean bloody,' she said in sudden anger. 'Bloody, bloody, bloody, and I want to do something about it too, David. Perhaps now may be my chance.'

He was alarmed. 'What can you do? You've got Deborah to look after.'

'So I have,' she said. 'So I have.'

At Bagleigh Samira had settled into a routine that left little time for brooding. She filled every minute with furious action. She did all the housework and most of the sewing, and there was a lot of that. Clothes must be fashioned out of old garments that she found in chests in the attic or sometimes from curtains. If there were any new things to be bought with the sparse clothing coupons it was usually the children who benefited. She often thought of the lovely embroidered dresses that she had left in Palestine and when she looked at herself in the mirror she usually managed to laugh and wondered what her mother would think of these ugly clothes.

The gay twenties-style dresses that Harriet had given her were put away for special occasions. She usually wore a thick tweed skirt or a pair of old slacks and an assortment of nondescript jumpers against the cold, one in summer and two or even three in winter. And her shining dark hair was forced now into a roll around her head with an upswept curl at the front. A Victory Roll, Mary called it. Very patriotic, she said. Colin once told her that he did victory rolls in his aeroplane and so she kept the unbecoming style and only allowed her hair to flow freely on to her shoulders at night when the work of the day was over.

Mary did most of the cooking at Bagleigh for Samira was still wary of the kitchen with its large cooker and vast assortment of pans and dishes. She was glad to be free of this chore for it gave her more time with the children, her own two and the irrepressible Dougie who seemed now to be a permanent fixture at Bagleigh. When she was with them she was happiest and most fulfilled.

She had promised Diana that she would regularly exercise Merryon and Rollo and so whenever there was a moment to spare and Mary was free to look after the children, Samira would ride out on to the moor whatever the weather, exulting in the wind and the rain and the lonely expanse of hill and moorland. Very occasionally she would walk to the secret place between the two rocks and would sit down for a moment and think of the time when Colin had made love to her there. Then the tears would come.

She had longed for another child, had hoped and prayed passionately for a son for Colin. Surely a lovemaking as perfect as that would have given her her heart's desire? But Allah had obviously not wished it. She had been brought up not to question the will of Allah. So she would sigh and walk slowly down again, looking now and then at her ugly shoes. She was beginning to like them, for Colin had bought them for her. 'Walking shoes,' he had called them, and they made her smile through her tears, made him seem nearer somehow. She still preferred to ride, but to walk up to the tor as they had done on that last leave helped her to feel closer to Colin.

When she heard about her mother-in-law's offer of accommodation to the Jewish woman, David Halprin's wife, she was apprehensive. She remembered Rachel vaguely. She had seen her once or twice on the kibbutz and thought she had been at the wedding, but they hadn't spoken. But Samira would never forget the debt of gratitude she owed to David as long as she lived. He had saved her life on that terrible night when her brothers had nearly killed her. She thought back to the terror as they had dragged her along the road, and could still hear in her imagination, David's cultured English voice piercing the velvety darkness of the warm Palestinian night. 'What the hell...you bastards!' he had said.

Yes, she owed her life to David Halprin. Even if it was difficult she would do all she could to welcome his young wife and little daughter to Bagleigh.

CHAPTER 24

Diana was working in Egypt when she heard the news of Rachel's move to Bagleigh. She greeted it with disbelief and horror. What on earth could her mother be thinking of? David's wife and child installed in her own precious home! It was unthinkable. They must have been there for quite a time for the letter had been slow to reach her.

Now that she had banished David from her mind, or believed that she had, came this astounding news from Devon. She read the letter three times before she could really believe that it was true, before she could imagine David's wife living, actually living, at Bagleigh. Rachel and the child had been bombed, nearly killed, her mother wrote, and she had offered them a temporary home. Samira and Rachel had become firm friends. They were good for each other. Rachel had helped Samira over her grief at Colin's death, and no one was in any hurry to find alternative accommodation for them, Mary continued, even had it been available.

Diana was furious. She felt supplanted by the news, pushed out by Rachel for the second time. First of all she had lost David to her, and now she seemed to be losing her mother, her friend, and unbelievably her home. She was consumed with jealousy and also with shame for being jealous which made everything much worse.

Thelma laughed at her when she heard about it. 'Hope she likes dogs,' she said. 'Bounder will keep her busy.'

Before leaving England Thelma had been more worried about her dog than about any of the other complicated arrangements that had to be made. Eventually she had been persuaded that he would be well looked after at Bagleigh, and she and Diana had gone to Devon to leave him in Samira's welcoming care.

'I've no idea whether Rachel likes dogs,' Diana replied somewhat belligerently. 'Probably not. I think she's a town person.'

Thelma looked at her gloomy face. 'I don't know why you're behaving like a wet week,' she said. 'You've got the job you wanted, a rich and pleasant fiancé who doesn't appear to be very demanding, and a nice home to go back to after the war. You're jolly lucky. Good Lord, girl, count your blessings and pass the ammunition.'

'Home?' Diana grunted, for once irritated by her companion's hearty manner. 'I don't really feel that it'll be my home much longer.'

'What on earth are you talking about?'

Diana hadn't really meant to say that, but thinking about Bagleigh, and Rachel's presence there, had brought that other gnawing dissatisfaction into her mind. Matthew. Her small nephew whom she loved, whom her brother had loved, and whom her father adored. Matthew, the son of a Palestinian Arab, was one day set to take Bagleigh away from her unless she did something about it. But what? For many conflicting and heart-rending reasons she felt powerless to act.

She frequently wondered if her brother had made any arrangements before he died for he had been just as aware as she was of Matthew's true paternity. She knew that some day the facts would have to be told, Samira would have to face them, damaging though they would certainly be to the whole family.

It was strange how the dreadful news of Rachel's living at Bagleigh brought it all into even sharper focus in her mind, made her feel doubly wronged. Bagleigh seemed quite remote and completely beyond her reach now, for with David's wife and his precious child living there, she felt it to be totally out of bounds.

Not that she was likely to be in England for a long time anyway she told herself with angry satisfaction. Thelma had managed to inveigle a photographic commission at last. 'You need a woman's perspective on war,' she had repeatedly told her editor. 'The war in the Middle East particularly.' To the delight of both Diana and Thelma, he had fallen for the suggestion.

'Right,' he had said. 'Give me a record of everything that goes on behind our lines, from a woman's point of view. That should be original. Thought of it myself a day or two ago, as a matter of fact.'

Thelma had laughed, secretly triumphant. 'I shall need to take my assistant with me, of course.'

So here they both were, not official war correspondents but with a brief, and furnished with all the necessary passes and documents. Diana knew that it was the chance she had longed for and she was determined to make the most of every opportunity. But in the heat and the dust she frequently dreamed a little of Bagleigh. She would picture riding Merryon again, watching Rollo bounding ahead up to the tor. In her imagination she could almost feel the welcome tearing of the cold wind in her hair and on her face, and she would be comforted with the thought of the house, solid and welcoming, waiting for her to return. But now all that was gone. Rachel was there. Bagleigh was no longer the lovely dream.

Only this burning desert remained, the constant defeats of the Eighth Army at the hands of Rommel and his Afrika Korps, the death and the destruction, the smells and the wounded. The British troops had been pushed back to Sidi Barani. Even the naval base at Alexandria was threatened.

Diana tried to concentrate her thoughts on Philip. His letters arrived in batches now and then, full of love for her, full of concern that she had left the comparative safety of England, and sometimes he added a few comments about his own life. But he revealed little, and many words were slashed out by the censor. He was unreal to her now. Even the ring he had given her so proudly was hidden away in her bedroom at Bagleigh. She had thought it unwise to bring such a valuable piece of jewellery out here. Sometimes she regretted this decision for it was a tangible thing, reminding her of security and peace. The solid opulence of the diamonds flashing on her finger had always given her great pleasure. Yet this was combined with a niggle of unease too, a disquiet which had grown stronger over recent months. She thought back to the day she had promised to marry Philip. Already more than two years had passed since she had seen him and in spite of his letters he often felt a stranger to her.

To combat all these conflicting and disturbing emotions she concentrated more vigorously than ever on her photography, pushing herself to the extreme of her endurance. She photographed everything she could and as well as photographs of soldiers and battles, she went into the villages, made friends with the women and the children, recorded their lives.

'You'll make a name for yourself one day,' Thelma told her. 'Glad you've got the energy, dear child. All mine has gone since we came here. Must be getting old. Find the heat a bit unbearable. Looking forward to getting to Cairo after all. Plenty of decent hotels there.' Thelma had at first refused to join most of the press in the capital, preferring the excitement of life here where the action was, but she sometimes regretted her decision, and knew that she would remedy it later on.

Meanwhile a daily siesta was a necessity, a longer one than in London. A few days later, during this welcome midday break, Thelma was unable to sleep so picked up an out-of-date newspaper that had found its way into their camp. She fanned herself with its pages and then sat bolt upright. 'The bastards!' she said. 'The murdering bastards! They're loading men, women and even kids into trucks fitted with poison gas and murdering a hundred or so at a time. Seven hundred thousand in Poland alone, it says here, and they're still at it!' She thumped the page so that it fell out of her hand on to the floor.

Diana heard the words through a haze of sleep in which she had been dreaming about moors and heather and sheep. 'What are you talking about?' she mumbled. 'Who's murdering who?'

'The Nazis, of course. Jews. They're murdering thousands of Jews.'

Diana was wide awake suddenly. 'David,' she said aloud. 'Oh, please God, don't let his plane come down in occupied territory.' Then she thought of Rachel. She couldn't help a measure of shame at her feelings about David's wife, and unaccountably her body became cold in spite of the heat. She shivered. 'Rachel too,' she whispered. 'Keep Rachel safe too.'

Thelma was looking at her oddly. 'The desert does funny things to people,' she commented. 'Never heard you praying before, dear girl. Send one up for me, won't you, and for those poor bloody Jews.'

'They're supposed to be the Chosen Race. Chosen by God and all that.' Diana picked up the discarded newspaper and read the item for herself. 'Why do you suppose God is letting Hitler get away with it?'

Thelma rose unsteadily to her feet. 'No idea. Something about killing Jesus, isn't it? Don't know that I believe all that stuff myself, but some folks do, more's the pity.'

Diana was still reading. 'This report was smuggled out by a Polish underground group and sent to London. It looks as though we don't know half of what's going on.'

'No wonder they want a country of their own,' Thelma said. 'Always been persecuted.'

Diana looked at her, surprised. 'If I can ever do anything to help that dream come true, I'll do it with all my might,' she said.

'Because you're still in love with that

361

Jewish chap, I suppose? Foolish child!' Thelma shrugged her shoulders but her voice was kind. 'Forget him and concentrate on your own nice young man or you'll land yourself in a heap of trouble. Let the Jews fight their own battles.'

Diana carefully smoothed out the crumpled pages of the newspaper, folded them and placed them on the table with exaggerated care. Thelma had, of course, exposed her innermost emotions. She tried not to be angry. 'Perhaps you're right,' she said. 'I'm trying to forget him, I have forgotten him.' But she knew that it wasn't true, wasn't true at all.

In Devon a few months later the church bells were ringing out into the November sky. Samira listened in amazement and ran into the kitchen. 'That noise?' she asked. 'The bells? What do they mean? I thought they would only ring if we were being invaded?'

Mary was ironing. She looked at her daughter-in-law and smiled. 'It's for Monty,' she said. 'You heard the news on the wireless last night, didn't you? The bells are ringing all over the country because he's won a great victory in the desert.'

Samira stood still. The desert. Egypt. It was almost like hearing about her own country, about Palestine. And of course Diana was in Egypt. There had been letters, mostly gloomy ones. But that had been before the advent of Monty. Lately she had written that General Montgomery was changing things.

Samira went to the door and opened it and

362

the joyful peals sounding over the hills entered the kitchen and filled her heart with wonder. It was beautiful. She supposed she must have heard church bells when she first came to England, but they had made no impression on her then, and at the beginning of the war they had been banned, and were only to be used as a warning that Hitler's troops had landed on the English coast. Samira had no idea how moving they could sound. She had never heard them in Palestine for there were no churches anywhere near El Admah.

James Stanmore was sitting near the Aga reading the newspaper. He looked at them over the top of it. 'El Alamein,' he announced. 'Rommel's Afrika Korps has been hit for six. That's what Monty told the Eighth Army they had to do, hit them for six, and by God they've done it!' He was obviously hugely excited. 'Probably saved the whole of the Middle East.'

Rachel came into the kitchen at that moment. She too had heard the bells but was an avid follower of the news so she was well aware of their significance. 'The Middle East,' she said thoughtfully. 'I wonder what's going to happen there now?'

'I don't know,' Samira said. 'It belongs to a part of my life that's past, almost dead.'

'But I can't wait to get back,' Rachel replied.

The following afternoon the weather was fair for November and Samira and Rachel snatched a precious hour away from the house while Mary was in her element looking after the children.

They always enjoyed this time together and Major and Merryon needed the exercise, so they told themselves that it was not entirely selfish.

When they reached Greatcombe Rocks Rachel reined in her mount and stared at the expanse of moorland that lay all around. The skies were clear and still with no mist, but heavy black clouds threatened in the distance, looking as if a great thunder storm would burst upon them. There was little sign of human life in all that vast wilderness.

'It's so dramatic,' Rachel said. 'David sometimes told me how incredible Dartmoor was, but I could never quite imagine it. Now I know what he was talking about.'

'I love it whatever the weather,' Samira replied. 'At first I was quite overawed but I've become used to its moods. I should miss it terribly if I had to leave.'

Rachel looked at her in surprise. 'But that won't happen surely? You belong here. Matthew will inherit Bagleigh one day, won't he?'

Samira felt shock waves sweep her body. There it was again, the impossible problem which she knew she must do something about soon.

'I don't know,' she hedged. 'There may be difficulties, and anyway, Father-in-law is only in his fifties. I'm sure he hasn't any intention of dying for a very long time.'

Rachel laughed, ignoring or perhaps not even registering Samira's doubts. 'I like Colin's father,' she said. 'He's accepted you fully, hasn't he? You had some trouble at first, I believe?'

'He hated me, called me a wog. I think he imagined me in a yashmak or something. It was seeing me ride Major one day that brought him to his senses.'

'Very odd. You rode in Palestine, didn't you?'

'Yes, a wonderful horse called Jazi. Harriet still has him.'

For a moment Samira remembered that terrible ride to her wedding, when she had been dressed up in those awful robes and had ridden so unwillingly to Eshref's home. She wondered how much Rachel knew of her past.

'Will you ever go back?'

'I should like to visit my mother, but I don't know how it could be managed. Without Colin's protection, I think I should be too scared.'

'You could come with us.'

Samira laughed. 'Well, perhaps I could. Now there's a thought. That would make my brothers pretty mad again! You know about all that, don't you? David must have told you how he rescued me from them?'

'Yes, I heard.' Rachel was silent for a time, and then she spoke again, slowly, unsure of herself. 'There's a favour I want to ask of you, Samira. I don't know what you'll think of me for asking, or for the plan I have, and I can't tell you much.'

'A favour? What kind of favour? I owe my life to your David so I could never refuse whatever you asked.'

'Would you look after Deborah for me?'

The words came out in a rush and Samira stared at her companion as if she hadn't heard correctly.

'Of course. She's lovely. It would be an absolute pleasure, but I don't understand.'

'I have to go to London, just for a couple of days initially, but it could be much longer.'

Samira was surprised and very curious. 'You mean you want to go into the forces or something?'

'Sort of. It grieves me to say so, Samira, but I'm just not a natural mother. Our kibbutz system would suit me fine. After the war I shall be able to have as many babies as we want, but I shall not have to look after them for twenty-four hours a day. Our children are brought up mainly in the children's house. Living in a kibbutz is voluntary, of course, but for me it's wonderful.' She paused for a moment, wondering how this must sound to such a motherly woman as Samira. Impossible to understand probably. 'Debbie loves you,' she continued. 'She turns to you more often than to me in fact. You must have noticed? I can't stay here feeling useless any longer. Have you heard the latest news about Hitler? He intends to exterminate the whole of the Jewish population of Europe. How can I sit around and do nothing while that's going on? I speak fluent Dutch and pretty good French. I can probably be of use in lots of ways. Anyway, I must offer myself.'

'What about David?'

'He doesn't know yet.'

'And your parents?'

'My mother is dead. My father married again some time ago. There's no one in either of our families who would want to look after Deborah. David's mother is an officer in the WAAFs and his father is busy with his work. And I wouldn't let her go to anyone but you anyway.'

Samira smiled at her. 'I didn't mean that, Rachel, and thanks for the compliment. I'd absolutely love to look after her for you if you really think you could bear to be parted.'

'It'll be a wrench, but I know she'll be happy. And I'll give David lots more children after the war, hopefully all the sons he wants. I expect I'll be able to have them without much trouble. It's the looking after them I'm not so happy about.' She laughed a trifle ruefully. 'Well then, we'll see, won't we? I'll go off for my interview and find out if they want me for anything worthwhile. Sure you don't mind? It's an awful cheek.'

'Mind? Of course not. I wanted more children of my own. I longed for a son for Colin.' Samira's voice was sad.

'But you have a son.'

Samira felt the colour rush to her face. Again the words had slipped out, words that she feared could one day betray her and Matthew. 'Another son,' she said quickly, covering her mistake. 'Men always want lots of sons. My mother had six.' Then she pulled gently on the reins. The horses had been cropping the short winter grass. 'We'd best be getting back,' she said. 'Mary might have had enough of the children by now.'

367

They turned their mounts and prepared to walk them slowly down towards the house. They passed the ancient hut circles and Samira remembered Colin telling her about them. 'Bronze Age,' he had said. 'Around 1,500 to 500 BC. Impressive, don't you think?'

'Look,' she pointed out the rough granite stones to Rachel. 'They've been here for more than three thousand years. You can only see them clearly in the winter. The bracken almost covers them in summer.'

'I wonder where I'll be in the summer?' Rachel said half to herself.

Samira, in front of her, caught the words, understood the emotion. 'Perhaps the war will be over,' she said with a deliberate attempt to cheer both herself and her companion. 'Then you'll be on the way back to Palestine.'

'Perhaps,' said Rachel.

CHAPTER 25

1943

Diana came back from Egypt exhausted but triumphant and the proud possessor of a portfolio of as yet unpublished photographs that she hoped might be the basis of her future career. 'But,' she said to Thelma, 'I have no job right now and no home to go to.'

'Absolute piffle,' Thelma told her. 'You've

got both. If you're still too stubborn to go to Bagleigh, I shall have to get there on my own somehow to bring Bounder back.'

They had managed to get a flight on a transport plane from Egypt the previous day and Thelma was seated at her desk with a large pile of unopened mail in front of her. 'As for a job,' she continued, 'you won't be without one for long. You'll be kept busy writing the bumph to go with all those photographs you brought back. There's enough material for about a hundred articles, I should think. Scarcity value too. How many women could write about the things you've seen and heard lately?'

'Not many, I suppose,' Diana replied absent-mindedly. She was standing in front of the large mirror that Thelma had installed in the sitting room to reflect the view of the garden. She turned this way and that, looking at herself critically. 'I haven't much in the way of looks either after all that sun and hard work,' she said, half to herself and with an element of wry amusement. 'My freckles are terrible and I'm as skinny as a beanpole.'

Thelma glanced up from the letter she was reading. 'You'll do,' she said. 'A bit of good food will soon fatten you up.'

'You make me sound like a Christmas goose. But where are we to get good food? Don't you know there's a war on?'

Thelma laughed at the overworked expression. 'I expect there's plenty of good grub at your dear old Bagleigh. The Ministry can't count every egg

369

the chickens lay and every ounce of cream, can they?'

'I'm not going to Bagleigh.'

'Of course you are. I thought you were too adult to keep up this ridiculous vendetta?'

'Vendetta?'

'Well, something like that. You'll have to meet Rachel one day, whether you like it or not.' Thelma picked up the next letter from the pile. 'For you,' she said. 'From Devon.'

Diana ripped open the envelope and drew out two pages in her mother's handwriting. She read them through eagerly and then flopped down on the nearest chair. 'Rachel isn't there after all,' she said. 'She's upped and come to London to work, left her child with Samira if you please. Can you imagine it?'

'Seems odd certainly, especially for a Jewish woman. I always thought they were mothers before anything else.'

Diana read the pages again. 'Apparently she isn't the motherly type, never has been. Samira adores children, of course, and Deborah...' She paused a moment over the name ...'Deborah, Rachel's little girl, has become very attached to Samira. That's what my mother says here anyway. She seems to be making excuses for Rachel's behaviour.'

'I wonder what job can be so important?'

'It's all rather mysterious apparently. She's told everyone that it's something to do with translation work. She speaks fluent Dutch and pretty good French.'

Thelma grunted. 'Translation my eye! More

likely to be something much more dramatic.' She paused and shook her head. 'We'd best not talk about it. Careless talk cost lives and all that.'

'Do you think...?'

'I don't think anything and neither must you. But now I presume you'll go down to Bagleigh with me to fetch Bounder?'

Diana grinned at her friend. 'Yes, I suppose I will. I can't object to a three-year-old child, can I? In fact, I think I shall rather like to meet David's daughter.'

Diana found that her clothes coupons had accumulated while she had been abroad and she set out to buy some new dresses before returning to Devon. The two she chose were shorter than she had worn before. 'Utility, to save on material,' the shopkeeper told her. There were large shoulder pads too which she found uncomfortable at first. One dress was in a green linen with short sleeves and a tightly belted waist and the other was bright red gingham. She managed to find a warm jacket that matched both and that too possessed padded shoulders.

'I feel like a wrestler,' she said as she paraded her new finery for Thelma. She put her hands on her enormous shoulders and made a face at herself in the mirror. 'What a stupid style, and they call it attractive! I thought that fashion had gone out for the duration.'

'I suppose it's because we want to make ourselves look like men with nice broad shoulders,' Thelma said. 'Quite ridiculous, but there it is. You could always cut them out.'

'What? The men?'

'The shoulder pads, foolish child.'

'No,' Diana said firmly. 'I intend to follow the latest fashions from now on, and I've decided to have a perm. I saw an advertisement in a shop window. A Eugene costs twenty-five shillings. I shall give it a go.'

'But you'll be strung up to a machine by all those fearsome curlers. If there was an air-raid you'd be in a pretty pickle. Your hair isn't straight anyway.'

Diana made a face at herself and ran her hands through her hair so that it stuck out in all directions. 'It's thin and straggly and I need a new me before I face Bagleigh. I'll risk an air-raid.'

Thelma shrugged. 'Can't be bothered with such fripperies m'self, but you go ahead, dear girl, if it'll give you a boost. Not that you need one,' she added. 'You seem to be full of confidence and enthusiasm as you are.'

They arrived in Devon during May, and as their taxi wound up the steep road towards the moor, the first thing Diana saw from the smeary window was the gorse. The hillsides were once more aflame with its golden beauty. 'I'm glad to be going home after all,' she said. 'It's ages since I was here, nearly a year, and it feels good. The air is different...'

'Of course it is. I can't think why you want to be in London at all.'

'You know perfectly well. I like to be where the action is.'

'You sound as though you want the same things as this Rachel Halprin.'

Diana grinned. 'Well, that's a thought! As well as wanting the same man, we want the same things! Yes, perhaps you're right!' Her voice became thoughtful. 'Maybe it isn't so odd after all that she needs to do something important. But there's one great difference, isn't there?' She paused and could feel the old bitterness, the old jealousy. 'She has a child...and a husband.'

Deborah Halprin's fair hair was plaited in two little pigtails that jutted out each side of her head. She was standing just inside the gate and turned and ran towards the front door as the taxi pulled in at the end of the drive.

Diana stared at her. So this was David's Jewish daughter, looking as fair and blue-eyed as any of Hitler's master race.

'She takes after her mother completely,' Samira told her later. 'Rachel is fair. She's Dutch and she told me that quite a few Northern European Jews are fair.'

They were seated round the kitchen table enjoying cups of tea and large slabs of cake. Diana smiled to herself as she compared this informal set-up to the long-discontinued silver teapot regime in the sitting room. 'How's it all working out?' she enquired of Samira. 'Is it too much work with four small children around?'

'No, I love it.' Samira's eyes glowed with

pleasure. 'Even Dougie can be charming at times. He's at school at the moment. He fits in and is very good with the little ones. I've a feeling that he won't ever go home.'

'He doesn't seem to have a home to go to now. He's completely abandoned if you ask me,' Mary said. 'It's very sad.'

'I'm going to school soon, Auntie Diana,' Matthew contributed. 'Dougie said it's good. You learn lots of things.'

'You're a big boy for four,' Diana replied. 'You've grown a lot since I last saw you.' She couldn't help feeling a pang of grief as she looked at him. He was so handsome, a small replica of his mother. If only he could have been Colin's son. If only she could have seen, in his dark eyes and the way he smiled at her, a trace of her brother.

'I'm big too,' Deborah said, her mouth full of cake. 'Nearly as big as Matthew.'

'No, you're not, stupid! And you're a girl anyway. Girls aren't big.' Matthew straightened his back and glared at her.

Kaffa-Mary was sitting next to Diana. She had milk around her mouth like a froth of snowflakes. 'I don't want to be big,' she said solemnly. 'I want to be just like my mummy.'

Diana smiled at this little niece. Of all the four children this one was her own flesh and blood, her brother's true child, and she was filled with a quick surge of love for her. 'You have a very pretty mummy and you look like her,' she said. 'But I think you're a little bit like your daddy too. He had big brown eyes

374

just like yours. And yes...' She gently touched the child's dark waving hair. 'Yes, you've got that gingery tint in your curls that your daddy always had in summer. The sun gives you little fair bits amongst the dark.'

Matthew looked at his sister's hair with interest. He put his hand up to feel his own. 'Have I got gingery bits too? I want to be like my daddy more'n anything. He was brave. He shot down Germans.'

Diana met Samira's eyes across the table and felt that her heart would break.

'No darling,' Samira said gently to her son. 'I don't think you have, but that doesn't stop you growing up brave and strong just like he was.'

'I'm going to fight Germans when I'm grown up,' Matthew said. 'Can I get down now, Grandma?' He turned to Mary. 'Grandpa promised to take me out on Popeye after tea.'

'Yes, dear,' Mary said. 'Be careful you don't fall off.'

Diana decided to stay at Bagleigh for two or three weeks, but after a few days Thelma declared that she had work to do and must return to London. 'The countryside isn't really my favourite place,' she told everyone. 'I miss the noise.'

She was hugely delighted at the mode of travel which had been suggested for her journey to the station. She and Bounder were to be taken to Newton Abbot in a neighbour's pony trap.

James Stanmore helped her into it with elaborate ceremony. 'Think we'll have to buy one,' he said. 'It's the only way to get about now with petrol a thing of the past.'

'Back to nature,' Thelma replied. 'Well, it's been nice seeing you again, James. We haven't met for umpteen years and then twice in a year.'

'Bring Bounder down if you go off gallivanting any more,' he told her. 'Nice little dog, no trouble, and try to persuade that daughter of mine to stay home here for good.' He wagged a finger at her. 'You and my sister have made her into a discontented hussy.'

Thelma laughed. 'Absolute rubbish!' she said. 'Harriet always told me what an old stick-in-the-mud you were long ago when we were girls. As a matter of fact, she told me to beware of you.'

'You were never in any danger,' he said. 'I was looking for a nice quiet submissive little wife.'

'Then I was certainly not a candidate,' she called cheerfully back at him as the pony ambled away along the lane.

James watched until the trap was out of sight and then he went into the house grinning to himself. Thelma had visited Bagleigh a few times with his sister when they were all young. He had indeed fancied her once. He shook his head in relief. What a fate he had been saved from! Mary was the wife for him. Submissive, that was what women should be.

He had long ago decided that this was the most important attribute in a woman. Samira was submissive. He had changed his mind about his daughter-in-law. In spite of his early misgivings he had to admit now that she had turned out well on the whole. His son had not chosen so badly after all. He must talk to her soon about Matthew and his plans for his education. He was sure that she would agree with any decisions he might make.

The following evening he summoned Samira and Diana into the sitting room. The children were in bed and Mary was ironing and listening to the wireless which they had recently installed in the kitchen.

Diana came in first and flopped on to the sofa. She looked at her father and wondered what could be the meaning of this formal request. Samira was obviously uneasy when she joined them and Diana sensed her apprehension. Immediately her own foreboding deepened. Her father stood in front of the old granite fireplace, his hands behind his back. The fire had been lit an hour ago for the evenings were chilly and it was just beginning to give out a little heat.

'I want to talk to you about Bagleigh,' James said without preamble. 'As you know the house and land is entailed upon the male line. When I died it would have been Colin's, with certain quite valuable shares to you, Diana. You would also get the cottage. Still do.'

He paused and turned away from them for a moment and Diana felt herself trembling. So this was it! This was the horror that had been waiting to break about their heads. She looked at Samira who was sitting with her hands tightly clasped and her eyes cast downwards, staring at the intricate pattern on the carpet at her feet as if it held some magical power that would save them all from the catastrophe to come. She thought of Matthew asleep upstairs, so young and quite unaware of the awful truth he would soon have to face. For a moment she considered that it would even be worth losing Bagleigh if she could save her whole family from that damaging truth.

'So,' James was saying, 'I have been to see my solicitor and everything is in order. There is nothing more to be said. I think you also know that I have put Matthew's name down for Wellington. He will go to the village school here until he is seven and then away to prep school. That too is all arranged.'

Samira's thoughts were only with her son and for a few seconds she almost failed to grasp the totality of what was being said. At first the second edict about boarding school took precedence over the first and she wanted to scream at her father-in-law that he couldn't send her child away at seven years old as was the manner of these strange middle-class English. But then her frozen mind began to work again and she realised that he wouldn't want to do so when he knew the truth. He would throw Matthew out, anywhere, but certainly away from Bagleigh, totally out of his sight for good. Everything she valued most was at stake. She wanted to sit there and keep quiet, say nothing, give in as she had done almost all of her life. It would be so easy to allow the lie to go on. But she had promised Colin! She could almost hear his words, see his face as he had told her what he wanted to happen if he should die. Tears slid down her cheeks, but she brushed them impatiently away. The terrible facts must be told now, this very minute, if she was to be true to her husband's memory. There was no other way. There must be no more deceit, no more pretence.

She stood up and forced herself to look straight into the eyes of the man she feared now more than any other. 'None of what you have said can be so,' she said quietly.

There was silence in the room, a silence so dreadful that Rollo who had been lying asleep at the side of the fireplace woke and looked around from one to the other. Then slowly he got up and walked towards the closed door, his tail dragging between his legs. He stood there immobile and Diana got to her feet automatically and let him out. She did it all in slow motion, her mind reeling from what she had just heard.

James stared at his daughter-in-law in total incomprehension. 'Explain yourself,' he said. His voice was iron-cold. 'Why can it not be so?'

Diana closed the door quietly behind the dog and then stayed just where she was, her hand on the brass knob. She looked at her father and held her breath. The expression on his face was quite frightful. She knew she would never forget this moment.

Samira had her back to her. She was still standing in front of the sofa, her body very taut and straight in the ugly tweed skirt and

379

thick jumper. Diana wondered at her sudden courage. She must have loved Colin very much for it could only be loyalty to the promise she had made to him, that would force this truth from her lips, a truth that would destroy all the security she craved and worse, would devastate her son's life.

'Matthew isn't Colin's son.'

Diana heard Samira speak the dreadful words in level guarded tones, unemotionally.

'He is the son of an Arab sheik to whom I was married for one day before my wedding with Colin.'

Diana felt herself trembling now and knew that Samira must be terrified in spite of that calm exterior. She had no idea how her father would react. He had never, to her knowledge, been violent although she could imagine that he might be capable of violence. She looked from one to the other and felt that she was about to witness an explosion of the worst rage and grief that she had ever seen.

But James Stanmore said nothing. He merely stared at Samira, or rather right through her, and then marched to the door. He pushed Diana aside and opened it and walked slowly up the stairs. Both girls heard each footstep and the creak as he reached the bend near the top.

Then suddenly Samira was galvanised into action. 'He's going up to Matthew. Oh, please, not that. Please God, don't let him hurt Matthew.' She was out of the door and running up the stairs two at a time before Diana could collect her wits and follow.

As Samira reached the landing James opened Matthew's bedroom door and walked towards the bed. Filled with terror, and heedless of her own safety, Samira was about to tear over and put herself between them, but Diana, close behind her, saw what was happening and understood.

She gripped Samira's arm. 'He won't hurt him. Wait,' she commanded.

They stood breathlessly, staring at James' back as he looked down at Matthew. The little boy stirred in his sleep, said something and turned over. Then Samira could hardly credit what she saw. Her father-in-law bent over the bed, but his action was gentle, full of love. She thought that he kissed Matthew, but she couldn't be sure for she could only see his back and he straightened up very quickly. He stood for a moment more in the quietness of the dimly lit room and then turned round and walked towards them.

He ushered them out and followed, closing the door silently behind him.

Once outside on the landing his whole manner and bearing changed. There was no gentleness in him now. When he spoke his voice was quiet but in deadly earnest and there was a fierce anger in his eyes that made Samira flinch in renewed terror.

'Matthew is my grandson and my heir,' he declared, 'and anyone who says otherwise or who breathes a word of the disgraceful matter I heard tonight will never be allowed to spend another night in my house. Is that clear?' He looked from one to the other and his eyes now were cold and calculating. 'My son is dead. I have his son to replace him. If you contradict me, Samira, you will leave this house and you will never see either of your children again. That is all I have to say, and the end of the matter.' He pushed past them and went down the stairs without looking back.

CHAPTER 26

Sleep refused to come to Diana that night. She felt completely rejected, a non-person of no importance whatsoever. It wasn't merely the loss of Bagleigh that hurt her, for she had grown up knowing that her brother would inherit. It was the way her father had rejected her so completely, so coldly, accepting a lie as the truth, taking a foundling child instead of his own flesh and blood, that distressed her so much.

As she tossed and turned angrily on her bed she came gradually to see that her father had blocked out from his mind the unpalatable facts that he had heard last night. He couldn't possibly have doubted Samira's integrity for he must have known that she would never have made up such a story. But because the truth was so terrible to him he had dismissed it totally, refusing to acknowledge it in any way.

She awoke the following morning feeling crushed and wretched. Although she considered herself to be fairly strong and independent, her father's rebuff hurt her more than she cared to admit. She was so upset that even riding Merryon or Major was out of the question. They would feel her distress too much. After breakfast she called to Rollo and trudged out of the house.

'Can I come, Auntie Di?' Matthew ran after her. 'Mummy's all quiet today and the girls want to play sissy games. Can I come up to Greatcombe Rocks with you?'

'Not this morning, Matty,' she said. 'I want to go on my own today.'

'You look sad,' he said. 'I could come and cheer you up.'

She wanted to be alone, desperately needed time to come to terms with what had happened, and Matthew of all people wouldn't exactly be the best companion just now, but she looked at the little boy and reminded herself that nothing was his fault. She loved him, had loved him from the day of his birth. She relented. 'All right then,' she said. 'Come on. You'd better tell them you're coming though. I'll wait.'

They walked in silence for a time and eventually she felt Matthew's small hand creep into hers. She gripped it and was comforted. This was the child who was going to usurp her and any sons she might have in the future, who would have Bagleigh. If only he had been Colin's true-born son she would have accepted it happily. But she must accept it anyway. 'If only' were terrible little words that should be banished completely, she thought. They only brought self-pity and misery.

Rollo rushed ahead, picked up a stick and brought it to them, laying it at their feet. His tail wagged expectantly and Diana threw it as best she could with her free hand.

Matthew laughed. 'Grandpa is going to give me a dog of my very own. He promised 'cause I was sad when Bounder went back to London. Dougie said London's no good for dogs.'

With the wind in her hair and the child's company Diana could feel her distress ebbing slowly away. 'Bounder will be all right. There are parks in London for him to run in,' she said.

'Auntie Rachel's in London,' Matthew volunteered. 'It's a secret.'

Diana took a deep breath. She didn't want to think much about Rachel Halprin. She never did. 'You mustn't talk about it then if it's a secret.'

Matthew loosed her hand and skipped ahead. Then he turned back and looked at her. 'Debbie's lucky 'cause she's got a daddy as well as a mummy. He's coming to see her soon. He comes a lot. He flies aeroplanes like my daddy did and drops bombs on Germans.'

Diana felt her heart miss a beat or two. 'He's coming to Bagleigh?' Why had no one told her?

'Yes, and he promised to bring me a model bomber, a Wellington I 'spect. I like Uncle David. He's fun.'

Diana closed her eyes for a second. Oh, and I like him too, far too much. This was another

384

grief, perhaps an even bigger one, another 'if only' in her life that she mustn't allow.

When they returned to the house an hour later there was a letter waiting for her on the hall table. From Philip. She picked it up and held it in her hand for a moment, staring at it, suddenly full of guilt. Why? Thoughts of David coming here: the everlasting passion that she couldn't cast out however hard she tried? She must get back to London, back to the blessed oblivion of work and more work. Thelma was a good antidote to self-pity.

She opened the letter slowly and scanned the pages. 'He's getting shore leave,' she said to her mother who had just come into the hall. 'His ship's coming into Plymouth for refit.' Her voice was flat, bemused.

Mary looked pleased. 'Well, that's something to cheer us all up,' she said. 'Everyone seems gloomy this morning. Samira has hardly said a word and I haven't even seen James. He was out before I was awake. You'll be able to go over to Maddacombe to stay for a while if Philip is going to be home for some time, won't you? That'll be nice. You'll have to get to know his parents a bit better if you're going to live there after the wedding.'

Wedding? What wedding? Maddacombe? Live with his parents? It sounded like Samira's first awful marriage arrangements. Diana twisted the bright engagement ring on her finger. She was wearing it again now that she was at home. Why on earth had she accepted it? She knew perfectly well, of course, but so much had happened since. Her mind flitted back over the past year to the fascinating months she had been abroad.

After Alamein she and Thelma had moved to Cairo and there, for a short time, she had met the members of the Press who had followed the whole progress of the Desert War. They were not all men either. She had been surprised by that for she'd heard that Monty didn't like women reporters. They had stayed in one of the big hotels and had been part of the glittering life there for a short time. Cairo was the centre of everything, a place for fun, full of smart exciting people, glamorous hotels and night clubs. And there was, in contrast, the brooding intensity of the Nile and the pyramids, and over all of this the restlessness and excitement of war. It had whetted her appetite for something more than Maddacombe, even perhaps something more than Bagleigh.

Philip was taller than she had remembered, bronzed and fit and incredibly handsome in his Lieutenant's uniform. They were to have a night in Plymouth he had told her when he had telephoned. 'Just the two of us without the family. After such a long time apart we need to get to know one another again.' She had been taken by surprise, acquiesced without thinking, and now here they were.

He had booked two single but adjoining rooms, the best the hotel could provide, both with a view of the sea. There were flowers on her dressing table.

'I've been dreaming about this for ever,' he told her as his eyes explored her face. But his kiss was restrained, waiting, she felt, for later. She shivered.

They ate, drank champagne, and she felt her tension gradually draining away. Was it just the champagne? Could this man to whom she had given her promise, whose ring she wore, ever replace that other destructive passion? Why was she consumed with desire for a man whom she could never have, a man who had only one thought in his head for most of the time, and that an impossible dream for a country he called Eretz Israel? Such a place didn't even exist anyway. Perhaps her wayward heart was living in a dream world too just as David was, longing for something completely unobtainable. Philip was here. Philip was real, no dream, and he wanted her, loved her. Wasn't that of more value than any fantasy? She knew with a deadening certainty that it was not.

After dinner they wandered on the Hoe. It was quite dark for there was no moon tonight and the blackout was total.

'The single rooms,' he said at last. 'I didn't want to presume.'

His arm tightened around her. She could feel his fingers pressing into her shoulder, his emotion communicating itself clearly to every nerve in her body.

'Let's go back,' he whispered. 'We'll have another bottle of champagne in my room.'

It's wartime, her mind dictated, he's going away soon, give him pleasure. We all need a little pleasure in this nightmare war. But then she knew that for her at least it wasn't a nightmare war. She was enjoying it, actually enjoying her part in it. More guilt! But, oh, the bliss of no ties, no marriage yet, certainly no babies. Let the future take care of itself. She would remain free, her own person, at all costs.

'Will you marry me before I go back, Diana?'

The words cut into her thoughts like a shaft of ice. No, oh no, not that, please don't ask it of me. I don't want to hurt you. Tears sprang to her eyes. She felt humbled, unworthy of the man at her side. 'Not yet, Philip. Please, not yet. After the war.' Dear God, what was she saying? How was she to survive this night, the next few days?

She couldn't bear his so obvious hurt when she kissed him briefly outside her bedroom door, pushed the key firmly into the lock. Please let the door open easily, no difficulties. It swung inwards and she turned and looked into his pain-filled eyes. She was aware of the movement he made, one step towards her into the room. 'No,' she said. 'Please, Philip, no.'

With the door finally closed between them she threw herself on to her bed and sobbed her disgust with herself into the hard and unyielding pillow until it was damp with her misery.

Back in London a few weeks later she tried to take up the reins of her life.

'How's Bagleigh? How's your impossible father? How's Philip?' Thelma fired the questions at her over the inevitable cup of tea on that first afternoon.

Diana laughed a trifle grimly. 'Where shall I begin?'

'With Philip.'

'Philip? He's handsome, good, wholly admirable, loves me in spite of my awful behaviour, still wants to marry me, I think.' How could she add: dull, dull, oh so dull, to me at any rate.

'And you're having second thoughts about marrying him?'

Diana looked at her companion in surprise. But Thelma had always been perceptive. 'Everyone likes him,' she said, not answering the question, but it was not really a question, more a statement. 'Father and Mother think he's quite wonderful, Samira considers him the bee's knees. I almost believe she's jealous of me. And the children all adore him.'

'Did you see David Halprin?' Another perceptive query.

'No. He didn't come when I was there. A good thing, I suppose.' She picked up her cup of tea and drained it to the bottom, getting a mouthful of tea leaves. 'What's happened to the strainer?' she asked, spitting them back into the cup and making a face.

'A hole, dear girl, and no others to be had for love or money. I suppose they've all gone to make Spitfires. You'll have to put up with tea leaves from now on.'

'I suppose we're lucky to get tea,' said Diana.

Samira had secretly been very cross with Diana during Philip's leave. She had watched him carefully when they were all together, had seen the frequent hurt look on his face when Diana was cold towards him, and had marvelled that anyone could spurn such a kind and attractive man. He had not stayed as long as they'd first expected. The ship had only needed repairs and not the refit that had been expected.

After he had gone back to sea Diana hadn't remained very long at Bagleigh either, but the night before she left for London they had talked a little—not about Philip, although Samira, for some obscure reason that she couldn't fully understand, longed to ask Diana whether she loved him. They had discussed the future of Bagleigh and James Stanmore's strange behaviour over Matthew.

'What are you going to do about it, Diana?' Samira had asked with a degree of diffidence. She realised that her father-in-law's edict worked in her own favour. The only loser was Diana.

But she had seemed almost disinterested, the first bleakness quite spent. 'Do?' she had replied. 'Nothing, of course. There is nothing to be done. My father has made up his mind and that's that.'

'But it wasn't what Colin wanted.' Samira often tortured herself with that thought.

'We'll make a pact,' Diana had said. 'We'll do nothing, tell no one as Father ordered. Perhaps in the future...well, who knows what may happen in the future? My mother must certainly not be told. It would destroy her.

I promise you, Samira, that I'll never say a word, do anything, unless we are both agreed upon it.'

Samira had been wildly grateful and her irritation at Diana's treatment of Philip had been thrust aside. She had kissed her sister-in-law and cried a few tears of relief. For the time being everything was secure and normal again. There was only her loneliness to manage. Since she had watched Philip's rather sad farewells to Diana she had begun to feel the burden of her own solitary life. Caring for the children was some compensation, but not enough. Diana was self-sufficient, needed no one really, but...I'm different, she thought. I need someone. Colin's memory is always with me, but I can't live with a ghost.

No one knew of Samira's unhappiness. She continued outwardly to appear completely content.

One day in August she was picking runner beans with Mary in the kitchen garden. She was intrigued by the way her mother-in-law salted them down in big glass jars for use in the winter. Samira had never learnt to do anything like this at home in Palestine.

'We put them in layers,' Mary had explained the day before. 'One of salt and one of beans and so on. That way we'll never run out.'

Privately Samira wished that they would run out. She could happily do without boiled runner beans with every meal. They were nice raw though. She put one in her mouth and crunched it noisily. 'I don't know why we cook them,' she said. 'They're better like this.'

The children were playing in the orchard, but at that moment they came tumbling into the kitchen garden and helped themselves to the longest, juiciest beans. 'We're playing war,' Dougie announced, pointing a bean at her as though it were a gun. 'But the girls won't do what I say. They're no good at war.'

'War's horrid,' Kaffa-Mary objected. 'It's silly.'

'I like war 'cause while it's on I can stay here,' Dougie said. He was eight years old now and seemed a permanent fixture at Bagleigh. The other evacuees had returned to their homes a long time ago, but Dougie's father appeared to be non-existent and his mother had abandoned him completely, disappearing into the war-time chaos of London. 'What'll I do when there's peace?'

'You can stay here as long as you like, Dougie,' Mary assured him. 'But now carry those buckets in and we'll have a drink of lemonade and a biscuit.'

They trooped into the house and Samira, coming last and holding the hands of the two little girls, wondered what peacetime would bring for all of them. Deborah was gripping her hand tightly. She had obviously been thinking about Dougie's words.

'Can I stay too, Auntie Sam, for ever and ever?' she asked.

Samira shook her head. 'You won't want to,' she said. 'Not when your mummy and daddy come home for good.'

'I will, I will, I will,' said Deborah. 'For ever and ever.'

Rachel's training had been long and arduous, but now she was to have some well-earned weeks at home before her first assignment. At the end of August David too had a long leave.

'We'll take Deborah off your hands for a time and rent a cottage or something,' he had said to Mary on the telephone. 'You're too good to us.'

But Mary loved having visitors. She craved a house full of people and children and wouldn't hear of them going elsewhere. 'As long as you bring your rations,' she had told him, 'we'll be fine. I've told the hens to lay more eggs!'

Much to Matthew's delight David arrived in his RAF uniform. He was now a Flight Lieutenant and had been awarded the DFC. He refused to talk about the reasons for this honour but Matthew and Dougie were both round-eyed with admiration. He had brought each of the boys a model Wellington bomber.

There were American servicemen everywhere lately and Dougie was constantly trying to copy everything about them, but the Yanks paled to insignificance beside Deborah's glamorous bomber-pilot father.

'Oh, boy! Gee whiz, that's really something,' he exclaimed as he held his 'plane aloft and raced around the room with it. 'Thanks a lot, Uncle David.' He paused for a moment in his headlong flight and stared at David with sudden awe. 'I wish I had an important dad who flew bombers.'

'Mummy does 'portant things too,' Deborah said. 'I got a 'portant daddy and a 'portant mummy.'

Later on that first day when the children were in bed Rachel and David walked up to the tor. 'What actually are you doing?' David asked. 'A husband ought to know what his wife is up to, Rachel. I'm very frightened for you.'

'All I can tell you is what you already know,' she whispered.

'A Radio Officer in the Intelligence Corps of the British Army,' David said. 'And I thought it was to be translation work.'

'It is. It's that too, and just think how valuable I shall be to our country, David, after the war. The new Israel is going to need all the abilities we have, and if the British are willing to train us, well then, we should take the opportunities offered.'

'The new Israel is going to need plenty of sabres too, little citizens born in Palestine,' David said gently. 'I'd hoped that was what you wanted to do.'

'Between us we shall breed a super race,' she declared, laughing. 'There'll be plenty of time for that as well. We're young, and don't forget we have children's houses on the kibbutz. Our admirable system won't force me to look after all these children we're going to produce.'

'And before we do any of that,' he said, catching her optimism, 'we'll buy a little motor car and tour the whole of Eretz Israel from Dan to Be'er Sheva. We'll see it all.'

Hand in hand they swung jauntily down the hill again, feeling the excitement of a world that lay before them full of challenge and fulfilment and wonderful promise.

Christmas arrived in Bagleigh with the normal damp misty weather that Samira was used to now. The autumn had been uneventful with only the usual country things to do, the children to look after, the horses to exercise, and the chores that seemed endless in such a big house with no help to be had at all now. Samira was usually too busy to fret much about her loneliness, but still she worried about the future.

Sometimes she was fearful, wondering how a teenage or grown-up Matthew would react to the news that he was the son of a Muslim Arab, for surely one day he would have to be told the truth? When her thoughts went in this direction, Eshref would come vividly to mind. Could he ever claim Matthew? It was something too horrible to contemplate.

When these fears predominated, everything about her life here seemed to Samira to have a dream-like quality, as if the past was reality, the present unreal. She felt this occasionally when she first awoke in her warm feather bed. Then she would turn over for another five minutes, delighting in its security, dwelling on the positive things. Usually this strategy worked and the worries disappeared.

There was no dream-like quality about the way the war was going however. James Stanmore kept everyone up to date with the news. General Montgomery, he announced, was to be appointed Field Commander, but under a Yank of all people. 'This Dwight D. Eisenhower would be the Supreme Commander,' he said. 'Why couldn't they have had Monty?'

'Supreme Commander of what?' Mary asked. She liked to assume ignorance of these relatively unimportant things. It gave James a sense of his own superiority and made him easier to live with.

'The allies' biggest operation yet,' he said. 'We're going to invade Europe, woman, free Holland and France and the rest of it.'

'Oh.' When her husband made this announcement Mary was sitting at her desk making lists of things to do and buy. She gave him scant attention. 'That's good then.'

Samira, listening, immediately thought of Rachel. Although nothing had been said, she was quite sure that Rachel was not in England any more now. She had not been back to Bagleigh since September and there had been only scant news. Samira guessed, with a shiver of fear whenever she thought about it, that Rachel was probably doing something connected with espionage or the resistance movement. It was a terrifying thought. David never talked about his wife's movements and this confirmed her fears.

How could she leave her little daughter and go off to do such a dangerous thing? Samira often wondered. But it was wonderfully brave and noble. She was full of admiration, and gave Debbie more than her share of affection and cuddles to compensate.

In London Diana too had her suspicions about Rachel's work. Nothing specific was said in any letter from Bagleigh, but there were the odd hints now and then.

'I believe that David's wife is working in Europe, somewhere behind enemy lines,' she said one morning to Thelma after reading the latest letter. 'My mother says that David goes to Bagleigh as often as he can, every leave in fact, to make up for Deborah not seeing her mummy very often now. Funny that our paths have never crossed.'

'She must be a very exceptional woman, this Rachel, especially being Jewish,' Thelma said. 'I wouldn't give much for her chances if the Jerries get hold of her.'

Diana sniffed. 'Yes, she is exceptional, I believe. Everyone seems to think so anyway.'

By the spring of 1944 David was really worried about his wife. There had been no news for weeks, and when in early-June his squadron was detailed to pound the German batteries all along the Normandy coast, he put all his anger and fury into every sortie. As the flames lit the night sky he thought of Rachel down there, possibly in the hands of the Gestapo, being interrogated, tortured probably. She would never give in. Would they discover that she was Jewish? Her fair hair might give her some protection. It was a pretty vain hope but he clung to it desperately.

God, don't let her die. The words went round and round in his head constantly like a litany. But he had little hope of any deity hearing him for hadn't thousands of Jews perished in the fiendish Nazi camps and the Jewish God had done nothing.

CHAPTER 27

'I was at Bagleigh this time last year,' Diana said. She looked out of the window at the May garden where Thelma had just been planting out dahlias for the summer. The large lilac tree behind the new plants was in full bloom, the scent creeping seductively into the room. She breathed deeply of the bewitching perfume. 'I've only been home twice since. I feel guilt about it.'

'Shouldn't worry too much,' Thelma replied. 'You have your own life to lead now, and they're all right down there, aren't they? If there was a problem you'd be off straight away.'

Diana smiled to herself. Yes, they were all right. Samira had almost taken her place as daughter of the house. She was just the kind of daughter that Diana's parents had always craved: domesticated, contented with very little, submissive.

'Father has come to be very fond of her,' she

said. 'He forgets that she's not English but if you want to believe something badly enough it often becomes fact in your mind. That's what has happened to him.' With Matthew too, she thought. Matthew is Colin's true-born son to my father, probably always will be. The unpleasant facts of his birth that Samira confessed to him on that never-to-be-forgotten day last year were banished completely from his mind just as though they had never been.

'You've been jolly successful lately,' Thelma said, cutting into her thoughts. 'Don't give up now.' She pointed to the latest copy of *La Mode* which lay on the table. 'Saw your last article. Great pictures, good writing. Keep it up, girl.'

Diana blushed with pleasure. 'Philip asked me to marry him during that last leave. I managed to put him off.'

'A choice you'll have to make one day, dear child,' Thelma replied. 'Life's full of difficult choices.'

'We're engaged so I suppose I've made my choice.'

'Things change.' Thelma grinned at her and waved her muddy hands in the air. 'Must go and wash and make some coffee. Thank God for coffee.' She went into the kitchen, turned on the tap and plunged her hands into the water. 'Don't make irrevocable decisions in a hurry if you can help it.'

By the August of 1944 Diana was abroad again. To her delight, and to her father's disgust, she had managed to secure accreditation from the

399

armed forces as a war correspondent and now she found herself in France a few miles behind the allied lines.

She wasn't prepared for the ravages that the war had inflicted upon so many of the towns and villages there. She had been twice before in peacetime, once on a short holiday and the second time just the journey through on her way home from Palestine. She remembered on both occasions being impressed by the country's beauty and serenity.

It was all so different now. Worst of all was Caen. The town appeared to have been almost completely obliterated. She photographed as well as she could from the back of the army truck in which she was travelling, but once asked her driver to stop. She had seen a teddy bear sitting atop a ruined wall with a cigar fixed in his mouth and a British Army helmet on his head. Two small tattered flags were pinned to him, the French tricolour and a Union Jack. Nothing that she had seen so far had made her cry. She was determined to be the tough woman journalist, no feminine weaknesses ever showing, but that bear in that place brought the tears. She jumped from the truck and photographed him from many angles but kept her face turned away from her amused companions. Before she returned to the vehicle she brushed her hand quickly over her eyes. It wouldn't do to be emotional just now. Her sturdy slacks, army shirt and jacket, and her careful disregard for her appearance, mustn't be discredited by any tears.

In every newly liberated village the people were jubilant, and Diana was welcomed with enthusiasm and gratitude. In spite of all the devastation, wine was usually brought from secret places amongst the ruins where it had been hidden from the Germans during the occupation, meals were prepared with dedication and skill in spite of all the shortages and difficulties, and celebration was everywhere.

But memories of the brutality of the feared SS were still vivid, and in most villages Diana saw frightened or defiant women with their heads totally shaved. These were the collaborators. Some had babies in their arms or in battered prams. 'German bastards,' she was told. 'They're whores, those women. We spit on them.'

'I should like to get some of their stories,' she confided to her driver, a cheerful cockney, Private Sam Fairweather.

'If you want to write about a lot of bloody whores, darlin',' he said, 'we'll see if they'll play ball, but be careful. Nobody loves 'em. They're damned lucky to get away with just their bloody heads shaved. Fraternised, didn't they, with the boche. Deserve to be shot along with their damned brats.'

Diana had long since given up being shocked by anything she heard from the men she was travelling with. She looked at the kindly soldier who had just said those awful things and guessed that he didn't mean a word of it.

'What about that place we just 'eard about?' Sam went on however. 'Ordure-sur-something or other. Been smashed to bits by the SS because one of their ruddy officers got killed.'

Diana too had just read the report. The whole village of Oradour-sur-Glane had been obliterated, the men rounded up and shot and the women and children burnt to death in the church. She sighed, unable to think of any suitable reply.

The truck was bumping over the pot-holed surface alarmingly and Sam Fairweather kept his eyes firmly on the road. 'Then there's them concentration camps,' he went on relentlessly, his large hands gripping the steering wheel as if he was frightened that one moment's lack of concentration would land them all in the ditch. 'Killing Jews and Gypsies and the like by the thousand they say. I never liked Jews, nor Gypsies for that matter, but slaughtering them like animals ain't right.'

'I have a...a Jewish friend,' Diana said, 'who I think has been working for the resistance somewhere. She's jolly brave. There's been no news for a long time now.'

Sam grunted, but still didn't turn to look at her. 'She's 'ad 'er comeuppance then if she's one of them ruddy Jews,' he said.

By the end of August Diana reached Paris. The city, just liberated, was overflowing with excitement and high spirits. In spite of the years of occupation there was a vibrancy and sparkle that Diana found difficult to describe.

Letters from Thelma in London told her about the new science fiction-like terror that Londoners were having to cope with now, the loathsome and pilotless flying bombs. They came out of the sky without warning, flames spurting from their tails, and Londoners of an imaginative turn of mind named them devils from hell. Compared to the despair that these had brought to the English capital, Paris was pulsating with life and colour, an electrifying place to be. The atmosphere gave Diana a feeling of wild exuberance.

'I've been kissed and cheered all day long,' she confessed to Linda Milson, a fellow journalist when she returned to her hotel on the first night in the city. 'And everyone was willing, anxious in fact, to pose for the camera.'

'Same here,' her companion said. 'Gosh! Can't imagine how I'd feel after all those years of occupation. The girls' clothes really took me by surprise. I suppose I'd thought of the people as starving and dowdy.'

'Not Parisiennes,' Diana said. 'But where on earth have they found those wonderful fripperies? I thought all that kind of thing went out long ago. I've taken some fantastic photographs that'll shock the people back home. They won't believe it.'

'Might give the wrong impression. Best be careful what you send in.'

'You mean they'll be jealous?'

Linda laughed. 'Some'll no doubt think that we Brits have been doing all the fighting while the folks here have had things easy.'

'Then they ought to see the rest of it,' Diana said. 'They will, of course. I've got some horrific shots that'll go in alongside the cheerful ones.'

She thought of the teddy bear, the piles of rubble, the refugees.

'Paris was always glamorous before the war,' Linda said. She frowned at herself in the mirror as she spoke. 'I came here on holiday in '37. Seems years ago now. I was even slightly glamorous myself then. I suppose they kept their gayest things hidden while the Germans were here.'

'Except the shaven-headed ones!'

'Oh, those.' Linda sniffed dismissively. 'The collaborators. Did you get any photographs of them?'

'A few. One of them talked to me. Made me jolly sad in fact.'

Linda looked up, obviously interested.

'Why sad?'

'She said he was a good man, her Kurt, an officer. She loved him. She insisted that some of the ordinary Germans were honourable, not like the SS.'

Linda shrugged. 'She was still a traitor though. Are you going to publish all that? In a sympathetic way, I mean?'

'Perhaps. I'd like to do my own book after the war.'

'What are you going to do when it's all over?' Linda flopped down on the bed, lighting a cigarette. 'I've thoroughly enjoyed these last few years, though I feel a bit guilty saying that. Suppose I've been lucky, but I'd have been stuck in some dead-end job at home or married with kids if it hadn't been for Hitler!'

'The same goes for me,' Diana agreed. 'And

if I do what my family expect, I shall marry Philip and become a contented farmer's wife.'

'Marriage snuffs out everything,' Linda commented. 'Not sure that I want to get married actually.'

'Not everything.' Diana was looking out of the window. The hotel was in a typical street of tall shuttered buildings with ornate balconies at most of the windows. Flags fluttered from many of them. She thought of the view from her window at home, so different, wild hills and great rocky outcrops. 'I know someone who's left her husband and kid and gone off to join the secret service or resistance or something,' she said quietly. 'It's all very hush-hush. There's been no news of her for weeks as a matter of fact.' Why do I have to keep talking about Rachel Halprin? She wondered. Why is she so often in my thoughts?

'You mean she's been captured?'

'Looks like it. She's Jewish too.'

'Heaven help her. You've heard about Maidenek Concentration Camp, have you? The one in Poland that's been liberated?'

'Yes, the gas chambers!'

'It doesn't seem possible. It's like the Middle Ages.'

'Much worse. They didn't have gas in the Middle Ages!'

Diana shivered in spite of the hot stuffy room. How could she get Rachel out of her thoughts? Was it because of David? She closed her eyes. Oh, please God, let me not think of David so often. With his wife in...in goodness knows what terrible plight, it's absolutely obscene.

She returned home only twice during the next few months. Her reports and photographs were acclaimed as brilliant, and she travelled widely in Europe, usually a day or so behind the victorious liberating armies, in search of stories and photographs. She was delighted when, in April of 1945, she was joined for a short time by Thelma.

'Everywhere is in a pretty awful state, dear girl,' her friend remarked unnecessarily. 'I've just done some gruelling hundreds of miles in a frightful vehicle. I hope never to repeat such a journey.'

They were staying in the usual press hotel, commandeered by the British, for this was Germany now, a frightened and defeated Germany. Diana took Thelma's battered suitcase and dumped it on the bed next to hers. 'I'm afraid it's the only mode of transport and we're lucky to get that. You've seen the thousands of refugees, of course?'

'Where on earth are they all going? It's frightening.'

Diana sighed. 'Thousands are trying to get home or to track down lost relations. The Jews who are capable of anything other than just lying down and dying, dream of getting to Palestine, and lots more are just wandering with no idea where they want to go.'

'Any news of Rachel Halprin?' Thelma said. 'I don't suppose you've heard anything?' She opened her suitcase and frowned at the dusty and creased pair of slacks on the top. 'I took Bounder down to Bagleigh before I left England and I met her husband. He was visiting little Deborah, a sweet child.'

Diana shook her head. 'No, I haven't heard a thing, but then I wouldn't, would I? What did David say?'

'Say?'

'About Rachel. What do they think? Is the government doing anything?'

'Nothing they can do. The Red Cross are doing their best to find out what's happened to her. David is frantically worried, of course, but she seems to have disappeared completely. His squadron bombed Dresden by the way.'

'Some people say that we shouldn't have done that.'

'David said he might have felt marginally guilty if he'd known that Rachel was safe, but thinking of her in the hands of the Gestapo made him so angry that he didn't care.'

Diana remembered those words when she stared with chilled horror and unbelieving eyes at the camp they called Belsen. And, dear God, the smell! She knew she would never forget that smell as long as she lived. She walked beside a great trench full of naked emaciated bodies. Some of them seemed to move, an arm, a stick-leg, even a head or trunk. The man beside her was an officer of the Guards Armoured Division which had arrived two days before. 'No, they're not alive,' he said in a strangled voice. 'It's the gases in their putrefying bodies. We're doing our best to get the trench filled in, but the living need all our attention first.'

'But how?' Diana could get no further. She rushed away and was violently sick.

'You didn't know?' he murmured when she returned.

'I'd heard.' She groped for a handkerchief and wiped her face. 'But knowing is very different from seeing.'

'You reporters are here to tell the world.'

Diana shivered. 'How can I? How can I calmly position my camera and photograph all that indescribable agony and horror?'

She had never needed to worry about taking photographs before. It was second nature to her, her camera part of her, like her eyes almost. She usually saw everything that she encountered in terms of photographic frames, but this was different. This took your very being, everything you were, and tore it into shreds so that nothing whole or sane remained. Nothing could ever again be as it was before today, before this hour.

'You must,' he said. 'You have a duty to record it so that it never happens again.'

For the next two days she lived through the most horrific nightmare of her life. She wandered the camp, helping the medical teams whenever she was able, photographing the dead and the living-dead. And all the time thoughts of Rachel haunted her. News had come through at last that she had been captured and since then had disappeared completely into this great Nazi horror machine. Was it to a place like this that she had been taken?

The jealousy Diana had lived with for so long swiftly evaporated in the unrelenting hideousness of the things she was witnessing every hour. The only emotions she had left were admiration and searing grief, admiration for this woman who had risked everything for an ideal, and grief for her terrible fate. But combined with these things was a sense of her own unworthiness. In every skeletal face both of the living and the dead she saw Rachel's face, and in each small child who had survived this hell she saw Deborah Halprin. For the people here were mostly Jews. She knew that millions, not merely Sam Fairweather's thousands, had been slaughtered, by starvation, by the gun, by senseless beatings, by medical experiments, and in the gas chambers. Never again would she resent David's longing for a country of his own, his fierce determination to have a place where his people could be secure and free. Since Belsen she understood more fully than ever before. Since Belsen her world had been turned on its head. Since Belsen she was a different person.

Philip's ship came into Plymouth again in early-May and as he left the docks he saw flags hanging brightly from windows and red white and blue bunting decorating the streets. He telephoned Bagleigh only to find that Diana was still somewhere in Germany. Disappointment shot through him for although he understood how important her work was to her, he'd hoped that she might have managed leave. He'd told her that he expected to be home at the beginning of May.

He arrived at Maddacombe in time to hear Winston Churchill declaring on the wireless that:

...the representative of the German High Command...signed the act of unconditional surrender of all German land, sea and air forces in Europe. Hostilities will end officially at one minute after midnight tonight... The German war is therefore at an end. Long live the cause of freedom. God save the King!

With only his parents at home, he longed for some brighter company of his own age. This momentous day needed celebrating. There was some petrol hoarded by his father in one of the barns and his motor car still serviceable. An hour later he was on his way to Exeter, but decided to call in at Bagleigh first to find if there was any more news of Diana's whereabouts. He was still feeling frustrated that she was not here to share the excitement with him.

He found Samira pulling down black-out curtains, the children tearing round the garden inappropriately playing soldiers, and David on a short leave sitting in the kitchen talking to Mary.

'Anybody going to celebrate then?' he asked after they had briefly shared their news over a glass of blackberry wine. 'The war's over. In Europe at least it's finished.'

410

'I don't really feel like celebrating,' David said.

Philip could have kicked himself for his insensitivity, but Samira smiled at him.

'We can't be too joyful, Philip,' she said. 'Not until Rachel is found, but I think I should like to do something to mark the day.'

'I'm sorry,' he said. He could feel his face reddening. He shouldn't have come here, of course, with things as they were. Victory was great if you hadn't lost anyone, but here at Bagleigh there had been two losses. He knew that although the fear was unspoken, no one held out much hope for Rachel's safe return.

'Don't feel guilty,' Samira comforted. Her voice was soft and calming. 'Of course we must all be thankful for today. It's wonderful. What do you suggest we do? There'll be a party for the children tomorrow in the village, but this evening is free.'

'I was going to Exeter just to see what's going on. There'll be something happening for sure.'

'Could I come?'

Both Mary and David stared at Samira for a second as if she had gone quite mad, but then Mary laughed. 'A very good idea,' she said. 'You go off and enjoy yourself. You don't get much fun. It's all work lately.'

James Stanmore burst into the room at that moment. 'What's all this then?' he asked.

'Philip is going to take Samira to Exeter to join in the fun,' Mary explained, mentally daring him to interfere. The war had changed her into quite a different person too. She was

411

frequently surprised at herself. Even after four years of organising the WVS in the area, her authority was still a marvel to her. She was no more the quiet little wife of long ago.

But today she had no need to fear that her husband would object.

'Good idea,' he said. 'If that silly daughter of mine hadn't rushed off to God-knows-where taking her ridiculous photographs she'd be here to enjoy herself too. Go and have a good time, Samira.'

It was a hot thundery evening, but nothing could dampen the excitement of the crowds in the busy streets. Philip parked the car in as safe a place as he could find, helped Samira out and then they both hurried towards the singing and cheering. The centre of the town was one mass of hysterical rejoicing. There were bonfires in the roads and people dancing wherever there was space to do so.

'Keep tight hold of me,' Samira said. 'Don't lose me in this lot, will you?'

Philip laughed and gripped her hand firmly. Breathless and excited, they danced the hokey-cokey so many times that Samira felt she would never forget its tune as long as she lived. Then there was the Lambeth Walk over and over again, and an attempt to waltz to the enthusiastic singing of 'There'll Always Be an England'.

At last, at midnight, someone shouted that this was the official end of the war. People became suddenly quiet and from the open windows of several houses the chimes of Big

Ben on the wireless boomed out into the Devon night.

Samira cried. Philip put his arms around her and held her close to him.

'Colin should be here,' she whispered. 'And Rachel and David and Diana.'

He took out his handkerchief and gently wiped the tears from her eyes. There was nothing he could say to assuage the grief that followed so quickly and naturally after the elation. Others must have felt the sadness of their own losses too, for the mood changed. Some were still dancing, still cheering, but the rejoicing was quieter now.

'Shall we go home?'

'Yes, please, Philip. It's been wonderful, but now I think I'd like to go home.'

They walked together through streets still cheerful with lights switched on everywhere after the long years of blackout, and bonfires with the flames dying down now but the embers glowing red-hot and quite destroying the road surfaces beneath them.

In the car Philip tucked a blanket around Samira. And then he kissed her, gently at first and finally with more passion. She looked at him in surprise, but responded eventually with equal enthusiasm. Then he drew away from her and started the engine.

'I'm sorry,' he said for the second time that day. 'But you're very beautiful, Samira, and this has been a wonderful night.'

They drove back to Bagleigh without saying very much but they both felt a surprising closeness. Samira guessed that the kiss meant little more than a friendly gesture, something to mark this very special time. It was a day to remember for ever.

Philip was Diana's fiancé. Neither of them would do anything to hurt her. Samira was sorry that Diana had not made an effort to be here and had to admit that she felt the smallest trace of jealousy. She knew that if she had a man like Philip she would always be there for him, whatever happened. He would be first in her life and nothing of her making would ever be allowed to come between them.

CHAPTER 28

One June evening David came late to Bagleigh. Samira heard the sound of his old motor car and, surprised, glanced at the clock. Quarter past ten. He usually came about tea time so that he could be with Deborah, never at this hour. Immediately sensing bad news she jumped up, the jersey she was knitting for Matthew still in her hands. She ran to open the front door and one look at his face confirmed her worst fears.

'I've heard,' he said. He walked past her into the sitting room and slumped upon the settee. 'Rachel was taken by the Gestapo. She was tortured, taken to a camp called Saarbruken and then to Ravensbruck. The Russians got there a few weeks ago but the details are scanty. They think she was shot as a spy. The authorities believe it was not the gas chambers.' His voice broke and he put his hands over his face. 'Not the ovens,' he murmured. 'Thank God not that.'

Samira couldn't trust herself to speak. She had read about the things that happened in the horrendous Nazi camps, and Diana had confirmed all of it. She was standing immobile at the sitting-room door, but then she quietly crossed the room and sat down beside him.

He glanced up at her at last. 'I waited until I knew the children would be in bed. I couldn't face Deborah, not yet.'

'No, of course not.' She thought of the child peacefully asleep upstairs in the large double bed that she shared with Kaffa-Mary. Then she put her hand over David's. 'I'm very, very sorry.'

He managed to smile weakly at her. They sat for a while without saying anything more, both staring at Mary's elaborate flower arrangement in the fireplace, yet not seeing it. There were no tears in their eyes. The pictures in both of their minds were too dreadful even for tears. Samira was the first to break the difficult silence.

'Rachel will always be a heroine to Deborah,' she said quietly. 'She's been that for a long time in fact. I think she'll grieve more in the future than now. Don't worry too much about her. Five is very young to understand.'

'Thank you for everything,' David said. 'For all you do for Debbie. You don't know how grateful I am, Samira.'

'It's nothing.'

Another long silence. No sound in the house.

'Do you know what Rachel was doing?' David's voice was low, without emotion.

'I've made guesses, as we all have.'

'She was parachuted into German-held territory to help set up escape routes for Allied Airmen and for Jews who had managed to hide until now. Her languages made her invaluable to the resistance.'

Samira closed her eyes and remembered Rachel, remembered the buoyant assurance and optimism. She knew that it wasn't only her fluent knowledge of Dutch, French and English that made her outstanding. She was brilliant, exceptional in so many ways, one of those people one meets perhaps only once in a lifetime, and in whom all the greatest gifts seem to be concentrated. Samira felt suddenly proud to have known her so well, for they had become good friends during the time she had been at Bagleigh.

A great cloud of misery swept over her for Rachel's terrible and untimely death. She had perished in such a dreadful and meaningless way when life held so much for her, when the war was practically over!

She could say none of those things to David, not now anyway. Instead she rose quietly and went to the sideboard and poured some of James Stanmore's precious brandy. She had lived long enough in England to know what to offer in times like this.

David drank it quickly. The golden liquid slipped down his throat and he hardly seemed aware of it. Then he held the empty glass in his hand, twisting it this way and that.

'I think my squadron is going to the Far East,' he said slowly, surprising her by his abrupt change of subject. His voice was controlled now, but iron cold. 'Got to finish the job. The Japs won't surrender easily.'

Samira thought that he looked lost, like a child who suddenly had no idea what to do next.

He put the glass carefully on the coffee table and stood up. 'D'you mind if I go to bed now? I need to be on my own. Could you tell Mr and Mrs Stanmore?'

'Of course. Do you want anything? Another brandy? Ovaltine?' She longed to do something, yet knew that there was nothing she could do that would be of any help at all.

He shook his head. 'No, thanks.' He picked up his bag which he had thrown on the floor and went straight upstairs to the room that was kept for him, that he and Rachel had shared, their only home since the bombing of the cottage.

Samira sat quite still and thought back to the day she had heard of Colin's death, but that had been so different, so sudden, even glorious in a way. She packed up her knitting and went into the kitchen to tell her mother-in-law.

'She was a wonderful person, a shining star,' Mary said in an unexpected burst of poetic licence.

They were impressive words. Samira felt slightly comforted by them. She would write them down so that they shouldn't be forgotten, use them when she talked to Deborah about her mummy's death.

James was working in his study. When he heard the news he registered no emotion at first. He reached for his pipe, packed tobacco into it, and lit it slowly before replying. 'A damned good woman, as brave as a man in fact,' he commented eventually. It was high praise for James.

In the morning Deborah let out a hoot of delight when she was told that she was not to go to school today. She'd been surprised to find her daddy here and was prattling away to him over breakfast. He sat quite still, toying with the bowl of porridge that Samira had set before him.

'I like school though,' Deborah said. 'I'm learning to read. I can read lots of words. C-A-T and S-A-T and M-A-T. I can write them and my name, though that's hard. Deborah's hard to write.'

Samira glanced at David and wondered how he would manage to break the news to his little daughter. She'd offered to do it for him earlier when she'd taken him a cup of tea, but he had shaken his head. 'No,' he'd said firmly. 'It's my job, Samira. I won't shirk it. I'll take Debbie out somewhere.'

'Why's Debbie not coming to school?' Kaffa-Mary wanted to know, her mouth full of scrambled egg.

'Because her daddy's here.'

'It's not fair.' This was from Matthew who idolised David and wanted to be with him whenever he came to Bagleigh.

Dougie scowled at them. He was eleven now and was anxious to get into the grammar school. He had surprised them all by his bright intelligence. 'Sillies,' he said. 'School's good. You learn things.'

'You're all going to school except Deborah, and that's that,' Samira said firmly. As soon as breakfast was finished she ushered them out to the hall. 'Get your satchels and blazers quickly.' She always walked with them to the next farm and they continued their journey in the neighbour's trap.

When she returned to the house she found David and Deborah mounted, David on Major and Deborah on Jinny, her new pony, a present for her recent fifth birthday. Samira checked Deborah's saddle automatically and smiled at David. He was pale and there were deep rings beneath his eyes. She guessed he'd been awake most of the night. She cast about in her mind for something suitable to say, but there were no easy words, nothing that would be of any comfort.

She watched as they wound their way up the curving path, the large stallion walking carefully beside the small pony. Then she turned and went inside, wondering how she was to get on with the small ordinary things of life when the world held so much tragedy and suffering.

On the lower slopes of the moor the bracken was tall now, its green fronds waving in the gentle wind, and the branches of the rowan trees were laden with fairy-like blossom. David

419

saw the beauty but it depressed him further. He had seen photographs of the Nazi concentration camps and superimposed that indescribable horror on to this scene of peace. His mind couldn't make a leap between the two.

'Is this a special treat?' Deborah asked suddenly, breaking into his misery. 'And why are you all quiet and sad, Daddy?'

'It's not a treat, Debbie,' he said. 'I have some bad news. I wanted to tell you when we were on our own.'

'You're not going to make me leave Auntie Sam?'

'No not that. It's about Mummy. She isn't with us any more. She's been very brave, and some bad people have killed her.' The words came out in a rush and it wasn't at all what he had intended to say.

'I know she's brave and special,' Deborah said. 'Auntie Sam keeps telling me that.'

'We won't see her again, Debbie.' He realised that she had not fully understood what he had said. 'She won't ever come back.'

There was silence for a time and he turned round to look at her, wondering if she could really comprehend her loss. But when she eventually spoke her words sounded shocking to him.

'Then I'll be able to stay with Auntie Sam for ever and ever, won't I, and be Matthew's real sister?'

It was only later that Deborah began to understand a little more. 'I haven't got a mummy now, have I?' she said to Samira one day the following week. 'She's up in the sky with Jesus. Matthew told me. Will you be my mummy now? Can I really and truly call you Mummy?'

Samira longed to gather her up in her arms and tell her, yes oh yes, of course you can, but instead she replied, 'You had a very special, very brave and wonderful mummy and I'm not a bit like her. Go on calling me Auntie Sam, just like you do now, and I'll be just like a mummy in everything else. You can only ever have one mummy who was as wonderful as yours. She was like a shining star.'

'She's a star up in the sky with Jesus,' Deborah repeated. 'Daddy said he doesn't believe in Jesus, but I do and I 'spect Mummy does if she's up there with Him.'

Samira smiled in spite of her sadness. It was incongruous, a Jewish child going to an English Sunday School and brought up by a Muslim Arab, for Samira had to admit that she was still secretly Muslim in spite of her regular attendance at the Parish Church week by week. She wondered how it would all turn out in the end.

'A star up in the sky with Jesus.' Deborah affirmed her interesting and new-found belief over and over again during the next few days. She could be heard telling her dolls, her teddy, and even Rollo. She would put her arms round the dog's neck and whisper in his ear so that sometimes he would shake his head violently from side to side before licking her enthusiastically.

Her father smiled indulgently on his next visit.

'Should I stop her going to Sunday School?' Mary asked him. 'I mean she's Jewish, isn't she? You don't want her growing up a good little Anglican, do you?'

'She won't,' he said, 'and it would be wrong to separate her from the others. I'm not worried about what she believes really. Knowing what has happened to six million Jews, I doubt if there's a God at all, let alone a good one. It's only the country that's important to me now, Israel. To be Jewish doesn't mean you have to accept a religious creed. At least that's how I see it. Plenty of people wouldn't agree.'

Mary saw a great bitterness in him that hadn't been there until recently. 'No one can understand it,' she said. 'But it's sad not to believe in anything.'

David laughed grimly. 'You're right of course,' he said. 'So let Debbie go on with her picture of Mummy, a star in the sky with Jesus, if it helps her. In fact it's rather nice. Perhaps I'll try to share the fairy-tale.'

David's expected move to the Far East didn't come to pass. On August 6th a massive bomb was dropped on a thriving Japanese city called Hiroshima and three days later another on Nagasaki.

'It'll save thousands of lives,' James said as he read the reports. 'Serves the Japs right.'

Mary wasn't so sure about his last words, but it would certainly save a vast number of our lads, she agreed, if the Japs were forced to give in quickly. And David wouldn't have to go away now surely. He'd be home for good, would want to go back to that outlandish place he called Eretz Israel, she supposed. She thought of Debbie and was slightly ill at ease.

They had to wait a few more days for the wonderful news that the war was at last completely over.

It was Samira who first heard. She was listening to the wireless while she put cutlery on the table for supper. She stood transfixed, and then ran to the door, knives and forks in her hand. She had already called to the others that the meal was ready and now she called again jubilantly. 'Unconditional surrender,' she shouted. 'Japan has surrendered. It's all over.'

They came quickly, Mary first, followed by all four children.

'The King is to speak to the nation at midnight,' Samira continued, 'and Mr Atlee as well.'

James, following the others into the room, snorted at this last revelation. 'Should've been Winston,' he said angrily. 'Dirty trick chucking him out at the last shambles they called an election. Labour government, pah!'

Mary wanted to shake him. 'The war's completely over,' she said. 'Did you hear! It's really over this time, James, and all you can think of is politics.' She wiped emotional tears from her eyes. 'Almost six years of war! That's how long it's been, nearly six years. I can't believe it.' She grabbed Samira's hands, cutlery and all, and danced right round the kitchen table, and Rollo barked, and the children all rushed to join in the fun. Then Mary ran into the sitting room and sat down at the piano and vamped out 'There'll Always Be an England'. They sang as loudly as they could, following it with 'Land of Hope and Glory', 'God Save the King', 'Run Rabbit Run', 'Roll out the Barrel' and then 'There'll Always Be an England' again and again until they all collapsed on the floor or the settee. James brought out a bottle of the inevitable home-made wine and even poured small amounts for the children. They had celebrated three months ago for Victory in Europe Day, but this was better still. With the surrender of Japan, peace was assured for ever.

It was Dougie who cut into the euphoria like a blast of cold air. 'Where'll I go?' he said.

'You'll stay here, love,' Mary replied. She put her arms round him and hugged him close. 'As long as you like.'

'Certain sure?' He disentangled himself from her. 'Can we all stay just like we are?'

Mary smiled. 'You'll grow up and you might want to go then,' she said. 'But this is home for as long as you want it to be, home for all of us, Dougie.'

'And me,' Deborah stated. 'I'm staying too, for ever and ever.'

Suddenly Samira's happy little world fell slightly apart. I'll have to lose her, she thought. David will take her back to Palestine... Palestine...home. Could she too go and visit her mother and possibly ease Deborah's transition from slightly pampered little English girl to kibbutz pioneer child? She thought of Beth Haron, heard the cicadas in her imagination, saw her mother's face. Would it be safe to take Matthew and Kaffa-Mary as she and Colin had promised her mother on that long ago day, show them her birthplace?

'Perhaps we can all go and visit Auntie Harriet now the war's over,' she said, without really thinking about the complications.

Immediately James' benevolent attitude changed. He turned furious eyes upon her. 'If you do that, my girl, you'll leave my grandson here. Matthew will never go to that God-forsaken place as long as I live.'

During the following months Samira often pondered those words of her father-in-law. The end of the war had bred a restlessness in her, an edginess that was hard to control. She couldn't talk to Mary about the loneliness and frustration she was feeling for although she was, on the whole, a good friend, they only discussed simple superficial things, never anything serious.

Then in November, much to her delight, Diana wrote to say that she was coming to Bagleigh for a few weeks. To work, she said.

Three large trunks arrived first. They were delivered in an ancient Great Western Railway van. James, and one of the newly demobbed farm workers, were summoned to help carry them up to her room.

'They feel as though they're filled with bricks,' James grumbled.

Mary anxiously watched the procession. 'Diana said to be careful. There are cameras and breakable things in them,' she told the men. 'And books.'

Diana herself arrived a few days later. 'I won't have much time to spare,' she announced. 'I've got work to do, loads of photographs that I'm going to get published if I can. I shall have to spend ages in my room writing the stuff to go with them. I'll need a big table.'

When she had unpacked and laid everything out to her satisfaction, Samira stood at the door and looked at the piles of photographs all carefully stacked and labelled. A large black typewriter sat importantly in the middle.

'Come and see some of these,' Diana invited. 'You'll be interested in the prints I took in Egypt.'

'There's been a riot there,' Samira said. 'I saw something about it in the newspaper.'

Diana looked up at her. 'Arabs all over the Middle East are angry because the Jews want a homeland in Palestine. There's going to be a lot more trouble.'

Samira sighed. She thought of El Admah surrounded by its scrubby barren hills, and again of her mother. She frequently longed for Kaffa but had said nothing more of a visit. She remembered Beth Haron and the new ideas that the Jews had brought, the crops growing green and healthy because they were watered. 'Irrigation,' Harriet had told her. With a pang of foreboding she thought about the trouble that Diana predicted, and imagined Deborah there. 'Do you think David will really want to take Debbie back?'

'Of course he will, some time, but goodness knows when.' Diana shrugged her shoulders, not realising the hurt that her words caused. 'He's not likely to be demobbed for a bit, is he? Heard anything?

'Not yet. He can't wait to get out of the Air Force now the war's over but it's a slow process. What about Philip?'

'He has a definite date. In January.'

Samira stood looking down at the photographs of Egyptian villages very similar to El Admah, but she was thinking of Philip Briscoe and of Diana's unenthusiastic response. 'You don't sound very thrilled about it?' She couldn't help a critical tone creeping into her voice.

'Don't I? Perhaps that's because I'm not.'

'Oh, Diana, how can you?'

'How can I what?'

'Be so cruel to him?'

Diana was shocked by the words. 'Am I being cruel? Is that what I appear to be?' Without answering the question, and asking another instead, she said, 'You've seen him more recently than I. He came here on VE Day, didn't he?'

'Yes. I told you in my letter. We had a good time in Exeter.'

'You like him, don't you, Samira?' There was no disapproval in her voice, just a flat statement of fact.

427

'Yes, I do. I think he's kind and...sort of vulnerable. He loves you. I don't want to see him hurt.'

Diana was sorting through another pile of photographs, not concentrating at all on what she was doing. Philip's ring on her finger sparkled in the light from the lamp which she had placed on the table. 'I sometimes think that I should break off our engagement.'

'Oh, no,' Samira said quickly. 'He'd be heart-broken.'

'Better now than later though.'

'Is it still because of David?'

Diana put down the photographs in her hand so quickly that some of them spilled on to the floor. 'Don't say that, Samira.' She couldn't stop the anger. 'Please never say that again. Since Rachel died, since I saw Belsen, all my feelings for David have...' She couldn't finish, couldn't find the right words. It was strange and yet completely true that she no longer felt any passion for David Halprin. Or perhaps for anyone? All her sensibilities seemed to have been buried there at Belsen, buried in the trenches along with the pitiful skeletal dead. She functioned automatically most of the time now, coldly and without emotion. Only at night in her disturbed restless sleep did she begin to feel again, and that was more dreadful than the paralysing indifference of the day. The nightmares had not diminished. How could she tell Samira or anyone all of this?

She bent and retrieved the photographs that were scattered at her feet. 'I don't think I'll ever love again,' she said. 'Love and decency and everything worthwhile and beautiful all disappeared at Belsen.'

After that first day Diana became very secretive about her work. She shut herself in her room for hours at a time, only emerging to eat a little now and then or to walk or ride up to Greatcombe Rocks. There she would stay as long as the weather allowed, often standing in the centre of one of the ancient hut circles, or on the highest outcrop of rock where she could see a great expanse of moorland stretching in every direction. Here all was loneliness and silence, broken only by the evocative call of curlew or snipe and the cracking of dry bracken as Rollo enthusiastically searched out yet another stick to lay at her feet. Here she usually experienced a measure of peace that lasted until she was back in her room, until she was confronted by her photographs again, until she saw afresh the accusing dead crying out to her for their stories to be told. And then she would sit at the typewriter and hammer out the angry words that had been omitted from her earlier work.

Eventually she had a great pile of manuscripts and labelled photographs and knew that she must return to London soon and find a publisher.

David's visits to Bagleigh were as frequent as ever. He came to see his daughter whenever he had leave. Diana tried to avoid him as much as possible for every time that she saw him, she saw Belsen afresh, saw Rachel's face yet again superimposed upon the piles of grotesque and stinking corpses. It didn't make for pleasant conversation.

Samira, watching them, marvelled that they had loved each other once, had been light-hearted, happy in each other's company. Each had suffered and obviously found it impossible to find any comfort in the other now. Those long-ago days in Palestine seemed like a distant dream. The war had changed everyone, except perhaps Philip Briscoe, she thought. She remembered, with continuing pleasure the time she had spent with him on VE Day. Compared to everyone else she knew, he was uncomplicated, easy going, a perfect companion. Companion? Was that all? She smiled a little to herself and then the smile turned to sadness. Philip Briscoe could never be anything other than that.

CHAPTER 29

Diana decided that she must return to London after Christmas.

'But Philip's coming home in January,' her mother objected. 'You'll want to be here then, surely? You told me he was to be demobbed. You'll be planning your wedding.' Her tone was aggrieved.

'Not yet. I've things to do. He'll come to see me in London.'

430

Mary sighed. Diana was quite impossible to talk to lately. In fact everyone seemed to be gloomy. If it wasn't for the children's light-hearted chatter she sometimes felt that she would go quite mad. With the war over these four months now they'd all hoped for a few little miracles to cheer up the dark nights and cold weather. Ample food would have been nice, petrol for everyone, and bananas! How Mary longed to give the children bananas. The three younger ones had never seen any. But the shortages appeared to be getting even worse.

'I can't understand it,' Mary had complained. 'We won the war, didn't we, and now there's less to eat than ever.'

'Got to feed the damned Germans and all those displaced persons, would you believe?' James had answered in disgust.

David was to be demobbed soon, before Christmas in fact, and when Mary heard the news she decided that she would have a party for him. 'To cheer us all up,' she said hopefully.

But when she told Diana of her plans she was met with even more gloom.

'That'll be nice for him,' was all the response she could get. 'Where are you going to get the food for a party?'

Samira too refused to greet the news of David's imminent freedom with much enthusiasm. 'He'll want to take Deborah to Palestine,' she said.

He arrived one Friday evening and the party was arranged for the following afternoon. It was planned mostly with the children in mind and Mary had made jellies and blancmange, and she'd even managed to bake some little chocolate cakes with cocoa that she had hoarded for a long time for just such an occasion as this. There were egg sandwiches, and a few of salmon from one precious tin, another of her secret treasures. They would be strictly rationed, one each. She laid the feast out on the big dining-room table and then shut the door firmly until tea-time.

'We have a couple of hours to spare,' she said. 'Do you want to play games or go for a walk? It's a nice day for December.'

'Let's have a sing-song,' said David. 'I'll teach you some of our Yiddish tunes. They're very go-ey. I learnt them at Beth Haron.' He went to the piano and Diana, who had reluctantly come to join them all in the sitting room, looking at him, realised that she had almost forgotten that he was a musician. He'd not been able to play his violin much in Palestine. No time, he'd said, and his hands were too rough anyway from working the land.

Now they were smooth again, the long sensitive fingers white and the nails well-groomed. He was just as accomplished on the piano as the violin and she looked at his hands as they travelled the keyboard and for one betraying second felt a flicker of the old magic. But she banished it quickly. How long would it be, she wondered, before she could obliterate Belsen from her mind? For while she felt the sick need to transpose Rachel's face onto the horrific putrefying dead, she would not be able to feel anything for Rachel's husband.

Deborah was standing beside her father. 'I'm learning to play the piano,' she told him. 'Granny teaches me a bit.' She had long ago given Mary this title, copying Kaffa-Mary and Matthew.

'You'll be able to have lessons at Beth Haron,' David said. 'We have some clever musicians there.'

'I like Granny's lessons best,' Deborah objected. 'I'm not going to that place. I'm staying here for ever.'

Matthew, nearly seven now, looked at her importantly. 'Mummy told me that you'd have to go away one day,' he said. ' 'Cause Uncle David belongs to another country. She told me about it. It's hot and there are lots of soldiers. I don't want you to go though.'

Deborah turned frightened eyes upon him. 'Well, I'm not going. Never, never never. I'm staying with Auntie Sam.'

There was a tense moment of silence in the room. Samira was the first to speak. 'You'll like it at Beth Haron, Debbie love,' she said. 'It's nearly always warm, and there's a swimming pool, and you can wear pretty summer dresses all the time.'

'I don't want pretty dresses. I want to stay here with you. I can, can't I?' She ran across the room and grabbed Samira's skirt. 'You promised to be my mummy always. You did, you did.'

Gently Samira leaned down and put her arm around the shaking child. 'No, darling. I said

433

that I'd be just like a mummy until the time came for you to go home with Daddy.'

'This is home, not that horrid old Beth place.'

David had stopped playing. He looked at the two of them and his face was white.

Diana, still watching him, thought he looked suddenly old, just as he might look in thirty or forty years' time.

Then he spoke. 'You'll get used to it, Debbie. There are lots of children to play with. You were born at Beth Haron. Your mummy loved it very much. She'd want you to be there.' His voice was quiet. He hadn't moved from the piano.

'Auntie Sam's my mummy. She is, she is!' Deborah burst into tears and, suddenly detaching herself from Samira, grabbed at the door handle and pulled the door wide open. They heard her going up to her room, stamping on each stair. Samira was about to go after her, but David sprang into life.

'Leave her to me.'

He spent ten minutes with her and when he reappeared was more tense and pale than he had been before. 'Don't go up yet,' he said to Samira. 'I've told her that she must come to Palestine with me after Christmas. There's no choice. She'll get used to the idea.'

Samira felt that her heart would break. She longed to run up the stairs and cuddle the little girl in her arms, but Deborah was David's child. She had no official right to her at all.

Mary looked round the room and hoped that the party was not going to be spoilt. She wasn't

434

too concerned with Deborah's tantrum for she had been brought up to believe that children had to know their place and fall in with their parent's plans.

'Take Major out, David,' she suggested with sudden inspiration. 'He needs exercise and the ride will do you good. We'll have tea later, when you return.'

The rest of the afternoon was not easy for anyone. There was no sound from Deborah's room. 'I think she's fallen asleep,' Mary announced after she had gone upstairs and listened outside the closed door. 'I didn't go in or she would have wakened. The sleep will do her good, bring her to her senses.'

At five o'clock David returned, colour in his handsome face now but his eyes still haunted. Diana felt momentarily annoyed with Deborah. It was incongruous that such a small child should have the power to disconcert him so. He had been promoted to Wing Commander early in 1945, had won a DSO with a bar added later towards the end of the war, and yet she guessed that his little daughter meant more to him than all these honours. She thought of the millions of other Jewish children brutally murdered during the past five years. Those horrific thoughts and images clouded her judgement over so many things, but she couldn't banish them, and they prevented her from feeling much sympathy for Deborah.

But everything changed when Samira went to call the children for tea. She came clattering down the stairs. 'She's not there,' she said. 'I can't find Debbie anywhere. Matthew's gone too.'

James was the first to come to his senses. He rushed to the back of the house, grabbed the large torch which was always on a table near the door, and shouted to David to come with him. Mary had come running as well. 'You search the house, we'll do the outside,' he said to her. 'They can't have got far.'

Dougie had been doing his homework in the dining room and, hearing the commotion, he too came into the kitchen. 'What's up?' he enquired. When told he merely shrugged his shoulders. 'I 'spect I can find them,' he said in a matter-of-fact voice. 'I know our secret dens.'

'Then for goodness' sake, show us,' Diana said.

Samira grabbed a coat from the row of hooks in the passage way and threw it on. She draped another over Dougie's shoulders and turned to Diana. 'You stay here,' she directed. 'Look after Kaffa-Mary. When we find them, I want to be there.'

Dougie led her straight to one of the sheds in the second yard. There was a loft above it with a ladder permanently in place. It was home to a motley crowd of farm cats and they scattered in alarm as Samira hastily climbed up. She shone her torch around and saw two frightened faces looking at her in the farthest corner. The two children were sitting close together on a pile of hay with an old blanket up to their chins.

'She says she won't go. I was helping her to

436

hide.' Matthew's voice faltered a little as if he recognised the futility of the plan.

'You must come down,' Samira said gently. 'Then we can talk about it sensibly. Hiding away here won't do any good.' With some difficulty she scrambled out of the trap-door and made her way cautiously towards them but they got to their feet and backed away from her like frightened animals.

It was Dougie, following close behind, who managed to diffuse the situation. 'Don't be daft,' he said. 'You're spoiling everything. I want some of them jellies.' His cheerful cockney voice seemed to bring the two younger children to their senses, but it was a little while before they could be persuaded to abandon their false security and follow him down the ladder.

Samira shepherded them into the house, brushed the hay from their clothes and cuddled the now weeping Deborah in her arms.

'Daddy won't take me away, will he, Auntie Sam?' she sniffed, but Samira didn't reply. She merely held her tighter on her lap and rocked her back and forth in the old rocking chair and wanted to cry herself.

Dougie had been despatched to find David and James, and when they all came back into the kitchen Samira could feel Deborah stiffen in her arms.

'Thank God they're safe,' David said. His face was full of conflicting emotions. 'Where were they?' He turned to Samira.

'I found them,' Dougie said. 'We've got secret dens.'

437

'Good lad.' This was from James who couldn't bring himself to speak to the two children. Deserved a good hiding, he thought privately. If they were his, they'd be sent straight to bed.

'I'll make a cup of tea,' Mary muttered. No one seemed in any mood to partake of the party goodies yet. She thought gloomily about her jellies and sandwiches as she lifted the kettle over on to the hottest part of the Aga.

David watched her blankly. He refused to look at his daughter. 'Well, that's that then,' he said to no one in particular.

'What's what?' Diana stared at him, at his white face set in angry determined lines.

'I've been offered a job as a test pilot. In Bristol. I shall take it.'

Mary clattered about with cups and saucers, irritating everyone.

'You mean, you won't go back to Palestine?' Diana couldn't believe it.

'That's just what I mean.' He stamped out of the room and they heard his motor car revving up outside and the sound of the engine as he drove along the lane away from the house.

He didn't come back that day and the party food was consumed mainly by Dougie and Kaffa-Mary. During the escapade Kaffa-Mary had said little, just watched round-eyed. Deborah was her sister—well, not a real one, Mummy said, but almost. Usually she forgot that she was not. It was frightening to think that she was going away for ever to some place with a funny name. It made her frightened

438

for herself too. Perhaps they'd take her away as well?

Samira had a hard job that night when she put the two little girls to bed. She had no idea what David's plans were now. Bristol! Like Diana, she couldn't believe it. Palestine was all he lived for, or Eretz Israel as he insisted upon calling it. She stayed with them until they fell asleep and then crept out of the room.

Diana was with Matthew. 'No,' she said, stroking his dark hair. 'I don't think she'll have to go after all, not until she's bigger anyway.'

'Because we ran away?'

This needed some consideration. It was a difficult question. Was it really because they had run away that David had given up his dream, his whole reason for being? It had certainly shown him how dreadful it would be to take Deborah away from everything she knew and loved, especially from Samira. Thanks to Dougie the affair had been quickly resolved but the shock remained.

'Will you read me a story?'

Matthew interrupted her thoughts. Perhaps she need not answer his question after all. Children were easily diverted.

She took the first book she saw from the top of the chest of drawers and opened it at the bookmark. 'This one?'

'Yes, that's the place,' Matthew said. 'They're Bible stories. It's one of my best books.'

And every day Goliath threatened the armies of Israel, and no one was brave enough to fight him. Then David, a young shepherd boy, came out of the ranks and said, 'I'll go. Why are none of you brave enough? This Philistine is defying the armies of God.'

So David took his sling and chose five smooth stones and he went down into the valley and said to Goliath, 'You have come against me with sword and spear, but I come against you in the name of the Lord of Hosts, the God of Israel whom you have defied.'

'I think about Uncle David when Mummy reads me that story,' Matthew interrupted, his eyes glowing with hero-worship which had surprisingly not been at all dented by the afternoon's events. 'He could've said that to old Hitler, couldn't he?'

'I suppose he could.' Diana's mind made the jump from the picture of a ruddy-faced youth with his sling to David in his uniform. She couldn't help a quick smile.

'Why does he want to go away?'

So Matthew had not been diverted so easily after all. She groped for a simple answer to this second question. 'Palestine is his country, like this other David,' she said, indicating the book on her lap. 'You said that your mummy had told you that.'

'Yes, she did, but I didn't understand it really.'

'Shall I go on with the story?'

'All right.' Matthew settled himself more comfortably on the pillows.

So David fought the Philistine and struck him down with his sling and stones, and he killed him, and all the soldiers of the Philistines saw the fate of their champion, and they turned and fled, and the men of Israel and Judah pursued them all the way to Gath. And David was proclaimed as a great hero. Everyone came out and cheered him, and when he returned to the town the women and girls brought tambourines and danced in the streets for David had saved Israel.

'Uncle David says that his country is called Israel,' Matthew said. 'You said Palestine.'

'It's the same place,' Diana said. 'Its proper name is Palestine. Uncle David would like it to be called Israel.'

'Why?'

'No more questions. You must go to sleep.'

'But I want to know.'

Diana sighed. 'Ask Uncle David,' she said wearily.

'He's not here. He went off all angry with us for running away.'

'He'll come back.'

'I hope he comes soon. I wish he'd take me instead. Debbie doesn't want to go, but I'd like to. It's a place for boys not girls, isn't it, Auntie Di?'

Diana tucked the eiderdown more firmly

round him. 'Go to sleep, Matthew,' she repeated, and shivered. It was cold in the unheated bedroom.

'All right,' he said, his voice already becoming slurred with sleep. 'But I'm going to see this Palestine-Israel place when I grow up. Perhaps I'll go and live there with Uncle David.'

As predicted, Philip was demobbed from the Navy in January and after a few days at Maddacombe, rushed up to London to see Diana.

She met him at Paddington. They didn't fall immediately into each other's arms but stood for a time like polite strangers who had just been introduced. Then he kissed her. She returned the kiss but without enthusiasm, and as they walked from the station to a small restaurant in the road outside, their conversation was stilted and difficult.

Diana didn't know how to tell him that she couldn't come back to Devon, couldn't marry him. She'd been putting it off, not wanting to write the damaging words in a letter, feeling it was better to see him, but now she was doubtful about that decision. She remembered how she had felt long ago over the loss of David and her face grew pale at the thought of inflicting such suffering on a man whom she liked so much. She and Philip had been good friends, had written long letters to each other throughout the war, yet she still couldn't submerge her life in his. Friendship alone wasn't enough.

They ordered tea and toast and when the waitress had put it on their table and left them staring at the cracked cups, they both started to speak at once.

'Sorry,' Philip said. 'You first.'

'Thelma has offered me a partnership,' Diana said. 'She's doing well, lots of commissions of various sorts, and she can't manage on her own.'

'And what are you going to do?'

'I must take it, Philip. It's a wonderful chance.'

'What about us?'

She put milk into the cups, stirred the tea, found the strainer and started to pour. 'You won't want to wait?' It wasn't what she really meant to say, but it sounded less harsh somehow.

'Wait? For how long?'

She put his cup and saucer in front of him, pushed the sugar in his direction. 'I don't even know if you take sugar,' she said.

'Thank you. Diana, for God's sake, answer me. For how long? What are you trying to say?'

She hadn't meant everything to rush along like this. She had wanted to take more time, talk about their relationship, explain how she felt, but she realised that way was no good. An amputation had to be quick. There was less pain. She looked round to see if anyone could overhear their conversation. There was only one old man reading a newspaper, and a couple of girls giggling and intent on their

443

own lives. 'That I can't marry you, Philip,' she whispered.

He sat quite still. 'I suppose I guessed after Plymouth.'

Slowly she took off her ring and held it out to him.

He shook his head. 'No. I don't want it.'

'You must.'

Still he refused. 'Give it away then.'

She opened her handbag and dropped it into the inner pocket and stared at the white mark on her naked finger.

'I shall go back on the next train.'

'Oh, Philip.'

For the first time he looked angry. 'What in hell's name do you expect me to do then? Go and watch Brief Encounter with you at the cinema, drag out the agony? Is that what you want?'

Of course it wasn't what she wanted. She hated herself.

He swallowed the tea in one swift action, took out a ten shilling note and pushed it beneath the milk jug. Then he stood up and strode to the door.

She watched him go, and when he was out of sight she closed her eyes in despair. What is the matter with me? For a second time she had turned away from a relationship, first from David because she couldn't accept the challenge he offered, and now from the kindest man she had ever known because she couldn't adopt his life either. Dear God, why am I like I am? Women have always submerged their ambitions, given up their private dreams when they married. But I'm not like that, she declared to herself. I cannot be. Perhaps I shall never marry. She sat at the table for more than an hour, ordering more tea when the waitress hovered, and then she got up, paid her bill with Philip's money and went out into the bitter cold.

She couldn't face going home just yet. She walked until she found herself outside a cinema. She stared at the pictures on the wall. Then she went into the blessed oblivion of warm darkness and celluloid figures living out their own heartbreak on the screen. Celia Johnson and Trevor Howard on a railway station, in love and knowing that their love was hopeless. Brief Encounter! The film Philip had obviously wanted to see.

She thought about David and Philip, the two men she had cared for. There had been no brief encounter with either of them, no totally impossible situation. In both cases it was her own need for independence that had made the relationships unacceptable.

She watched the film through twice and then staggered out into a night that felt even more bitterly cold. She walked all the way home through the freezing January streets, back to Thelma and sanity and work.

'Am I really as selfish as I think I am?' she asked again, this time aloud. She was ensconced in the depths of the armchair in which Thelma had installed her. It was pulled close to the blazing fire and Diana was just beginning to feel some warmth penetrating her frozen limbs. She cradled a cup of tea in both hands.

'Of course not, child,' Thelma said firmly. 'When you fall in love you'll know it and then the sacrifices won't seem like sacrifices.'

'But...but I was in love with David, yet I couldn't marry him.'

'Stop torturing yourself. Maybe you were. Maybe you weren't. Let the past go. There's the future to live for.'

Diana stared into the flames and knew that Thelma was right. She must let the past go, the good things and the bad. The war was over, she was free, the world could look exciting again if only she would let it.

'When you've recovered the use of your hands,' Thelma said, 'there's some post for you.' She got up and fetched two small white envelopes and put them on the coffee table.

Diana quickly put her cup of tea down in the grate and picked up the letters. The envelopes were typed.

When she had opened the first one she let out a whoopee of joy. 'They're going to publish my book.'

The second envelope too bore good news. 'From *La Mode*,' she told Thelma as she read it. 'They want more pictures. Of women having to give up jobs to our returning heroes. There's an irony, back to the kitchen sink and all that.'

'Not for you,' said Thelma. 'You'll never be chained to the kitchen sink.'

'No, I don't think I will,' Diana replied.

CHAPTER 30

Even James had to admit that Diana's book was good. 'Perhaps she'll make a go of it after all,' he grudgingly said to Mary when they unwrapped the pre-publication copy that she had posted to them.

Mary turned it over and looked at the large photograph on the back. 'We've a famous daughter now,' she said. 'I'm proud of her. Fancy having your portrait on a book.' She leafed through the pages, print after print of carnage and ruin, but nearly all taken from an unusual angle, interspersed frequently with humour and with personal stories. *The Other Face of War,*' she read as she passed it over to Samira. 'It's a gripping title. There's lots here that we didn't hear about while the war was on.'

'Right and proper,' James said. 'We had to keep going. No point getting despondent.'

'Diana told me that they call this kind of thing photo-journalism,' Mary said knowledgeably. 'I think she means pictures with some writing to go with them.'

Soon after publication day in June Diana started to get reviews, and nearly all of them were good. One day at the end of the month Thelma was beside herself with excitement when Diana came home.

'You missed a telephone call, girl,' she said before Diana even had time to take off her coat. 'From the new editor of *The Weekly News Review*. Mr Leivick he calls himself. Strange name. Anyway he was raving about your book, wants to speak to you urgently. You'd better telephone him now.'

He was a tall handsome man and he unwound himself from behind his desk to shake her hand warmly when she was shown into his office the following day.

'Nice to meet you, Miss Stanmore. Please take a seat.' He looked her up and down and then offered her a cigarette which she refused. 'Sure you won't smoke?'

She shook her head. 'Thank you, but no.' A cigarette would in fact have been very welcome, but she wanted to concentrate on this interview, wanted no distractions.

He returned to his side of the desk and seated himself in the high-backed swivel chair. 'Mind if I do?'

'No, of course not.' She watched him inhale deeply and wondered what he wanted of her.

She was not to be kept in suspense for long.

'I'm very impressed with your book,' he began. 'You mean to tell me you took all those photographs yourself? You went through France and Germany, and before that to Egypt?'

'Yes, of course.'

'Not bad for a woman.'

Diana immediately bridled at this remark. He sounded like her father. 'Why for a woman?'

448

she asked, trying not to appear as annoyed as she felt.

He laughed. 'Not many women war correspondents, you know. Too dangerous. Congratulations.'

'Thanks. I like danger. I always want to be where the action is.'

'And do you still?' He appeared to be summing her up, trying to judge the truth of what she had said.

'Certainly. But where is there any action now?'

'Palestine!'

The word took her by surprise. She could feel colour flooding to her face. Was she hearing correctly? She stared at him, quite speechless.

'Would you be willing to go there? Not an easy assignment, of course. A lot to ask in fact.'

She clasped her hands together, felt for Philip's ring which had long gone, but which she still imagined to be there now and again in moments of stress. Was this man actually asking her to go back to the place which had once won her heart, back to Harriet? Still she said nothing. Visions of Khanhaven, Beth Haron, the barren hills and lush valleys, the olive groves, all passed in quick succession before her eyes.

'I see you're hesitant,' he continued. 'I understand that, of course, and I hadn't even considered asking a woman to go until I read your book.'

She shook her head. 'Not really hesitant,' she said. 'Just amazed. Why do you particularly want a woman for the job though?'

'I liked how you approached your subjects. A woman's angle on war is original, and we have a great number of women readers for our paper. There's a special section devoted to them.'

'But there's no actual war in Palestine.'

'My dear girl, you disappoint me! Europe is brimming over with thousands of Jews wanting to get to their Promised Land. They're the survivors of the German camps as you know. Six million ended in the ovens, remember. The rest have world sympathy at the moment, apart from the Arabs and, strangely, the British. The Arabs don't want them in Palestine and so we only allow them to emigrate there in very limited numbers. That's the situation in a nutshell, but you must know all this?'

Diana nodded. 'I saw many of them, in Germany mainly. Displaced persons, we call them. A convenient term.'

'Quite so, and they're tramping through Europe, desperately trying to get on to illegal boats to take them from Italy or other Mediterranean ports to Palestine. When they get there our warships intercept them, turn them away and put them in camps on Cyprus. A lot have been drowned.' He stubbed out his cigarette and opened a file on his desk. 'Heard about the Irgun, have you?'

'The Jewish terrorists? Yes, I have.'

David had talked about them. She remembered that he'd told her that they'd not stop at any outrage if it would further the cause of a Jewish state.

'I know a lot about the Haganah too,' she said. 'They're not quite so violent. I had a friend who wanted to join the Haganah.'

He looked at her with renewed interest. 'Not Jewish, are you?'

'No, I'm not Jewish.'

'So would you care to go, see what you can find out for me? Write it up in your unusual fashion? I can get you a pass, organise contacts, and possibly even arrange a flight. It's not easy but it can be done. Better than going by sea.'

'I've been to Palestine.'

He nodded. 'I thought you might have. You don't say anything about that in your book though. When were you there?'

'Before the war. I have an aunt who runs an animal clinic called Khanhaven.'

He roared with laughter. 'Well, I'll be damned. An animal clinic! If this isn't my lucky day.' He slapped the desk in delight and sent pens jigging around on its surface. 'So, Miss Stanmore, can I say that we're on? You'll do it? And a special bit about the clinic for light relief?'

'Prepare me a contract. Tell me exactly what you want and I'll agree if I find it acceptable,' she said, surprised at her cool calm voice. Thelma's training was paying off. 'But I shouldn't want to go for long. I have a business here. I couldn't desert my partner for more than three or four weeks. And I shall need a day to think about it, of course.'

He appeared not to have heard this last remark. 'Do you know that two Irgun terrorists have been condemned to death by the British,

451

and so they've taken three British hostages? They're threatening to kill them if we hang their men.'

'I was at Belsen just after it was liberated,' Diana said. She suddenly felt great anger with the government and its implacable rules. 'I'm inclined to be sympathetic to the Jews. I can understand why they want a place of their own.' She was thinking of Rachel again. Recently she had begun to hope that the haunting nightmares were diminishing, but now, with this new assignment, they were likely to come back in full measure.

'I knew you were at Belsen,' he said. 'From your book.'

'I'd hoped to blot it from my memory, but I shall never be able to do that.'

'Do you have any sympathy for the Arab side, for their dislike of Jewish settlers?'

Diana smiled. She knew that her next piece of information would amaze him further. 'My sister-in-law is a Palestinian Arab,' she said.

'By Jove, I don't believe it. You have to be fibbing?'

She shook her head. 'No it's quite true. My brother fell in love with her when he was on a dig out there. He was killed in the Battle of Britain.'

'Then get out there, for Christ's sake. Get out there as fast as you can, woman. I'll pay you a fat salary, or commission, whichever you like. This calls for a celebration. Wish I had a bottle of champagne. Come out to dinner with me tonight and we'll have a couple?'

She shook her head. 'Sorry, no time, but I'd like that cigarette you offered me earlier.'

He handed his slim silver case to her, clicked open a matching lighter. 'Sorry you won't come out,' he said. 'It would've been fun. It's not often I meet such an interesting and enterprising woman as you, Miss Stanmore.'

Diana laughed. She didn't know whether to be flattered or insulted. 'Another time perhaps,' she said, not meaning it at all. 'I'll let you know what I've decided tomorrow.'

She wanted to be alone, to think about this amazing offer and all the repercussions it would have on her life.

Palestine! Harriet! And David not there, David here in England. And Colin not there either. Palestine meant Colin, meant seeing him on the dockside at Beirut, showing her the wondrous ruins at Baalbec, and introducing her to Samira for the first time at Khanhaven all those years ago. Suddenly she wanted to cry for him all over again, but wouldn't allow herself that luxury until she was home in her little attic bedroom at Thelma's. Here in this scruffy little office she was the tough career woman, the ready-for-anything pioneer. She got up and went to the door.

'Tomorrow then,' he said. 'Come round in the morning and I'll have the contract and details ready. No time to lose. I'll buy you lunch.'

Diana wanted to surprise her family with the news, and needed to fetch things from Bagleigh, so two days later, when the contract had been signed, she went down to Devon.

Her father, already furious with her for the broken engagement, fumed and complained, told her that it was even more dangerous now than it had been before the war, and that if she was a dutiful daughter she wouldn't think of doing such an outrageous thing, giving them all such cause for worry. The war was over now. She had no excuse. Her mother merely sighed and said to take care of herself.

Matthew was full of envy. 'That's Uncle David's country, isn't it?' he said. 'I want to go there. And I'd like to see Aunt Harriet's animal hospital. I want to be a doctor when I grow up.' He'd been talking about becoming a doctor ever since he was able to understand what it meant and Diana had often wondered if this childhood passion might one day come to fruition. It wouldn't please her father.

Samira too was envious. 'You're making me feel so homesick,' she confided. 'Take lots of photographs for me, won't you Diana? Take my mother and the places we used to love, and Jazi and Ghazala and...' She paused and there was a wistfulness in her large brown eyes. 'Perhaps I'll be able to go some time. Colin and I promised my mother that we'd take the children to see her. I don't know how I'm to keep that promise without him, but I mean to try.'

Diana remembered her father's words about never taking Matthew to Palestine, but said nothing. Instead: 'Round the children up and we'll go outside and I'll do a special lot of photographs for your mother, Samira. That'll

454

be the next best thing,' she said brightly.

'Philip is coming over later,' Samira said. 'Could we wait until he arrives. I'd like...' Then she stopped and clapped her hand over her mouth. 'Sorry, Diana. I haven't told you. I was a bit afraid.'

Diana looked at her in surprise. 'Told me what?'

'That Philip and I go out together now and then.' She spoke diffidently and colour rushed to her face.

For a moment Diana was silent as the full implication of what Samira had said dawned on her. Was she pleased? For a second time she had rejected a man only to see him find happiness with someone else. History was repeating itself. Yet surely here was the perfect match? Samira, with her home-loving domestic ways, and Philip longing for a wife who desired nothing more than to settle down happily at Maddacombe and have babies. Surely it couldn't be better?

Samira was looking at her, seeming to plead for approval.

'I'm pleased for you,' Diana said. Then she smiled and kissed her. 'Yes, I'm really pleased for both of you. I hope you'll be very happy.'

Diana arrived in Palestine two weeks later to be greeted by a slightly older-looking but just as energetic Harriet. They sat for a long time in the cool living room at Khanhaven, looking at photographs, sharing news and talking about the troubles that Diana was to report upon.

'It won't be easy,' Harriet said. 'The British

Authorities don't want the world to know how repressive its policy is towards the Jews.'

'I'll do my best to be open-minded. I'd like to talk to Samira's mother. She's an intelligent woman. She'll help me to see the Arab point of view perhaps, and I'll go over to Beth Haron as soon as I can.' Diana felt a sudden pang of misery as she thought of the kibbutz. She remembered swimming in the little pool with David, recalled the care-free lives they lived then.

'They'll want to know all about David,' Harriet said. 'I still go every week to take English lessons. They often ask me when he's coming back. Some of the young men talk about starting an Air Force one day in the future. Ludicrous at the moment of course. You can't have an Air Force without a country. The British Army won't even allow them to have weapons to defend themselves against the Arabs, let alone aeroplanes, but they have great dreams for the future. Someone like David would be invaluable.'

'What can I tell them?' Diana sighed. 'Of course he should be here, not test flying for the British Aeroplane Company! But Deborah made a great scene about leaving Samira, threw hysterics when the subject was discussed a few weeks ago. She ran away in fact. Dougie found her and Matthew hiding in one of the barns.'

'Just a childhood escapade. David should have more sense. Children have to fit in. She'd get over it.' Harriet couldn't understand David's behaviour either.

'I think it's something to do with the feeling of obligation he has to Rachel. He doesn't want to do anything to harm their daughter.' Diana was trying to make excuses for David now.

'He's wrong of course,' Harriet said. 'Rachel would be the last one to allow anyone to flout all their dreams for Palestine. She stayed here for the birth so that her child would be a sabre.'

'I know that.' There was just a trace of residual bitterness in Diana's voice. 'It was so important to both of them.' She didn't add that because she couldn't give him Jewish children she had felt herself to be an unsuitable wife for David.

'So why don't you tell him that he must come back?'

'You mean, when I go home?'

'Yes. Or better still, write to him at once. Tell him how much he's needed here. Not many Jewish refugees are allowed in as you know. That's what all the trouble is about, the rigid quota, but as a British Citizen I don't suppose he'd have any trouble. They desperately need people of his calibre.'

'What about Deborah?'

For a few moments Harriet was silent. Then she smiled slowly and a look of delighted conspiracy spread across her face. 'Samira could bring her, couldn't she?'

The idea was a novel one and Diana was immediately intrigued. 'How would she manage that, and what about Matthew and Kaffa-Mary?'

'I think I could arrange for all of them to

457

come. I have many contacts in high places.'

But Diana saw the difficulties. How could Samira make a journey like that with three young children? And there was the big problem of Matthew.

'My father said that he would never allow Matthew to come here. He was quite adamant about it.'

Harriet only laughed. 'I shall write to my stupid brother and tell him that Samira's mother wants to see her grandchildren and has a perfect right to do so. Just as much as James himself in fact. Leave him to me.'

She has more right, Diana thought, over Matthew anyway. How much did Harriet know or suspect about his birth? It was something she could quiz her aunt about later.

'In fact Kaffa hasn't been well lately,' Harriet continued, giving more strength to her argument. 'Samira should definitely come soon. And of course David would be travelling with them if the plan is to work. Otherwise there would be no point in Deborah coming.'

Of course, Diana thought. Her aunt had it all worked out. But there were still problems. 'Samira would have to go back eventually,' she said. 'What then?'

'By that time Deborah would have been eased into kibbutz life. She could go to live there with her father at Beth Haron while the others were here. That way the break with Samira would be gradual.'

Diana looked at her aunt in amazement.

'You probably think I'm an interfering old

woman,' Harriet said. 'I suppose I am.'

'Not old and not interfering,' Diana replied. 'It's a brilliant idea. It solves everyone's problems all at one go. Samira is longing to visit her home, her mother is longing to see her and the children, and David has this dilemma over Deborah. You're fantastic, aunt. I'd never have thought of it.'

'By the way,' Harriet said, 'how did you get on with Thelma?'

'Admirably. I can never thank you enough for the introduction. We're business partners now and doing very well.'

'Will this escapade in Palestine interfere with it too much?'

'Not really. We share profits, so if this doesn't work out I'll have the other to go back to.'

'Excellent. You know that James and Thelma were sweet on each other for a short time when we were all young?'

Diana laughed. 'I know. I heard him telling Mother that he'd had a lucky escape.'

Harriet chuckled too. 'A very dominant character. You and she seem to have hit it off though. Let's have some tea, shall we? I continue to enjoy my English tea.'

'It's still rationed at home.'

'Yes. I can't believe it.'

Harriet got up and went out to draw water. Watching her, Diana suddenly realised that they hadn't talked about her life at all. What about the nice Arab doctor she used to know? Just before she'd left for England Diana had thought that romance might be in the air for them.

Dared she ask? Yes, of course she dared!

'By the way, Aunt,' she said when Harriet returned. 'Do you still see anything of that nice Dr Habib?'

'Of course. He calls two or three times a week. We are great friends.' She fetched cups and saucers and placed them on the little table. 'He asked me to marry him actually, but I wasn't prepared to lose my freedom. He's well-educated and a Christian Arab, but Arab nevertheless. All men change when they've captured you and...' She laughed again. 'You know me, Diana. I'm like you. I've no wish to be dominated.'

The following morning Kaffa came over to Khanhaven.

'She helps me with records and things,' Harriet said.

But there was little work done during the next hour or so as Diana produced her albums of photographs taken at Bagleigh. Samira and the children smiled up at them from almost every page and Kaffa had tears streaming down her face as she looked.

'Please tell them to come and visit when you return, Diana,' she pleaded. 'I long to see my daughter just once more.'

'You shall. I promise you that they'll come before next winter,' Diana said. She looked up at Harriet for confirmation.

'Of course,' said Harriet. 'We'll get them all here if I have to go to England and fetch them myself.'

CHAPTER 31

David read the letter from Diana many times.

> You should be here. This is your country. It needs you. I have never understood how you could allow a child's whim to deflect your purposes when your love for this place is so fierce.

He paced up and down the sitting room of the flat he had rented in Bristol and could find no peace. Then he flung the closely written pages down on the settee and stared out of the window. He could just see the Avon Gorge from here and the gracious span of Brunel's suspension bridge. Bristol was an agreeable city, he had decided, if only you hadn't a great gnawing passion for quite a different place. His job at the Bristol Aeroplane Company was acceptable too, in fact he acknowledged that it could be much more than that if only he could allow it to be. As a senior test pilot he had a lot of responsibility and there was endless challenge and excitement. But always, deep inside him, there was this nagging discontent, the secret feeling that he had failed, failed himself, failed Rachel, and most of all failed his country.

'I did it for Deborah,' he said aloud, turning back to the letter again, picking it up and addressing the pages as if they were Diana herself. 'It would have destroyed Debbie to separate her from Samira while she's so young, to take her to Beth Haron where she knows no one.'

Diana seemed to speak from the pages.

Harriet thinks that Samira should come to visit her mother. Kaffa isn't well and longs to see her and the children. Things seem very quiet around here and Harriet believes there would be no danger. She has written to Samira suggesting she comes out soon. Of course my father is bound to object but Harriet has written to him too! There is one other small problem. Deborah! She wouldn't want to be left behind in England. Do you perhaps see any possibilities in this situation?

Did he see possibilities? Most certainly he did! He'd been seeing them and thinking about them ever since he had received the letter. But what was Diana getting at? What was behind her sudden desire to get him out to Palestine? Did she still have any feelings for him? Surely not for she wouldn't be persuading him to go back there if that was the case. She had longed for him to settle in England years ago when they had loved each other. They had separated mainly because she couldn't share his passion for Eretz Israel. He said the words over to himself. 'Eretz Israel, the Promised Land.'

Then suddenly he was galvanised into action.

He would go down to Bagleigh and suggest that he and Deborah went to Beth Haron for a short holiday. Holiday? The idea made him laugh. One didn't take holidays in a place as fraught with problems as Palestine just now. But he'd tell people here at work that it was a holiday, keep his options open.

He could travel out with Samira and her two children. That might make James Stanmore give in more easily. Samira would need a man around to help in such a difficult journey anyway. How did one go about it? How did you get to Palestine now? He had deliberately not kept up to date with things like that, had not wanted to think about it until now. With his connections though he'd probably be able to get a flight of some sort he mused, although he guessed that it was difficult.

First of all he must see the estate agent and stop all plans for buying the house he'd been thinking about. He was amazed at his own stupidity. The very idea of anchoring himself with property here in England seemed preposterous now.

What was happening to him? Was it just this amazing letter from Diana? He must get to Bagleigh and talk to Samira first before he became too enthusiastic. Without Samira the plan wouldn't work. Debbie would only go happily to Palestine if Samira went too.

At Bagleigh two letters from Palestine had caused ructions. Harriet had written to Samira and also to her brother.

'I told you I wouldn't allow Matthew to go to that heathen place and I still won't,' James declared, waving Harriet's pages at his wife and daughter-in-law.

Mary laughed. 'Heathen? Have you taken leave of your senses, James Stanmore? It's the Holy Land you're talking about. The Holy Land. Jerusalem, Bethlehem, Galilee... A dreamy look crossed her face. 'In fact, I'd like to see it myself. I shall go on a pilgrimage one day like all those brave people of old.'

He grunted. 'You'll have to wait until I'm dead and gone then. Holy Land it may be, but there have always been wars there and always will be. Just like I said years ago when Colin and Diana first set their hearts on going, it's not safe for decent ordinary folk.'

Samira was so nervous, so anxious to go, that she clenched her hands together until they almost ached. She knew that she must stand up to this man. She had done so once before and she could do it again. Her own letter from Harriet had told her that her mother had been ill, that she really ought to visit soon, that Kaffa longed for her, and wanted very much to see the two children.

'I must go, Father,' she said. 'I've longed to go for so long, and now that the war's over and Diana is out there, I think it's the right time.'

James looked at her scathingly. 'That's as maybe. You go and take Kaffa-Mary if you wish, but Matthew, no. Matthew stays here.'

'Colin promised my mother that she would see our son one day,' Samira persisted. 'I can't go without Matthew, and what would he think if I suggested leaving him here anyway?'

'What he thinks or doesn't think is beside the point. He's my grandson and I say that he's not going.'

'I don't think you have any power over us. Matthew is my son first and foremost.' Samira marvelled at herself as she spoke. Is this truly me saying this, Samira el Hamid? She laughed suddenly, a laugh that owed more to intense nerves than to mirth. No, she was Samira Stanmore. She had her own money and the right to direct her life and that of her children as she thought fit.

James was silent for a long and terrible minute and Mary held her breath.

'If you take Matthew against my will,' he said at last, 'you don't come back. I will not have you under my roof again, and I may even make other decisions about Matthew's inheritance. You would have that on your conscience for ever.'

Then Samira did laugh, and it was a bitter almost frenzied sound. The stresses of the past months and years took precedence over commonsense and control and when she spoke she hardly knew what she said. 'You have no rights over him at all as you well know. He is Eshref's son, not Colin's. He has no legal right to Bagleigh anyway. We've been living a lie for too long. Perhaps now is the right time for me to speak out. Bagleigh should be Diana's or Kaffa-Mary's. I love my son, but he isn't your grandson, isn't Colin's child. I told you a long time ago and you chose to ignore it. Well, you can't ignore the facts any longer.'

Both James and Mary were looking at her in shocked amazement. She glanced from one to the other and had no idea what their separate reactions would be. Sudden fear replaced boldness as the moment of rebellion disappeared as quickly as it had come. She rushed out of the kitchen and into the garden and flung herself down on to the bench that stood outside the back door, slumped her head on her arms on the old scrubbed picnic table and sobbed as though her heart would break. Rollo pushed his wet nose on to her lap, tried to comfort her. 'What have I done?' she said through her tears. 'Oh, Rollo, whatever have I done?'

Mary came out to her eventually. She sat down on the bench.

'I knew about Matthew,' she said simply. 'You've done the right thing, child. I'm glad that it's said and that we can begin to put things right at last.' She put her arm round Samira's shoulders.

'But I don't understand?' Samira looked up at her, searched for a handkerchief and wiped her eyes. 'How could you have known and kept silent?'

'It was often hard, and perhaps I was wrong to say nothing.'

'But who told you?'

'You thought that I was ironing and listening to the wireless that night when you confessed to James about your first marriage, but I was not.

Oh, yes, the wireless was on and that was why you imagined I couldn't hear. It's very simple really. I'd gone into the dining room to fetch something and I heard the first part of your conversation even though the sitting-room door was shut, and then of course I listened. That partition wall is very thin. The room was divided long after the house was built.

'I was very ashamed of myself but I put my ear to the wall to hear more easily. Listening at walls isn't something that I feel very proud of but I became quite numb with shock as you talked and couldn't tear myself away from what I was hearing. It all sounded so terrible. I knew how much your father doted on Matthew and I was too paralysed with fear to take any action. I just stayed where I was. The dining-room door was open a little, but I hadn't switched the light on because the black-out curtains weren't drawn.

'I heard James go upstairs and like you I wanted to run up after him, but I stayed just where I was. I was shaking with fear while he was in Matthew's room, but then he came out and shut the door and I heard clearly what he said to you on the landing, that Matthew was his true grandson and that no one was to contradict him. Later I managed to slip back into the kitchen and I tried to continue ironing as though nothing had happened.'

Samira was sitting as if turned to stone but her tears had stopped. 'You mean you've known and not turned me out?' she whispered. 'You were still prepared to have me in your house as your daughter?'

Mary smiled at her then. 'Why should I turn you out? You've been a wonderful daughter to me, and none of it was your fault. I kept silent partly for James too. I did a lot of thinking during the following days and realised that if he had been aware that I knew, it might have made it more impossible for him to reject the facts. That's what he did, of course, and I judged that maybe it was for the best just then. He rejected the truth completely, cut it right out of his mind. I'm sure that he believes Matthew to be as much Colin's child as Kaffa-Mary.'

'You knew I was speaking the truth though?'

'Why would you have lied about something so harmful to your security and happiness? Yes, I believed you, and the more I pondered, the more some other things began to fall into place.'

'What things?' Samira felt a small shiver of alarm.

'Just little niggles that I had wondered about but put at the back of my mind like the date of Matthew's birth, and the way he looks—no trace of Colin at all. He's so dark, especially in the summer. And there was something in the way Colin used to look at him, a sort of faraway musing kind of look that occurred to me as odd.'

'What are you going to do?' Samira's mind was quite numb. She couldn't think what effect all this would have on her life and, more important, on her son's life.

'Do?'

'About Matthew? Will you tell him? He adored Colin.' She closed her eyes with the horror of what she had done, of the near-impossibility of telling her child that he wasn't who he thought he was. In one blinding moment of panic she thought of Eshref.

Mary took both of Samira's hands in hers. 'Colin was his adopted father, wasn't he? We can cling to that.'

'There was nothing official.'

'But he loved him, Samira. I always knew that. I think that when Colin remembered about Matthew's origins it was more disappointment than anything else that he felt. Maybe that was what I saw in his eyes. It certainly wasn't rejection.'

'No. He never rejected him.' Samira remembered Colin's words when he first saw her new-born baby, and her own tremendous relief.

'So,' Mary said, 'you'll do what Harriet says. Go to Palestine for a short visit and see your mother. It'll do you good to get away just now. You must insist on going, whatever James says, and while you're away I'll try to talk to him about the future. We'll sort something out. Meanwhile get away and forget your problems for a bit.'

But James and Mary never had that talk, and there was no time to arrive at any conclusions about the future of Matthew and Bagleigh and the other problems that had arisen.

James died as he had lived, still presuming

that he was in charge, still dominant and sure of himself, still in his full strength, with no warning and no weakness. As far as anyone could tell he knew nothing of his death. He had stormed out of the house after Samira's outburst, had saddled Major and was riding up to Greatcombe Rocks.

Rob, now demobbed and working on the farm again, found him. 'Not thrown, Sir,' he said to the doctor. 'I think he must have fallen from the saddle. He was dead when I got there. He'd been lying like that for quite a long time, I suspect, for Mrs Stanmore expected him home a good three hours before I went out to look for him. Major was standing nearby grazing as if nothing had happened.'

'A heart attack,' the doctor pronounced. 'I'm pretty sure that was it. We'd best get him back to the house.'

With some trouble they finally achieved the difficult task of carrying James' heavy body to Bagleigh and laying it upon the bed. Mary stood white-faced in the room looking down at the shell of the man who had been her husband, the man who had completely dominated her early years, moulded her life absolutely, until the war had given her a new freedom.

Samira stood beside her, also speechless. Was it her fault? She felt that she would always blame herself.

'He came to see me some time ago,' she heard the doctor saying. 'I told him he had a weak heart and must slow down a bit, but he utterly refused to do anything of the sort. I also assured

470

him that he was asking for a heart-attack sooner or later if he continued as he was doing but he just laughed at me. He refused any treatment and always said he wanted to go quickly. He had his wish. He'd have hated a long dependent illness.'

Diana and Harriet were unable to get home for the funeral for no flights were to be had in spite of all Harriet's efforts, but Thelma came down from London, looked at the large coffin that held the man she had once quite liked long ago, and shed an unusual tear.

James was buried near the memorial to his son in the quiet churchyard. Samira, who thought that she had recovered a little from that long-ago loss, shed tears again during the committal. Philip Briscoe had come over for the service and he was standing beside her. He took her arm and walked with her to the waiting car and she was glad of his support.

David too was there. After the funeral meal when the house was full of guests he took all the children out on to the moor, and later he gathered them all together, Dougie included, and read them a bed-time story. He had said nothing about his letter from Diana and the plan to go to Palestine. James' sudden death had put everything on hold for the time being. Samira certainly wouldn't want to leave her mother-in-law alone just yet.

The will had been read after the guests had departed and there were no surprises in it. Later after the children were asleep and the house quiet again, Mary and Samira were in the sitting room not quite knowing what to do, what to say to each other. David, who was staying, for they still kept a room for him at Bagleigh, looked from one to the other. He too was lost for words.

Mary was the first to speak. 'I expect you're wondering what I'm going to do,' she said. She put her handkerchief firmly away and straightened herself in the deep armchair. 'The house and estate is in trust for Matthew, but the house is mine for my lifetime, so there's no need to change the way we live immediately.'

Samira looked at David. She supposed that he knew nothing about the circumstances of Matthew's birth so she couldn't discuss the will with Mary just now, and it wouldn't have been the right time anyway. Diana must come home and sort all that out with the solicitor. The only thing she must do was prepare Matthew in a few small ways for the shock he was bound to suffer when the facts had to be told. He was only seven years old. The full impact wouldn't hit him for a long time, she hoped.

'Diana says that she's coming home as soon as she can,' Mary continued, cutting across Samira's thoughts. 'But Thelma and I have other plans. Thelma is cabling her from London telling her not to rush back.'

'Why, and what has Thelma got to do with it?' Samira had not talked much to Diana's strident partner, being a little in awe of her. But Thelma had stayed at Bagleigh the previous night and had been closeted for a long time in

472

the dining room with Mary.

'I'm going to London to stay with her,' Mary announced. 'We talked last night and she has offered me the use of part of her house for as long as I wish. I shall go during the school holidays so that Dougie can come with me. Rollo too.'

'Dougie?' The mystery was deepening.

'For a long time I've felt that we should make some effort to find out if he really is quite alone in the world. If he is, if we can't find any trace of anyone who has a claim on him, then I hope to adopt him. I've become very fond of Dougie and now that he's been offered a place at the Grammar School I think we should sort things out for him. He needs security.'

How could she sit here and calmly talk about things like this, Samira wondered, with her husband not long in his grave? But perhaps Mary felt a new freedom rather than a sense of devastating loss. During the last year or two Samira had often thought that their marriage hadn't been very close.

'How long will you stay with Thelma?' she asked.

'Until you return from Palestine probably. Rob can take charge of things here. He's very capable.'

'You still think I should go then? I thought I shouldn't leave you just now.'

'Rubbish. You have your own mother to think of. And I'd like you to go while Diana is there. Thelma says that Deborah can come to London with me. There's room for all three of us, she says, especially if Diana is away.'

David had been listening to this conversation with increasing amazement. His own plans for going to Palestine had been shelved immediately he heard of James Stanmore's sudden death.

'No need to take Deborah to London,' he said quickly. 'I've been thinking of going to Beth Haron, that's the kibbutz where I used to live. I should go initially for a few weeks, and of course I should take Deborah.' He looked at Samira. 'We could travel together. It would be easier for you, and Deborah would come more happily if you were with us.'

'It all fits in very well, just as if someone had planned it,' Mary said.

Someone did, David thought. Diana and Harriet between them in fact had hatched the whole plot. The only unexpected element had been James' death, and even that had not interfered with it too much. In some ways it had made things easier for Samira. He still couldn't understand why Diana had written to him in the way she had. He would find out when he arrived in Palestine.

So the plans were made, passages booked for the last week in July, and Mary spent hours packing for herself and Dougie to go to London. She was very excited. It was the first time she had ever been to the capital, the first time she had been away from Bagleigh to sleep for almost ten years, she said. And then it had only been for family holidays to Chy Morvah.

Diana agreed to remain in Palestine for

August. She would come home in September, she said, with Samira.

Philip Briscoe was the only one to be worried about the arrangements. He came over to see Samira two nights before they were to leave.

'Are you sure you'll be all right?' he said. 'I shall worry about you the whole time you're away.'

They were walking on the moor. Samira loved the cool English summer evenings. 'Of course I'll be all right,' she assured him. 'It was my home, remember.'

He laughed. 'Of course, but it's difficult to realise sometimes. You seem so English.'

'That's a compliment,' Samira said. 'I am English now.'

Suddenly Philip stopped, turned to face her. 'Will you marry me, Samira?' he said quietly. 'I've loved you for a long time.'

She knew that he loved her, had long known that she loved him, and this proposal wasn't altogether unexpected.

'Yes,' she said. 'Yes, Philip. I will marry you. I love you too. I think I've loved you ever since that night when we went to the Victory celebrations in Exeter.'

He pulled her into his arms, and they each knew that they'd come home at last. This was perfect and right. After so much suffering they had at last found happiness.

They swung along the path together, hand in hand. 'On Saturday we'll go to Exeter and I shall buy you a ring,' Philip said.

Samira glowed. 'I shall be able to show it to

my mother, tell her that I am to be married to the most wonderful man in the world!'

'I wish you weren't going to Palestine,' he said. 'I don't want to lose you so soon, and what about David Halprin? You won't fall in love with him during the voyage, will you?'

She laughed, knowing that he was teasing, and reached up to kiss him quickly on the cheek. 'Of course not, you ninny, and it's only a week, hardly a voyage as you call it.'

When they reached the top of the tor he pulled her down on to the grass beneath one of the great rocks and held her close again. She responded to him with all her heart and body, but they didn't make love. 'We must keep that for our wedding night,' he told her. 'I want it to be perfect.'

For a moment she thought of Colin. She knew that he would always have part of her heart, but Philip was her man now. This marriage was going to be perfect. Philip knew all about Eshref, all about Matthew, and yet he loved her as though she came to him fresh and new.

She glowed with happiness when they announced their engagement later that evening, and when at the weekend he placed his ring on her finger she knew that she would go to Palestine with a new confidence. The only thing that bothered her was telling Diana!

'We could be married in October,' Philip said. 'No need to wait, is there?'

Samira shook her head and kissed him again. 'No need at all,' she replied.

CHAPTER 32

Samira, brim full of emotions which changed minute by minute, stood on the deck of the little ship that was bringing her home, for Palestine would always be home. As they sailed into the Bay of Acre she could see the Mount Carmel range shimmering in the clear morning air and the houses of the picturesque town of Haifa clustering round the harbour. It was from here that she had embarked with Colin eight long years ago. She had watched those same mountains fading into the distance as the ship then bore her away from everything she had ever known.

She remembered Colin's protectiveness, the way he had cared for her. She could almost feel the touch of his arm around her shoulders as they stood on deck together. But she was also a little amused as she recalled the trepidation she had felt at the thought of going to England. She remembered clearly too her pleasure because she had become pregnant so soon and would, she hoped, be able to give Colin a son.

She held Matthew's hand tightly as her thoughts roved over all that had happened since, and glanced down at her left hand, at the large diamond glinting in the sunlight, Philip's ring. Colin's rings were on her other hand now. She smiled to herself thinking that she was very blessed indeed to have won the love of two such splendid men. She was returning to the land of her birth a very different creature from the timid girl she had once been.

David, with Deborah clinging to one hand and Kaffa-Mary the other, had very different thoughts. He had seen, out in the bay, five tattered-looking vessels, all proudly flying the Star of David. He knew that they were crowded with desperate and hungry refugees, Jews like himself, yet so unlike himself that the comparison was almost obscene. The pathetic men, women and children on board those boats were the pitiable remnants of Hitler's camps, and wanted only one thing—to get to their Promised Land, the haven they had dreamed of in the hells of Auschwitz, of Belsen, Buchenwald and all the rest. And there, ranged against them, preventing their entry, was all the might of the British Navy.

Rage boiled inside him as he stared at the little boats and then at the blockade of warships. He turned to Samira. 'Look at them,' he said. 'Can you believe that any government can be so callous and bloody-minded as ours? A British passport gives me the freedom to come here unmolested and yet I'm ashamed to own it.'

Samira shook her head, not knowing how to reply. She knew that the British were limiting immigration in response to fierce Arab objections to too many Jews entering the land. Yet when she thought about Diana's description of Belsen, and about Rachel's horrific death, and when she looked at David beside her, she understood only one thing. Whatever the politics, those poor wretches out there on their pathetic little floating prisons should be allowed to dock at once before they perished either by drowning or by disease. Hadn't they suffered enough?

She had been able to see on to the deck of one of the small boats for they had passed quite close. It was a tramp steamer and obviously not meant for the open sea.

'Poor sods,' one of the sailors had remarked in Samira's hearing. 'That old tub's likely to sink sooner or later if you ask me. His Majesty's bloody rotten Navy ought to be bloody ashamed. First we fight Hitler, then we turn on Hitler's ruddy victims.' He had shaken his head in disgust and stalked off, leaving those who heard him visibly shaken. Samira guessed that some of her fellow passengers hadn't given the refugee boats more than a moment's thought until then.

Their own ship sailed through unmolested and was allowed to dock without trouble, but Samira's pleasure was severely dented by what she had seen. There were long and complicated checks of their passports and papers and she became nervous hoping that all was in order, fearing that they too might be refused entry and forced to go straight back again.

David's passport and that of his daughter held no clue that they were Jewish. Wing Commander David Halprin, it said, test pilot. The minor officials who were checking looked at him with respect and even with a certain amount of awe. Deborah's fair plaits looked totally

English. When Samira's turn came her papers and those of her children were examined with more care. She found herself being scrutinised suspiciously. Stanmore was a good English name, but maybe they thought it was a cover. With her dark Semitic looks she could very well pass for a Jew, although her smart summer dress and box-shaped jacket were obviously expensive, a far cry from the rags worn by the poor wretches in the flotilla of misery out there beyond the harbour, she thought.

Advised by David, she had chosen her clothes with care for this journey. Her children were carefully dressed too, in true English middle-class fashion. Matthew wore short grey trousers, white shirt, and a tie and blazer that was part of the uniform for his new prep school. There was even a smart new school cap on his head. He'd complained bitterly about this in the heat, but Samira had insisted and she looked at him now with pride. But at the same time there was pain in her heart for the children on the boats who were denied all the things she and her family were enjoying.

Their careful appearance obviously bore fruit, for the necessary papers were stamped at last and they were all ushered through. And there beyond the barrier was Harriet waiting to welcome them. She folded Samira in her arms and kissed her heartily on both cheeks, then she stood back and looked at the three children who were clustered shyly behind her. She shook hands solemnly with Matthew, for he held himself aloof, but the little girls suffered a kiss from this rather exuberant and strangely dressed lady.

David grasped her hand in a vice-like handshake. 'It's been a long time,' he said. 'You look well.' He looked round expecting to see Diana.

Harriet, guessing his thoughts, said, 'Diana is in Jerusalem. She'll be home in a few days' time, all being well.'

They needed two cars to get them and their luggage to Khanhaven. Raif Habib was waiting outside the customs and passports office for them. 'I've arranged a meal, lunch, for all of us at the Carmel House Hotel,' he said after he had greeted them. 'I expect you need a little refreshment. Then we'll drive home.'

Home! It meant different things to each of them. For David it was the land, Eretz Israel, and for Samira it was her mother. She was quite overcome by the thought that she was to see Kaffa again so soon now.

'I shall fetch your mother this evening,' Harriet said. 'She has more freedom than she used to and can come any time. She works for me every morning, in fact, just a little paper work, so you'll see plenty of her.'

'You said that she had been ill?'

'Nothing serious and she'll be all the better for seeing you!'

'And my father and brothers? Do they know that I'm coming?' In spite of the security of her name, her position, her British passport, a small shiver of fear passed through Samira.

'Yes, they know. But they've changed. Don't worry about them. Abdulla does a few jobs for

481

me now and then, heavy work that I couldn't manage. There's only one black sheep in the family now, Zeid.'

Zeid. He was the one Samira had always disliked, always feared. 'What has he done?'

'Don't ask. I'll leave your mother to tell you about Zeid.' Harriet's voice was grim, but dismissive. 'Now what shall we eat? They do very good food here.'

After the meal they piled back into the cars but not before David had seen the barbed wire that was strung all along the harbour wall. Harriet saw his angry face and understood. 'It's to prevent those poor souls out there from swimming ashore,' she told him. 'There are camps just a little way inland too with about three thousand or so Jewish refugees behind more barbed wire.'

He gritted his teeth in rage. 'I think it's time I came back,' he said.

'That was why Diana wrote to you. She's investigating all this for her paper. She's angry too.'

They reached Khanhaven in the early evening. The children were tired and fractious but Ghazala, older now and very stately, welcomed them enthusiastically, and there were two baby donkeys in the field behind the bungalow to further beguile them. Once outside and fortified with ample orange juice, their spirits began to revive.

'I shall fetch your mother after we've unpacked and sorted ourselves out,' Harriet said. 'Your

482

rooms are ready, one for you and the two girls, Samira. David, I thought you could share the little one with Matthew.'

'I was going to Beth Haron,' he objected.

'If you wish, but I wondered whether it wouldn't be better to stay here tonight. Break Deborah in gently.'

David smiled at her. 'You're a marvel, Harriet,' he said. 'I'll abide by what you say. You always know best.'

She laughed at him. 'Old age, my dear. It comes to all of us, I'm sorry to say.'

Samira was strangely nervous about seeing her mother after so long, but when she heard Harriet's car on the track outside she ran to meet her and the two women, after one initial moment's pause, threw their arms around each other and their eyes were full of tears. Then they started to talk, Kaffa in quick Arabic, and Samira, who had not spoken her native language for almost eight years, replying more slowly. They went into the house together.

Harriet drove the car around to the back where she always parked it now and wanted to cry herself. She beckoned the children to come inside. 'Your grandmother is here,' she told them simply.

Kaffa-Mary was the first to run into the room. Then she stopped and stared at this strange lady with the beautiful smile and the lovely dress. She had never seen a garment like it. There were shining patterns embroidered all over the front, little pictures of birds and flowers. On her head the lady wore a strange scarf thing, just as beautiful.

Matthew hung back as he had done when Harriet had greeted him.

Samira quickly reverted to English. She smiled at them, got up from the sofa where she and her mother were seated. 'My children,' she said, taking their hands and pulling them gently forward. 'Kaffa-Mary and Matthew. And this is Deborah, David's daughter.'

Kaffa greeted them all carefully, allowing them to come to terms with her appearance and her strangeness. Then she looked at Matthew again, examining his features, and Samira knew in that instant that her mother guessed the secret of her son's birth. It was only a quick look of affirmation perhaps, followed by a barely perceptible flicker of sympathy.

The first emotion Samira felt was relief that her mother knew the truth. She wished they could be alone so that they could talk about it. She needed her mother's wisdom and counsel, something she had missed for a long time. She wanted to tell her about the inheritance of Bagleigh, a problem not yet resolved and waiting for her when she returned to England.

The following day they did find themselves alone. Perhaps Harriet had deliberately arranged it. She packed the three children into the back of her little car and David in the front, and drove over to the kibbutz. 'For a swim,' she told them brightly.

Before Samira could bring herself to mention

the problem that was foremost in her mind, she and her mother talked about all manner of other things, tried to catch up on all the news of eight years. Then eventually there was silence between them. They were sitting outside in the shade of a vine that Harriet had trained over the porch at the back of the house. Ghazala was lying quietly at their feet and there was only the contented sound of the donkeys grazing in the field just beyond the fence.

'Tell me about Matthew,' Kaffa said gently. 'Your husband? Did he know?'

'Yes. He knew the very first day,' Samira replied. 'Colin was a wonderful man. He accepted him as if he had been his own.'

'I saw the likeness to Eshref when Harriet showed me the photographs,' Kaffa explained. 'I was frightened for you for many reasons.' She was silent for a time, the embroidery in her hands quite still. Then she added quietly: 'Eshref has no other son.'

No other son! They were simple words but to Samira they held a terrible threat. A man with no son was a desperate man, especially one like Eshref, a respected sheik, rich and influential, a leader in his society. To have no son was to suffer unthinkable disgrace.

'As soon as he hears that you have arrived, I have no doubt that he will come,' Kaffa continued. 'I hate to frighten you, child, but you must be prepared. He won't come to threaten or anything like that, of course. He's much respected by the British now. The District

Commissioner has made him Mukhtar for his area. But he will be very persuasive. He has vast resources.'

'Why has he no son?' It was difficult to imagine any rich Arab with no son. 'With four wives surely...?'

Kaffa shrugged her shoulders. 'His first wife is barren. The second produces only daughters, the third bears only dead sons, four so far. He's quite desperate.'

'I'm sorry. What do you think he'll offer? Will he suggest that I become his fourth wife?' Samira's voice was full of scorn.

'Hardly. He knows that your husband is dead, however, so he might possibly think that you would be glad to accept him.'

Samira immediately saw Philip's face in her imagination, saw Bagleigh, and then Madda-combe waiting for her. Philip's parents were to move into a smaller house nearby after the wedding. She twisted the diamond on her finger.

'Well, he'll just have to be disappointed, won't he?' Then sudden fear shot through her. 'But he has no legal right, has he?'

'You can deny that he's the father of course,' Kaffa said. 'But looking at Matthew, how would anyone believe that?'

'But there's no proof, and how will he find out anyway? He won't see Matthew.'

'He knows already, I think. Abdulla brought home one of the photographs you sent. Zeid saw it. He's the only one of my sons I don't trust. I saw his face when he looked at it, and then the photograph disappeared. I think I know where it went!'

Two days later just after the midday siesta Eshref came. Samira heard the car on the track outside and when she looked out and saw the tall impressive man uncoiling himself from the driving seat she could feel her pulse racing and knew that all colour had drained from her face. Matthew had been the first one up after his rest. He hated this period of inactivity in the middle of the day and had gone out to the field with Ghazala. Samira hoped that he wouldn't run round to the front of the house to see who their visitor was. The arrival of a motor car was something of an event.

Harriet immediately came into the room, straightening her hair and her dress. She smiled at Samira. 'Don't worry,' she directed. 'Stand your ground. He isn't the ogre you believe him to be.'

He stood waiting at the door without knocking, aware that they would know he was there, and Harriet eventually, and with deliberate slowness, opened it and stared at him. 'Sheik Eshref el Nasim,' she pronounced, giving him his full name. 'What can I do for you?'

He inclined his head slightly before replying. 'Peace be to you, Mrs Clayton,' he said in Arabic, and then continued in English, which he had learned to speak with a little more fluency since his appointment as Mukhtar. 'I would like to speak to Mrs Stanmore, if you would permit it?'

Harriet was not surprised by his attitude. He was coming to beg for something that he wanted above all else, and the power to give it was in the hands of the woman whom he had once abused and humiliated and who was now a British citizen, rich and independent. She guessed that he hated this subservient role. It was one that he had probably never assumed before. 'Come in,' she said.

Samira was standing in the living room and held herself proudly erect as he entered. She was wearing a long traditional gown that her mother had given her that morning. It was a beautiful thing embroidered with all the skill that Kaffa could command. But her head was bare, her beautiful hair loose on her shoulders. 'No, I shall not wear any headdress,' she had told her mother. 'To cover my head denotes submissiveness, and I shall never be that again as long as I live.'

She thought of those words as she confronted this man who had haunted her memories for so long. He was wearing a spotless white djellaba and she wondered for one surprising moment what feminine hand had laboured over this garment to achieve such a pristine state.

He was looking at her, his eyes roving over her body from head to foot, and she wanted to drop her gaze to the ground before him as she had been brought up to do, but forced herself to look him straight in the face. During her years in England she had learned, with much effort, to eradicate this habit of docility and obedience.

He greeted her in Arabic, and she replied in

the same language, but then she quickly changed to English. She felt more at home with English now and wanted to have the advantage.

After formal enquiries about her health, he came straight to the point. 'You have a son,' he said.

'Yes. Matthew.'

'I believe that...'

'That you think he may be your son also?' She would surprise him by taking the words out of his mouth.

He inclined his head. 'I have been told that there are many indications that this may be so. May I meet him?'

They were both still standing. Samira had not invited him to sit down. Her heart was pounding furiously and in spite of her brave stance she wondered yet again if he really had any power over her, any legal right to Matthew.

Harriet had been hovering in the background and at this point she came to the rescue. 'You may see him, of course, but only on condition that you say nothing to him of your suspicions. In British law he is the baptised son of my nephew, Colin Stanmore. Moreover he is the legal heir to Bagleigh Hall in England, and there is no question of your having any rights in his life whatsoever.'

'I understand,' Eshref said, obviously not believing a word. 'You said that I may see the boy. I agree to your condition. I shall say nothing.'

'Very well.' Harriet turned to Samira. 'That is, if you're willing, of course, my dear?'

'I shall tell all three to come in,' Samira replied. She was glad to escape from the room which seemed to her oppressively hot and uncomfortable. She walked as calmly as possible out of the rear door and called to the children. Deborah had not gone to the kibbutz with David today and she was the first to obey the summons. The other two came quickly behind her for it was almost tea-time and they expected some of the home-made cakes that Harriet always produced at this time in the afternoon.

'We have a visitor,' Samira told them. 'Go in quietly and say hello.'

Deborah went straight into the living room and stared at Eshref and then smiled at him. 'Hello,' she said brightly, for she was seldom shy, possessing all the self-assurance of her mother. 'I like your dress. I told my daddy that he should wear one of those.'

Harriet wanted to laugh but with some difficulty restrained herself.

Eshref hardly glanced at Deborah. He seemed not to have registered her remark. He was looking past her to the other two who followed. When he saw Matthew he ignored the little girls completely.

Matthew was wearing a cotton shirt and short trousers, but these very English clothes failed to hide the dark good looks, the features that were so obviously a legacy from the man standing motionless there.

Samira looked at father and son and held her breath for wonder and fear. There could be no doubt now, if indeed there had ever been. Every line of Eshref's handsome face seemed to be repeated in the little boy.

'You are Matthew,' Eshref said, and held out his hands to him.

But Matthew ignored the gesture. 'Hello,' he said politely as he had been told and then he turned to Harriet. 'Can we have tea soon, Aunt?' he asked. 'I'm starving.'

Kaffa-Mary pushed to the front and stared at the stranger. 'My name's Kaffa-Mary,' she announced, 'after my two grandmothers.'

Eshref was forced to look at her then. 'Kaffa is an Arab name,' he said. 'I wish that your brother too had a name that befits him.'

Matthew was temporarily diverted from his desire for cakes by this remark. He examined the newcomer afresh but said nothing, and Harriet, sensing trouble, quickly ushered them all out of the room and into the yard for tea.

Samira watched them go and longed to join them, but instead she renewed her stance in front of the heavy wooden table. She put her hands behind her, feeling its sturdiness and praying for strength. 'You promised that you would say nothing,' she accused.

He smiled briefly at her. 'And I did not. To be named for his mother's race would have been acceptable.'

She shook her head. 'Never. He has a name from the Christian Bible and he's baptised into the Christian Church as Mrs Clayton told you. That was how I wanted it to be.'

He didn't comment further on this. 'My wives

491

have given me no sons,' he said, and there was sudden sadness in his voice. 'As you must know this is a great grief to me, but at last I have found my son, the son I've prayed Allah to grant me for so long.'

'But he can't be your son,' she stated firmly. 'He's English, and can never have any part or interest in this country.'

'I can offer you much. You could live here as my wife, Samira. I would marry you again, make you my chief and honoured wife. I would even divorce the other three if that was what you wanted. Or you could live in my house free and independent, and you would be rich. You could have anything you wished. I could build you a house of your own nearby. Only give me my son.'

Samira bowed her head and for a moment wanted to cry, but then a wave of anger swept over her, replacing the trace of pity that she had begun to feel.

'It's out of the question,' she said fiercely, straightening her back and standing to her full height. 'I could never allow Matthew to be brought up here. And I am to be married again when I return to England. You'll no doubt marry a fourth wife.' Her words were scornful. 'You'll have sons eventually, but none of that is my concern. You humiliated me and divorced me with no thought of my wellbeing. I was nearly murdered by my brothers. Did you know that, Eshref el Nasim? One of your hated Jewish neighbours saved my life, and Colin Stanmore married me in spite of my disgrace at your hands. No, you shall never have my son. He is Colin's son by right of acceptance and adoption. He's English and always will be. Now go.'

She gripped the table behind her with both hands as though her life depended on it, and watched as the man she had always feared turned abruptly away from her and strode out. She remained motionless as she heard the car revving up furiously outside and then the tyres scrabbling to get a grip on the stones of the rough track.

When all was silent she collapsed on to the sofa and closed her eyes in horror at what had been said during those past terrible minutes. She had as good as admitted to him that Matthew was his child. Colin's son by right of acceptance and adoption, she had said, and yet she knew that there were no official adoption papers, nothing that a court could accept. She had no idea how she stood officially. The only thing she was sure of was that she must get back to England as soon as she could, take Matthew to the safety of Bagleigh, to the protection of Philip Briscoe, and to the normality of his English prep school, where, at her insistence, he was to be a weekly boarder rather than a termly one. James Stanmore had not beaten her in this and Eshref el Nasim would not get his own way either. But she must never bring Matthew to Palestine again.

She could hear the children laughing out in the courtyard and went to join them, but suddenly and unaccountably she thought of her

493

brother Zeid. She had no idea why she should think of him at this moment. It was almost like a premonition of something bad. With so many other things to think and talk about she had forgotten to ask her mother what Harriet might have meant when she had referred to him as the black sheep.

Deborah looked up from her tea as she stepped into the little courtyard. 'Come on Auntie Sam,' she said. 'Come and have some of Aunt Harriet's cakes. They're even better than the ones you make.'

CHAPTER 33

Diana was in Jerusalem when they had all arrived, and on her return she hugged the children enthusiastically and gave each of them one of the little presents that she had bought there. For Matthew there was a replica oil lamp just like the real one that Colin had given his mother long ago. Debbie had a chain with a large green shiny stone hanging from it and for Kaffa-Mary she had chosen a little Jerusalem cross on a similar chain.

'So how do you like Palestine?' she asked them as they sat on the verandah eating Harriet's biscuits.

'It's wizard,' said Matthew. 'I want to stay.'

'You can't stay,' Deborah told him. 'It's me that might have to stay, and I don't want to one bit.'

494

'I like the donkeys,' Kaffa-Mary said. 'Aunt Harriet said that she's going to call the new baby one Kaffa, after me.'

Later when the children were playing in the field just outside the bungalow Samira told Diana about Eshref's visit and she mentioned her uncomfortable feelings about Zeid.

'He can't do anything to harm you now, especially as you're engaged to Philip.'

Samira had sent a letter to Diana telling her of the engagement. It had arrived only a few days before their own arrival.

'You...you don't mind about Philip and me?' Samira had been dreading this moment.

Diana was brisk. 'Mind? Why should I? We weren't suited. You and Philip were made for each other.'

'You really think so?'

'Of course I do.' Diana smiled at Samira and gave her a quick kiss on the cheek. 'I could never say that about him and me. You'll be very happy.'

They sat for a long time over a further pot of tea for there was much to talk about. Her father's death had been a shock for Diana, and the fact that she couldn't get back to England in time for the funeral gave her a great sense of uselessness.

'Are you quite sure that Mother is all right?'

'Fine really. Gone to London with your Thelma. She's taken Dougie with her, and Rollo too.'

Diana had known this, had been surprised, hardly seeing her quiet little mother and Thelma

495

Barrington-Smith making a good pair.

'I'd never have thought it,' she said, trying to imagine the two together. 'Rollo won't think much of London parks after the moors,' she added with a grin. 'Oh, well, it won't be for long and then we'll all be home again.'

Samira looked searchingly at her. 'I don't think David wants to go back.'

'Probably not. He's needed here.' Diana jumped up. 'I've to go and see him as a matter of fact. Lots of news about things happening in Jerusalem. Want to come?'

'No, thanks. I'll stay with the children.'

Harriet offered to drive her over to Beth Haron.

'What did you do in Jerusalem?' she enquired as she manoeuvred past various clucking hens on the road.

'Took endless photographs. Got some good ones of the bombing of the King David Hotel as a matter of fact.'

'We heard about it and were worried for you.'

'Well, I did have a near miss actually. I haven't said anything before, didn't want to frighten Samira. It was Jewish extremists who set the bomb.'

Harriet nodded. 'I know. They're getting more and more militant. I don't agree with it, of course, but I can sometimes see their point.'

'So can I,' Diana said. 'Britain won't allow more than thirteen thousand Jews to come here each year, and Europe's crammed with them trekking south with all their belongings in wheelbarrows—they're lucky enough to have wheelbarrows!'

'Pray for the Peace of Jerusalem,' Harriet quoted.

Diana gave a hollow laugh. 'Well, there's plenty of praying done,' she said. 'Bells are constantly ringing from umpteen Christian shrines, the Muslims call from their mosques every four hours, and there are the Jews of course. One presumes that they pray, but they're more private about it. Except of course at their Wailing Wall.' She turned to look at her companion. 'Do you really think that God is dead, Harriet?'

'My, what a question for a hot afternoon. I have absolutely no idea.' Harriet laughed and shrugged her shoulders. 'Some people think he is. Who's to tell? Certainly not me.'

Their car was familiar to the guards at the gate of the kibbutz and they were ushered through. Harriet drove to the main building and stopped. 'I don't know where you'll find David,' she said. 'He's probably doing some highly unsuitable manual task and wasting all his vast abilities. Anyway I'll come back for you just before supper. I have to bring Deborah over then.'

Diana hauled her bulging briefcase from the back seat and climbed out of the car. 'Why isn't she here?'

'She stays at Khanhaven every other day. It's an arrangement we have. She sleeps here though, in the children's house. David insists on that.'

She found him eventually in the cow shed. He laughed when she told him of Harriet's remarks. 'It's good to get a bit of muck on your hands,' he said. 'Cuts one down to size.'

'You don't need to be cut down to size.' Her voice was serious. She stared at him. He was wearing the usual kibbutz gear of old trousers and patched shirt. 'Where did you get those awful clothes?'

'Standard issue. My RAF uniform wouldn't go down very well here, would it, with all those British troops around persecuting Jews?' He grinned at her and wiped his hands on an old towel. 'Come on. I've finished as a matter of fact. I want to hear all about Jerusalem. I'll get cleaned up and we'll go for a walk.'

'I need to discuss my latest copy with you. That's what I came for.'

'Fine. I'm flattered. Dump it all in my billet and we'll relax a bit first. That suit you?'

'Perfect. I've hardly had any time off in days.'

While David washed Diana stood in the sunshine and listened to the sounds of the kibbutz: children singing from the schoolroom, hens clucking, and the wind gently playing through the branches of the pines that stood like sentinels around the perimeter fence. On the surface nothing much appeared to have changed since she was last here before the war, yet if you probed a little deeper, she thought, you would see that everything had changed. Since Hitler's camps nothing could ever be the same again.

When he reappeared they swung along the path together, in step, in perfect accord, but carefully not touching.

She told him about the King David Hotel. He knew the facts but she gave him an eye-witness account. 'Over ninety people were killed,' she said. 'Jews, Arabs and British, including women and children. It was frightful, like the blitz all over again, only worse in some ways.'

'It was the Irgun,' David said. 'Not a group I support. Terrorism seldom achieves anything.'

'Then how is your precious Jewish state to come about?' She plucked a piece of rosemary from the bushes that grew in abundance here but could only be persuaded to grow in very sheltered places at Bagleigh. She crushed the spiky leaves in her fingers and the aromatic fragrance filled her nostrils. Rosemary for remembrance! The evocative words flashed into her mind and for a moment she wanted to have nothing to do with this tormented land. Yet for one traitorous second she felt a glimmer of the old magic. She wanted David again, but David without his country.

A moment of despair! Surely that part of her had been banished for ever? She mentally shook herself. She was a career woman, here to do a job, send reports to London.

'By negotiation,' David replied, turning her thoughts abruptly back to the question she had asked him. 'But if the British won't negotiate, there will have to be other methods.'

'You mean terrorism after all?'

'I didn't say that.'

She sighed. 'What else is there? Will God do it? Harriet wouldn't give me an answer when I asked her if he was dead.'

David stopped and stood quite still. He shaded his eyes and looked beyond the perimeter fence to the hills, hazy now in the afternoon heat. He started very quietly to quote some lines and Diana, listening, stared at him as though she had never known him before this moment.

For behold the days are coming, says the Lord, that I will bring back from captivity my people Israel, and I will cause them to return to the land that I gave to their fathers, and they shall possess it.

He started to walk again. 'Jeremiah,' he said. 'One of our prophets.'

'But I thought you were a secular Jew?'

'In many ways I am, but I believe that we have a right to be here, that this land was promised to us by God.'

'Then you must believe in Him?'

He laughed, the serious moment gone as quickly as it had come. 'Have you brought your swimming things?' he asked. 'The pool is still here. A bit murky, but acceptable.' He took her hand and soon they were both laughing and running together along the path. She felt the problems, the horrors of the past years and weeks dropping swiftly away.

When it was time for Harriet to come with Deborah they both waited at the gate for her. David loved this hour with his daughter. She was just beginning to enjoy some of the pleasures the kibbutz had to offer. The pool was her favourite, and there were swings and organised games for the children every evening before they went to bed. She had made friends with another little girl and David confidently expected that soon she would ask to stay at Beth Haron for the rest of their time here instead of at Khanhaven. He still hadn't made up his mind about the future.

They heard the motor car coming before they saw it, and as Harriet screeched round the corner and pulled to a halt in a cloud of flying dust they jumped swiftly back. Diana felt a sudden shiver of fear for Harriet never drove like that. Behind her was another car, a British Police vehicle.

'Deborah? Where's Deborah?' David shouted, peering into the back seat as he pulled open the door for Harriet to get out. 'What's happened?'

Harriet was pale and dishevelled and Diana looked at her with rising alarm.

'We can't find her,' Harriet said. 'But it may be nothing—a prank perhaps.' The tone of her voice told them that she didn't think it could be anything of the kind. 'Everything is being done to find her, David.'

'What happened? When?' He was more terrified than he had ever been during the war. He almost wanted to shake Harriet. She'd

501

been in charge. He made an effort to control himself and looked at the Inspector who was just getting out of the second car.

'Wing Commander Halprin?'

'Yes.'

'Can you help us? Tell us anything that might give us a lead in the search for your daughter?'

'Don't worry too much,' Diana said. 'She ran away one day at Bagleigh.'

'This isn't Bagleigh,' David said grimly.

Zeid had hatched his terrible plan during the long night hours when he couldn't sleep. He was the only one of the brothers not to have been successful in life. The others all had jobs of various sorts and were moderately contented. Abdulla, Nasir and Gasim had wives too, pretty girls, all very seductive and fruitful. He watched them with envy, his eyes following them about, looking at their rounded figures as they swelled with his brothers' children, then watching the babies at their breasts. His own wife had died when their first child was born, the child too. Everything he touched went wrong. And now he was making bombs secretly in the old shepherd's hut in the hills. Bombs to kill Jews and British soldiers, for he believed that both were against him, both wanted only to thwart all his plans. He had recently joined an Arab terrorist group and this was giving him much needed status.

But this latest idea was quite different. He needed money. It was a way to get it. Easily! He'd thought it all out when he'd heard about Eshref's visit to Samira. He'd had the photograph of Matthew, stupid name, for a long time and it was obvious that the child was Eshref's. Eshref had no other sons, was desperate for sons!

Zeid decided that to achieve his aim he must first take the Jewish child. He mustn't touch Matthew, or for that matter the sister. She was his own flesh and blood after all, and named after his mother. He was slightly superstitious and wouldn't harm little Kaffa. But what did the life of a Jewish child matter? Nothing at all. The fewer Jews there were in Palestine the better for everyone.

Once he had the child he would be able to threaten his sister, tell her that if she didn't give in to Eshref the girl would be killed. It must seem as if the message came from Eshref of course. Once the boy was handed over he'd go to Eshref and tell him what he'd done, why his sister had been willing to give in. Then he'd demand payment, and if this was refused he'd threaten to tell the British authorities that it was Eshref who was behind the kidnapping. The Sheik was very proud of his position and of the respect in which he was held. Disgrace would be unthinkable. He'd pay up. Zeid's plans went no further than that.

But how to get the girl? He waited and watched, saw that during siesta Deborah usually crept out of the house and sat in the shade of the olive tree beside the two donkey foals. He prepared a thick gag to prevent her screams. He had no transport, but perhaps that was a good thing, for his feet made no noise, and he was strong. And he knew how to quieten her.

He was pretty sure that she hadn't gone to the kibbutz today. The heat was intense and everyone was inside with shutters drawn against the sun.

He sweated and watched, his heart beating furiously. Then she came. With bare feet and thin dress she crept from the house and walked over to the two little donkeys. She sat down beside them and began to stroke their soft noses. He approached her normally and she showed no fear, smiling at him. This disconcerted him a little, but in one swift action he clapped his hand over her mouth and before she could make a sound he was away out of the gate which he had left open, and down the track which led into the hills.

He tied the gag round her mouth when they were out of sight and she pounded him helplessly with her small fists, but he laughed. She was like a little goat, a chicken for slaughter. Eventually he dealt her a blow to the head and she slumped over his shoulder as he strode out to his hideaway. It was built into the hillside, hidden now in the undergrowth. No one would ever find her here. To his own secret surprise and satisfaction his plan appeared to have worked.

Inside the hut there was an array of bomb-making equipment, several blankets rolled up beside the wall, a pitcher of water and a rough wooden table. He threw the child viciously down on one of the blankets and peered at her. A little light came in through a crack in the wall. There was no window. She began to whimper and then she opened her eyes and started to scream.

Zeid couldn't bear the noise. He had not counted on this. He was tempted to hit her into silence again, but if he killed her too soon his plan would fail. He must offer her life in return for Samira's compliance. 'Stop it,' he shouted in English. 'Stop it or I will kill you.'

Deborah stopped. It was all a nightmare, a bad dream. It couldn't be happening. Daddy would come soon. Daddy was brave and strong. Or it might be Mummy. She was brave too. She was a shining star in the sky with Jesus and He'd send her down. Or Auntie Sam might come. She wasn't brave like the other two, but she wouldn't let Debbie stay here in this awful bad-story place.

'Be quiet and you'll be all right,' the fierce man said.

She couldn't see his face. It was covered with a funny scarf-thing, only his eyes showing.

'I'll bring you bread.'

She didn't want bread. She wanted to be back with Auntie Sam and Matthew and Kaffa-Mary.

Then he went away. She heard the door shut and a thump on the outside. When he'd quite gone she staggered to her feet and groped her way to the door and tried to push, but there was something stopping it, something heavy and big. Her head hurt. She sank down on the smelly blanket and started to cry, small quiet sobs in case the man came back and killed her.

For the frantic adults two agonising days and worse nights passed and there was no news, then Samira found the first message. It was written on a piece of thick white paper and had been pushed through the window of Harriet's car. It was written carefully in a round childish hand, but it was in English.

If you want the child to live, give up your son. If you go to the police with this letter she will die. Bring your son to his rightful father and the Jewish child will be returned to you.

She ran to find Harriet and thrust the paper at her, panic quickly giving way to anger. 'Will he stop at nothing then?'

Harriet read the words twice over and then she looked at Samira. 'I don't believe this is Eshref's doing,' she said.

'But who else? And he says, bring your son. It must be from him.'

Harriet shook her head. 'He isn't that kind of man. Desperate for a son, yes, an Arab despot, yes, but a criminal most definitely not.'

'Then what are we to do?'

Harriet had slumped on to the sofa and was silent for a time, considering. 'If we went to Eshref he would deny all knowledge of it and would insist on going to the police to clear his name.'

Samira paced back and forth in the room and wondered how to cope, how to do all the ordinary things that must be done, while

506

Deborah was suffering unimaginable horrors and while her life was in such terrible danger. It was important, for the sake of the other two children, to try to maintain an outward calm that she was far from feeling.

Matthew and Kaffa-Mary had been frightened and shocked by Deborah's disappearance. Diana took them out riding every morning to help divert them from their fears, but Harriet insisted that she take a pistol with her. The comparative peace of Khanhaven had been shattered. They were all nervous now.

They had decided nothing by the time Diana returned from the morning's ride. She flung off her coat and put the pistol back in Harriet's desk. 'Any news?' she enquired.

'This.' Harriet gave her the note.

She read it quickly, her face visibly paling as she did so. 'We must tell David,' she said. 'Do you want me to go?'

Matthew had come in and was listening. 'Is Debbie found?' he asked. He looked hopefully at all three of them in turn.

'Not yet, darling,' Samira told him. 'But we know that she's safe.'

'How do you know?'

Harriet was the first to think of a suitable reply. 'Someone has taken her away for a few days, but they're going to give her back soon. Now go and see to the horses,' she directed briskly.

David had organised parties in the hills and valleys surrounding Khanhaven and Beth Haron.

507

The British police had a great number of men out too, but nothing had been found that gave any lead to Deborah's whereabouts. The brief note was the first clue, but David was adamant that the police should not be told of it in case it further endangered her life. He was beside himself with grief and remorse and fear. If it had not been for his insane passion for this country, his precious daughter would be safe and sound now at Bagleigh, or in his home in Bristol. He cursed Palestine, Eretz Israel, and himself even more, for her fate.

Diana too felt a great weight of self-reproach and anguish. If she hadn't told him that he ought to come here, almost engineered events, none of this could have happened. Deborah's life now assumed more importance to her than anything else. In this one child she saw personified the whole Jewish race, persecuted, maligned, homeless. She knew that her reasoning was faulty, that Deborah had probably been kidnapped for purposes that had nothing to do with politics, but the feeling remained. If Deborah died, then Diana felt that she too would die, mentally anyway. It was an extravagant sentiment but she was unable to banish it.

At night sleep came to her with great difficulty. She saw Debbie in her imagination and sometimes in her dreams, tied up, terrified, starving. Then the pictures of Belsen would return to haunt her. It was in the middle of one such dream that she awoke suddenly to hear a noise at her window. She was instantly alert, wishing that the pistol was beneath her pillow instead of in the desk-drawer in the living room. She sat up in bed and saw a man's shape etched against the window. The moon was bright behind him. He tapped gently on the glass and her first fear gave way to surprise. No one intent on some evil purpose would knock. Silently she padded over to the window and then flashed her torch full on his face. He put his hand to his lips and she saw that it was Abdulla, Samira's brother, the one that they all liked, the one whom she had met here at Harriet's when he came to help with the animals.

The window was open a crack. Diana had never been able to sleep in a shuttered room and in spite of the dangers of leaving it open, she had insisted on having fresh air.

'If you come,' he whispered, 'I can lead you to the child.'

Why me? she wanted to ask. And why now? But with her horrendous dreams still vivid in her mind there was no choice. 'Wait,' she whispered back. She pulled the curtain across the window, threw on some clothes and picked up a pair of sturdy shoes. Then she silently opened her bedroom door and went into the living room. Ghazala opened her eyes and looked at her sleepily. She was old and deaf now and hadn't heard Abdulla. Diana patted her briefly so that she shouldn't think anything was amiss, then she slid the desk drawer open, removed the pistol and tucked it into her jacket pocket.

Abdulla was waiting for her at the edge of the front path. They didn't speak until they were out of sight of the house. Then Diana paused. 'Now, tell me,' she said.

'I've found her. She's terrified. I tried to bring her, but she screamed so much I had to fetch someone. It was the only way.'

'Where is she? Who took her?'

'Come,' he said. 'Hurry. I'll tell you as we go.'

The moon was very bright and they needed no torch. Diana, feeling both terrified and hopeful, walked behind him. She kept putting her hand down into her pocket to feel the comforting shape of the pistol.

'It was my brother Zeid,' Abdulla said, and as soon as Diana heard the name she understood. Why had no one thought of Zeid? He was embittered, strange, a man with an insane hatred of Jews and British alike. She shivered with fear for Deborah. What awful unspeakable things might he have done to her?

She had no idea how long they walked and stumbled along the rocky path which led ever deeper into the hills. The moon cast strange shadows, making terrifying images of ordinary things. She had no choice but to follow the man in front of her. He walked swiftly over the stones like a mountain goat but occasionally he turned to see if she was keeping up.

'We have to go fast,' he said. 'Zeid will return at first light.' Eventually he paused. 'Speak to her. Call her name.' His voice was very low. 'She mustn't make a noise. If I go to her first she'll scream again.'

'But...where is she?' Diana could only see

510

bushes and scrubby undergrowth.

'Just call to her.'

'Debbie?' She felt weak with fear and tension. Could this be a further plot? But there was nothing she could do except obey. With her hand firmly on her pistol, she called again. 'It's me. Auntie Di. I've come to take you home, Debbie love.'

'She may be asleep,' Abdulla whispered. 'We must go in, you first.'

He pulled some branches aside and directed the beam of his torch on to an old wooden door. Diana saw a crude wooden bolt across it and a large stone leaning against the bottom edge. Abdulla silently rolled the stone away and pulled at the bolt. But this was not silent. The noise it made was truly fearsome in the hush of early dawn. Diana heard a whimper from inside and it was enough to banish all her fears. She pulled at the door and rushed in. 'Darling Debbie,' she said. 'It's me, Diana. I've come to take you home.'

The child didn't move at first, but then she got up and hurled herself into Diana's arms. Diana held her tightly, rocking her gently, becoming wet with her frenzied tears.

'Come quickly,' Abdulla said. 'We shan't be safe from Zeid until we're back at your aunt's house.'

Diana picked up a blanket from the floor and was about to wrap Deborah in it, but the smell was so terrible that she dropped it in disgust and took off her own coat and folded it tightly around the little shivering body.

How they got back to Khanhaven she would never know, but they arrived just as there was a glimmer of light in the Eastern sky and the first cockerel was crowing his delight to the morning. Abdulla vanished as though he had never been and Diana carried Deborah inside.

'Harriet, Samira,' she called gently. 'Come quickly.'

Full of sleep they came and there were tears and kisses and hugs until Deborah said, 'Please wash me. I smell so bad.' Then she burst into tears all over again.

CHAPTER 34

Devonshire—October 1946

A gale had been howling around the Dartmoor hills all day, but towards dusk there was a spectacular sunset, the wind dropped, calm descended and all was quiet. A good omen for my wedding day, Samira thought as she looked out of the bedroom window at the weird shape of the tor etched against the red-gold sky. She remembered how those rocks had scared her when she first came to Bagleigh. They held happy memories for her now and had no more power to disturb or frighten.

She turned to the two little girls who were sitting up in bed eating biscuits, a special treat. Two identical dresses hung on the outside of the

512

wardrobe door, both made in bright pink satin, both floor-length.

'I can't wait,' Deborah said. 'Being a bridesmaid is the most excitingest thing I've ever ever done.'

'And me. I'll never go to sleep.' Kaffa-Mary finished her biscuit and brushed crumbs from the eiderdown. Her dark hair was bound in long conspicuous white rags so that she would have ringlets for the great day tomorrow.

Deborah was similarly coiffed. Mary had spent a long time with each child, winding each prospective curl carefully and tying the pieces of material as her mother had done for her own hair years ago. 'You're going to be beautiful bridesmaids for a beautiful bride,' she had told them. 'So if it's uncomfortable to sleep in you'll just have to put up with it.' Then they had all laughed, the little girls had inspected themselves in the mirror, and Matthew and Dougie had said that they were glad they were boys and hadn't to suffer such torments.

Samira read them a story, helped them to settle, making grooves in the soft feather pillows for their uncomfortable curls, then she kissed them, put out the light and went downstairs.

This was her last night at Bagleigh, her last night as Samira Stanmore. Tomorrow she would be Mrs Briscoe. She thought of Philip and was filled with happiness and pride. She had no regrets, no fears and no worries.

Bagleigh was full, every bedroom occupied. To everyone's delight Harriet had managed to get a flight on a Dakota, a difficult feat but accomplished with the aid of much pulling of strings in high places. She had performed another miracle too and had succeeded in bringing Kaffa with her, and what an accomplishment that had been! There had been endless threats and bribes before Jebel had grudgingly given permission for his wife to go to her daughter's wedding. Then they had driven to Haifa to buy clothes, for Kaffa adamantly refused to go to England wearing her traditional Palestinian costume, beautiful though some of her outfits were. 'No,' she had said. 'I will not disgrace my daughter. I shall wear European dress.'

Samira had marvelled when she saw her mother in a smart skirt and jacket, her legs conspicuous in stockings for the first time in her life. 'You look wonderful, Mother,' she had said. 'Whatever did Father say?'

Kaffa laughed. 'He didn't see. I changed at Harriet's just before we left.'

'Do you like yourself in these things?'

'I'm not sure. I feel embarrassed, but I should have been quite humiliated to wear my ordinary clothes here in England.'

'But they're beautiful,' Mary had said. 'I've seen some of the things you made for Samira.'

'In Palestine yes, but here, no.'

The two women had got on well from the first day they met, a week before the wedding, and this added to Samira's happiness.

David arrived after the children were in bed but Deborah heard his car on the drive. She went to the door of her room and called to him. 'Daddy, Daddy, come and see my funny hair.'

He ran up the stairs two at a time and hugged her. 'You look like a goblin,' he teased.

'Goblins don't have rags in their hair.'

'Well, no, perhaps not. But you should be asleep. You've an important day tomorrow.'

When both little girls were kissed and tucked back into bed he went down to the kitchen. Matthew and Dougie were playing chess and Diana was washing dishes.

Both boys looked up when he came in, their game momentarily abandoned. 'Got your uniform?' Dougie asked.

'Yep. All complete and correct.' He gave a mock salute.

'I'm being a page-boy,' Matthew said. 'I've got sloppy shiny trousers and a lace thing instead of a collar.'

Diana's heart had missed a beat or two when she heard David arrive. Since they had returned from Palestine she had seen little of him, for most of her time was spent in London now. She knew that he was occasionally at Bagleigh, but that Deborah went to stay with him in Bristol at weekends. He had bought a house there and hoped to make a home for her. The kidnapping had affected him deeply, seemed to have changed the course of his life.

But something had changed in her own life too. She remembered telling Samira that after seeing Belsen she would never be able to love again. All decency, all the good things, had disappeared in the ovens of the holocaust. But was she beginning to come alive again now, was she able to feel once more? The shock of Deborah's kidnap and her part in her rescue had affected her deeply. Perhaps that had been the catalyst that had unlocked her heart.

'All set for tomorrow?' David enquired. 'Anything I can do?'

She shook her head. 'Everything's ready. I've made some sandwiches for you. I'll just finish these dishes and we'll take the tray through to the sitting room. The others ate earlier.'

'Where are they all?'

'Harriet's driven them over to Maddacombe for pre-wedding drinks. Except Samira of course. She's gone to bed. Wants to look her best for the great day.'

He picked up a tea towel. 'I'll dry.'

His nearness disconcerted her and she rubbed viciously at the burnt-on marks round the edge of the glass casserole.

The boys had returned to their game and apart from the ticking of the clock the room was quiet. There was so much she wanted to say to David, so much she had thought about during the past weeks, but she couldn't speak. Not yet.

When the washing up was finished, the draining board wiped and everything put away she made a pot of coffee, put cups and milk on the tray beside the sandwiches.

She smiled at him. 'Thanks. We'll go and sit down now. It's been a hectic day. I'm tired.'

He took the tray and followed her.

'How's Bristol?' she said, a banal question meaning nothing.

'A good place to be on the whole. I hope Debbie will settle.'

'You've made arrangements then?'

'I've got a live-in housekeeper. A nice sensible grandmother type. She'll do for a bit. Debbie likes her.'

He finished one of the sandwiches, drank some coffee.

'She's going to miss Samira.'

'Of course, but she can't go to Maddacombe to live. That's out of the question.'

Diana thought of all the changes that had to be made because of Samira's marriage to Philip, and she thought of her own life too.

'How do you feel about this marriage?' David asked suddenly.

She was taken by surprise. 'I... What do you mean?'

'You were engaged to Philip Briscoe.'

She looked down at her lap, wondered how to reply, how to say that she had given her broken heart to Philip hoping that he would be able to mend it. It hadn't worked.

'It was a mistake,' she said. 'I'm glad I realised it soon enough, and I'm very happy for him and Samira. They're made for each other.'

'I too have made mistakes.'

She looked up at him sharply. 'What do you mean?' Surely he couldn't mean Rachel. She hoped that he'd truly loved Rachel. To think of her tortured and dying in a Nazi hell-hole and

517

not having been loved would be unendurable.

He took another sandwich, ate it slowly. 'Putting an ideal, a dream, before the people I love. That's the worst mistake of all I think.'

'You mean...'

'Yes I mean Eretz Israel. I shall not go back to Palestine to live until Deborah is happy to go. Perhaps I shall have to wait until she's grown up. I don't know, but I shall put her interests first. I think Rachel would want me to do that.'

'She didn't do it herself though.' It sounded cruel after she'd spoken and Diana was ashamed that she'd said it.

'That's precisely why I must. No child should have two parents who put their ideals first. One parent doing noble deeds, sacrificing everything for a dream is OK as long as there's another left to care. Because Rachel made that sacrifice I must make up for it to Deborah. It's simple really.'

Diana stared at him in amazement. He'd changed so much. Where was the starry-eyed visionary she had always thought him to be? 'Was it the kidnap?' she asked quietly.

'It brought me to my senses, showed me many things.' He finished his coffee and took out a packet of cigarettes. 'Smoke?'

'No, thank you.'

'You've changed too,' he said.

'Yes.' She could feel the colour rising to her face. 'I had my dreams, my ideals, still have I suppose, but they're subordinate now to other things. Is that what you mean?'

518

'That's just what I mean.' He laughed gently. 'I think we've moved together, haven't we? Is the old magic still there, Diana?'

Her whole body wanted him, wanted to cry out that, yes, oh yes, it was very much so. She could feel tears begin to course down her cheeks. 'It's still there, David,' she whispered. 'I think it always was. It was just hidden a bit, that's all.'

She was sitting on the settee and he came to sit beside her. He pulled her into his arms and kissed her with all the passion that had been building in him since he had realised how much he loved her. And when had that been? The night of Deborah's rescue perhaps, or was it long before that? Yes, he decided, long before. I had been just hidden a bit, that was all.

The little parish church was as resplendent as Diana and Mary had been able to make it. They had brought vast quantities of chrysanthemums, dahlias, and michaelmas daisies over from the Bagleigh gardens and every corner of the ancient building was bright with colour.

Kaffa looked about her with amazement and gratitude that she should be here, that her daughter was so happy, so free. Her eyes kept returning to the bridegroom waiting at the altar. He was very handsome in his naval officer's uniform. Fleetingly she thought of Eshref and that terrible first wedding day. Her wildest dreams then could never have imagined a future so golden as this for her favourite child.

Her own life too had improved. Jebel had

mellowed considerably, partly because of the flourishing of her little business. The clothes she made were more in demand than ever. She had her own money, and even her own little workroom built on to the side of the house, and she employed two other women. England was beautiful, but she wouldn't mind going home with Harriet in a couple of weeks' time.

Mary, beside her, was thinking of very different things as they waited for the bride, but she too was content with the way everything had worked out. Dougie, now giving out prayer books and importantly telling guests where to sit, was to be her adopted son. She was proud of him and they were fond of each other. They would continue to live at Bagleigh for the time being.

She would miss Samira and the children but Maddacombe was only a few miles away across the moor. Then there was little Debbie. She couldn't help feeling a bit sorry for little Debbie.

As for Bagleigh and the inheritance, well, that had been sorted out too. Matthew was still too young to learn that Colin hadn't been his father, but he seemed not at all concerned about Diana inheriting the house.

'I don't want it,' he'd said. 'I'm going to be a doctor and live with Aunt Harriet. I like it in Palestine.'

Except for his mother they'd all laughed. Samira had not been pleased.

'Just a childish dream,' she'd said, but Mary

was not so sure. Perhaps there was some sort of destiny about it.

Diana had declined to be senior bridesmaid. 'Pink satin wouldn't become me at all,' she'd told Samira. She was sitting in the pew behind her mother and Kaffa. She was still glowing from last night, still wondering and a little fearful about the future. But she was quite sure now what her answer would be when David asked her to marry him. She would be quite happy to give up her career, her independent life, to go with him to his Eretz Israel when the time came, for she was sure that he would go there one day.

Meanwhile Bristol would be quite pleasant as long as David was there, and she would enjoy being a mother to Debbie. Since she had rescued her from Zeid on that terrifying night back in August she had become a sort of heroine to Deborah. The little girl had transferred some of her affection for Samira to Diana.

Diana looked towards the ancient rood screen where Philip was standing with his best man, a friend she didn't know. She was totally happy for Philip and Samira.

Then she stared at the screen itself. All the saints' faces had been viciously scratched out. Although she had been in this church many times she had never noticed that before. It was presumably done by Cromwell's men hundreds of years ago during the Civil War. So much fighting, so much strife. She thought of

Palestine. Yes, she was happy to go back there, to fight alongside David if need be. It was an extravagant idea, but the faceless saints on the screen seemed to focus her thoughts.

Then the organ thundered out the wedding march and she turned with everyone else to see Samira, radiantly beautiful, walking down the aisle on David's arm, for he was to give her away. He was wearing full dress uniform of a Wing Commander of the Royal Air Force and he caught her eye and smiled a special smile that she knew meant many things. Her heart was overwhelmed with love for him.

Debbie and Kaffa-Mary came behind in their identical shining dresses, their ringlets, the fair and the dark, bobbing as they walked. Then there was Matthew resplendent in his page boy outfit that Mary had spent weeks making, and which he hated. Diana, looking at him, saw in spite of the clothes the strong resemblance to his father, for she'd seen Eshref while she was in Palestine, and she had a premonition that one day, when he was grown, Matthew would go to him. She tried to shrug it off, but she'd felt it before. As her mother said, sometimes there was a pre-ordained path for you that had to be followed. Thinking of her own life, she was inclined to agree.

After Philip and Samira had left in a hail of confetti and laughter for their honeymoon, David and Diana slipped out of the house and walked up to Greatcombe Rocks. It was almost dark but they swung along the path hand in hand and reached the ancient hut circles just as the moon rose over the distant horizon.

'Do you remember the first time we came here?' Diana said. 'You and Colin were at Oxford. It was the summer vacation.'

'And I was crazy about only one thing.'

'Palestine.'

'Yes. How foolish I was, how self-centred.' Then he grinned at her. 'But there will be a Jewish State there one day, Diana. I'm convinced of it. I want to help create its first Air Force.'

She laughed aloud. 'So much for all your high ideals of yesterday.'

He took both of her hands in his. They were standing right in the middle of the circle of stones. 'Will you marry me?' he said. 'I love you, have loved you deeply, for a long long time. I've no idea what the future holds, but share it with me. Help me to do the right things, make the right decisions. I need you, Diana.'

'I love you,' she whispered. 'I've loved you since we stood here all those years ago. Yes, I'll marry you, David.'

He held her tightly in his arms and kissed her until she had no breath left. Then she disentangled herself from him and put her hands on the magical enduring granite. 'And this place is a symbol of our love. Wherever we are in the future, we'll remember that we made our pledge to each other here in this ancient circle of stones.'

He laughed at her affectionately and together they made their way along the silvery moonlit path back to Bagleigh.

* * * *

Author's Note and Epilogue

On May 14th 1948 David Halprin's dream came true. British rule in Palestine ended and Ben Gurion made his historic statement:

> By virtue of our natural and historic right and on the strength of the resolution of the United Nations General Assembly we hereby declare the establishment of a Jewish state in Eretz-Israel to be known as The State of Israel.

There was great rejoicing, and free access was granted to all Jews who wanted to come. The refugees from Nazi persecution could enter their promised land at last. After two thousand years of exile the Jews had returned.

Tel Aviv was savagely bombed the following day, however, and the avowed aim of all the surrounding Arab nations, Lebanon, Syria, Iraq, Saudi Arabia, Trans-Jordan and Egypt, was the extinction of the one-day-old state. With pathetically few weapons or trained soldiers, the new State of Israel was fighting for its very existence. But by July 1949, to the amazement of a watching world, the Jews had not merely beaten off the Arab armies who had boasted they would drive them into the sea within a week, but had expanded their own territories far beyond the original boundaries allotted to them by the United Nations.

This was the end of Arab Palestine, which led to thousands of Arabs leaving their homes and becoming refugees in their turn.

An Israeli Air Force was soon formed, and the greatest irony was perhaps that pilots, many of them trained in the RAF, were flying German-made fighters against Spitfires which Egypt had bought from Britain.

Old Jerusalem, including the Wailing Wall, was lost to the Jews in the fighting of 1948 and not regained until the Six Day War of 1967.

Now in 1994 there are hopes of peace at last between the State of Israel and the Palestine Liberation Organisation.

Pray for the peace of Jerusalem.

BIBLIOGRAPHY

The Handbook of Palestine & Trans-Jordan, Edited by Luke and Keith-Roach, Macmillan & Co, 1934 (from the Parks Library, Southampton University)

Rabin of Israel, A Biography, by Robert Slater, Robson Books

My Life, by Golda Meir, Weidenfeld & Nicolson

Weizmann, Last of the Patriarchs, by Barnet

Litvinoff, Hodder & Stoughton

Moshe Dayan: Story of My Life, Weidenfeld and Nicolson

England In Palestine, Bentwich, Kegan Paul, 1932

Palestinian Costume, Shelagh Weir, British Museum Publications, 1989

New Guide to the Holy Land, Fr. Barnabas Meistermann, Burns, Oats & Washbourne, 1923

Through the Holy Land, Leonard T. Pearson, Pickering & Inglis, 1937

In the Steps of the Master, H. V. Morton, Methuen & Co, 1945 (originally 1934)

Palestine Unveiled, Douglas V. Duff, Blackie & Son, 1938

Hannah Senesh, Her Life & Diaries, Sphere, 1973

Seven Pillars of Wisdom, T. E. Lawrence, Cape, 1941

The Untempered Wind: Forty Years in Palestine, Christina Jones, Longman, 1975

Children of Bethany: The Story of a Palestinian Family, Said Aburish, I. B. Tauris & Co, 1988

The Haj, Leon Uris, Corgi

The Last Enemy, Richard Hillary, Macmillan & Co, 1942

The Spitfire Log, 50th Anniversary Tribute—Battle of Britain

Battle of Britain, Len Deighton, Jonathan Cape

The Few and the Many (Battle of Britain), Imperial War Museum

A Nurse's War, Brenda McBryde

Heroines of World War Two, Eric Taylor, Robert Hale

The Girls Behind the Guns, Dorothy Brewer Kerr, Robert Hale

Tale of a Guinea Pig, Geoffrey Page, DSO, DFC

How we Lived Then, Norman Longmate, Hutchinson, 1971

Front Line, Clare Hollingworth, Jonathan Cape

Carve Her Name with Pride—Story of Violette Szabo, Fontana, R. J. Minney

Talking About the War, Anne Vallery, Isis Large Print. Also Michael Joseph 1991

Women Photographers—1900 to Present, Val Williams, Virago

Lee Miller's War 1944–45, Lee Miller, Condé Nast Books

Britain 1945–1985, S. R. Gibbon, Blackie & Son

This Large Print Book for the Partially sighted, who cannot read normal print, is published under the auspices of

THE ULVERSCROFT FOUNDATION